HAUTE CUISINE

HAUTE CUISINE

Barney Broom

www.hautecuisinenovel.com

Book Guild Publishing
Sussex, England

First published in Great Britain in 2014 by
The Book Guild Ltd
The Werks
45 Church Road
Hove, BN3 2BE

Typesetting in Scala by
Norman Tilley Graphics Ltd, Northampton

Printed and bound in Spain under the supervision of
MRM Graphics Ltd, Winslow, Bucks

A catalogue record for this book is available from
The British Library.

ISBN 978 1 909984 32 5

for

Katherine and Richard

Domine, dirige nos

Prologue

Staring out of the window at the distant glow of Manhattan, its multitude of lights flickering magically in the night sky, the chef turned back to his large kitchen high up in the building – a kitchen that had taken him two years to build. Its immaculate layout was finished to perfection: counter space, triple sinks, fridges, freezers, hobs and ovens, all of the very finest quality and several items designed and made to the chef's unique specification. It was a wonderful room, a culinary paradise. In its centre was a console at which he had conceived some of his finest creations – dishes that were being spoken of in the city and beyond. Right now, though, laid out on its smooth, clean surface was the biggest challenge the chef had ever faced – a human body.

He looked down at the corpse. He had already cut away and removed the man's clothing, now lying on the floor, and the body was completely naked. The man had been a ginge, coppery-coloured stubble covering his chest and legs, his underarm and pubic hair a crinkly dense auburn. Inspecting each limb, the torso, loins, the chef was fascinated by the man's skin – its follicles, texture, down and bristle.

Moving the clothes away, he carefully laid out black bin liners around the console base, then ensured plenty of cloths and several stacks of kitchen roll were to hand. There would be blood, though right now he didn't realise just how much.

I

Arranging the corpse with arms resting beside the trunk, legs slightly splayed, the chef walked over to an array of magnetic, wall-mounted blades, including some very large kitchen knives and butcher's cleavers. Selecting several, he opened a drawer and removed two fine boning bistouries.

The chef stared at the body: where to begin? Surely it made sense to separate the limbs from the torso as one would any other carcass. Perhaps the arm sockets first and work down?

As he contemplated the first incision, the chef honed his blade to a razor's edge using a steel. Beside him the monkey chattered away; it was going to be a long night.

Chapter 1

A young man gently guided his ancient T-Bird convertible down a New York side street. It was a Sunday morning in late autumn and the leaves on the trees, having turned their golden brown, had begun to fall. Raymond Babchuk – for that was the driver's name – was relaxed. He was listening to his favourite composer, Bartók, who reminded him of home, Budapest, Hungary. Not that Raymond was homesick, far from it, but there were some things that were in your blood, that you could never rid yourself of – indeed, didn't want to.

Raymond was of medium height and build, his hair shaggy and lank and he sported a little wispy beard. His dress erring on the scruffy, neither the ragged T-shirt nor the jeans he wore had seen a washing machine for several weeks, but his appearance didn't bother him. He was, ostensibly, on his way to work at *Le Chat Noir*, one of the most fashionable restaurants in Lower Manhattan's East Side, where he was vegetable chef de partie. But Raymond's job wasn't really work at all, more an extension of his existence. For Raymond Babchuk, food, its provenance and its preparation, made up his entire life. He lived for nothing else. He cared for nothing else.

At twenty-eight, Raymond had lived in New York since he was eight, he and his brother István having made their way to America from their native homeland after their parents were both killed. The Babchuk seniors' departure from life was particular, their circus trapeze act coming to a climactic finale when, while performing a triple twist somersault manoeuvre, they collided with each other head-on in mid-air, crashing to the ground through an insecure safety net. The circus lion, although a mangy animal, also happened to have escaped that morning and the whole scenario, as reported in the *Szeged Star*, came to a bloody conclusion.

Although at the time of their parents' death István was at a more impressionable age than Raymond, being ten years older than his little brother, the younger boy felt the loss of his father and mother profoundly, not least because he was now subject to the largely irresponsible whims of his elder sibling.

The story of István and Raymond's journey to America was not without incident. While Raymond was just a child, his brother was a youth of some spirit. The nomadic life of the parents having stranded the boys homeless in the south of the country, István, with Raymond in tow, made his way to Budapest, arriving on the doorstep of distant Uncle Zsigmond's restaurant, which reportedly served the finest goulash in Hungary. To Raymond's mind, the experience of the months spent living there was how the love of his life began – food, and all things about it; turning food made from simple ingredients into droolingly delicious cuisine; creating dishes that made people travel for miles to taste a soufflé or *truffes à la bombe*. The process connected with his infant brain; it would change his life forever.

Aunt Vilma, Uncle Zsigmond's wife, was a large woman, big in spirit, laughter and natural cooking ability, for she was a self-taught chef. Little Raymond would be at her side morning, noon and night watching as she kneaded dough or cut vegetables, which to the child's eyes seemed to miraculously segment, her pudgy fingers holding a carrot or turnip, the razor-sharp knife moving up and down along the root with almost magical speed.

While the child Raymond (or Radomér as he was known then) experienced a religious inculcation in the kitchen, his elder brother was hanging out with Uncle Zsigmond – a situation that was to lead István into murky waters. For, as well as being a restaurateur, Uncle Zsigmond was a small-time crook and, unlike his culinary enterprise, which relied largely on the talents of his wife, his underworld activities were amateurish and incompetent. He'd had several brushes with the law, his latest scam being some lottery con, and the young István was an active gofer, running errands for the gang – a role he greatly enjoyed.

However, very soon, all was exposed. A greedy member made a stupid slip (it was one thing to siphon off a tiny percentage per ticket, quite another to openly defraud purchasers, taking all their money and paying out nothing) and the police moved in on the operation. Uncle Zsigmond simply disappeared, which made little difference to Aunt Vilma; indeed, with her slothful husband out of the way the restaurant business became more successful. However, István only escaped prosecution because he was a minor and in further discussions with other relatives it was decided the best course of action would be to ship the boys out – literally.

America: home of the brave, land of the free; if they couldn't get a clean start there and make something of themselves then they wouldn't amount to anything, in the old world or the new.

The decision to head for the New World suited István perfectly; the principal concern was little Radomér. Who would look after him? Other relatives (in Hungary more than most places everyone appears closely related to everyone else) wrote to family in New York, and because Hungary was at that time behind the Iron Curtain, the young Babchuks could only emigrate if they had a relative living in the United States. Enter Aunt Renais.

Although the Hungarian Babchuks were not Jewish, several decades previously, an aunt had married a Hungarian Jew and their daughter, Renais, married Harold Rinegold in 1966. Whilst not Hungarian himself, Harold had Slavic antecedents and had been deeply committed to the nationalist uprising ten years previously. Sadly meeting an untimely end (he was run over by a reversing tractor while on a farm in Nebraska, attempting to introduce a genetically modified form of Balkan wheat to America), Harold left the childless Renais a young widow. Whether because of the tragic loss of her husband or simply because it had been subjugated during marriage, her natural wildness now came to the fore. Renais Rinegold hit Manhattan. Racy parties and risqué behaviour led her into a life of the debauched.

What was it, then, that drove this dissolute woman to welcome these distantly familial émigrés into her life? Money.

It turned out that Rezs Babchuk had not been quite the crazy circus acrobat he'd generally been portrayed as, having sunk his cash into some interesting American stocks. Television, a dynamic young industry he had invested his big top earnings in, grew at a fantastic rate during the fifties, subsequently paying out serious dividends. These shares, along with others in several American airline companies, meant Rezs would have been quite a wealthy man had he lived.

Rezs's investments had come to light in Budapest and Renais Rinegold was made aware of them, but in a final parting shot of financial sanity, Aunt Vilma managed to set up a trust fund, which meant that, whilst being able to draw money for the boys' keep, neither Renais nor István could touch the capital until little Radomér reached twenty-one. Oh, that Aunt Vilma could have remained a presence in the children's lives for longer. Anyway, the teenager, with his small brother in tow, said goodbye to their Hungarian homeland in the summer of 1986 and set sail on the Star Ship *Oceanic* – a voyage that would change their lives forever.

Even on the passage István got up to plenty of tricks, amongst other things attempting to make money at cards. Alas, his pathetically amateurish skills at cheating only got the lad into trouble with the authorities, but it was always Radomér who saved him.

'My poor little brother. We're alone. I'm the only person he has in the world to look after him.' But István's conscience did not hold him back.

The ship was finally relieved when, entering the East River and coming alongside Pier 17, they could be free of the elder Babchuk boy, but it wasn't perhaps the best of omens no one was there to meet the young migrants. Their papers were in order and they cleared immigration satisfactorily thanks to the help of a Hungarian official who was assisting a number of his countrymen into America, but had Aunt Vilma not had the foresight to sew Mrs Rinegold's address into an inside pocket of Radomér's jacket, they might have had problems being directed to their new home. As it was, two tired, footsore children finally showed up at Palmetto Street, Queens, having walked across the Brooklyn Bridge carrying their battered cases.

István liked what he saw. It appeared that Aunt Renais had a whole brownstone house and to his juvenile, Hungarian eyes the place spelt money. How wrong he was. As would quickly be discovered, Renais Ringold owed cash all over town. Their present predicament was more immediate, however, in that no one was home, so the boys sat down on the front doorsteps.

'You guys waitin' for someone?'

István and Radomér stared at the speaker blankly. It hadn't really occurred to those in Budapest that English might be necessary by way of communication in New York. But luck was at hand.

'Egy rokona miénk itt él.' A relative of ours lives here.

'Ah, fiúk Budapeströl mi?' Ah, you boys from Budapest, huh?

And so began a conversation with one of New York's great Hungarian populace, that city having the second largest such community in the world.

'But yer can't speak Hungarian all the time. Yer got to learn English pronto.'

István nodded.

'Yer said you're waiting for a relative? Is that, er...?' The boys' homeland comrade was hesitant.

'Mrs Ringold.'

'You're related to her?'

'By marriage.'

'Yer never met her?'

István shook his head. 'What's she like?'

'You tell me. Here she is now.'

A yellow cab pulled up in the street and the blowsiest-looking woman – top too tight, skirt too short, with mock leopard skin jacket, clutching a miniature poodle complete with pink bows – clambered out of the vehicle.

'I'm tellin' yer, shit-face, it's eight bucks from the club!'

'Lady, the meter never lies.'

'Oh yeah? Well yours does.' The woman handed over several dollar bills. 'Keep the change, yer Bronx Bull.'

'There is no change!'

The driver clearly dissatisfied, the cab screeched off. Mrs Ringold turned and teetered on her high heels towards her steps. Noticing her neighbour, Balázs, she nodded in his direction.

'Hiya Balsy. And you two. Yer refugees or somethin'? Move yer asses.'

'They say they're relatives.' It was Balázs who replied.

'Ha! Don't they talk?'

'Not English.'

'Wha'? Relatives who don't speak English!'

'Didn't you know they were coming?'

'Aw, mebbe. Move yer butt, kid.'

This last comment was directed at Radomér; the boy caught the side of Mrs Ringold's shoe as she unlocked the front door, leaving it open whilst switching off the alarm. The two boys gaped into the house which was crammed with furniture and painted lurid colours, shades of pink predominating. The boys entered. Renais reappeared from under the stairs.

'Yer really don't speak no English?'

István, who immediately liked his aunt, stuttered, 'I... I...learn.'

'Yer better, and damned quick. What about Little Boy Blue here? He talk at all in any lingo?'

'He small...kid.'

'I speak a little.'

Whilst his brother appeared to somehow connect with Renais, Radomér had taken an instant dislike to his

American relative. Nevertheless, it was difficult to know who was more taken aback by his first utterance in English. Mrs R approached.

'Well, well, well. The boy speaks a bit after all. I can see I'm going to have to keep an eye on you. What's yer name?'

'Did you know we visit?' Radomér stood his ground.

'Don't get smart with me, kid.'

The three looked at each other. Again, it was Radomér who led.

'Me Radomér.' Then, pointing to his elder brother, 'István.'

'Yeah, yeah, yeah, the little delinquents from Hungaria. Well, if you're so smart with the lingo, let's get talkin' right away.' And without further ado, Mrs R slammed the front door, turned on her heels and teetered into the depths of her home. For once unable to lead, István looked down at his brother. Radomér, who had found some inner attitude, followed Renais along the hall, István reluctantly following. Entering a messy kitchen – dishes left dirty, the kitchen table cluttered – Auntie opened her fridge and poured herself a large glass of white wine into a previously used wine glass, the rim stained with her bright, garish lipstick.

'So, you're here, then. Where's yer money?'

This was a struggle for Radomér but he understood 'money', got her drift and turned to his elder brother. 'I think she's asking for money,' he told him in Hungarian.

István actually smiled. 'An account's been set up with the Bank of Hungary. We have to go and see the manager. The amount due to her has already been agreed but they need to be notified back home. Manage that, smart ass?'

István turned to Aunt Renais and smiled his most

winning smile. For the first time she appeared to eye him with a little more appreciation.

'Money in Hungary bank here. We need to...'

István looked at his brother, but Radomér couldn't think of the English word for 'visit'.

'Go there?' His aunt finished the sentence. 'Yeah, yeah. Well, I ain't doin' nothin' the rest of the day and you ain't stayin' here without me gettin' some dough.' She quaffed her wine. 'What's the address?'

Before Radomér could attempt an answer, the doorbell rang.

'What the...?' Banging down her glass, Renais left the room.

István hissed, 'What's with you speaking English?'

'I can't, not really. Aunt Vilma's recipes. Some books were in English. She spoke a little. I learned some words.'

'You and food. Make me sick.' István didn't get the irony.

Mrs Rinegold opened her front door.

'Balsy, you again? Gonna think you've got a crush on me, or is it party time?'

Balázs Malursk could never really understand his neighbour. To him she was a repulsive woman – gaudy, ill-mannered and lewd – yet he had occasionally seen a different side to her, one that showed kindness, though he had to admit such glimpses were rare.

'The language. I wondered if you needed any help.'

'We're doin' just fine thanks, Balsy, though yer don't happen to know where the Bank of Hungary is, do yer? Guess there ain't too many branches.'

'Not only do I know it – I bank there. Want me to take you?'

'No, no – we'll be fine. Just an address'll do.'

Radomér had appeared in the hall and feeling in the inside pocket of his jacket, pulled out a piece of paper. Balázs looked down at the little boy and took the proffered note.

'Ha! This is the address: West Forty-fifth Street. I can still take you; the manager's a friend.'

'Nah, nah, we'll be fine. Thanks for comin' by, though. Appreciated.'

'Well, if there's anything else I can do... You need any help...'

Mrs Rinegold began to close the door, almost forcing her friend back on to the street. 'Thanks, Balsy, I'll remember that, but we'll be okay won't we, Ray?'

It was the first time Radomér was called the name he would become known by in the New World. The boy didn't respond.

With a last glance at the child, the door was closed on the helpful Balázs. Mrs R turned to the lad and said, 'See here, yer little jerk. Somethin' tells me I don't like yer. Somethin' tells me I'm never gonna like yer, and as long as yer livin' under my roof you'll do exactly as I say. Got it?' She slapped Radomér hard across the face, but the boy only stared back at her, his big eyes impassive. 'Yer little jerk,' she slurred and slouched past him into the kitchen.

Chapter 2

The unlikely group making their way across New York towards downtown Manhattan where the National Bank of Hungary had a branch within the Hungarian tourist office, seemed unrelated in every way. Radomér was wide-eyed at the sights, sounds and smells of the city, the eight-year-old being especially enthralled by the markets. His elder brother, too, was excited but that had rather more to do with the Big Apple's population, particularly its younger female contingent. Big lusty Hungarian lad that he was, this factor wasn't lost on Aunt Renais, who being well past the first bloom of youth herself was sensitive to such things.

If her mood was agitatedly unpleasant when leaving Palmetto Street, it was positively belligerent by the time they arrived at the Empire State Building. On entering the Hungarian tourist office, Mrs R went immediately to the information desk and barked the words 'Money' and 'Banking'. Then 'I got these two kids here from Budapest. There's a transfer set up.'

'I'm sure we can be of assistance. If you'd like to take a seat.' The woman assistant was polite.

'I ain't leavin' here without no money.'

They were shown into the office of Mr Gáspár, the banking manager, who was all obliging, but the fact was that the trust in Budapest (Aunt Vilma's work) had to be notified.

However, he assured her that everything would be author-
ised within a few days.

'So how'm I gonna feed 'em? Huh? You tell me that?'

'I really can't say, Mrs...' The manager looked down at
his notes. 'Ringegold.'

Without another word, Aunt Renais got up and stalked
out. For a second the manager looked nonplussed then
hastily exited himself. Catching sight of Mrs R leaving the
building, he hurried after her.

'Madam! Madam!' The manager caught his breath as
he ran out into the street. 'Madam, may I just say that the
documents I have – if you don't comply with the care of
these two young people, if there is any suspicion of your
not doing so, then the terms of the trust will be nullified.'

'Speak English, yer jerk!'

The manager looked at her hard. 'If you don't care for
those boys now, you...' He held himself in check. 'Then
you'll receive no funds – ever. At all. Clear enough for you?'
And with that he turned on his heel and left her on the
sidewalk.

It was Radomér who again came to the rescue when
his aunt returned sullenly. He excused himself to go to the
men's room, in the privacy of which he reached into
another of his mysterious inside pockets (what hadn't Aunt
Vilma secreted in that jacket?) taking out $500 in small
bills. He removed $50, folded it into his hand and put the
rest back inside the pocket. When he returned to the
manager's office, he found his brother and Aunt Renais
sitting alone, both shrouded in cigarette smoke. He sat
down beside István and whispered in Hungarian, 'Some
money. I've got some dollars.'

István shot out of his chair. 'Where d'you get it? You sly
little... Speaking English and stuff.'

'I told you, some of Aunt Vilma's cook books were in English.'

'Aunt Vilma. Aunt Vilma this, Aunt Vilma that! Bet she gave you the money. How much?'

'Fifty dollars.'

'Yeah? And the rest!' He pushed his brother hard. Radomér just waved the money in his face.

'What's he got there?' Aunt Renais was sharp enough at the sight of Ulysses S. Grant.

'He... I...er...' István's lack of English rendered him useless.

'Yer need to learn English, stud boy!' And with that, Renais snatched the money from Radomér's hand and stalked out.

A $17 cab ride took them back to Palmetto Street, where the boys were deposited at Aunt Renais' house, while their aunt went straight out with their thirty-three bucks. István appeared crestfallen.

'You got any more money?'

Radomér shook his head.

'Liar.'

The younger brother didn't reply.

'You're a dodgy little bugger.' István was in a Balkan mood. 'New World! They can keep it!'

Radomér remained silent.

'I'm going to bed. Let's look round the house for somewhere to sleep.'

It was actually a spacious property – a basement and three floors above – but the place was crammed full of bric-a-brac; tasteless, gaudy chairs and sofas, stained carpets and Mrs Ringold's two poodles' – Pussy and Hard – shit generously littering every floor. They even found dog turds in their aunt's bedroom. At the top of the house was a box room, where the lads came upon some camp beds and sleeping bags, and on these they lay down side by side, the street lights' flicker only partially penetrating the sheet they placed across the window.

'You don't really mean it about New York. You like it.' Radomér sought reassurance.

'S'not Budapest, though,' István answered then immediately began to snore.

'No, it's not Budapest. It's New York! New York...' Radomér's breathing also became regular and within seconds he was fast asleep. Aunt Renais didn't return for another nine hours, almost dawn the following morning, and not only was the $33 gone, she had to borrow the cab ride home. But Giorgio was so forgiving and he was great in the sack.

Chapter 3

Several significant things happened during that early period of Radomér's life in New York. After some weeks, when it was established the two Babchuk lads were living in Palmetto Street, funds did come through for their keep and, though she constantly complained it was never sufficient, Mrs R spent it quickly enough. The second event involved István shipping out a short while later, never to return. It wasn't long before Auntie Renais had taken István to her bed and the Hungarian youth was happy to service his distant American relative, but, perhaps unsurprisingly, a short while later he took up with a travelling fairground passing through Coney Island, becoming besotted with an Afro-American Wall of Death motorbike rider. However, before his departure, he managed to drive a near-irrevocable wall of resentment between Renais and Radomér, achieved through cunning and spite, always inferring to their aunt what a scheming so and so his little brother was – a suggestion Aunt Renais was all too ready to believe. Mrs Ringegold was only partially mollified when the little boy agreed to keep his mouth shut about the departure of his brother, allowing her to continue receiving the money for his care, although István had bolted.

Given Aunt Renais was completely hopeless at doing anything practical for the boys, Radomér, or Ray as he was quickly becoming known, and his elder brother had also started school at this time. One day when they were idly wandering around the neighbourhood, Mr Balázs stopped them and asked what they were doing about education.

'Dunno. Ask Auntie,' was István's only response.

Balázs did and found the answer to be nothing. Taking the lads under his wing, he walked them round to the school of St Stanislaus Ignatius to meet Father Tolnay, the senior friar and head teacher.

'Of course the boys must be admitted. We'll find a place for them somehow.'

The senior pupil assigned to show them over the school – a property hemmed in by other larger buildings, typical New York fashion – was a youth named Feydor Gaultier, who one day Radomér would work under, then employ, in a world neither could imagine. Attending the school would never have much significance to István, he shortly after-wards skipping out of their lives, but Radomér would spend the next ten years with Father Tolnay, thanks to the financial assistance of the Hungarian Youth Foundation.

After István left and Aunt Renais persuaded Radomér to keep quiet about his brother's disappearance, much went on in the little boy's mind. Now nine (his birthday had come and gone, its only recognition being a card sent by Aunt Vilma from Budapest), Radomér decided it suited him to carry on living in the top floor of his aunt's house in New York, although he had largely to fend for himself. This required him to get his own food, which sometimes meant stealing money from his aunt; money which, as time went by, he came to figure was really his own anyway. Never-theless, the two settled down to a life together which, in an odd way, came to suit them both.

An independent child, the one facet of Raymond's

character that never wavered was his passionate interest in food and all things to do with cooking. When out one day browsing a bookstall (never monitored, Ray spent hours, even days and weeks on his own) he came across a battered copy of Escoffier's *Le Guide Culinaire* in its original form, which the bookseller gave him:

'No one speaks the French lingo. Get it off the stall.'

From then on, Raymond's culinary library grew dramatically. His one and only friend at this time was Mr Balázs who, after István's departure, kept a weather eye on the boy and the pair discovered a mutual interest in cuisine. Mr Balázs was a keen amateur chef, enjoying classic traditional Hungarian dishes, and their friendship blossomed. In fact, it was cooking that made Ray's life at Palmetto Street tenable and by his early teens he was a very accomplished cook. He could produce any sauce, make any dessert and even experimented with his own recipes. Because his aunt appeared to be only interested in drinking and fucking herself into oblivion, Ray gradually took over the kitchen. First of all he cleaned it from top to bottom, then he arranged the utensils, pots and pans in some order so that he could work. The night Mrs R came home and discovered the transformation, all was initially explosive aggression, until Bad Boy Mullins – her current late-night beau – saw a pie on the table which he quickly began to devour.

'Goddamn me, Jesus! What the fuck? This is the best goddamn pie I ever tasted, Renais. You cook this?'

Vaguely mollified, Mrs R gulped her wine. 'Little jerk upstairs. Gotta nephew stayin' here spongin' offa me.'

'Ha! Spongin'? If his sponge is as good as his pie, I'd pay him! Goddamn well delicious!'

'Okay, okay, Mullins, the kid can cook.'

'I'll say he can.'

Later that night when he was leaving:

'See yer tomorra, hunk.'

'Sure will if there's another pie on the table.' Laughing, Mullins slammed the door behind him.

'Goddamn men. Money, sex, food. That's all they ever want.' Renais wasn't much on self-reflection.

The next step in Ray's culinary development came when, in his teens, as a thank you for making canapés for a party his aunt gave (every single guest had raved about the food), Renais agreed to let the boy 'do some work upstairs'.

'I'd like to make another kitchen on my floor.'

'Ain't your floor, yer louse – and yer ain't gettin' yer hands on this house, neither.'

However, this outburst came to nothing. She relented, allowing him to begin work, and Ray started creating his kitchen. It took nearly two years. Unbeknown to his aunt, while she made a trip to Kansas for a month, he knocked down two stud walls, creating one massive room for his culinary paradise and leaving only a modest bathroom and tiny living space for his bedroom. He then set about plastering and kitting out his cuisinier's dream. Ray had also begun quietly doing some work on the home catering front and was picking up useful money. Now seventeen, he was of a leaner, wirier frame than his brother, medium height and neither particularly good-looking nor bad. Because Ray was unobtrusive, his clients liked the way he conducted himself, coming and going with a minimum of fuss and serving up some of the best party food in Manhattan. All the money he earned went on materials for his kitchen and he compromised on nothing. Only the finest quality products were installed, be they an enormous fridge-freezer, professional hob or counter and cupboard units. In Ray's eyes it was the best kitchen in New York – and quite probably it was.

Eventually, the day came when he felt he should perhaps invite his aunt to see what he'd been doing. Initially she refused to come up and so the first person ever to view the finished kitchen was Mr Balázs, who so admired the work he asked if he could take photographs. Mrs R finally agreed to make a visit – she hadn't been up to the top floor of her house in years – but then still didn't appear. It was weeks later, when Raymond was out one day, that she made her way up the stairs to the young man's domain and, inexplicably, freaked out. She went crazy. She smashed many things in the magnificent kitchen (there was little to break in Ray's bedroom or bathroom), but the damage she caused was so irrational as to be insane. Raymond contemplated murdering his aunt when he discovered what she'd done but, running out into the street, he fortunately found Mr Balázs who was so overcome he wept when he saw the devastation.

The only thing that kept Ray from breaking down was his acceptance to the French Culinary School, located off Broadway. With guidance yet again from his Hungarian mentor (though his natural abilities had shone through winning him a place), two years later he graduated with *cum laude* honours. It took all that time to repair his kitchen, the destruction had been so great. As a precaution, Ray also made the whole top floor secure and self-contained, fitting separate locks. Interestingly, after she'd all but destroyed his kitchen, Renais disappeared for nearly two months and when she returned never made mention of what she'd done. Neither did she ever attempt to approach his floor again. It was as if doing what she did had been some strange, exorcising rite. In any event, the next few years saw Renais and Raymond's relationship more or less maintain equilibrium. For weeks at a time neither would speak to the other. It suited them both.

Aunt R didn't attend Ray's graduation from cookery school, where he passed out best in his year, achieving marks no other student managed before or since. Indeed, his senior tutor, Monsieur Lebeau, considered Raymond little short of a culinary genius.

When it came to applying for a position in a restaurant, Ray had no difficulty in securing employment at *Le Chat Noir*, an exclusive establishment in Lower Manhattan under the direction of Maestro Pierre-Auguste Etienne, an erratic character who bore a remarkable resemblance to Salvador Dali. It was here he also re-encountered Feydor Gaultier, now assistant maitre d', though it was a while till both realised they'd attended the same school. Entering the kitchen as a commis, Ray quickly rose to the position he now held as a chef de partie, though recently his progress appeared to be slowing down. Some said it was due to jealousy on the part of rivals; some said Ray might have lost his edge. But he knew better.

However, one member of the kitchen staff, Tabitha, was definitely cheering his corner and had shown him an article in *International Chef* magazine about the 'Chef de France' competition, open to young chefs around the world. Held in Paris, the event ran for two weeks and involved every aspect of cooking. It was *the* global competition.

'Hey Ray, seen this?'

A new commis herself, Tabitha McKindrick was a redhead and quite talented. Not overly attractive, Tabi, as she was known, had a natural exuberance which helped her through the sometimes bitchy and stifling kitchen atmosphere.

Ray looked at the article but said little.

'You should go for it. You're the one person here who could just do something. Never know, you might even win!'

Sous-Chef Charlie Reardon approached. For some reason Ray and Tabi felt mutually secretive.

'What's going down? Little secret squirrels are we? That's not on the menu tonight, though monkey brains will be coming in shortly.' Good looking and arrogant, Reardon was a bully. 'Some mangetout, Babchuk – now!'

Gathering the vegetables, Ray began preparing them as required, his face impassive, his knife hand working so quickly nicking and cutting the pods it was impossible to see his fingers at work.

That night he'd taken the article home then, organising some leave (the first he'd ever taken), Ray applied to enter the competition. Rather than give Maestro Pierre-Auguste as a reference, he listed Monsieur Lebeau at the French Culinary School. On the internet later, acknowledgment of his application came through electronically and a few days after he'd applied Ray received formal written acceptance. However, there were problems from the word go. Ray nearly had to cancel because for some reason his application to take leave, while granted by management, hadn't been cleared with the Maestro.

'I said he could have time off, Pierre; he applied months ago.'

'I am "Maestro" to you. "Management *écume*".' Pierre-Auguste faced a man in his late thirties who seemed to be straight out of the Mafia – swarthy, apparently reasonable but sharp and expensively dressed. Sitting at a desk, Frank Chesson, co-owner and manager of Le Chat Noir, cleaned his fingernails with a paper knife. He barely looked up.

'Just 'cause, to you, I'm an ignorant person with a lack of

sophistication when it comes to food don't mean I don't have a brain, and don't mean I don't understand other languages. Comprenez, poubelle?'

Pierre-Auguste looked apoplectic, flouncing about, but his hot-air bluster had zero effect.

'The kid deserves a break.' The conversation was terminated.

However, when that was sorted, on arrival in Paris – a city Raymond instantly liked – there had been a mix-up with his registration. Ray's French – learnt entirely through his profession – was reasonable (though with a food bias) and his application was eventually found, amidst a flurry of Gallic confusion. Because of some further committee complications, the whole event was forty-eight hours late in starting, a factor that was to have particular repercussions subsequently. When granting Ray's vacation, the stipulation *Le Chat Noir*'s management had conceded to Pierre-Auguste's petulance was that Ray be back the following Saturday week. A special celebrity party was coming in and his services would be required.

The first week of competition passed quickly, Ray moving easily through early rounds, his *fricassée de frango* being remarked on with particular praise. An especial admirer was the deputy head of the competition, Louis Blanc. On the panel of international judges no one was more influential than the suave and silver-haired Blanc, French by origin and training, but now residing in the US, where he owned the exclusive Michelin-starred restaurant, *L'Escargot,* in Beverly Hills. The competition was meticulously planned to push the competitors' abilities to their limits, requiring all-round expertise in every aspect of cuisine from *démarreurs* to a variety of delicate and difficult main dishes and exotic deserts. There were also freestyle challenges, where contestants were allowed to present their own dishes from original recipes they had created. Showing no favouritism, Blanc had an eye for talent, and whilst no one in the group of twenty-five top under-thirty chefs was lacking in ability, there were only two or three who stood out as having that special something, that indefinable flair which would take them to a heightened level. A Brazilian lad created a fabulous *ovo de cordona* and a young French chef from Gascony made the most wonderful *onglet à l'echalotte*. These two and Raymond were in a league of their own, which is why Ray's abrupt disappearance during the closing rounds was so surprising. He simply vanished, not telling anyone why he wasn't present that last day and officially forfeiting his place in the final. However, when the panel of judges sat down to adjudicate (the Brazilian won with a brilliant *Filet de Boeuf aux Champignons et aux Truffes*), they were so impressed with Raymond's work during the two weeks they elected to award him a special prize for innovative creativity. This was largely instigated by Louis Blanc who, having checked out Raymond's submission details, decided to drop by the French Culinary School in New York when returning to the States, and see if he couldn't track down the elusive young man. Having other business to attend to in France, it was several weeks before Blanc was able to head back to America, but he was careful to pack Raymond's special award in his overhead bag the night before he checked out of the Hotel Georges Cinq, taking a cab to Charles de Gaulle Airport the following morning.

Chapter 4

Parking his dilapidated car in a side alley near the restaurant that Sunday morning, Raymond prepared to join his colleagues in the preparation of lunch. He was late and it wasn't the first time. Making his way to a small room at the back of the kitchen Ray began changing into his chef's uniform. Two colleagues, Luke and Aldo, were already mostly in theirs – jackets, trousers and neat chequered hats.

'Whoay, Raymondo – you're here, dude. Charlie-boy was screaming for yer.' Ray didn't respond but continued changing. 'Heavy night last night, Ray-Ban? Cookin' up somethin', were yer?'

'Meat balls and grits. That's what she loves.' Aldo smacked his lips; a southerner, he was lankier than his best friend, the stocky Bronxian, Luke. The two young men made for the door just as Sous-Chef Charlie Reardon appeared.

'Little meetin'?'

'On it, Chef.' Luke was unperturbed.

'Yeah, yeah, 'way to it, boy! As for you...' He turned to Ray. 'You're late. Yer always late Sundays and I'm recommendin' dockin' yer money. I've warned yer, Babchuk. Yer gonna be on yer way soon.'

'On whose sayso?'

'On my sayso.'

Ray looked at Reardon, his face impassive.

'And before you say I have no authority...get pushy with me, kid, and you'll get more than yer cards.'

'Yer want me to go now?'

'Sure – the fuck I want yer to go now!'

Completing his dressing, Ray adjusted his hat. 'Was there anything else, Chef?'

Reardon suddenly grabbed Ray and slammed him against the wall. He was quite a fit guy, with a toughened hardness. 'Don't try it with me, kid.'

Ray didn't allow himself to be intimidated.

Aldo, popping back to the changing area, walked in on the bizarre scene: Reardon, ludicrous, pinning Babchuk up against the wall. For a moment Aldo simply stared then Reardon let go of the young chef and growled, 'What yer starin' at?'

'Nothin', chef.' Aldo went to his locker and took out his neckerchief.

Reardon moved towards the door. 'Get fuckin' started. Coupla jerks, the pair of you,' he barked and slammed the door behind him.

Ray and Aldo looked at each other then Aldo burst out laughing and Ray smiled. Aldo mimicked, 'Coupla jerks, the pair of you!'

Activity in the kitchen was rapidly getting underway. Key components of dishes having been prepared, starters were readied and vegetables cleaned. Being a top Manhattan restaurant, *Le Chat Noir* had a menu that was carefully considered. Traditional roast lunches were much in demand, but culinary delicacies such as pig's trotters and a variety of eel were also available. Because he found the preparation of food all-encompassing, Ray was one of the few chefs who hadn't been squeamish when a live monkey arrived at the request of a particular customer desirous to partake of its brain as a speciality dish. However, the patron suddenly had to take a business trip out of New York and the kitchen staff, including Raymond, had become attached to the monkey now living in their midst. Naming him Tutti Frutti on account of the macaque's ability to blow very large bubble gum bubbles, they were becoming uncomfortable about the pending requirement to terminate the life of the little creature who kept them company as they toiled over every detail of their Sunday service excellence.

At around 12.30p.m., the first orders started to come in and to the untrained eye the kitchen became chaotic. But it was very far from being such. On receiving his or her instruction, each chef went to work with an intensity that defied intrusion. The work and skill required in the preparation of each dish was what gave *Le Chat Noir* its Michelin status, and the rivalry between chefs was palpable. Of all the people at work, it was Raymond who shone, possessing an air of sublime confidence. Although his position was relatively lowly, it was as if this were his domain. Raymond appeared to exude command, not by anything he said – indeed, he said very little – but his phenomenal abilities added another dimension to every dish he prepared. The envy of his colleagues, he was regarded jealously by his peers. A *fricassée d'agneau à la grecque* appeared as effortlessly as if it had been beans on toast, and a serving of *cerveaux au gratin* seemed to take no more effort than a Welsh Rarebit. This was, of course, an illusion. It was because Raymond only really lived for the creation of food, spending every waking moment, whether at work or home, living, eating and breathing cuisine, that his talent had risen to the heights it now attained. He was a wonderfully gifted chef, imaginative and subtle; it was little wonder others were either envious or resentful of him – or both.

Chapter 5

Louis Blanc loved New York. Sitting in his first class, Air France seat, coming into JFK, he watched the city loom up in the early morning fall light like a spectral apparition, watery rays reflecting from the glass of its skyscraper landscape. Although his main home was Southern California, in many ways Louis preferred the dynamic of Manhattan, but the opportunity to open in Beverly Hills had been too good a chance to miss. One day, he told himself, he'd also have a top restaurant in the city below.

A few hours previously, whilst dozing on the plane, a random thought entered his head. It being Sunday, the French Culinary School would be closed; why not drop by and see his old acquaintance Feydor Gaultier at *Le Chat Noir*? Perhaps he might have heard of young Babchuk? Besides, annoying that poser Pierre-Auguste Etienne would be fun. Theirs was a strange relationship, Blanc and Etienne (it wasn't his real name). Having known each other for years, Blanc realised Pierre-Auguste was a sham, but had some admiration for the bizarre front he presented.

A limousine met Blanc at the terminal and the Frenchman gave the driver *Le Chat Noir*'s address. The car swept off, transporting the suave gastronomic auteur down the New Jersey turnpike, across the Brooklyn Bridge and into the city. Moving deeper into Manhattan, towards its Lower East Side, Blanc sucked in NYC's vibrant atmosphere. It felt good. The limo stopped outside the exclusive restaurant, a flunky immediately opening his door. Carrying his parcel, Blanc strolled into the restaurant. Almost immediately he saw Gaultier, immaculate in maitre d's tails, moving away from a small booth, the expression on his face a slight smile of recognition.

'To what do we owe this honour?'

'Pleasure and I hope some assistance.'

'Are you dining? I can—'

Shaking his head, Blanc turned slightly to see a rotund diner put a beautiful piece of fish into his gargantuan mouth. 'Is there...somewhere we can talk? Two minutes.'

It was Gaultier's turn to swivel away and snapping his fingers, summon an aide. 'Take over for a few minutes. I'll be in the nook.'

Recognising Blanc, the aide nodded and Gaultier led his visitor through to the back of the restaurant. The maitre d' entered a space that wasn't much more than a closet, but had a one-way glass, enabling the occupant to look out but not be seen. There was just room for Blanc to squeeze in.

'A surprise, huh? When are you going to come and work for me?'

'When are you going to open in New York?'

Blanc laughed then stopped abruptly and said, 'You know I sit on the Chef de France panel?'

Gaultier nodded.

'A young man from New York was one of the competitors. Does the name Raymond Babchuk mean anything to you?'

A look of vague recognition crossed Gaultier's face. 'Well, yes. He's an assistant chef de partie.'

'Here?'

'Oui.'

Blanc slapped his leg and sat back. 'He's a genius.'

Gaultier looked startled. 'Babchuk?'

'You are surprised.'

'If it's the same young man, well...'

'What's the take on him?'

The maitre d' took a quick furtive look outside. 'He *is* good. I've watched him. I don't know *how* good, but you know Pierre-Auguste Etienne?'

'Who calls himself Maestro? Unfortunately.'

'Well, there are issues. Babchuk is–'

'Temperamental?'

'Wouldn't call him that. He can be withdrawn, uncommunicative.'

'With Pierre-Auguste that might not be so dumb.'

'You say...genius?'

'Feydor, his *mousse de canard* had some other almost magical taste, a touch of mint-fraise perhaps – something indefinable. And his *tarte surprise aux pommes*...he'd added, I'm pretty sure, a point of *Noyau de Poissy*. Phew! It was so different. I couldn't speak!'

Gaultier looked at Blanc appraisingly. 'So he's a genius and you want him to come and work for you.'

'*Certainement*, but that's not why I'm here.' Blanc broke off at some commotion outside. Gaultier immediately left to sort out the issue. When he returned he was preoccupied.

'Monsieur Blanc–'

'Louis, please.'

Gaultier calmed himself. 'Louis, is there anything else?'

Blanc said, 'He comes to Paris and enters the competition. It starts two days late because of organisational complications. Of the twenty-five global contestants – and remember, these are already regarded as highly talented in their own countries – two others are exceptional, but he is not just outstanding, he's in a class by himself. One only sees this a few times in life. On finals day he is not there. He disappears. The panel are astounded, but are so impressed they make him a special award for *innovation creative*.' Pulling back some of the wrapping, Blanc revealed the top of what was obviously a very smart award.

Gaultier sighed. 'Who would have known it? Yes, he is talented, but... And you want to make this presentation here, now?'

'I've flown from Paris to do so.'

'Not an ideal time.'

'I can wait, and it will take but a moment.'

'The management are upstairs; I will see them.'

Although gone for only a few minutes, it was still longer than Gaultier had anticipated. Taking out his cell phone, Blanc was scrolling through his inbox when the sight of Pierre-Auguste waving his arms at a cowed waiter caught his attention. How anybody could work with such an overblown prima donna was beyond him. Suddenly the door burst open and the theatrical cuisinier stood there, his Dali-like moustache perfect in its imitation.

'Manifestation from hell. Get out!'

'What a welcome, Pierre-Auguste! Are you under pressure or simply being your normal courteous self today?' Closing down his cell phone, Blanc smiled sweetly.

'You...you get out of my restaurant, now!'

'*Your* restaurant, Peter? *Your* restaurant?' Blanc retorted, belittling him by using his real name.

Frank Chesson suddenly appeared beside the apoplectic chef, suave, cool and more than able to defuse the situation. 'I think it would be sensible if you returned where you belong.' He spoke calmly.

Departing, Pierre-Auguste's blustering rant surrounded him like a cloud of meaningless vapour. It was farcical and pathetic to behold.

'How can I help you, sir?' Addressing Blanc, Chesson was polite and courteous.

'I explained to Monsieur Gaultier I have come from Paris to present an award to a young chef working in your kitchen.'

'From Chef de France, huh?'

Blanc bowed slightly.

'Babchuk – young Raymond? Pretty damned good. Didn't know he'd entered.' Frank looked thoughtful. 'Was this a few weeks ago?'

'Nearly two months.'

'He had a vacation. Good for him. When do you want to give it to him?'

'I can wait.'

'Give it to him now. Won't take long, will it?'

Shaking his head, Blanc looked at Frank but said nothing. Reading his thoughts, Frank said, 'Do PA good. Spike him up some!' and, laughing, indicated Blanc to follow him. 'Peter! Ha! And to think he doesn't think we know.'

The backstory to Pierre-Auguste Etienne's origins were murky and originally known only to a few but the truth ultimately always emerges. The maestro's recent histrionics had led several people to enquire about him and had revealed his real name to be Peter Anthony Everard, whose birth was registered to a mid-western town far from Paris, France or haute cuisine.

Now Frank Chesson and Louis Blanc walked along a wide, carpeted passage to some swing doors marked 'in' and 'out'. Entering the noisy kitchen, Frank clapped his hands.

'Excuse me, Chef.' He nodded briefly to Pierre-Auguste, but didn't wait for an acknowledgement. Taking a heavy ladle, Frank banged on the counter, making Tutti Frutti screech in his cage. Frank grimaced; some quiet began to descend on the busy scene. Chefs and several waiters who had come in for orders stood waiting. Pierre-Auguste appeared temporarily stunned.

'As you know, I rarely enter this magical place where you guys create. However, we have an esteemed visitor today: Monsieur Louis Blanc. I'm sure you'll all know Monsieur Blanc has his own Michelin place out on the coast, and you'll prob'ly also know he's on the panel of judges for the world-renowned Chef de France competition.' Frank paused. He had their attention now. 'A month or so ago one of you took a brief vacation.'

Whilst no one interrupted, Frank played it as though there had been some response, putting his hands up. 'I know, I know – who here can have time to take a vacation, you say? Must be one lazy chef!'

This drew a slight laugh. Tutti Frutti screeched some more.

'But this guy didn't really take much of a break. He went to Paris and entered the annual competition. He did good. He did so good he made the final, but because he was contracted to return and the competition ran late, he missed the last day.' Frank paused for effect. 'So good had his work been throughout the two weeks, the Chef de France judges decided to make him a special award for his outstanding abilities, and requested Monsieur Blanc come by and present it. He knows who he is – Ray Babchuk, come up and receive your award.'

Led by the chattering Tutti Frutti, there was clapping all round, most of the kitchen being genuinely pleased at

Raymond's triumph. As he stepped forward, Maestro Pierre-Auguste had already exited through the swing doors and Charlie Reardon's expression was one to freeze piss. Raymond shook Frank Chesson's hand, the director smiling and clapping him on the back. Having unwrapped the award, which was a stylish glass affair, Blanc presented it to the young man. Several people produced small cameras and their cell phones, digitally clicking away, recording the event for posterity.

'One of you bring me up some of these pictures, huh? Have 'em on the wall. Celebration of success.' Smiling, Frank turned to Blanc, who now stood beside Gaultier, the maitre d' having quietly materialised from the restaurant.

'Wanna have a few minutes with the kid?'

Blanc nodded.

'Okay,' Frank looked at Gaultier, 'What shift's he on?'

'He's working tonight.'

'Let him finish lunch and give him the rest of the day off.' Frank grinned at Gaultier's tense face. 'It won't do him no harm. And if it does, we could have ourselves a new maestro!'

'He's—'

'Upstairs waiting for me? Can't wait. Good to meet you, Mr Blanc. Kid did good, huh?'

'The kid did very good, Mr Chesson. He has a lot of talent.'

Frank nodded and left the kitchen. It was Blanc who took charge.

'I am sorry to have taken up so much of your time. I know you must get back to work. *Allez! Vite!*'

Activity was immediately resumed in the kitchen. Just as he was turning away, Raymond was stopped by Blanc.

'Young man.'

Raymond turned back.

'You are being given some time off this afternoon. I would like to meet with you and discuss some things.'

Whilst Ray's face was one of pleasure, his expression became alert. He didn't immediately respond, then said, 'Things?'

Smiling, Blanc was smooth. 'Yes Raymond, presenting this award to you is very special. The panel have never done such a thing before.' The young chef and the master of the art looked at each other. 'I would like to talk to you, about cuisine.'

Ray's face broadened to a smile. He looked endearingly attractive. 'In that case, Mr Blanc, I'd be delighted.'

'My car will be outside.'

Clutching his award, Raymond backed away, his natural diffidence returning, and began walking towards his bench.

'Hey, Raymondo – one cool dude; that's some award, man!' Luke was genuinely impressed.

Aldo, too, chimed in: 'Dark horse, my man. An award-winner. Michelin next, huh?'

Raymond just smiled at their appreciation. Arriving back at his place, he positioned the award carefully to one side.

'Hey, Ray, that's so beautiful. You're just so brilliant.' Although gushing, because Tabitha was genuine in her praise, her compliments somehow didn't come out as cloying. She admired the glass trophy.

Raymond Babchuk
in recognition of his outstanding contribution
Chef de France Special Award
for
Originality and Innovation

'So awesome. Where yer gonna put it?'

Raymond shrugged. A cry went up.

'*Boeuf en croute*, twenty minutes.'

'Chef!' Raymond was immediately assertive in his response. Gaultier appeared beside him.

'Maestro Pierre-Auguste and Sous-Chef Reardon are both upstairs. Can you take over?'

'Unnecessary, Monsieur Gaultier. If you can handle front of house we'll all manage the rest.'

'Sure? You don't need to control?'

'Preparation is done; the session is half through.'

'All right. If you're concerned about anything, let me know immediately.'

Busy with his *en croute*, Raymond smiled briefly. Gaultier departed. Tutti Frutti let out a screech.

Upstairs, Frank Chesson appeared remarkably relaxed as he sat lounging in a swivel chair, his colleague and business partner, Alain de Lange, gazing out of a window, apparently indifferent to the raging Pierre-Auguste.

'Never have I been so insulting – never! This leetle piece of shit, this leetle piece of dung here goes behind my back. I, Maestro Pierre-Auguste Etienne, who taught him everything he know!'

Charlie Reardon appeared at the door. Sitting back, Frank began cleaning his fingernails with a paperknife.

'Come in. You may as well. Anyone left in the kitchen?'

'Babchuk's running it – the little shit who's such a goddamn genius!'

'You betray–!' Pierre-Auguste's colour was rising fast.

Frank held up his hand. 'I take it you side with "Maestro"' – Frank smiled – 'Pierre-Auguste...'

Charlie Reardon gave a terse nod. Pierre-Auguste pulled

himself up to his full 5 feet 6 inches. The effect was comical.

'Either the upstart go or I!'

'This award he won–'

'Tcha! It is nothing!'

'The Chef de France is not an important competition, according to you?'

Pierre-Auguste appeared to ignore the question.

Frank continued, 'But you having taught him everything he knows, he went off and won this, to you, "unimportant" award, but one of international renown.'

'Crap-head!' Reardon snarled out the words.

'A crap-head who wins an award.' Frank didn't raise his voice but the effect of his words was much stronger than Reardon's obvious animosity.

'He is nothing. Tcha!' Pierre-Auguste clicked his fingers.

For several seconds the room was silent. Reardon stood immobile. Even the maestro seemed powerless. Frank Chesson continued cleaning his fingernails, and Alain de Lange gazed out of the window. But it was he who finally spoke, turning to the chefs.

'That's not quite how we see it.' De Lange picked up some papers from the desk. 'Covers were down last month, Maestro. You think that's a reflection on the food?'

Pierre-Auguste looked apoplectic. His head shook; he appeared to be having a fit. De Lange reached down to an intercom on the desk and flicked a switch.

'Marjorie, would you tell Mr Gaultier we're confirming Mr Babchuk's having the night off?' He didn't wait for a response, immediately removing his finger from the intercom button and turning back to the window. 'Maestro, if you're thinking what I think you're thinking, don't do it, huh? Let things calm down a little.'

Pierre-Auguste looked from de Lange to Frank and back to de Lange again. Then, muttering words of outrage, he turned on his heel and headed for the door. Frank looked up.

'Cool it, Mr Everard. You think your food's the greatest. Just make sure the Great American Public thinks so too, huh? Continues payin' for it?'

Replacing the paperknife on his desk, Frank inspected his cleaned fingernails. Pierre-Auguste and Reardon left the room.

Chapter 6

Walking from the restaurant, Raymond felt in a strange state. He'd heard about people who, having experienced some euphoric surprise, found themselves feeling light-headed as a result. Staring down at his award, his present frame of mind was certainly something he'd never known before. Approaching a limousine parked outside *Le Chat Noir*, a chauffeur opened a door for him. Raymond climbed in, taking a seat opposite Louis Blanc, who sat languorously on the back lounger. Raymond was still in a partial out-of-body state as the car moved off, only waking from his reverie when Blanc produced an expensive store bag. Peering inside, Raymond took out several shirts and ties.

'I thought your attire might not quite befit where we're going. Still, a new shirt and tie should help. The jeans; I believe they've recently changed the rules regarding *denim*.' He pronounced the word the French way.

Selecting the brightest items from the batch, Raymond handed back the bag. Heading up town, the car glided through busy streets but his eyes saw none of it. He was still transfixed, gazing at his award which he turned over endlessly with his long fingers.

'Don't wear it out. You'll need to change before we get there.'

Placing the glass statuette between his legs, Raymond took off his T-shirt, revealing his white body with its modest chest hair. Then taking the shirt, he undid a few buttons and pulled it over his head. Thrown by the young man's indifference to expensive clothes, Blanc stared at Raymond, who now picked up the tie. It quickly became apparent he was none too familiar with the item, unable to begin, let alone complete, a knot.

'Here. Let me.' Leaning forward, Blanc expertly tied the tie and straightened the shirt collar. By the time he'd finished, the top half of Raymond looked okay, but in strange contrast to the bottom. Blanc sighed. 'Ah well, I know the doorman. Perhaps we can have dispensation if we stay in the bar.'

They were lucky. Whilst not impressed by Blanc's suaveness (he saw that every day), doorman Blenkovitch had just had a row with management and found the idea of admitting the bizarre-looking young man through the hallowed portals of the Cabot Club completely to his liking. The two men strode up the grand staircase. On the landing, Raymond asked for the men's room, leaving Blanc to enter the lounge alone. It was a magnificent saloon, all button-backed Chesterfield sofas and worn leather chairs. Blanc requested the wine list and sat down on a stool. After studying the selection, he ordered, and in due course the wine arrived: a vintage white. Blanc checked its temperature then tasted it, holding it in his mouth for several seconds. He gave a slight grunt of appreciation. Babchuk finally appeared, now looking even stranger. He'd plastered down his hair and cut off the bottoms of his ragged jeans, creating a pair of long shorts. Blanc stared open-mouthed, as did the bar steward. Clearly the man had never seen such a sight at the club. Smiling, Raymond placed his award on the bar.

'It's okay; they were old jeans anyway.'

Blanc closed then opened his mouth. Raymond said, 'What yer drinkin'? D'Yquem?'

Working furiously to regain his cultivated composure, Blanc indicated the steward pour his guest a glass of the wine he'd ordered. Raymond stared hard at the pale gold liquid, swilling it slightly before taking a sip. Like Blanc, he also held it on his palate.

'Sixty-two or maybe...? Thirty-seven?'

In spite of himself, the steward was impressed.

'Sixty-two, sir.'

Raymond smiled.

The steward looked at the award. 'This...is impressive.'

'Just won it!'

'You?!' The steward couldn't help the force of his words. 'You, er, won this?'

'Just said so. Presented to me by Monsieur Blanc himself.'

Blanc made a little head movement and picking up his wine glass, gave a small smile of indulgence. 'To your present and future success.'

Raymond also picked up his glass and sipped some wine. Neither spoke for a little then Blanc said, 'I am sorry if my presentation caused any trouble.'

Raymond didn't respond. His manner could be disconcerting.

Blanc continued, 'I rather think Pierre-Auguste won't forgive you.'

Sipping the vintage wine, Raymond still didn't react.

Blanc cleared his throat. 'I've known' – He hesitated – '"Pierre" for many years. Whilst he is indeed a man of some talent, forgiveness isn't a quality I would associate with him.'

Blanc had some more of his wine. Putting down his

own, Raymond turned to face him in that very particular and direct way he had.

'Mr Blanc, I really couldn't give a Godzilla's ass what the "Maestro" – ha! – thinks or does.' Raymond turned the stem of his wine glass. 'He don't figure.'

Blanc considered. 'You know, I would like you to come and work for me. I have a restaurant in Beverly Hills, *L'Escargot*.'

'Yeah – you have Head Chef Pirradi.'

'He wishes to go to Paris.'

'Can't say I blame him.'

'Hmm! Are you interested?'

'Dunno. I'm very flattered, Mr Blanc.'

'Louis, please.'

'Er, Louis. But right now I'm unsure what my plans are.'

'This is your best time to make a move. There will be publicity.'

'Yeah, sure. Look, I–'

Blanc cut in forcefully. 'I wanted to ask you about your *mousse de canard*. Several members of my panel said it was–'

'Exquisite. They said it was exquisite.' Raymond was quick to supply the superlative term.

'That is exactly what they said.'

'They liked the touch of aspic and mint.'

'Inspired.'

'Okay, then. Well, if you're gonna talk food!'

The two men rapidly became absorbed in their subject. For the younger man, it reflected his total being.

Hours later, Louis and Raymond – the latter still clutching his precious trophy – were the last to leave the Cabot Club. The evening had obviously been a good one. As if by magic, Blanc's limousine appeared before them. West 42nd

Street was quiet at the Sunday midnight hour.

'And I must tell you, when I had added the anise hyssop, the dish... It was fantastic!'

The two men tumbled into the back of the car, which glided off. Sprawled on the sumptuous seats, the mood became comfortably affable.

'You know, Raymond, I love New York. There's no city like it.'

Raymond, who had been continuing to gaze at his beloved award, looked up and giggled. 'You're right there, Mr Blanc.'

For a second a look of great intensity swept over the older man's face. His mood was interrupted by an intercom voice.

'Say, 'scuse me, sir, but can you tell me where we're headin'?'

Blanc turned to Raymond. 'You wish me to take you home?'

Raymond smiled. 'Oh, no, The Cat'd be fine.'

'Do you need to get in? It'll be closed now; even the clearing up will be done.'

'No, no; left my car there.'

'Are you driving?'

'If it'll start.'

'Hmm! The wine?'

'Pretty good.'

'I mean, driving...'

Raymond had one of his non-responsive moments; Blanc gave a slight shrug.

'*Le Chat Noir* – Park and seventy-four.'

The car accelerated and the two cuisiniers were quiet for a minute.

'So...you'll consider my offer?'

'Your offer?'

'*L'Escargot.*'

'Ah. Beverly Hills. Yeah.'

'When can you start?'

Raymond laughed. 'When can I start? I don't know, Louis. I just don't know.'

'You will be Master Chef.'

'Uhuh! Well, it's a thought.' Raymond laughed some more and Blanc caught the moment.

'It's a prestigious restaurant. You're twenty-eight years old. To be a maestro at that age...you'd be doing well.'

'Guess I'll have to shoot for a Michelin.'

'You have the ability.'

'I know.'

Blanc chuckled. 'The conceit of youth.'

'No conceit about it, Louis. I'm great and I intend to be the greatest – the greatest that ever lived.'

The car glided along.

'You know, Raymond, confidence is a wonderful thing, but arrogance – you must be careful. Conceit on the way up can alienate people and if you ever come down...'

Raymond snorted his odd-sounding high-pitched chuckle. Smiling, Blanc looked across at him again.

'Do you have other interests?'

Raymond made no immediate response, then, 'What other interests would I have?'

'I don't know. A girl, maybe?'

Raymond sniggered. Arriving outside *Le Chat Noir*, the limousine glided to an effortless stop.

'That's a no then, is it?'

Raymond opened the car door and got out. He looked back at Blanc.

'Mr Blanc, it's none of your business. Thanks for the

drink...and the award. So long now.' Closing the car door, he began walking away.

Blanc depressed the electric window button. 'If I cleared it with Maestro Pierre-Auguste, would you come?'

Sighing, Raymond turned back. 'I've told you, I don't know what my plans are right now. Thanks for the offer, but I don't know.'

'I'm in town for a couple of days. Like to meet up again?'

'Maybe.'

'I'll call you.'

Raymond waved but said nothing, moving toward a side alley. As his car moved off, Blanc sat back.

'You can have the shirt and tie on me.' His mood was reflective. 'Godzilla's ass! Hmm!' He flicked the intercom switch. 'The Village. I'll tell you where when we're nearer.' He straightened his tie; he'd been flustered. 'I'll have you – little upstart!'

Chapter 7

Loosening his collar as he passed the closed *Le Chat Noir*, Raymond turned into the side alley, at the back of which his old convertible T-Bird was parked. Although at this hour it was a dark and shadowy place, anything sinister was lost on him as he danced amongst the trash cans and steam-emitting manholes, his award clutched to his breast. Suddenly a scream rang out, but it wasn't a human scream. Charlie Reardon stepped into the dim light of a single alley lamp, holding a cage-like contraption which contained Tutti Frutti, head held tightly in a vice, causing the little monkey great distress. Reardon was clad in a leather jerkin and swung a steel bar. He gave a hollow laugh.

'Looking interesting tonight, Raymond, though I don't know about the jeans. Been out with the man, huh?' His tone was sarcastic. 'Offering yer a job, was he, yer talentless little jerk?'

'What are you doing with Tutti?'

'Thought he could do with a little air... Come to see his friend.' Reardon looked into the cage. 'Ha! What am I goin' to do to yer both? Monkey brains, the pair of yer – or will be!'

'Let him go. He's hurting like that.' Raymond approached his car and, putting down his award, began fiddling with his keys, trying to unlock the vehicle. Swinging Tutti's cage in one hand and swishing the crowbar, which was chained to his wrist, in the other, Reardon placed the monkey cage on the T-Bird's hood.

'Caring to animals, huh? An award-winner and animal-lover. Asshole!'

The crowbar smashed into the wing of the car, causing the monkey cage to jump.

'Hey!'

Reardon ignored Raymond, picked up the award and read off the inscription:

'Chef de France... Outstanding originality and innovation. Asshole.'

A disturbance in the alley's darkness caused Reardon to look round. A hobo sat up, scratching himself, peelings and detritus falling from his filthy clothes.

'Can't yer pick another adjective? We're gettin' kinda bored over here.'

'Wha...? Shut the fuck up! Can't yer see we're havin' a conversation?'

'Well, have one then. Use a greater variety of words, can't yer? Gets kinda tiring, the anal orifice constantly repeated in its crudest form.'

'Will yer get this? Listen, pal, if yer don't park it you'll get this up yer.'

The hobo fell back, the sound of trash cans and burping rupturing the night air. 'Yeah, yeah, yeah.'

Having opened the car door, Raymond now took hold of Tutti's cage and put it inside. 'Have you got the key for this?'

'What are yer doin', man? Who said you could have that?'

'I don't want him getting hurt.'

'What is goin' on around here? Are people not payin' me enough attention?'

'Yer fuckin' right they aren't, asshole.'

The words came from the alleys depths. Banging down the award, Reardon turned towards the shadows. Without waiting a second, Raymond grabbed the glass trophy and jumped into his car. Excited, Tutti Frutti began chattering loudly. Swinging round to see Raymond trying to start his ancient motor, Reardon smashed the metal bar into the car's side.

'That's very stoopid, Raymond – very stoopid. I ain't finished with you yet.'

Raymond's engine caught, oil fumes pouring from the exhaust, causing Reardon to cough.

'Jesus H! Yer got any emissions on this thing?'

Raymond floored it; the engine screamed. Quickly recovering, Reardon leapt towards the car and began to beat it crazily. Raymond engaged 'Drive' and the old car shot forward. However, by some bizarre chance, Reardon's wrist was caught in the T-Bird's wing mirror. The sous-chef barely had time to utter an oath before he was slammed into the alley lamppost, causing it to fracture. The force of this collision catapulted him skywards and his return to earth penetrated Raymond's tattered and torn convertible roof. Raymond pumped the brakes and the car came to a standstill, Reardon's legs protruding grotesquely skywards. Tutti Frutti appeared overjoyed, his monkey voice screeching into the night.

'Ooohoo. That's a very nice sight. A sight for sore eyes, that is. Hahaha!' All the excitement had rendered any further sleep for the hobo impossible. He now stood up in all his muck and filth and began to walk round the car.

'He's... He's...' Raymond's shock made him incoherent.

'Looks like it to me – as a dodo.'

Raymond got out of his car as the bum, whose name was Hikey Homaster, peered inside.

'Yup! He's a dead 'un all right. Neck broken. Heeha! Well, he sure had it comin' to him, the–' Homaster broke into eruptions of laughter.

'But...but, I didn't mean to kill him!' Raymond was beside himself.

Homaster was easy, indifferent. 'Sure yer didn't, kid. Good job, though. Good riddance. Nasty piece of work.' Homaster laughed darkly.

'What should I do?'

'Well I wouldn't advise yer drivin' around like that, though personally I like it. Kinda different.'

One of Reardon's legs flopped crazily against the canvas roof. Another hobo appeared: Leon. Seriously inebriated, Leon staggered into the scene, falling against his compadre.

'I guess yer ain't too keen on goin' to the police. Been drinkin', haven't yer?' Leon burped.

'Yer...yer can't leave me with him.'

'Won't do that. Yer comin' with me, ain't yer, Leon?'

Leon retched.

'Jesus! Time and place, Leon. Time and place.'

The two began lurching down the alley.

'What am I gonna do?' Almost in a swoon, Raymond leant against his car. Homaster swung back.

'That's a question. Try feedin' him to the crocs and cut yer lights.'

Leon suddenly spun round. 'Yer can't eat 'im alive, can he, Hikey?' He had a funny little cackling voice and now laughed like a hyena. 'Eatin' alive, eatin' alive – he bein' dead an' all!' Leon danced around Homaster as they staggered out of the alley.

Cutting his headlight beams, Raymond stared after their departing silhouettes. Tutti Frutti began to chatter excitedly. Initially ignoring him, the racket Tutti made was such that it ultimately permeated even Raymond's addled brain.

'Ssh! Ssh, Tutti! You'll wake the–' Raymond gagged against the side of his car. When he finally managed to pull himself together, he was staring at the little monkey who played with some keys. Fallen from Reardon's jeans pocket, the dead chef's wallet and some cigars also lay on the car seat. Taking the keys from the monkey's fingers, Raymond unlocked the cage and released the vice. Tutti screeched away.

For several minutes Raymond sat in the darkened alley, the distant sounds of the late night city throbbing in his freaked-out head. What was Tutti doing now, dancing round the back of the car? Raymond stood up and walked towards the trunk, where the monkey was tapping the lock and chattering. Although still in something of a stupor, Raymond took in the scene. What followed was as unreal as the accident. Raymond attempted to free Reardon's inert body from his coupé roof, but the ripped canvas tangled around his legs and torso. Because the roof clips were worn, Reardon's weight caused them to snap and the roof crashed back. Muttering and sweating amidst Tutti's row, Raymond was at last able to extricate the body, lugging it round to the back of the car where the monkey, perched on the collapsed roof, appeared almost to be directing things. Opening the trunk, Raymond hauled Reardon's body into it, the crowbar still dangling from one wrist. He then slammed the trunk shut and got into his now open-top convertible. Tutti scampered up beside him in the passenger seat.

'Okay, wise monkey, let's get outta here.' Starting the

car, Raymond engaged gear and the T-Bird lunged away.

Guiding his old vehicle along, Raymond turned into 33rd Street, gently nursing the wheel and doing his best not to lane-drift. As he pulled up at the lights, he became aware of several young women in a cab alongside, laughing and giggling. Looking across at them, he discovered Tutti smoking a cigar and blowing smoke rings at the girls.

'Tutti! Stop that! Stop that right now!' Raymond desperately tried to remove the Havana from the monkey's clutches, which only made the girls laugh more. Tutti loved it. The lights went to green and the T-Bird rocketed off. Never a particularly good driver, Raymond's road skills were now erratic.

'You kiddin' me, man? What are you like? Attractin' attention to ourselves – and us with a dead body in the trunk? You'll get us arrested!'

Tutti chattered hysterically; Raymond had to concede it was how he felt, too.

They trundled out of Manhattan into suburbs. Whilst Raymond wasn't really aware of anything much, least of all what time it was, he drove on mental autopilot heading for Queens and home, the streets becoming darker and the traffic thinner. Unbeknownst to the young chef, a gang of robbers had been raiding a bank less than a mile away and were now pouring into their getaway car with swag, before roaring away from the crime scene. Raymond was driving along a bit too fast and swaying about. Hearing police sirens, he became even more tense, sweat running down his face. As he crossed an intersection, the car suddenly spun round in a half-circle, it being clipped by the gang's vehicle. The trunk flipped up, and the hoodlums were dumbfounded to see the open eyes of a dead body gazing back at them, one arm dangling from the car. The trunk lid thumped down, cutting through Reardon's wrist. The crowbar shot free, with the dead chef's hand still attached, its flight unerring in accuracy, piercing the getaway car's windscreen and squarely impaling the driver's forehead. Out of control, the robbers' motor slammed into the front window of a store. Still preoccupied with his earlier troubles, Raymond was unaware of the fate of the thieves and correcting the T-Bird's direction, he and Tutti continued on their way. What an evening – it seemed to him like a hellish dream, but although Raymond didn't know it, his night had only just begun.

Chapter 8

The rain started as Blanc's limousine entered Greenwich Village, cruising through side streets and stopping outside what looked like a small church. Instructing his driver to park up, Blanc got out and dashed towards the apsidal door, pressing the button of an entry phone. Hugging the arched entrance to avoid the increasingly inclement weather, the Frenchman cursed. Finally there was an electrical buzz; Blanc spoke into the little speaker.

'Pierre, I'm getting wet.'

The speaker went dead.

'Merde!' Blanc shook his head in frustration. The buzzer went again and this time, so did the door latch. Blanc entered. At first glance, the interior was that of a Gothic church, but although organ music flooded the building, a closer inspection revealed it to have been converted for domestic use. However, elements such as the presbytery and altar had been left and, walking down the nave-like hall, Blanc found it hard not to genuflect. Perhaps that was the effect the owner desired? The music abruptly stopped. The church-like impression was augmented by the figure of Pierre-Auguste, looking more like Salvador Dali than Dali ever did and dressed in long robes, staring down from a triforium. Blanc burst out laughing.

'Ah there you are, Salvador. What fugue was that?'

Pierre-Auguste made no reply.

'Don't know? You should have mugged that up by now, Peter.'

'Manifestation from–'

'Yes, yes, yes! Bizarre how people will use the same expressions over and over. So unoriginal, but then you always were a copyist. Aren't you going to offer me a drink? It's been a tedious evening.'

Continuing along the hallway, Blanc turned off into a room resembling a small chapel. However, amongst crucifixes and statuettes it housed several sofas and other furniture, some pews being restyled into a bar with brightly coloured bottles and mixer shakers on display.

'This chapel looks more like a honkies' cat house every time I come here.' Helping himself to a large whisky and soda, Blanc sat down on one of the sofas. Pierre-Auguste appeared in the doorway. 'There you are. I helped myself.'

The maestro of *Le Chat Noir* swept in, looking completely ridiculous. Opening a fridge door, he removed a pre-prepared blue cocktail.

'I suppose it was your affectation that enabled you to get where you are.'

Before Pierre-Auguste could remonstrate, Blanc held up his hand. 'Don't do that Anthony – don't do that. You'll make yourself ill, and the arrogant little bastard isn't worth it.'

'He go behind my back!'

'You don't have to talk to me with that ridiculous accent, either.'

'The leetle piece of sheet. I teach him everything he know.'

Suddenly, Pierre-Auguste slumped down beside the Frenchman and started to sob. Blanc looked at him for several seconds then said, 'I'm sure you did,' and began stroking Pierre-Auguste's hair, calming him almost paternally. 'I'm sure you did.'

The phoney lay cradled against the other man's shoulder.

'You want rid of him and I want him.' The way Blanc said it had a ferocious edge. He gently patted the culinary pretender. 'We need to ensure we both get what we want, don't we? And we will.'

A mixture of smart and ageing housing, the Queens District of New York had originally been a poorer suburb of the city, but in the last twenty years the area had smartened up. The streets around Aunt Renais' location in Palmetto Street, though, had remained an island of old town – shops and restaurants serving minority cultures, the residences a hotchpotch of homeland and kitsch. Behind Palmetto Street were a series of run-down lock-up garages and it was onto this site Raymond now motored, rain pouring into the open car. Coming to a stop in front of one of the graffiti-covered garages, he got out, unlocked the padlock and raised the canopy door. Junk and bric-a-brac were piled high along the sides of the unit but after kicking away a kid's broken toy pram (what was that doing in there?), the central section was clear. Sopping wet, Raymond ran back to his T-Bird and guided it into the garage. Out of the car again, he pulled down the garage door using an interior lanyard. When it was closed, Raymond turned on a light.

Still wearing the tie Blanc had knotted for him Raymond wrung out the wet ends of the shirt. 'Got to get changed.'

Holding Raymond's award, Tutti Frutti chattered away.

'Come on, Tutti, let's get warm.'

Raymond took a torch from the car, turned off the garage light and partially lifted the door, so he and the monkey could slip under it. Outside, he closed the overhead and locked it. Huddling against the rain, the young chef and his monkey friend headed for the street.

Aunt Renais had had a tiring day dying her pubic hair. As she'd tell her male coterie, 'I like that Jean Harlow look, baby.' Now, as she reclined on a daybed inspecting herself, in her little TV box room off the hallway, a reality game show blaring from the set, legs akimbo and talking on her mobile, her full bizarreness was seen in all its ghastly glory. She was a revolting creature.

'You're coming to my soirée, Ruby? Yeah, Sunday.'

Raymond and Tutti entered, dripping wet and cold.

'Mamie'll be there and she's bringing her boy, Arnold. He's so successful, unlike the no-good scumbag of a nephew of mine who's just walked in. What are you doin', gawpin' and drippin' water everywhere?'

It was difficult to say who was the most grotesque – Raymond in his vivid shirt and sawn-off jeans or his aunt in her pink chemise and rou-rou slippers.

'Rubes, I gotta go.' An idle, aging slut she may have been, but Renais didn't miss much. 'Gotta sort out this son-of-a-bitch slime ball. See you a week today, 'bout five. Ciao.' She clicked off the phone and Raymond began to walk away. 'Come here!'

Raymond stopped.

'Where yer been? Hangin' out with the smooth Frenchie enquirin' after yer?'

'None of your business.'

'I'll decide that. What yer wearing? Is that a tie?'

Raymond just looked at her.

'You're… I don't like yer. I never liked yer. Whatcha got there?'

'An award.'

'Frog give it yer?'

'I won it.'

'Cookin', no doubt. Well, you can cook somethin' for me Sunday – somethin' decent, in sauce. And good meat. None of them miserly portions. Here, come and sit down.' Suddenly friendlier, she moved a frilled buttock to give him room.

'I'm wet. I'm gonna change.'

The look Renais gave him was unaccountable, suggestive, yet somehow desperate. 'Show me yer trophy.'

Reluctantly, Raymond proffered his Chef de France award, which Renais took, in the process somehow contriving to caress his hand. At that second Tutti, who had been scratching himself by the door, bounded into view. Renais shrieked and dropped the glass prize, which shattered on the floor. Tutti also let out a cry. Raymond stared, stupefied by what had happened.

'Get it outta here! 'Cept Pussy and Hard, yer know I don't let no animals in the house. Get it out! Out! Aagh!'

Raymond moved as if to hit her. Although scantily clad, Renais suddenly pulled out a little snub-nosed hammerless pistol from the folds of her short gown. Whilst shocked, Raymond couldn't help noticing how the Colt's handle and his aunt's chemise were of matching pink. He dropped down on his hands and knees and began collecting the broken pieces of his award, his face expressionless, his actions swift. Then he was gone, Tutti Frutti scurrying after him up the stairs. Behind him, his aunt's manner had returned to one of snarling aggression, her face contorted with hatred.

Opening the door to his self-contained apartment,

Raymond let Tutti scurry past before closing and locking it. He leant against the frame for several seconds, panting and trying to calm himself, before opening one of the internal double doors that led into his magnificent kitchen. Entering his *cuisine-de-paradis,* he placed the glass pieces of his broken trophy on the central console and got himself a bottle of water from the fridge. He knew beyond doubt now that not only did he hate his aunt with every fibre of his body, but she was sexually perverted and insane.

Raymond walked back into his tiny bedroom, crammed with its cook books and periodicals, piled high from floor to ceiling, even supporting the palliasse he used as a bed. On the small table beside it stood an ancient TV, the handset of which Tutti was fiddling with. As Raymond watched, the monkey turned on the set. One smart animal. Through a snowy image he could decipher the news was on. Tutti began changing channels.

The phone rang. Raymond let it, the ringing going to answerphone. It could only be his aunt – and it was.

'Yer little jerk! I've a good mind to come up and shoot yer! Yer out this time – yer out, hear me?' Renais' voice was a shriek, which prompted a similar row from Tutti though Ray didn't think it was of distress on the latter's part. 'Pick up, yer little turd.' Raymond swigged some more water. 'That rodent' – surely she didn't mean that – 'it's gone by dawn and you're gone right after it, Sunday night. Evicted! I'm callin' the law tomorr–'

The timer kicked in, cutting off Renais' hysteria. Raymond gulped down another swig of water and the phone rang again. Walking to the jack point, Ray disconnected it. Tutti was staring at the television. The picture quality had improved and a programme about the South Seas was now on the screen, the documentary revealing how the idyll portrayed can hide dark secrets. Moving aside a copy of Sabatier's *Cuisine Unique*, Raymond sat down on his bed and finished his water. Tutti climbed up beside him, resting his little head on the chef's knee. The television story continued, explaining how a young German couple had been sailing in the Pacific. Mooring their boat off the island of Papeete and having gone ashore, the man had got involved in a goat hunt and never seen again. A Polynesian had come out to the yacht and tried to entice the woman to accompany him. She had refused, and the native sexually assaulted her. Authorities later found charred remains of the man, but much of his body had been eaten. The narrator went on to talk about how, historically, cannibalism had been widely practised in those parts. Raymond idly rotated the recipe book in his hand. Tutti looked round. His monkey eyes saw a distracted human, a human who had much on his mind. Slowly, and with a strange look on his face, Ray turned towards the television. The presenter was giving details of this recent act of barbarism, leaving little to the imagination – burned bits of thigh and leg, human teeth-marks in the flesh... The images seemed to mesmerise Raymond, boring into his psyche. His eyes grew wider and his face took on a distracted look. Suddenly, he stood up and began pacing about the room in a fever of excitement. Up and down he went, sighs of intense excitation emerging from his lips.

'Yeah...and all eaten up!' He thought some more. 'Oh yes! Yes, yes yes yes yes yes! Triumph! Genius! I am – I will be! Oh, yes. Ooh, Auntie...your soirée. Ooh something decent – ooh, yes!' He then burst out laughing. 'Ooh, no miserly portions. You can pig yourself, you bitch. You can choke on it. Haha!'

Raymond was out of himself. Quickly, he went through

to his darkened kitchen. Walking over to a window, he peered round a blind at the rain outside.

'Perfect.'

Running back to his bedroom, he grabbed an anorak from his tiny closet.

'Clever Tutti! You stay in here now. Raining outside, huh? Raymond's got to go and get something, okay? Won't be long, then we'll have the time of our lives!'

Tutti screeched about, following Raymond to the fire door. It was now raining very hard as the young chef stepped onto the fire escape.

'See you in a minute, Tutti.'

He pushed the door so it was nearly closed and hunching his shoulders against the weather, set off down the iron stairs. When he reached the bottom, he dashed across to the lock-ups and opened up his own. Inside, he put on the light and lifted the trunk. Reardon's face smiled up at him grotesquely. The right hand was severed, but there was surprisingly little blood. Raymond gulped then bent down and pulled out the body.

'Goddamit, Charlie, you weigh a ton!'

Leaning the corpse against the side of his car, the torso flopped into the backseat. Raymond closed the trunk and moved to the light switch, flicking it off. Then, by feel, he began lifting the garage door from the inside. Hauling Reardon's body onto his shoulder, he stepped outside and pulled the door down behind them. Resting the dead sous-chef against it, he managed to snap shut the padlock. Shouldering the body again, he stepped out onto the muddy forecourt and began a lumbering dash towards the lee of the brownstone houses.

Arriving at a broken wall halfway across the rucked garage lot, a car's headlights suddenly appeared, their beams piercing the inclement night. The vehicle came to a stop on the other side of the wall. Raymond hid, crouched behind it with his macabre load. The headlights dimmed and music blared from the car. Peering round the wall, Raymond struggled to see why the vehicle had parked there. In spite of the rain, his inquisitiveness got the better of him and, leaving Reardon lying against broken bricks, he approached the vehicle. Peering inside, it rapidly became apparent what was going on – a girl straddled a guy who sat behind the wheel. The brunette loosened her blouse. Some other noise caused the man to sit up and Raymond to drop out of sight. The radio went off.

'Little jumpy, ain't yer, Bevis? Come on, honey, settle down. Have a play of these.'

Sounds of lascivious pleasure now came from inside the car. Getting an arm under Reardon, Raymond heaved the body up on his shoulder and, bracing himself, prepared to tackle the next bit of his tortuous journey. He had nearly made it to some shrubs at the bottom of the fire escape when his foot kicked a fallen dustbin lid. The interior car light went on as Raymond crashed into the undergrowth.

'There's someone out there, Darlene.'

'Too fuckin' right there is and I'm gonna find them. Give me more fuckin' action than you can!' The car door opened and Darlene, a bright plastic mac slung round her shoulders, emerged into the night.

'Darlene! Darlene! What yer doin'?'

'What does it look like, jerk?' Slamming the door, Darlene began to walk off. As she passed the shrubbery, Reardon's dead face and shoulder fell into her path.

'Fuckin' drunks.'

Darlene kicked the dead Reardon, who rolled back.

'What's this fuckin' town comin' to? Not fuckin', that's

for sure. Where the hell can a girl get laid around here?'

The car started up and began to reverse after her, Bevis's apologetic remonstrations bleating plaintively in the night air.

Raymond resumed his task. The sheer physical effort was quite difficult enough without having to deal with any further interruptions. The previous twelve hours had, for Raymond Babchuk, been the most unaccountable of his life, but events affecting his destiny were set to be even more so for the remainder of that night. Lugging Reardon up the fire escape, he managed to ease open the door into his kitchen and, dumping Charlie on the large central console, he closed and locked the fire door. He then put on some kitchen lights and straightened out the body, Tutti dancing about by his side. The TV was still on and Raymond walked through to his bedroom to stare at the screen. The South Seas programme was concluding: images of Paradise intercut with the horrific trauma of cannibalism.

'Paradise lost – devoured.'

Flicking off the television and walking back into the kitchen, the expression on Ray's face was intense. He adjusted the lights so that only the central console was illuminated and walked to the counter, above which was a row of wall-mounted Sabatier knives. Selecting several, he returned to Reardon's bedraggled corpse. Placing two of the blades on the counter, he began to walk around it.

'So she wants to evict us, huh? Breaks my award and pulls a shooter. She's a bad piece, Tutti – a very bad piece. She only took me in for the money and the thank you I get for not tellin' on István clearin' out and her keepin' all the cash for both of us – my money? She smashes up my kitchen! Two years it took. Work. Night and day. And all she does is play around. Even tried it with me – the lecherous depraved bitch. Well, now she's gonna have somethin' special to remember me by, somethin' she'll never forget. Ha ha!'

While he'd been speaking, the razor-sharp knife was at work, his skilled hands dextrously cutting away Charlie's ragged clothing, the fragments dropping to the floor.

'What type of cut do we have here? Perhaps the ultimate chef's challenge – homo sapiens!'

Reardon now lay naked on the console. Tutti clapped and chattered.

'I want meat! Give me meat!' Raymond mimicked his aunt. 'None o' them miserly portions – and sauce, lots of sauce.'

Raymond began work.

'Private parts for a private meal. Only one plate for those to end up on, auntie. Ha!'

Chapter 9

The kitchen at *Le Chat Noir* was busy readying itself for the day, but did not appear to have quite the usual air of efficiency. Whilst Tabitha was diligently involved in some preparation, apron and cap immaculate, Luke and Aldo were skylarking about.

'Love that pastry, bro.'

'My man!'

Luke flicked a ball of dough high in the air, it landing amongst some stacked saucepans. The front of house door abruptly swung back and Gaultier entered with a ranting Pierre-Auguste in tow.

'Everyone is out. I will have all new staff. I will have them out – all of them!'

Ignoring the maestro, Gaultier looked round the kitchen. Not seeing Babchuk he went over to Tabitha.

'Miss McKindrick, has Mr Babchuk not arrived?'

'Er, no, he – I haven't seen him.' Gaultier looked concerned. 'I could call him.'

She didn't have to, because at that moment the alley side door opened and the young award-winner walked in.

'Mr Babchuk.'

Ray went straight towards the changing area at the back of the kitchen, slipping his jacket from his shoulders en route. 'Yuh, I know.'

'Mr Babchuk.' Gaultier was insistent.

'I'm sorry, I–'

'You are required upstairs.'

Pierre-Auguste could still be heard carrying on in the background.

'Oh?'

'They want to see you. I don't think your clothes are important.'

Having already donned his chef's jacket, Raymond looked at Gaultier sharply; the maitre d' was playing it very cool. Neither man spoke, as Raymond headed off across the kitchen. Approaching the front work area there was no sign of the maestro, who seemed to have abruptly disappeared. Raymond climbed the stairs to the managers' office. He'd only been inside it once before. He knocked tentatively.

'Yuh?'

Raymond put his head round the door and was recognised by Frank Chesson who, along with Alain de Lange, sat with five other men and a woman.

'Raymond Babchuk. Come in.'

Raymond entered the room.

'This, lady and gentlemen, is the guy who, for his vacation, went to Paris and took part in the Chef de France competition, winning' Frank cleared his voice – 'a special achievement award for outstanding originality.' Frank got up from the table and came over to Raymond. 'Thanks for coming up.'

Raymond showed no sign of pleasure or surprise at this consideration. Frank guided him to a corner of the room.

'Ray, there's something very strange going on, something we don't get. We've just had a call from France. Apparently...' Frank paused. 'Apparently there's been some accusation of cheating.'

Raymond looked dumbfounded. 'The guy was very

apologetic, but till it's sorted you can't accept the award.'

All the macabre events of the previous night were as nothing against the shock that now rocked Raymond Babchuk. Or perhaps they compounded it. He went white; he shook. He looked like a man castrated. The emotions Raymond now felt far outweighed those he'd experienced either after his accidental killing of the sous chef or even what he'd since done to his body. This accusation profoundly insulted his professional integrity and being the obsessive he was, Raymond's mind simply couldn't cope with the defamation.

'Wha–?' He was near collapse.

'Hey, kid.' Frank moved closer to him.

'Wha–?' Raymond sounded strangulated.

'Don't take it too hard, huh? I know it means a lot to yer, but–'

'Don't take it too hard? Don't take it too hard? Mean a lot to me? Aah! What they're doing – that cannot be. It cannot be anyway, but it cannot be!' Raymond's voice rose, causing the other people in the room to look over. 'I'll call them. I'll sue them. They–'

'Listen, you'd better have some time off. It couldn't be worse timing, what with the sous-chef not turning up this morning, but you don't look so good.'

Frank's words didn't seem to permeate Raymond's mind. He staggered about like a man in a trance. Eventually he said, 'This just came out of nowhere, did it? What I mean is you just got this call?'

Frank looked steadily at him. 'Yeah, we just got this call. Like I said, we don't like the sound of it. We, er, wonder why now?'

Raymond steadied himself against the table.

'Look, kid, you may as well know, Maestro Pierre-

Auguste is gunning for your dismissal.' Frank obviously thought this would get a reaction and for a second was surprised that it didn't. He went on, 'Raymond, we think something stinks about this and we'd like to offer you the position of chef de cuisine.'

This did affect Raymond. Although still out of it, he stared at the other people around the table.

'You... You want to offer me head chef?'

'Yeah. We know your talent.'

Raymond began to shake. Then he began to laugh. Then he began to laugh hysterically.

Frank took hold of him. 'Kid! Kid!'

With an enormous effort of will, Raymond attempted to pull himself together.

'I can see how this has upset yer, but you've got to get a grip. If yer take the position, lotta pressures come with the job.'

It was hard to describe how Raymond looked. Bewildered, stunned, shocked – his face was a contorted mixture.

'Look, I think today you should take a break. Like I say, the timin' ain't good, what with Reardon not showing up.'

Sweat was now pouring off Raymond's face as if he were suffering a fever.

'But we've had bigger problems. In fact, if you take the job, no doubt you'd want Reardon to go anyway.'

Raymond said nothing.

'Split – have some time out. Just let us know what you decide in the next few days, huh? Meanwhile, we'll just say yer havin' a little leave to celebrate and if you take up our offer, you will be!'

'I...er...ha!' Faltering, Raymond managed to walk to the door.

'And, Raymond, don't go on a cookin' spree, huh? Give

yerself a break.'

The young chef left. Turning back to his colleagues, Frank looked bemused. 'Oh boy! Temperamental chefs! Gimme fast food any day!'

'You don't mean that, Frank. You love *haute cuisine*.' Alain de Lange was his usual cool self.

'Do I? Yeah, mebbe I do at that. It's just the bunch of egomaniac nutters that produce the stuff.'

'Could be right there. They make money, though. Talkin' of which...'

The meeting resumed.

It was still daylight, but where was he? As he lay on his bed, his eyes aching, his face ashen, Raymond's brain slowly clicked into gear. Oh yeah, that was it; he'd come back home and had had so much to do. He got up and stumbled to the kitchen door. Tutti, who had been sitting at the bottom of his bed, skipped up beside him. The normally immaculate kitchen was a scene of total devastation. Blood, bones, bits of carcass, and the rags of clothes were all strewn about. The place was a mess and he knew he'd have to clear it up – fast. But amidst the carnage there sat on the counter two dozen parcels of varying sizes, all perfectly polythene-wrapped and sealed. Picking one up, Ray studied it. It was hard to see exactly what piece of flesh it was. How impersonal; just meat. What was he thinking? *Just* meat? Meat could be so varied, so delicate. Strangely, the mess didn't bother him too much. His kitchen could be washed down quickly enough and returned to its immaculate state. Nothing – nothing could ever be allowed to contaminate its perfection. But the overriding emotion Raymond experienced was one of purity, the neatness of what he'd done. It had the kind of symmetry that so appealed to him. It gave him an almost overwhelming sense of achievement and satisfaction, pleasure even.

Raymond's thoughts were abruptly interrupted by a knock on the fire escape door. He dropped the package. There was silence, then,

'Ray! Ray! Open up!' a voice hissed through the door. He recognised it as Tabitha's. What was she doing here? She couldn't come here. He looked at the clock – 4.30 p.m. She'd finished her shift.

'Ray, I know you're in there. Heard yer.'

Fear in every fibre of his body, Raymond tiptoed over to the door and very carefully eased it open a fraction. He blinked at the light.

'Ray, let me in!'

'No, Tab, you can't come in – not right now.'

'Why not?'

'What yer doin' here, anyways?'

'I know you've got that nut aunt. But I've been here before, remember?'

Raymond didn't look as though he did.

'Why can't I come in? You doin' something funny in there? Place looks a mess.'

'No, er, yer just can't.'

'But I got news.'

Raymond looked at her. 'I gotta take a shower. I'll meet you somewhere – a café.'

Tabitha stared at him. 'You okay?' Raymond didn't reply. Tabitha shrugged. 'Meet me in Ralph's, then – coupla blocks from here.'

She turned on her heel and headed down the fire escape. As he let the door close, Raymond's whole body began to shake.

*

Ralph's was the quintessential New York café, and Ralph the quintessential New York café proprietor. Short, squat and compact, a no-nonsense savvy had seen him through fifty years of dealing with the great New York public in all its shapes, sizes, races, creeds and colours. Fancy delicatessens had opened up nearby, most of which had closed down again, but Ralph's place went on and on, immortalised by its indomitable proprietor. Ralph was the sort of man who liked who he liked and what he liked, and once his mind was made up nothing could ever change it. Little of this was Tabitha aware of as she sat sipping a *caffè macchiato* and reading a food magazine, but having seen her several times, Ralph figured she was okay. His über sixth sense told him she was all right. For her part, like others before her and no doubt after, Tabitha just enjoyed the place. It was New York – the New York she loved, the New York she might be leaving.

Ray entered. Even by NYC standards he was a man in bizarre attire; pale, his hair was plastered down and he sported a pair of striped jeans that looked more like pyjama bottoms. A torn T-shirt and old hunting jacket completed the ensemble. Blearily spying Tabitha, he headed over to her. She looked up.

'Hiya. How ya feeling?' Tabitha smiled at him. 'Not too good? That heavy a night, huh?' Ray nodded. 'Wanna coffee?'

'Er, iced tea, mebbe.'

Tabitha hopped off her stool and went to order. Ray rubbed his eyes. Ralph, who never missed a thing, watched him. Tabitha returned with the drink.

'Ray, it's fantastic – I'm plannin' on quittin' The Cat. Your friend Mr Blanc's offered me a job.'

'Yuh?'

''Course, he really wants you, but he said I could work

for him as an assistant sous, anyways.'

'You wanna live on the coast?'

'Hmm...well, it would make a change. I want to get away from Pierre-Auguste, and that Reardon. Talkin' of which, he's disappeared. Took Tutti with him.'

'I got him.'

Tabitha looked enquiringly at Raymond.

'Tutti. I got Tutti.'

'That's great! Haven't got that slime ball Charlie, have yer? I'd like to cut him up and serve him blood-rare, the piece of cat's piss.'

Raymond, who had been sipping his iced tea, suddenly shot a mouthful straight at the mirror backing the bar in front of them. Tabitha looked at him, dumbfounded.

'Hey, hey, hey, what's goin' on?' Ralph was round his counter faster than a hot rocket. 'You don't make a mess in my place. Clear it up.' Ralph waved a dishcloth at Raymond, whose face was buried in his hands.

'It's okay. I'll get it cleaned up.' The young woman took the cloth and began wiping.

'You don't do that – he does that!'

'He's...he's unwell.'

'Well, he can get better – pronto!'

Ray went to try and assist clearing up his mess.

''Sides, no one does that to Ralph's iced tea – the best iced tea in Manhattan. No one!'

Between them, Tabitha and Raymond finished wiping away Ray's liquid explosion. Tabitha turned to find Ralph holding a waste bin, into which she dropped the grubby cloth. Ralph looked at Raymond disparagingly.

'Yer want some more, yer have to pay for it.' Ralph gave Raymond another long look before turning back to his counter.

'You'd better get home, get some rest. All this has been too much for yer.' Tabitha was embarrassed, but understanding. 'I've given in my notice, Ray. I gotta get out of The Cat. I need a change.' Outside, looking at the kerb, she tapped a scuffed shoe against it. 'Mr Chesson was very nice. Said if things worked out with you and them he'd let me reconsider. I think I gotta go though. I just kinda had it with the place.' Abruptly, she pecked Raymond on the cheek. 'Take care of yerself, yer hear?'

For some reason Tabitha seemed close to tears, but with a wave she was gone.

Chapter 10

Having been given several days' leave, Raymond spent the rest of the week getting himself as sorted as he could. On Wednesday Blanc called his cell phone but when Ray didn't pick up, the restaurateur left a message, telling him Miss McKindrick's employment was imminent and again asking Raymond when he would start. Raymond did not respond.

From *Le Chat Noir* there was no word, no one enquiring as to his return or asking if he knew anything about the disappearance of the sous-chef. Indeed, the world seemed remarkably indifferent to Reardon's disappearance, reminding Raymond of the quote: 'Some folks come to this town *wanting* to disappear. What difference does it make if a person drops off the scale? One less mouth to feed.'

And, as had become their way, the major hiatus between Aunt Renais and her nephew subsided. Raymond repaired his broken award, his painstaking efforts producing such good results that, at first glance, the damage was barely visible. By the end of the week he had begun to prepare for her soirée, but deep in Raymond's psyche his relative's recent behaviour had left a searing mark. He would not forgive her and in his continued darkly distressed mind the delicacies he was preparing to serve Mrs Ringold and her guests formed part of some perverse retribution. How he would delight in serving the old bitch this very particular food.

In so doing, his brilliance and professionalism demanded he provide a complete *haute cuisine* meal – stunning vegetable dishes and subtle sauces supporting the unusual meat. By making it a 'supper to end all suppers', he intended Aunt Renais' guests to speak rapturously of his food long after they had devoured Reardon's delicious body. Looking at the neatly arrayed packages in his freezer, Raymond wondered at his own sanity. Was he weird? Was he abnormal? However much he had loathed Reardon, he'd done wrong in killing him – but hell, it was an accident. It had happened. The sous-chef was dead and Raymond hadn't reported the incident to the police. Three days had gone by with no repercussions. What difference was it really going to make now what he did with the body? Indeed, by having it eaten he was literally removing the evidence – Charles Augustus (Charlie's mother had once read a Roman history book) Reardon might never have existed. Dust to dust, ashes to ashes – in this instance the body would enter via the diners' mouths, pass through their intestines and leave as human excrement. Contemplating life and death, Raymond had to acknowledge that whilst not all mankind ended up on the plate, death in itself was a factor common to the entire human race – the one truly inevitable part of life.

Towards the back end of the week, Frank Chesson's PA, Marjorie, called Raymond's cell phone; could Ray tell them when he would be returning? Raymond replied that he was still considering the management's offer and would be contacting them the following week for sure.

At the weekend, Louis Blanc flew out of Manhattan, heading for the West Coast. While in America he needed to check on his Beverly Hills restaurant. Blanc wasn't entirely satisfied with the way things had been left in New York. Having sown the seed with Chef de France in Paris questioning Raymond's integrity in the competition, a representative had contacted *Le Chat Noir*'s management suggesting Raymond might have cheated, but instead of firing the young chef de partie, the restaurant seemed unmoved by the accusation. This in turn had required Blanc to spend hours placating his old acquaintance, Pierre-Auguste.

Theirs was an odd relationship. Once lovers, Blanc had become a formidable force in the international culinary world. A globally-renowned master chef and latterly, restaurateur, he had cut it at the very top of the fiercely competitive celebrity chef world. The same could not be said for Peter Anthony Everard, who had become Pierre-Auguste Etienne. Indeed, it was little short of a miracle the latter had reached the level he had at *Le Chat Noir*.

As Blanc sat in the first class lounge waiting for his flight, he reflected that Pierre-Auguste wouldn't be the first chef to rely on those below him to provide the talent, whilst he took the accolades. Pierre-Auguste just wanted Raymond out of there. Blanc – well, he wanted Raymond. He also wanted to break him, the arrogant little shit, but that could come later. He recognised the boy's genius and knew the strange little jerk had fantastic ability. So his and his old lover's desires had coincided.

He'd hoped the lad would be with him flying out now, but that would have to wait. As a lure, Blanc had hired the girl, Tabitha, who'd told him she'd already given in her notice and would join him in Southern California the week after next. That would help. He'd get the boy in the end, of that there was no doubt.

*

Around the time Blanc was jetting off on his travels from JFK, Raymond had begun preparation for what he intended to be the meal of his life. Well no, not *his* life. He chuckled as he readied his kitchen, chatting to Tutti.

'Good thing this old boy got nailed, not you, huh?'

The little monkey chattered away happily. Now he was embarked on his course of action, Raymond's calm had returned. There being no recipe book he could refer to regarding the cooking of human flesh, he had already tried a little, fried, boiled and grilled.

It was a milder meat than he'd anticipated (not unlike chicken, but stronger) and he'd opted to stew Reardon, creating a subtle lentil sauce and adding rare herbs with a touch of garlic to heighten his flavour. Like all animals, Reardon comprised white and dark meat. His chest and torso were 'breast', his arms and legs a more muscular flesh, like very large drumsticks. Then there was the offal. Heart, lungs, intestines, kidneys (he imagined the latter devilled for Auntie's breakfast one morning) – Raymond decided he would keep these and create various delicacies from them in due course; perhaps pickle some and brine-and-cure others.

One of the very few trips he made out was to trawl fruit and veg markets in his inestimable way, relentlessly in pursuit of the very best greens, the just-ripe fruit, an avocado of perfect firmness, a pomegranate at its most tender and succulent. Raymond's obsessiveness served him well.

It was after one such excursion he'd decided to confront his aunt and, returning to the house, went in search of her. She was out, so he left a little note simply saying he was preparing her Sunday evening soirée, which would be served at 5.00p.m. He would provide some canapés with cocktails beforehand, and he wrote down the names of some fabulous wines which would be way over his aunt's head, the white being a rare hock, the red an unusual burgundy. He received no response.

Invited to chaperone his mother, Arnold Riseveldt had been an extremely reluctant guest and now, walking into Renais Rinegold's dining room, he was astounded by the extraordinary contrast of the decor. Mamie's son, he was the youngest guest by thirty years and as his mother entered, talking with another elderly guest, he stared at the bizarre scene. The walls were a livid pink with what looked like white painted criss-cross garden fencing covering the lower portion of three sides. On the fourth was a lurid mural, depicting a female nude that had just enough to suggest it was a likeness of the hostess (in former years), the proportions exaggerated and voluptuous. Renais' body was bizarrely contorted, her torso twisted around what appeared to be a vine-covered pole. The tasteless artwork contrasted wildly with the table laid out before Arnold, which was immaculate and stylish. An Irish linen tablecloth, crystal glassware and silver candelabras were all exquisitely set out. It was the juxtaposition that invaded the senses.

Riseveldt himself was short and somewhat rotund, his flecked grey hair drawn tight to his head and the rear of his neck sporting a short pigtail. It had been said he bore a likeness to Danny DeVito – and he did.

'Yew admirin' my dinin' room?'

Arnold snapped out of his reverie. 'A stunning room, ma'am – unbelievable.'

Gazing at her naked portrait, Renais smirked and stroked Arnold's arm.

The elderly Wally, having seated Riseveldt's mother, sank

into a chair beside her, his teeth clacking and his face twitching slightly. Wally had very large teeth and they gave the old man's face the look of a laughing skull – a disconcerting appearance. Several other decrepits appeared, dropping dangerously into chairs. Extricating himself from his hostess's scavenging clutches, Arnold was relieved to find he was seated at the head of the table, opposite the aging strumpet.

'Okay, yer know it's a boofay – yer go help yerselves. Arnold, you'll serve the wine.'

Surprised he wasn't expected to wait on them as well, Riseveldt just said, 'Sure thing, Mrs Rinegold.'

'You sit down over there, Ruby Montgomery, and stop playing with Wilbur's parts. Indecent, that thing pokin' up between his legs.'

Panting, Wilbur held onto the side of his chair as he levered his skeletal body into it, the enormous bulge in his slacks protruding skywards.

'Didn't touch him up or nothin', randy old goat.' Ruby was querulous, which completely passed Renais by.

'Now then, food's on the side, laid out, and Arnold's servin' the wine. See yer gettin' stuck in there, young man.'

Riseveldt had picked up a decanter of white wine and was pouring for his mother. 'As you suggested, Mrs Rinegold.'

'Right on – mustn't have Momma dyin' of thirst. You just keep a-pourin'.' Renais sashayed towards her chair.

'Be glad to, Mrs Rinegold, be glad to.'

'Oh, yew must call me Renais, mustn't he, Mamie?'

Mamie Riseveldt smiled sweetly and raised her glass. Arnold carried on round the table, offering vin rouge or blanc and filling glasses.

'Quite some spread yer servin' tonight, Rennie.' It was

Wilbur who spoke, pronouncing her name the same as the indigestion tablet.

'Be the last for a while, stud. That punk nephew o' mine's on his way out.'

'The one who's the chef?'

'Only got one punk nephew – the little jerk.'

'Wos he gone an' dun?' Wally this time, teeth clacking in his denture plate.

'Got back late after some award thing, bringin' a great baboon into the house, that's what. Monkeys, the pair of 'em.'

'He lives here then, does he, your nephew?' Riseveldt looked up from his pouring.

'He has done, yes sir – punk! Livin' offa me, stealin' offa of me.'

'He decorate the table?'

'If you call it that.'

Arnold resumed his wine duties.

'Anyways, I'm kickin' him out along with the marsupial. Now, boys, get up and serve us girls.'

Wilbur and Wally staggered up and lurched towards the tablecloth-covered sideboard. Silverware was displayed, along with fine bone china plates and serving dishes, beautifully arrayed. Letting the senior citizens go first, Arnold returned to his place and sampled the white wine he'd been pouring. Something of an amateur wine buff, the nectar he now tried was quite beyond anything his palate had ever experienced before. It was astounding; it was fantastic. He held some in his mouth for several seconds then, staring at his glass, marvelled at the subtle gold colour.

'Magnificent! Fabulous!'

'Wos that yer sayin', Arnold?'

'Oh...I...er, Mrs Ringegold, this wine... You always serve such a wonderful vintage?'

'Dunno as I do. Guess so. Stuff we usually have when jerk Raymond's preparin'.'

'I... Well–'

'Yer like it, huh?'

'I like it, I certainly do like it. Don't know whether I've ever tasted such a fine vin blanc.' Serving such wonderful wine to these people who were so obviously philistines left Riseveldt dumbfounded. He had another sip. It wasn't simply superb; it was exquisite.

'Prefer red meself, but you enjoy it, then git and have yerself some food.' Mrs Ringegold looked down at the plate Wally had placed in front of her. Green vegetables were laid out beside potatoes and a large meat portion, which was covered with a light-coloured sauce. 'Least the punk's made some sauce. I like sauce with ma food.'

Wilbur was now getting stuck in and while chomping his way through a mouthful of food, spluttered, 'Wos the meat, Renais?'

'Chicken.' Getting started on her own mastication, Renais slurped an over-large mouthful of wine.

'Chicken?' Some gravy ran down Wilbur's chin. 'I'm not so sure. Tastes more like guinea fowl to me.'

'Guinea fowl? You wouldn't know a guinea fowl if it started up yer ass, Wilbur Fortescue.' Ruby was dogmatic in her opinion.

'Well, it ain't turkey. I forbid that bird on any other day but Thanksgivin'.' Renais was emphatic.

'Goose.' Wally's teeth clacked away.

'Oh, still alive, huh, Wally? Goose, yer say? May as well throw in duck while yer about it.'

The elderly chattering among themselves, Riseveldt

82

began serving himself. If the food was as good as the wine, he was in for a gastronomic treat to remember. Again struck by the immaculate layout of the spread before him, the vegetables looked fabulous, crisp and fresh. The potatoes were prepared *basquaise* – not that Arnold knew that – long French potatoes, with their centres hollowed out and stuffed with garlic-flavoured tomato, peppers and bayonne ham, breadcrumbed and baked. The effect was unusual and culinarily spectacular. The meat dish was magnificently housed in a silver serving dish. Resuming his place, Arnold unwrapped a perfectly ironed napkin, rolled the linen across his lap and prepared to begin. When he did so the tastes that hit his palate were unlike anything he'd ever eaten – and where the meat was concerned, of course it would be! The food was out of this world. The droning of the other diners largely lost on Riseveldt, tasting the meat and half-listening to their small talk, he understood why they couldn't decide what it was. He was almost certain it was beef, except the taste was sweeter and the texture softer. What was it? Whatever it was, it was fantastic. Someone was talking to him. What were they saying?

'Meal to yer liking, young Arnold?'

The grotesque image of Mrs Ringold swam into focus. Sitting before him, slurping her wine and belching, she really was repulsive. Riseveldt couldn't get his head around the fact that he was experiencing such incredible cuisine in such bizarre surroundings, and with such an unpalatable hostess.

'I'll say. Did I hear that yer nephew won some award?' Arnold's voice sounded far away to himself. 'Presumably it was for his cuisine – his cooking?'

'The son of a bitch! Gettin' rid of him.'

Why in the world would this ghastly friend of his mother's (he never could figure out why his mother tolerated, let alone appeared to like, Renais Ringegold) want to remove someone who was such a fabulous chef? This was the best meal Arnold Riseveldt had ever eaten – as he reflected, nothing else even came close.

'Could I ask why?'

Renais' mouth abstractedly chomped its way through an over-loaded forkful. 'Yer could. Then again, none of yer goddamn business.'

Arnold sipped some of the beautiful wine and said nothing. For several seconds it appeared Mrs Ringegold wouldn't speak either. Then she too lifted her Waterford crystal goblet, and downed its contents. Riseveldt looked at her aghast.

'You'll oblige me...' Renais indicated her empty glass.

Slowly replacing his own, Arnold went to pick up the chilled hock and a decanter of burgundy (he'd shortly try the red) and began to go round the table again, serving the other guests and his hostess.

'The louse has gotta go 'cause he's a good-for-nothin' Hungarian weirdo.'

'Now, Renais, don't go sayin' nothin' bad about our forebears.'

'Forebears? Forebears? Yer don't even know who yer forebears are, yer lecherous old sot.' This to Wally.

Clacking his teeth, Wally put some more food in his mouth.

'But Mrs Ringegold – Renais – he is a very fine chef; that I must say.' Riseveldt had reached Renais and was pouring her some more wine.

'Say wot yer like, he's still gettin' out. I'll have the police on him otherwise, by Saint Boldogasszony I will!'

'There yer go again, takin' our patron saint in vain.'

'Wally, if you don't shut yer teeth-clackin' gob you'll be departin' early.'

Whenever Renais spoke to Wally like this it always went completely over the old man's head. Like the other guests, he just kept on eating. It was hard to believe these skeletal geriatrics could put away the portions they did.

'He really sponged off yer, did he? Lived off yer – you say stole from yer?' Arnold was controlled.

'Thievin' little cuss!'

'But he cooks meals for yer, yeah? That's somethin'.'

'Impressed by his food, are yer?'

Replacing the decanter of Burgundy on the table, Arnold didn't immediately reply. When he did, he was turned away from Renais and spoke more to himself. 'Oh yeah.'

'Wassat yer say?'

Arnold didn't acknowledge her. Renais shrugged and threw some more wine down her throat.

'Let's eat!'

Forty-five minutes later, Arnold Riseveldt had enjoyed what was undoubtedly the finest food he'd ever tasted and decided what he needed was a cigar to round off the perfect feast; this meant some space in which to enjoy smoking it. Taking a large Cuban and a cigar clipper from his pocket, he sat back, watching his fellow diners. With the exception of his mother, who remained her serene self, the others now sat around burping, belching and farting.

'Mrs Rinegold-Renais, would you excuse me? I was going to enjoy a cigar and don't want to pollute your company or your dining room.'

'My, my, you do have the cutest turn of phrase, young Arnold. You can smoke where yer like.'

'Well, I could also do with a–'

'Oh, yeah yeah.' Renais was dismissive, indulging in more vino.

Riseveldt got up as Wilbur refilled his hostess's glass.

'Don't be too long – we gotta talk.'

Arnold was at the door.

'Oh, and if yer see that good-for-nothin' nephew tell him bring some more wine.'

Riseveldt went out.

'There's another bottle over there pretty full, Renais.'

Renais eyed Ruby watching Wilbur's attentiveness to his hostess.

'It's the red I want, Ruby, and don't worry; aimin' my caboose more towards a youthful interment!' She cackled at what she considered her witticism and glugged down the contents of her refilled glass.

Chapter 11

Closing the door on Mrs Rinegold's dining room, Arnold leant back against it and sighed. What a bizarre experience the whole thing was. He'd been reluctant to take his mother to the soirée, as she called it, only accompanying her because he knew she needed the company of her own age group and didn't often get out. But what a strange, teeth-clacking, erection-driven, randy crowd they were. To Arnold's mind the guests appeared to be on drugs – and not just the prescribed sort. On the other hand, who could blame them? Not many years left, and as far as he knew they didn't harm others so let them get on with it. Cutting the cigar, he ruminated that perhaps it was eating such wonderful food that gave them the vitality they seemed to exude. But the bizarre surroundings and the repulsive hostess – it didn't make any sense. He lit up. Gazing through the smoke, his mind was further intrigued by the interior before him. Quite unlike the lurid colours of the dining room, the lobby contained what had once been a grand staircase. Gothic-style, it was dark and shabby, its gloom shadowy and oppressive.

'The best meal of your life?'

It was barely a question. Arnold looked up. A young man dressed in chef's attire, accompanied by a monkey, descended the stairs.

'No doubt she's runnin' low on wine. The amount they

consume, they don't even know what they're eatin', let alone the quality of vintage.'

Surprised by the young man's arrival, Arnold recovered himself. 'Why do you do it then, if you know they don't appreciate your food, which was indeed excellent?'

'Excellent? Hmm! I'd say it was more than excellent. I'd say you've never had a meal to touch it.'

Opening a door beside the dining room, the chef entered a small parlour. Peering inside, Arnold watched as, with the confidence of a sommelier, the young man produced additional decanters for the Burgundy and chilled coolers for the hock, checking their temperatures and placing them in a dumb waiter. Closing its doors, he pressed a bell-button and returned.

'I do this so I don't have to see the repulsive bitch or her decrepit friends.'

'Careful, son.' Arnold exhaled a lung full of cigar smoke.

Tutti Frutti had hopped onto a bannister and began chattering away; he liked cigars. Apparently unconcerned, Raymond said, 'How do you come to be here? You're not so old.'

'My mother is a friend.'

'She warped or just crazy?'

'Hey!'

The chef and guest looked at each other.

'My mother doesn't get out so much; she needs company.' Riseveldt gave a little shrug. 'Anyway, she's here.'

'At least you and she've had a wonderful repast!'

'That's true. You have your own rooms here I believe.'

'And your hostess will've told you not for much longer. We're being evicted, aren't we, Tutti?'

'You don't get along, huh?'

'We get along fine.' Raymond put his finger under Tutti's chin. 'Just the vile bitch and I don't see eye to eye. We hate each other.'

He spoke matter-of-factly. As abruptly as they'd arrived, the chef and his pet began to climb back upstairs.

'Hey, wait a minute.' Riseveldt mounted the stairs and soon began to wheeze.

'You should work out.'

'Sure. Could I have a glass of water?'

'Still or sparkling's on the table.'

'Yeah, yeah – I kinda need not to be in there right now. Enough's enough. You must be Raymond. Arnold Riseveldt.'

The young chef looked at Riseveldt. 'There's more stairs – a lot more.'

'I can make it.'

Without further comment, Raymond disappeared up them; Arnold followed on.

Arriving at the upper landing, Raymond unlocked a door. Riseveldt noticed there was a metal grill behind it.

'Expecting a raid or something?'

'She destroyed my previous apartment.'

'Destroyed it?'

'Your hearing's good.' Raymond made to go inside and Arnold began to follow. 'I didn't invite you in.'

'Aw, c'mon. Have a little pity. Besides, I praised your food, didn't I?'

'Ha! Should think you did!'

'Okay, we could talk here, if you'd find me a chair.'

Raymond looked at Riseveldt for several seconds in his disconcerting way then abruptly entered his apartment.

'I presume that's an invitation to enter then.'

'Close the door and slip the catch.'

Muttering, Arnold stepped across Raymond's threshold. 'I've heard of security...'

'Which is insufficient.'

'Sure you're not paranoid?'

'No, I am not sure.'

'Fair enough.' Puffing slightly, Arnold began climbing up Raymond's stairs.

'Make sure that cigar's out.'

Arnold's initial impression of Raymond's apartment was 'surreal'; the tiny bedroom piled floor to ceiling with books, magazines, periodicals, journals and slicks; even the futon-like palliasse was supported by publications and cooking tomes. Then the kitchen; Raymond had gone through to his now-immaculate kitchen and was taking some water from the fridge. Entering, Arnold whistled.

'Yeow! This is somethin' else. This is...'

'Probably the finest private kitchen in New York City. Seein' as you're here, still or sparkling?'

Arnold seemed not to hear the question as he continued to gape at the magnificently accoutred culinary paradise. Raymond stood petulantly by.

'Oh. Oh, yuh – still. Sparkling gives me dyspepsia.'

'We can't have that.'

Raymond poured some chilled water from a decanter and placed the glass on his central counter. Arnold picked up the glass and downed most of its contents.

'You've...you've really got an amazing kitchen. I've never seen anything like it.'

Raymond appeared nonchalant, even arrogant.

'Why in the Lord's tarnation would your aunt want to get you outta here when she has a relative in her house who's so talented?'

'Because she hates my guts. Because she's nuts. Because I loathe the sex-crazed slut!'

'Phew! I can see you don't get along.'

'And she had regular money from my family 'n' all, over the years – only thing kept the old bat goin'.'

'How's that?' Arnold looked at Raymond, who didn't make eye contact.

'We're related by marriage. I'm a second cousin to her late husband, God rest his soul.'

'You're not from New York City?'

'Budapecht.'

'Buda...?'

'Pecht. Pecht – Budapest. Hungary.' Irritated, Raymond fiddled with a mixing machine on the counter.

'Hungary? Ha! What're you doing in NYC?'

'What's anyone doing in New York City?'

'Yeah, fair enough.' Arnold finished his water.

'My parents were killed. I was a little kid. I had an elder brother who got into trouble back home. Relatives thought it would be good for him to get out of the country. America. The New World. Land of opportunity. He could make it here. And me? Who was going to look after me, the runt? I had an aunt back home; I loved her cooking. But others thought maybe it would be good for me to start life early here. Anyway, we came and Auntie Renais, the laziest, bitchiest whore you see downstairs, was our "relative".'

'How old were you?'

'I told you, a kid. Eight.'

'That's a lotta years you've been livin' here, then.'

Raymond fiddled with his appliance, adjusting it, tidying it. 'My brother cleared out when I was still young. Auntie wanted the money, I needed to have somewhere; we kinda did a deal.'

Arnold waited.

'I wouldn't tell the family in Budapest István had gone and she'd leave me alone.'

'And still have the money. Hmm. So why the fuss now?'

'It's none of your business.'

'True. Could I have some more water?'

Sulkily Raymond went over to the fridge and removed the water decanter, pouring some more for his guest. Stoppering it, he returned the decanter to the fridge. ''Bout three years ago I'd just finished doin' all this.' He waved his arm expansively. 'She came up here and destroyed it. Wanted to kill the old crone, but a neighbour persuaded me otherwise.'

There was silence.

'Sensible.'

'Really? What possible use do you think the cow has on this planet? Better off without her.'

'And you'd be in the state pen, maybe death row. I deal in death. I know.'

Raymond appeared unimpressed. Arnold took out a black-edged calling card, which he proffered to the chef. Raymond ignored it, so Arnold placed it on the counter.

'Riseveldt's Interment Parlour – RIP. Competitive prices. Anything catered for; frozen, at sea, animals...'

Tutti picked up the card and twiddled it in his monkey fingers.

'Hey, even planning a service in space!'

Raymond idly watched Tutti flicking Riseveldt's calling card. 'Busy, are yer?'

'Busy? Jeez, never stop, not in this city. More people get blown away in NYC than die of natural causes in other towns. Yes siree, in this Gomorrah my business is gold, and those who aren't shot up either eat themselves to death or starve. For the rich or the poor, the Reaper – and RIP – never lose.'

'Passionate. Impressive.'

'Like you, I love my work.'

'I don't just love mine, I live it. It *is* my life.'

'Okay, okay, so I guess yer repaired yer kitchen?'

'To make it the best in New York, and me the best chef in town. One day I'll be world famous.'

'Matters to you, huh? Yer wanna be famous?'

'Only because of my cuisine. That's what matters to me.'

'But fame does as well, huh? Yer wanna be recognised.'

'My due.'

'So why in tarnation don't you keep Auntie downstairs sweet and stay here? You got everything yer need and yer created this fantastic kitchen.'

Tutti hopped around and scrambled on to Raymond's shoulder where he began stroking the chef's neck. Arnold picked up Raymond's award, sitting on the end of the counter.

'This the award yer won?'

'Very same – the one she broke! Geddit, man? She's vile! I hate her!'

Arnold replaced the trophy. 'Maybe I do, maybe I don't. Say, what's with you and the monkey? She said "marsupial", but I don't see no pouch!'

'One day it'll click for you. Not only is she a slut, she's a thick slut!'

Arnold drank down some more iced water. Raymond turned to Tutti and patted him. The two seemed intimate.

'The restaurant I've been working in...he'd been bought as a delicacy for a client. We got kinda friendly.'

'So yer love animals – still, not worth bein' evicted.'

Riseveldt prepared to go. 'Thanks for the water.' He then headed for the kitchen door. 'Oh, one thing; just what was that meat tonight? Downstairs was all guinea fowl this and goose that. Tasted darn good but I couldn't quite place it.'

For what seemed an eternity Raymond said nothing. Shaking his head, Arnold turned to the door.

'The extinct down there couldn't figure it, huh?'

It was Arnold's turn not to respond. Raymond began to laugh his weird hyena laugh.

'Extinct, that's what they are – like the dodo. They love my dodo food; all dead as dodos. Hahaha!'

'Be seein' yer, kid.'

'Dodo food – that's it!' Raymond was in hysterics, Tutti began his chattering. At this commotion, Arnold turned back.

'Mind lettin' me in on the joke, fellas?'

When he could speak, Raymond said, 'We already did!'

With an abandon brought on by his recent surreal experiences Raymond went over to his freezer and, opening a door, pulled out a tray on which sat numerous bulging freezer bags. Picking one up, Raymond actually tossed it in the air, catching and playing with it.

'Kid, you can be a very strange boy. My advice is stick to cookin'.'

'Oh, I'll do that all right. Dodo food – you've been downstairs eating my dodo food!'

Replacing the bag in his freezer, Raymond abruptly went to his fridge and poured himself out a glass of iced water. Inquisitive at what the chef had been looking at in his freezer, Riseveldt crossed the room and stared down at the immaculately laid out array of variously shaped and sized, sealed, polythene-wrapped parcels. The sound of a gong coming from below pierced the silence. Returning to the freezer and picking up several of the bags Raymond waved them about.

'Heart, brains, hindquarters, some leg. Ha!'

One of the packages wasn't quite as well-wrapped. Part of an arm, still just identifiable as being human, flopped out. As if struck by a thunderbolt Riseveldt got it.

Arnold went white; he shook, he gasped for air, he rushed to the sink and tried to vomit.

'Time and place. Time and place. I have a bathroom. And that after the best meal you ever tasted!'

Arnold gagged.

'Would you do that with guinea fowl? Or p'raps it was turkey...or goose – you were goosed!'

'Get away from me. Get away from me, you...you cannibal!'

'Not me, pal. You're the one that ate him.'

'Aghh! Aghh!' Retching, Arnold ran from the room screaming. On the landing he paused for breath, quite unable to contain his horror. The gong crashed again. 'Momma! Momma!' Galvanised, he stumbled down the stairs. In the lobby Renais stood, gong-stick in hand.

'There you are. Where's ma nephew? We want some service down here.'

Hysterical, Arnold rushed past her.

'Wos the scumbag bein' doin' to yer?'

'Momma!'

'Wos the matter boy? Punk hasn't tried to mug yer, has he?'

Panting, Riseveldt rushed into the dining room. 'Momma, we gotta get outta here – now!'

Turning back from the hallway, Renais was in time

to see the mortician retch. 'Poison! The bastard's tried to poison yer!'

Mamie Riseveldt got to her feet, an island of reserve in a deep sea of grotesqueness. 'Oh dear. You look pale, son. Is it yer ulcer playing up, honey? Shouldn't wonder, all the time yer spend with them preservin' chemicals.' She gathered her shawl about her shoulders. 'Maybe it's the rich food. Can have a powerful effect if yer not used to it.'

Standing in the doorway of Renais' dining room, Arnold was terribly sick.

'Oh! Better get you home, dear.'

Angry now, becoming crazed, Renais turned back toward the stairs and removed the little snub-nosed Colt from her suspendered fishnets. Brandishing it wildly, she began to climb the stairs. 'Son of a bitch! I've had it with the little shit. He's gonna get it and he's gonna get it now!'

At that moment, Raymond, accompanied by Tutti, smoking Arnold's discarded cigar, appeared on his landing looking down at the scene below.

'Goddamn primate!' she yelled and brandished the pistol in Raymond's direction, determination and anger forcing her features into something even uglier than usual.

Scampering along the banisters, Tutti swung from one side of the stairs to the other the very second Aunt Renais raised her gun. With uncanny timing, the monkey clipped the weapon with his tail, causing the pistol to somehow hook back in the woman's face as the loud retort of a gunshot filled the hallway. Having shot herself in the forehead, it was with a look of astounded disbelief Renais Ringold fell to the ground. Sitting atop the bottom balustrade, Tutti blew a perfect smoke ring.

Chapter 12

'Obviously it was a freak accident, officer.'

Morning light streamed in through the front door as a now-commanding and apparently recovered Arnold Riseveldt stood smoking a fresh Havana in the hall way, his smoke rings nearly as accomplished as those of Tutti Frutti. Several police officers and a forensic technician were present, along with two paramedics who removed Renais Rinegold's covered body on a collapsible gurney.

'Time of death was some hours ago. Mind telling us why we weren't called before?'

'Yeah, matter of fact I do.'

The sergeant looked round. Arnold exhaled a lung full of cigar smoke.

'Officer...Qwertle, isn't it?'

The police officer made a vaguely affirmative grunt.

'I didn't call the precinct station right off. We were all in shock.' Arnold took another puff. 'And when we calmed down some I called Captain Manifest. Known the Captain for years. He was very sympathetic, considerate.'

The sergeant didn't comment.

'Guess he called yer up.'

Qwertle still said nothing.

'How long d'yer think yer gonna need the body before I can prepare the deceased for interment?'

'What about you? It was your monkey that caused the

incident.' Qwertle shot a glance at the young chef sitting on a stair.

Raymond's expression was abstracted, yet when he spoke his voice was manic. 'You are wrong, police officer. You are incorrect on two counts. One: Tutti Frutti is not mine, and two: he did not cause my reviled aunt's demise. She pulled the gun to do bodily harm to me. Swinging by as he did, the monkey clipped the bitch's firing hand, causing her joyous demise.'

'You don't seem upset by this tragedy.'

'He is. It's just a reaction.' Arnold was smooth.

Qwertle seemed unimpressed. Then he said, 'And this murdering monkey – he's disappeared?'

'Swung out right after.' Raymond risked a smile.

'How? Where?' Qwertle was sharp.

'Well, he was up the stairs and gone. They can travel quickly, sir, and jump metres at a time.'

'Huh. Don't explain his escape.'

'My apartment has a back door. It was open.'

'Take a look,' Qwertle commanded his junior colleague. The younger officer headed up the stairs.

'Got a description?' he called back over his shoulder.

Arnold looked at the police officer. 'You gonna send out a warrant for a monkey? Fur, light brown, eyes close set, chatter high-pitched. That ought to do it.'

Qwertie looked from Arnold to Raymond. 'I should bring both you baboons in for questioning.'

'I believe he's a type of macaque.'

The look Qwertie gave Raymond suggested their incarceration imminent.

Arnold interjected, 'And what, pray, would that achieve? What else can we tell yer at the station we can't tell yer here?'

The junior police officer reappeared from Raymond's apartment. 'Clean, Sarge.'

'Of course it's clean! It's the cleanest kitchen in New York City!'

'Shut the fuck up will yer? We're the police here and we're askin' the questions. You'll speak when I say yer can speak.'

Arnold exhaled some cigar smoke. 'Are you wantin' to interrogate us, then, sergeant?'

After several seconds Qwertle snapped shut his notepad. 'Wouldn't exactly say I want to interview either of yer, but don't leave town. C'mon, Pinkerton, let's get back to the station.'

'We gonna look at that kiddie rape scene, Sarge?'

'Think I'd let yer loose on that? Enough monkey business you've had fer one day, boy.' The two policemen walked to the door. 'And, er, you can come by tonight and pick up the body. Say, what's in the bag?'

Arnold looked across at Qwertle. 'You know my line of business – measurin' up the deceased. Wanna take a look?'

Qwertle didn't respond.

Waving his cigar, Riseveldt said, 'As a matter of interest, why d'ya want to do an autopsy? You know how she died.'

'None o' your goddamn business.' Qwertle looked briefly at Raymond. 'Good coffee,' he said and left.

'Maybe we wanna see whether she blew her tits off. That'll give yer some nice reconstruction work for the embalmin'.' Officer Pinkerton sniggered and followed his boss outside.

For several seconds there was silence. The young chef fiddled with his hair; the mortician smoked quietly.

'Yer really know how to fix things good, don't yer?' Arnold's voice was low.

As if on cue Tutti appeared at the window, tapping on it and brandishing a cigar stub. Raymond got up and let him in.

'For a while I thought yer charm would mean he'd stay for another coffee then take us down.'

Raymond appeared indifferent to the comment. He offered the monkey a light and Tutti lit the remainder of Riseveldt's old cigar.

'Well, things'll be changin' now all right – changin' big time.' Arnold blew another smoke ring which collided with one blown by Tutti as he lit up. 'Jeez, your aunt was right – baboons, the pair of yer.'

'According to the officer that's more you and me.'

Arnold stared long and hard at Raymond. 'Don't tell me what that makes him, then.'

'Like I said to the officer, a macaque-rhesus, I think.'

Riseveldt just stared at Raymond then finally picked up the large holdall and walked to the door. 'Yer aunt will be residin' at RIP this evenin'. Be there.'

'And if I ain't?'

'Thought you paid attention to the officer. He also said don't leave town.' At the door Arnold turned back. 'We'll be havin' a serious discussion – and I mean serious.' He shook the bag slightly and left.

Tutti blew another smoke ring and scratched his little chin.

The evening light was placid as Raymond eased his old T-Bird out of the garage in Palmetto Street and headed south, taking the Queens Expressway towards Brooklyn, Tutti chattering away beside him. The mortician had told him not to bring the monkey, but fuck the mortician. Raymond had in fact nearly left his simian friend behind,

Tutti appearing more interested in watching an old episode of *The Simpsons* – Homer and Bart haranguing a police chief as to the ineffectiveness of an interrogation (Raymond didn't dwell on the irony) – than in accompanying him. The address Arnold had given Raymond was off Shore Parkway, near the Marine Park. To Raymond it somehow seemed a strange place for a mortician to operate, but what did he know? After all, an undertaker's could be anywhere. In any event his chipped sat nav directed him there.

A corner site, at its front stood a mock colonial style stucco house, complete with reception hall to welcome the bereaved. Beside it ran a driveway leading to a large court-yard where a series of low buildings housed the deceased, awaiting whatever preparation was required. Some 'clients' would have considerable work done to the viewable parts of their bodies, making them look sufficiently presentable for loved ones visiting while they lay in state. This might be necessary, for example, after an accident, which could render a deceased's face or hands so disfigured that restor-ation work was desirable in order to avoid any horror or unpleasantness for said relatives and friends. But interest-ingly, as Raymond was to learn, some people expressed a desire to have their bodies enhanced after they had expired, for reasons of perverse vanity. And not just their faces, but torsos, arms, legs – their complete anatomy, stipulating and ensuring this was carried out as laid down in their wills.

Raymond had never much contemplated the passing of life, but as he soon realised, the business of death was a considerable enterprise. Now, turning on to the forecourt of Riseveldt's Interment Parlour, an RIP sign flashing cheerily in the twilight, and pulling up in front of the mansion-style Hall of Remembrance, all this was in the future and much of it would come as unwelcome news to him when it did.

Ushering a mourning family into one of his 'In Praise of Passing' rooms, where relatives could view their embalmed loved one, encased in a white or coloured sateen-lined sarcophagus, Arnold noted Raymond's arrival and quietly dispatched an aide to direct the chef round the back. He gave the clients his mortician's respects and left them to their grief. Then, with surprising agility for a bulky man, made his way silently along the corridor to the rear of Remembrance House, emerging in time to meet his visitor as he arrived.

Arnold was blunt, curt even. 'Come with me.'

Leaving Tutti chattering away, Raymond climbed out of his dilapidated vehicle and ambled after the mortician.

'Thought I said not to bring the primate.'

Raymond ignored Riseveldt's comment. The mortician led him along a covered walkway. Entering one of the single storey units, to Raymond it seemed to have more the appearance of a hospital than a funeral establishment, clinicians' rooms running off a central corridor. The only thing suggesting a funereal setting was the number of covered gurneys guided purposefully about by people in white coats. A young woman wearing a smart uniform and carrying a clipboard emerged from a side office.

'Julie, can you tell me which ER Mrs Ringold is in? Mrs Renais Ringold?'

'Three, I think, Mr Riseveldt. Manny was doing her. Nothing too complicated. She only just came up from admittance. The precinct release forms took–'

'Yuh right. Thank you.' Guiding Raymond, Arnold began to move away.

'Oh, Mr Riseveldt, could I have a quick word?' Wiping a hair from across an eye, Julie pushed a pair of large tortoiseshell glasses, partly hiding her coquettishly attractive face, back up her nose. 'I, er, we need to discuss tomorrow's schedule.' Glancing briefly at Raymond, Julie Dominic's manner was professional and bright.

'Sure, Julie. I'll be tied up for a bit now. An hour or so?'

'Er, well– '

'Raymond Babchuk – Mrs Ringold's nephew.' Raymond stuck out his hand to Julie. Both Arnold and Julie looked at him then, slightly hesitantly, Julie shook it.

'Oh, hi. I'm sorry.'

Raymond turned to Arnold. 'Can I see my beloved relative now?'

'I'll take Mr Babchuk to visit his aunt. Number three, you say?'

'That's it, Mr Riseveldt. Would you like me to attend?'

'That won't be necessary, thank you. I'll catch up with you later. Come, Raymond.'

They walked on.

'Didn't know this was an emergency. ER?' Raymond sounded amused.

'Embalming Room.'

Julie watched the two men depart, her expression one of slight perplexity.

'Later, huh? Well, overtime it is...'

Embalming Room 3 was white, stark and clinical. Along one wall ran a laboratory bench with a sink. Underneath it were cupboards where formaldehyde and other preserving chemicals were kept. Laid out for embalming, Renais Ringold reposed on an adjustable gurney. Beside her stood a smart, sateen-lined coffin. As Arnold and Raymond entered, a man was washing his hands. Dressed in the *de rigueur* white uniform, Manny had receding swept-back hair and was of medium build. He wasn't quite the original Doctor Caligari, but moved in a smooth manner and had a reptilian presence.

'You about finished prepping her?' Arnold was brisk.

'Very nearly.' Manny drew out his words.

'No particular problems, were there?'

'Thirty-eight wound tidied up, compound crush abrasion to zygomatic and malar areas, corresponding extravasation.'

'Yeah, right; left cheek bone smashed.' Arnold's voice betrayed just a hint of mockery.

Manny arched an eyebrow, said nothing and continued to dry his hands.

'You'll give us a few minutes?'

'Sure. I just need to re-seal the lambdoid suture.'

'So you'll be cleaning up the back of her head? We won't look.'

Not to be hurried by Arnold, Manny gathered up a small case of surgical-looking instruments and glided past the two men. Riseveldt took out a cigar.

'Surprised yer allowed to smoke in here.'

'One of the privileges of bein' the boss.' Arnold lit up, drawing rapidly on his Montecristo. Finally satisfied with bringing it to a full smoke, he puffed contentedly and strolled around the open casket, caressing its material and timber. 'Trust you're satisfied with the sateen lining. Set inside the finest mahogany casket, complete with superior brass fittings, as befits a woman of her stature: popular member of the neighbourhood and hostess of some renown. I'm sure you'd only want the best that can be supplied by Riseveldt's Interment Parlour – oh, the plans I got! Seen enough? I can see you're grievin'. Let's go.'

Giving his aunt a final glance, Raymond followed the mortician out of the embalming room and as if on cue, Renais' head lolled to one side. Manny was right; her lambdoid suture did require some repair.

Arnold's office was at the far end of the building; it had several windows giving onto the corridor and an outer office normally occupied by his secretary. Mrs Dervish had finished for the day, leaving her desk as it always was, neat and tidy – unlike her boss's. Had it not been for Mrs Dervish, Riseveldt's room would have been a tip. Files, papers, cigar butts, old fast-food wrappers; left to himself, Riseveldt would operate out of squalor, which was interesting, as his company prided itself on cleanliness and immaculate presentation, albeit in a somewhat bizarre fashion.

'Impressive operation, huh?'

Raymond said nothing. Walking round to the back of his desk, Arnold picked up the big holdall he'd had earlier and plonked it in front of Raymond who sat down in a chair beside a coffee table.

'So what's with comin' down here, then? I had no great desire to see the reviled relative.'

Arnold was reflective and drew on his cigar.

'Do you have to do that?' Raymond was peevish.

'Shut up.' Arnold was unhurriedly commanding.

Raymond got up and headed for the door. 'Don't know what you're on, man, but I'm out of here.'

'That's exactly where you're wrong, son. Sit down.'

'You can't tell me what to do.'

'I can and I will, unless you want a stretch in Sing Sing. That is, if they don't chair you.'

'Sure it's only tobacco you're smokin'?'

'Upsets your sensitivities, does it? Shouldn't go worryin'

yer not-so-pretty little killer's head about my pollutin' the atmosphere. That's the last of yer worries. Lifers' protestations don't tend to get much listened to. That's what you'd get at the least – life.'

'Man, you're somethin' else. Whatever you're on, I want some.'

'Let's stop pussyfootin' about, shall we?'

Opening the holdall, Riseveldt took out a blood-soaked piece of Reardon's T-shirt.

'Enough evidence here to lock you up for a long time, what with yer culinary activities 'n' all.' He let the fabric drop back in the bag. 'I've been making some enquiries at that restaurant you work in.'

'Worked. I'm contemplating my future.'

'Oh? Are you indeed? I'll say you are!' Riseveldt drew heavily on his cigar. 'Buddy of yours has gone missin'.'

'Ain't no buddy!'

'No, I guess he ain't at that – but I'll wager these are his or I'm not dealin' in the life-ever-after. And I don't need no DNA test to prove it.' Arnold was calm, even casual in his manner. 'When I got home last night and...recovered some, I got to thinkin', and boy, I thought a powerful lot. For you to do what yer did there had to be some in extremis event' Another cigar puff. 'So, I'll tell you what I reckon could have happened. There was some fracas when yer won yer award. Maybe this guy was jealous or somethin' and he jumped yer. Must have been some place private to be kept quiet, but wherever it was you killed him accidentally; he gets it. Then I got to wonder, if it was an accident, why you wouldn't report it to the police? But yer didn't. Alcohol or dope maybe; you had your reasons. Then yer in a panic, yer got a problem. What are yer gonna do with a dead body on yer hands?' Arnold took another satisfying draw on his corona. 'You're following my reasoning so far? And auntie. You two didn't seem the best of friends and she was goin' to evict you...'

'You know I hated her guts.'

'Guts bein' the operative word.' For the first time Arnold looked a bit squeamish. 'Anyways, when yer beloved relative brought up...' Riseveldt took a deep breath '...the question of what was to be served at her soirée, that warped mind of yours had a bizarre idea. Using your culinary skills, why not serve up the evidence? In one foul gesture you remove the body – indeed, have it devoured – as well as gettin' off on some weird retaliation kick.' Arnold stopped smoking. Whether it was an excess of Cuban fumes or the subject in question having its effect was debatable, but either way he was turning a delicate shade of green.

'Yer said "accidentally".' Raymond's voice was hard. 'He was killed in an accident.'

Gulping, Riseveldt shook slightly and held onto the side of his desk. 'Sure. But it was no accident you cooked him up! Man, that's so sick they'd throw away the key!' Riseveldt slumped back in his office chair.

'Didn't choke yer, did it? Didn't affect your digestion? Best meal you ever had! Said so yerself. Wasted on the old bat and her crone pals.'

'Don't start that again. Remember, one of those senior citizens is my momma. But you're right, it ain't often I get the, er, privilege of experiencing such unusual cuisine and like I said, it set me thinkin'.'

'Never. You *never* ate such a meal.'

Arnold was regaining some of his normal colour. 'How right you are. And your skills are matched by my divine inspiration. The wider public will soon be able to enjoy your talents – in *my* new restaurant.'

Recovering from his temporary lapse, Arnold sat back and took another pull on his Montecristo. Raymond didn't seem to register what had just been said, but ambled back from the door and sat down in the easy chair.

'Unique in its gastro-funereal concept; revolutionary in its digestive climax; your business and my business. It has a perfect symmetry. Beautiful.'

'Mine isn't a business – it's an art.'

'Well, yes, sir, and in openin' up a restaurant we're gonna allow you to practise that art. What you did for auntie's dinner we're gonna provide to the great American public. Indeed, she can bequeath us the first meal.'

'Yer kiddin'?'

'Never been more serious in my life. What you did last night, Raymond, we're gonna do forever.'

Suddenly twitchy, Raymond stood up. 'Not with me you ain't!'

Prodding the bag, Arnold looked at Raymond. 'Let's not start arguing, son. You're in no position.'

'Okay, so you think you have it over me. You *think* I killed a guy and you *think* you ate him. Prove it.'

Getting up from his desk, Riseveldt went over to a small fridge which, whilst largely containing drink mixes, was also a temporary home to several small plastic containers. Snapping open the top of one, he proffered its contents to Raymond.

'Didn't think I'd go through yer bins, huh? I can prove this food was served yesterday evening. Apart from the other guests testifying, my mother was there, for chris'sakes!'

'You really think you can get away with this?'

'I don't have to *think* about getting away with it; I *know* I can, and so will you.'

'I said I'm havin' nothin' to do with it.'

'Apart from servin' time, what are you gonna do?'

'Already been offered another job. Not only that, been made chef de cuisine at The Cat, if I wanna stay.'

'Oh, my, my – chef de cuisine. Well, you're gonna be *my* chef de cuisine...unless yer really want a life inside – that is, if you have a life.' Arnold snarled out the words, but Raymond was casual. If he was calling Arnold's bluff he was playing it very cool. He didn't speak for several seconds, but his attitude was almost nonchalant.

'Fifty percent.'

'Huh?'

'You heard me. We know your hearing's functional. I'll take fifty percent.'

Gobsmacked, Arnold sat back in his chair and laughed. 'Haha! Gotta hand it to yer, kid, yer play a blinder!' Abruptly changing his manner, he sat forward. 'You may want fifty percent, boy, but you'll be lucky if I give yer five.'

Raymond wandered around Riseveldt's office and strolling over to the desk, picked up the container and studied its contents.

'A unique meal – one never to be forgotten.'

'And one that can be replicated day in, day out.'

'You're crazy.'

'Really? The ultimate business opportunity is crazy? A never-ending food supply free – indeed, they pay me for the privilege!'

'You'd never get away with it.'

Riseveldt sat back. 'Guess a young man like you don't know much about death, Raymond, but you'll come to see. When the deceased is laid to rest – once the relatives have checked out Pa's comfortable, Auntie's in her best doodads – that's pretty much it. Finito! Some folks don't even come by to pay their respects and anyway, whoever takes a look six feet under?'

'What about homicides?'

'Ha! You're the kid all right. Yeah, gotta be careful who we exhume. A guy cops it in suspicious circumstances, we pass on him. All we want is nice, innocent, little dead people, all tucked up in RIP.'

'And cremations?'

'Now yer thinking, aren't yer? Even easier. Ashes to ashes, dust to dust. Anyways, you leave that to me. Supply is my department; you just cook the damned–'

'Food! You were gonna say food, weren't yer? Well maybe these deceased of yours are already – but we *certainly* will be – damned! This idea of yours is immoral, Arnie.'

'Don't lecture me on morality, boy. I don't judge life, I just bury people. Maybe "commodity" is a better word for it.' Riseveldt was back to his hard voice again.

'Commodity? Commodity! That's the way you look at this, ain't it? It don't mean no more to you than that – profit and loss.'

'Just the profit will do.'

Raymond ignored Arnold's interjection.

'A subtle sauce, a fricassée – all meaningless to your gauche and callow mind. You're just a crazy guy who trips out on death, wrappin' people up in linin's, encasin' 'em in the finest this and the bootiful that. You say *I'm* nuts – *yer* fuckin' crazy!'

'Yeah, I'm so crazy I made Riseveldt's Interment Parlour the most successful morticians in Manhattan.'

'Well, I'm gonna be the best chef in the goddamned world!'

Riseveldt actually laughed then got up and came round

to face the young chef. 'Enough! I gotta wrap this up. Look here, Raymond, you'll love working at Renais. Your own place – what could be better?'

'*Renais*? You said *Renais*?'

'Why not? Thought it would be sensitive...in remembrance of...kinda cement our union. Don't forget it was she who brought us together.'

'I will not go workin' in any place called *Renais*. No way! Never!'

'Not even for twenty percent?'

'Not even for a hundred percent!' Raymond turned to head for the door again.

'Raymond. Don't be stupid, now.'

Raymond turned back. 'Yer not gettin' it, pal. You go to the police. You go tell 'em all about what I done and how you ate all that human meat up. Go on – pick up the phone! Oh, I'll do time all right. Doubt I'll swing, though. But I ain't gonna cook in no place called *Renais*!'

'Hmm! My, my – I had no idea you were so touchy.'

Raymond gaped at the mortician. There was a tap on the door. Julie put her head round it.

'Sorry to bother you, Mr Riseveldt. I did try your line but it just went to voice. A client needs me on site.'

'Be right out, Julie.'

Julie closed the door.

'Forty percent. That's my final offer.'

Raymond turned away and walked towards the door. 'Yer just don't get it, do you, amigo? I hated that old bat's guts. I did not like her and to name a place after her sure would insult my sensitivities.' He opened the door.

'I better see you off the lot. Amigos, huh? Hmm!'

Walking along the corridor, Raymond and Arnold passed Manny sliding his way into Renais' embalming room, gently rolling a covered trolley.

'Don't yer put stuff in 'em to keep 'em preserved? Formaldehyde – chemicals and shit?' Raymond's mind still weighed the options.

'I'll be workin' on that.'

They came out into the evening. In the distance, across Shore Parkway, ships' lights twinkled on the sea. Raymond walked towards his car.

'So long, Risey. Guess I'll be hearing from the cops.'

'Okay, okay – I'll go fifty-fifty with you. But I want results.'

'Results? Yer want results? I'll show you results, Arnie! Got a place in mind, have yer?''

'Sure have. I been lookin' to expand and I got just the site.' Raymond approached his car. 'Don't be late for the funeral.'

Chattering away, Tutti waved at Arnold as Raymond began to reverse away.

'Still can't quite work out who's the bigger monkey.' Riseveldt re-lit his cigar. ' "Arnie's"... "Risey's"...Hmm.'

Chapter 13

'Did Babchuk say why he wouldn't take the job?' In his office above *Le Chat Noir*, Frank Chesson sat back in his swivel chair.

'No, Mr Chesson. Just said he'd decided against your offer and wouldn't be returning.' Marjorie's voice was clipped.

Alain de Lange looked up from a pile of papers. 'What about working out his notice?'

'Never really had much of a contract.' Then to the inter-com, 'Did he say what he was gonna do, Marjorie?'

'He didn't. He's, er, not really the communicative type.'

'You're right there.'

De Lange put his signature to a couple of documents. 'We gonna keep the maestro on then?'

'For a while. Love to know what that kid's gonna do, though.'

'Is he really that interesting?'

'I think so. Any fella do what he did's got a future. He could just be something big and I want some of it.'

'Well, he won't be workin' for Luscious Louis, that's for sure.'

'Yeah – and what was that all about? Why'd Blanc do that shit – sow that cheatin' seed?'

'Jealousy?' De Lange put down his pen.

'Of the boy? You're kiddin' me.'

'Maybe he's in with the maestro.'

'Likely he is, at that. In spite of what they put out, they go back some; I been checkin'.' Chesson got up, stretched and stared out of the window. 'I reckon he wants him for one of his own places.'

'Sure funny way of going about it.'

'Not if he thought the kid would be out of a job, like he'd be needing his help.'

'But Babchuk rumbled it.'

'We told him! So it backfired. Shit happens.'

'Hmm. And we offered him number one slot.'

'Exactly! Which is why it don't add up he's passed on us.' Chesson was pacing the room, hands in pockets.

'The maestro?'

'We said we'd dump him.'

'What about the girl, Tabi – Tabitha?'

'What about her?'

'She's handed in her notice.'

Fiddling with a coin, Frank flipped and caught it. 'Side show. It's Master Raymond I'm interested in. Why didn't you take our offer, boy?'

Since her last encounter with Raymond, Tabitha McKindrick had been in a quandary. Two days after Blanc had made the award presentation, she'd received a cursory text informing her he'd let her know when her services would be required, but since then, nothing more. She knew it wasn't her that he was really interested in, but now she was getting concerned. She'd left *Le Chat Noir* and what was she to do? She didn't want to go back there – they might not even take her – but walking up Palmetto Street she knew she had to see Raymond again. When she'd last seen her friend he'd been in a bad way. Since then she'd called him, sent texts, but he hadn't responded. What had happened to him? Running up the steps of Mrs Ringold's house, Tabitha was about to knock on the door when she heard someone calling.

'Nobody home.'

Tabitha turned to see an elderly man dressed smartly in black on the pavement. Mr Balázs raised his hat.

'I'm afraid there's no one there. A bereavement.'

Tabitha must have looked shocked.

'The good lady whose house it was has passed away.'

'Ray's aunt?'

'Indeed.'

'Oh, I'm, er, sorry. Where is Ray, d'ya know?'

'Matter of fact I do. Right now he's headed for the Church of Our Lady of the Sacred Heart, then on to the cemetery. I'm on my way to join him.'

'Oh, er, mind if I come along?'

Tabitha was dressed in a collarless shirt, waistcoat, jeans and a pair of cowboy boots. Mr Balázs looked at her briefly and smiled.

'The pleasure will be mine.'

Taking his proffered arm, Tabitha accompanied the sprightly Hungarian down the street.

Those making up the congregation at the Church of Our Lady of the Sacred Heart were a motley crew. The usual suspects; Ruby Montgomery, Wilbur Fortescue and Wally Dimitrick, the latter's teeth still clattering away, making for some lively intercourse with Tutti Frutti, who sat opposite. Others present were boyfriends of Renais whose ages ranged from late twenties to the toupee-and-dyed-hair brigade. As her only relative present, Raymond sat at the front, clad in sober attire: worn leather jacket, off-white shirt and brown kipper tie. Beside him were Tutti and Mamie Riseveldt, who not only appeared unperturbed by the monkey, but spoke to him in a smiling and friendly manner. In stark contrast to the chief mourner, his new business partner was dressed in a shiny silver suit, RIP tie and patent boots. This was Arnold Riseveldt's show-time. Indeed, with Bruce's 'Born to Run' emanating from speakers, any bystander entering the building might have thought they were participating in some kind of jamboree rather than a funeral ceremony. Quite what the two rows of Hungarian elders, rather more conventional in their dress and manner, made of it all was anybody's guess.

Enter the Reverend Jesse-Lou Townsend – a black, gay cleric and quite a friend of Renais'; Raymond recalled the churchman coming by Palmetto Street with a handsome Swede that Mrs Ringold had taken a fancy to. Björn wasn't present today but maybe, like certain others, he was there in spirit. Most of the audience – for they were more of an audience than anything else – had no idea only the head, shoulders and hands of the deceased were present at her funeral service; the rest of Renais Ringold had, by that time, been quartered, hung and jointed.

Tabitha and Mr Balázs arrived just in time to enjoy the last bars of Springsteen:

Someday, girl, I don't know when, we're gonna get to that place

Where we really want to go, and we'll walk in the sun,

But till then tramps like us, baby – we were born to run.

The Reverend Jesse-Lou mounted the pulpit steps.

'My good brothers and sisters – I love yer! What do I do?'

Several cried out how he loved them.

'I do, I do indeed, and so does He who has taken her,

taken her to the land of milk and honey. She has gone from us but is now residin' in a place of love, a place free from hate and displeasure, a place where greed and bad shit are no more. We remember her – Renais – babe and goddess, beloved by those who are staying behind. What a broad!'

The Reverend Jesse-Lou was certainly giving it some and the gospel choir who had taken their places in the stalls beside Renais' catafalque were already beginning to respond with Hallelujahs and Good Jesuses, clapping and swinging their hips.

'I want to tell you about the Lord – He who has taken this girl to his special place; He who is just and kind and lovin'; He who knows us, cares for us, loves us. My, how He'll love our girl, Renais. That smile, that swing of those slinky hips – she's gonna wow that place! Good Jesus, they'll be a smilin' all day long! Oh yeah!'

And he'd only just begun. Such oratory ran for nearly twenty minutes, the Reverend Townsend building his eulogy to near hysteria, climaxing with the choir breaking into such a rendering of 'The Good Old Lord Jesus Christ' it had the plinth supporting Our Lady's statue rocking and swaying there was concern lest she topple over. Jesse's conclusion left the congregation drained and emotional. Some wept; some sat as if in a kind of trance (though whether this was shock or divine intervention was unclear), no one more so than Raymond himself. Tutti, however, was a great hit with the reverend, who invited him to come up and sit on the lectern as he preached and spoke the word. The monkey obliged, leading the crowd in their clapping and appreciation. It being announced the interment of ashes would take place on a subsequent date (Raymond was undecided quite where to sprinkle the few cinders that would remain of his aunt), proceedings finally came to a close when, cued by Arnold, six pall bearers dressed in RIP uniforms walked solemnly down the aisle, the choir singing 'Lay My Body Down', and placed the lid over Renais' face – all that could be seen of her in the sateen-lined sarcophagus. Then, while the organ thundered and her coffin descended to the furnace below, a 3D graphic of Renais dressed in leopard skin leotard and high boots appeared above the altar. Many in the crowd clapped and hollered, some spoke in tongues, others simply gawped. Several of the Hungarians appeared so moved as to have lost any speech or movement powers they may have had; all were rooted where they sat.

Such was their reaction mourners would have been there still, had they not been guided from the church by RIP officials, who ushered people in for the next service of cremation. It was, as Arnold said, a busy time to be in the funeral business.

'A moving ceremony and no mistake, Reverend.' An effusive Arnold spoke to the Reverend Jesse-Lou, who had his eyes on one of Renais' ex-boyfriends, a big hulking youth in tight T-shirt and leather pants.

'Glad you liked it,' the cleric answered before excusing himself to pursue the youth. 'Young man, with your permission, I'm desirous of prevailing upon your time for a little.'

The mortician lit one of his cigars and puffed indulgently. 'More like a couple of hours, I'd say.'

With Tutti on his shoulder and a small engraved urn in his hands, Raymond wandered out of the church. Several people tried to engage him, giving him their condolences, but the young man appeared remote and unapproachable.

That was until, through his reverie, he saw Tabitha talking to Mr Balázs.

'Ray.' Mr B raised his hat. 'This young lady came by looking for you.'

'Hope you didn't mind my attendin', Ray. Oh, you've got Tutti!' Tabitha smiled. Raymond twiddled the little urn in his fingers. The monkey chattered at the young woman.

'Gather we're going downtown...your aunt's wake.' Mr Balázs was his ever-polite self.

'Yeah.'

'Well, I'll get a car. See you in a while.' Nodding courteously, he headed off for the driveway where a number of black limousines were pulling up. Tutti hopped away, swinging amongst the headstones. Some folks were remembered simply, others more ostentatiously, winged angels and seraphs, scrolls, a stone fish and animals celebrating the deceased; one memorial was even a Saturn space rocket.

'You okay?' Tabitha was solicitous. Raymond gave a slight nod. 'Sorry to hear about yer aunt. What yer been doin'?'

'Hmm! Busy.'

'Yuh? Guess you have at that. I ain't heard no more from Blanc. When are you startin' work for him?'

'I'm not.'

'No? Yer ain't goin' back to The Cat?'

Tabitha looked tense.

'Nope – openin' up my own place.'

'Ray, that's fantastic! You got the money an' all?'

'Bein' taken care of.'

'Geesiree – that's wonderful!'

'Wanna come and work with me?'

'You serious?'

'Sure, why not?'

Tabitha suddenly flung her arms round Raymond's neck. 'Oh Ray!'

Looking round and not immediately seeing the chief mourner, Arnold suddenly spotted him with Tabitha, her arms draped around the young chef's neck and Tutti dancing beside them.

'Oh, boy – time and place. Alvin, go and collect Mr Babchuk and his entourage. That's him with the broad and the monkey.'

The RIP employee set off across the grass; Arnold got into the limo with his mother and Ruby Montgomery. Looking out of the window, he watched as Alvin guided Raymond and Tabitha towards another vehicle, the monkey skipping about at their feet.

In a quiet Lower Manhattan side street near Meatpackers' Wharf, the Hudson River just visible a block or two away, carpenters, painters and decorators were hard at work in an old warehouse, even as caterers were laying tables with canapés and drink. The premises had formerly operated as a slaughterhouse. Both interior and exterior contractors were cutting things pretty fine, for even as the last beverages were being stocked in the bar and two sign-writers made finishing touches to their work, the first funeral vehicles turned into the street, pulling up outside. Arriving in the first limousine, Arnold Riseveldt stepped out and studied the property, his air proprietorial. Ruby Montgomery was next to alight, helping his mother.

'We're goin' in here?'

'That's right, Momma. Party can't start without you.'

'I think we're the first, Arnold.'

'Then let me welcome you to my new restaurant!'

'This your place, honey?'

'Sure is.'

'Thought you was a mortician.' Ruby seemed unimpressed.

'I am, Mrs Montgomery, but I'm diversifyin'.'

As other cars approached, they began to cross the street.

'Funny name, ain't it?'

Riseveldt turned back as more mourners appeared. Their mood didn't seem overly downcast, the general atmosphere being one of 'let the party begin'. Of course, this could have been a reflection of the deceased herself, but most were smiling and talking – Mr Balázs with Wally and Tabitha, the Reverend Townsend already entwined with the youth in the tight T-shirt and Tutti, an obvious hit with young and old alike, dancing a jig with Wilbur Fortescue.

'What d'ya think?' Riseveldt put a hand on Raymond's shoulder.

Still clutching his aunt's remains, Raymond looked up. He didn't seem particularly impressed. 'Havin' the wake here, huh?'

'Not only that, it's where we open for business tomorrow night.'

'This the restaurant? You're kiddin'.'

'Never been more serious...partner.'

'Ha! What's with the name?'

'Inspired, ain't it? Heaven and earth and the flesh incarnate. A perfect symmetry of our interests.'

Completing the last 'e' of the name, the two sign-writers clambered to the ground. *Restaurant Incarnate* was open for business.

'Gotta see the kitchens.'

'Very best money can buy.'

The mourners were now entering the building and

climbing the steps to the mezzanine floor. Their reactions to the interior were a mixture of aghast and astounded. The decor comprised black and purple drapes, old pews for seats and coffin lids for tables. The same graphic of Renais that had played at the church was projected onto the back wall. The whole effect was that of a Hammer Horror movie set.

'Tad funereal, ain't it?'

'In keeping.'

'Interestin' location; perfect for a wake.'

'Dust to dust,' Arnold intoned quietly.

'Not in this case,' murmured Raymond.

Arnold turned away towards the guests, who were now tucking into the food and drink.

'Hey, I like it! You done this out special, Mr Babchuk?' Someone was talking to Raymond but he barely registered the question.

'Canapés going down well, Ray; you do the food?' Tabitha was smiling at him through a mouth full of vol-au-vent.

Raymond suddenly felt uncomfortable in the knowledge of some of the particular ingredients prepared in his kitchen the day before.

'Yeah...er–'

'Delicious. Best I ever tasted.'

'Would you excuse us a minute?' Arnold was politeness itself to Tabitha. 'Come with me.' He guided Raymond across the restaurant to a staircase. Descending to the kitchen below it was indeed state of the art. Spacious and with some natural light at its rear, high windows opened on to an alley at the back. Ignoring the mortician, Raymond began inspecting the kitchen in detail. Whilst he turned over arrays of pans, meticulously checked tools and implements, ranges and ovens, Arnold worked messages on his phone. Although criticising certain details, at length, Raymond pronounced himself satisfied. Alvin appeared at the door.

'Mr Riseveldt, you're wanted upstairs.'

'Oh, my speech.'

As he went up the stairs, Tabitha came down them, discovering Raymond checking an inventory.

'Wow, Ray, this is state of the art.'

'It's where you'll be workin'.'

'This the restaurant?'

'Sure is.'

'Wacky place.'

'Ha! You better believe it.'

'When do I start?'

'Now.'

Upstairs, Arnold was in full flow.

'And I know how much your respects mean to Renais, gone to reside in the other world so magnificently. May she rest in peace.' Arnold bowed his head for a second.

'You might all be interested to know that this here is my new enterprise, *Restaurant Incarnate*, and that you'll all be welcome back tomorrow evenin', the first night we're open to the public. You'll see some cards on the way out and if you bring one with you it's a ten percent discount on opening night.'

'Well, hey, goin' into the restaurant business then, Arnold? Will that be with Renais' nephew? We know he's a mighty fine cook.' Ruby knocked back her drink hard and taking several canapés, shovelled them into her mouth in much the same fashion her deceased friend had done.

Riseveldt was amazed at Ruby's digestion but all he said was, 'He produced this finger food.'

'Ha! Finger food! Don't see no fingers!'

It was on the tip of Arnold's tongue to suggest they look carefully, but he just laughed.

'We used to eat his grub – tasty. That last supper – some meal. Renais never liked him, though; reckon she didn't appreciate his talents.' Wally's dentures clacked away.

'Interestin' location. Ain't the sanitation department near here?' Ruby spoke with her mouth full.

'Just two blocks away with a fair breeze.'

'Don't smell nothin' today.'

Arnold laughed. 'Maybe you'll be back, then?'

Ruby finished her mouthful and drained her drink. 'Maybe I will at that. "Last supper". Tell that to the Reverend – ha! Jeez it was some meal.'

'Well, with the same chef signed-up, there's plenty more like it to come.'

Chapter 14

Sometimes an enterprise is destined to take off without a backward glance, its success seemingly preordained. So it was with Restaurant Incarnate. From the first night, when curiosity alone ensured a busy evening, the place just buzzed. Front of house was headed by Carmen, a stunning mulatto woman Arnold had found from Lord knows where. She knew her business, though, dressing as exotically as the surroundings in which she worked. The restaurant hummed with her vibrancy.

At first, things were fraught in the kitchen, chefs and serving staff frantic and barely coping under the pressure. But Raymond really did have great skill and, gaining in confidence, matters rapidly came in hand. When looking back at himself later, Raymond could never quite fathom exactly what it was that enabled him to remove the grotesqueness of what he was actually doing from his mind and turn it into the ultimate chef's challenge. He somehow transformed his situation into a unique opportunity and only being provided with one kind of *viande* (no lamb, pork, fish or fowl available to his kitchen), success would have to lie in a wide variety of preparations, unusual spicing, creative sauces and his own innate culinary skills. It would require genius to conceive delicate dishes within such limitations and in so doing, Raymond would be on the road to becoming a chef of renown – something he desired so very much.

Tabitha raised her own game, developing as a highly capable sous-chef to Raymond's chef de cuisine, but the biggest surprise of all was when one day, only a few weeks after opening, Feydor Gaultier entered the premises asking for Mr Babchuk. No one other than the two men was present during their meeting, but it was a grim-faced Raymond who emerged, announcing to the staff that whilst Carmen remained manager, the role of maitre d' had been created and it would be taken by Monsieur Gaultier. Being the admired professional he was, Gaultier's appointment met with general approval. Carmen continued her purple and black flamboyance, Gaultier providing super-smooth, black-tie elegance and adding a touch of class to Restaurant Incarnate's bohemian feel.

Diners varied in age; whilst youth led the way initially, as time went by an older clientele emerged, moneyed and greedy for more, people obviously enjoying the exotic style. Right down to Tutti's occasional appearance at table, folks found the place wacky and weird and the food sensational. They couldn't get enough.

One very particular rule that existed was Raymond, and only Raymond, selected the meat. The restaurant became known as a carnivorous establishment, offering not only conventional cuts but also featuring offal normally more popular in Europe – brains, heart and tripe frequently on the menu.

Writers and critics were generally enthusiastic in their praise for Incarnate, and complimentary on the quality of the food. Just how unusual the fare being enjoyed by the good citizens of Manhattan was, none of the clientele could possibly know.

The restaurant being closed on a Monday, Raymond

invariably took the opportunity to visit RIP for a late management meeting with his partner, followed by some time selecting upcoming cuts in the parlour's morgue. It was inevitable therefore that sometime he'd bump into Julie Dominic.

'Can I help you?'

Staring at a clipboard as though his eyes would bore right through it Raymond mumbled something about meeting Riseveldt.

'I think Mr Riseveldt was in the admittance area some-where.'

Julie eyed Raymond. 'Say, I gather your restaurant is doing real good. The hot place to eat.'

'Er, yeah. Er great.'

Raymond wasn't really coherent as he wandered away leaving a somewhat quizzical Julie staring after him. As RIP's senior embalmer, Julie Dominic worked the longest hours. Leaving Raymond, she got stuck into applying a final coating of glaze to the face and hands of a handsome young man whose life had been cut short by an assassin's bullet, after which she painted and polished his finger nails, finally standing back to admire her work.

'Hmm! Pity you had to go, pal. Pretty good-looking guy. Wonder what you were like?' She laughed. 'And what did you do to wind up so very dead?'

Putting down a brush, Julie picked up a spray can, apply-ing what looked like a fine mist across the deceased's body. The door opened and Arnold Riseveldt came in, pushing a gurney.

'Mr Riseveldt. You're working late.'

'You too.' He parked the trolley.

'This increase in business...'

'I know, Julie. A mortician's work...'

'Or a restaurateur's. Gather the new business is going good?'

'Ha! Yeah.' Arnold fiddled with the sheet covering the body lying on the trolley.

'Mr Riseveldt, if you don't mind me saying, you're looking a little tired these days. You mustn't overdo things, you know.'

'Well, standards must be maintained.'

'Indeed they must. I wanted to talk to you about that.'

'Can it wait? I'm collectin' a client.' Arnold began moving to the door.

'I don't think it can, Mr Riseveldt.'

The mortician made no reply. Putting down the spray can, Julie wiped her hands on a towel.

'I've been working here eight, ten months now, and when I started you advised me this was the finest, most distinguished parlour on the East Coast: an enterprise of the highest calibre.'

'So help me God.'

'Well, I'm sorry to take issue with you, Mr Riseveldt, but we have a disagreement here. Recently there has been a decline in quality of work: less attention to detail and, frankly, a greater concern for increased turnover at the expense of standards.'

'I'm sorry to hear you say that, Julie.'

'As an alumnus of the Herbert Biddlecombe Morticians School, I will not do second-rate work. Beautification of the bereaved is an art form on the highest level.'

'You and Babchuk...'

'I am sure Mr Babchuk has similar standards. I believe he won an award recently – the Chef de France, I understand.'

The door opened and Manny began his gliding entrance,

pushing another gurney.

'Whoa. I've just brought docket fourteen in here.' Arnold blocked his way.

'We're out of embalmin' rooms, Mr Riseveldt – queuin' up, they are.'

'Park it in the corridor. Make a start on this one. We'll continue in my office, Julie.'

Entering his office, Arnold poured himself a stiff drink.

'What can I get you?'

Julie closed the door. 'Not for me, Mr Riseveldt. I never drink at work.'

Ignoring any inference, Riseveldt took a slug of scotch. 'Julie, you're right. I know there's a lot of pressure right now and as you say, what with my diversification and all, things have been a little hectic. But I'm grateful to yer for bringin' yer feelings to my attention. We can't allow the fine standards of Riseveldt's – a byword in our industry – to slip any. But an increase in turnover does have its compensations and I'd like to offer you a little bonus, by way of thankin' you for all your hard work.'

Taking out a wad of $100 bills, Arnold began to peel off several, a process closely watched by Julie. Catching her eye, the mortician kept peeling off more. Finally she smiled.

'Why, Mr Riseveldt, that's very considerate of you.'

Arnold looked a little pale as Julie took the notes. 'Acknowledgement of perfection is always appreciated.'

'How true that is, Julie, how true indeed. In our profession, assisting clients in their passage from one life to another, no one can work hard enough.'

'I just didn't want you to think that because of our increased workload, standards should be allowed to slip any.'

'That must not happen, Julie. They must be maintained to the highest degree.'

'Good. Well, I'm glad we've got that cleared up then, Mr Riseveldt.' She was at the door now. 'I'll bid you a good evening.'

When halfway out, she turned back. 'Oh, Mr Babchuk was here a little earlier; did you find him?'

'Er...'

'Maybe he left.' Julie closed the door.

Arnold slumped in his chair, dropping the depleted wad of $100 bills on the desk.

'Standards mustn't drop! Less attention to detail! Alumnus of Herbert Biddlecombe!' he mimicked. 'Jeez! I'll give her Herbert fuckin' Biddlecombe!'

It was 1.00a.m. the following morning and the restaurateur-mortician had come to collect his cuisinier partner in crime, the black RIP Cadillac hearse pulling up in the lane at the rear of Restaurant Incarnate.

'Can't you leave that fucking monkey behind?' Tutti was feeling the rosewood dashboard. 'The little bastard's scratching the lacquer.'

Raymond ignored Arnold's plea. Tutti skipped over his shoulder and sat himself down on top of a roller-mounted coffin.

'Oh boy.'

'Why the late night squirrel?' Raymond seemed bored.

'We've gotta make a new plan. I don't want you comin' to the parlour no more. Pryin' eyes. From now on either you come and get supplies from where we're goin' or I bring 'em here.'

'Ain't it a bit obvious, this vehicle?'

'We're not collectin' tonight, dummy. We'll be unloadin' when we get where we're headin'.'

'And where exactly is that?'

'You'll see.'

It began to rain as the Cadillac glided away, its powerful V8 purring effortlessly into the night.

'Far?'

'Twenny minutes.'

Arnold was clearly not in a communicative mood, and as Raymond never was, their journey north through uptown Manhattan was a subdued one, the roads quiet at this late hour. Indeed, the district they entered, New York's South Side, although so near the most vibrant of all city centres, was eerie, its leafy streets deserted. Nearing Mount Vernon Hospital, the hearse passed several cemeteries before turning into a tiny back street off Amsterdam Place. Arnold reversed into a private drive with a shuttered docking bay at its far end. Getting out of the car, he walked back to the building and began unlocking various doors. Raymond waited in the warm comfort of the Cadillac with Tutti till he returned. The mortician activated a slide mechanism under the coffin and rollers slid out a shrouded body strapped to a collapsible gurney.

'Move your butt – and his. God!'

With some reluctance, Raymond got out of the car and Tutti off the coffin.

'What is this place?'

'Part of our new operation. Gimme a hand.'

The two men began trundling the collapsible gurney and its occupant inside the building.

'Some joint.'

'Old morgue. Perfect. You can work preparin' 'em in peace and quiet. Like I said, you don't come to RIP no more.' Riseveldt was business-like.

'D'you only deal in death?'

'One way or another.' Riseveldt lowered the loading bay

shutter and Tutti grabbed the arm of a mannequin, several of which were propped against a wall. Raymond laughed, which started Tutti off. Riseveldt grunted.

'Some guy was using the place as storage space for his shop dummy business – told him we got the real thing. Help me bring him through.'

The two men pushed the trolley deeper into the heart of the building which, whilst more antiquated, was not unlike RIP in layout. However, its age and emptiness made it much spookier, darkness and shadows playing across the walls. Under Arnold's guidance, they took the gurney to the old morgue's theatre, which had several operating tables at its centre and on the far wall a bank of cadaver drawers. Leaving Raymond to look around, Riseveldt entered a side room; fitted with sinks and cupboards, it also housed a kettle and some mugs. He filled the kettle, plugged it in and rifled around for a tin of coffee. In the theatre, Raymond had several of the drawers open and, clipboard in hand, began logging details. Arnold appeared in the door-way, his shadow falling across the chef.

'Busy already?' Arnold nodded at the covered trolley. 'Let's load him into one.'

With Tutti watching from an operating table, they slid the gurney's occupant into a drawer. Before closing it, Riseveldt checked an identity tag.

'Why're ya always checkin' dockets?'

'Good housekeepin'.'

'You're ticket obsessed. Worried I might make off with the stock?'

The kettle clicked off. Arnold finished making coffee and carried two mugs through to the theatre.

'Covers are up again, I see.' He sipped some of his hot drink. 'Hell, I didn't think when we started this thing it was gonna take off like this. People're eatin' a lot of people. I'm having to get business from out Jersey way.'

'Complainin'?'

'No, I'm not complainin'. This is New York City – lotta people die here, but we're consumin' 'em faster than they're goin' on the plate. Can't you cut down on portion sizes or somethin'?'

'Americans have big appetites.'

'Damn right they have! But we're runnin' a business here. This ain't some famine country.'

'Your idea.' Raymond shrugged.

'I know it was my idea, and we're gonna make a lot of money out of my idea, just so long as you don't go over-feedin' the great American public.'

Raymond sipped his coffee. 'Ain't the portion sizes that's the problem. We can't always use what we have due to the amount of formaldehyde Miss Goody Two Shoes fills 'em up with – unless, that is, you *want* to poison our customers...though I guess we could start usin' *them* the night after. Diners eatin' diners. Huh.'

'Ha ha! Very funny! What can I do? She's a very diligent young lady, talented; she takes pride in her work.'

'That's as may be, but she's costin' us money both ways – what yer pay her to make 'em look good and what we have to write off 'cause she makes 'em inedible.'

'You know, Raymond, you never cease to amaze me. Deep within that cooking-obsessed brain of yours lurk some hard commercial instincts.'

'Float.' Raymond held out a hand.

'See what I mean! Payin' out, always payin' out.' Arnold pulled out his much-reduced bill roll, peeling off most of the remaining notes. 'The prepped stuff you'd finished is over there. Let's get back and drop it off. Now we've got this place you can come and go as you want.'

Pocketing the cash he'd been given, Raymond didn't seem in an undue hurry to leave; he had some more coffee.

'Give me a hand.' Arnold sounded impatient.

'Need both mine.'

'Shut up.'

Putting down his mug, Raymond went over to Arnold who was stacking some nondescript boxes marked with meat descriptions: shoulder, neck, shin, etc. What they were doing was so bizarre, yet somehow strangely sterile. Everything seemed detached, remote from the reality of their macabre business model. Placing the boxes on a little trolley, they headed for the door.

'How can I help it if they're crazy about my food?'

'Give 'em less and we'll charge more. First rule of business, Raymond. With your rapidly developing acumen, you should appreciate that. Supply and demand's the thing. Supply and demand.'

Heading back to the restaurant, the men stopped at some traffic lights. An all-night mobile food kitchen was in operation nearby. As they looked at it a queue stood patiently waiting, collars turned up against the weather.

'You know, Raymond, it occurs to me we're doin' a considerable service to the community. I mean, what could be more important than feedin' people? Beats donatin' anythin' to science. They oughta give us an award.'

'Okay, so I reduce portion sizes but we're runnin' real low. You gotta sort out supplies.'

'I'm workin' on it, I'm workin' on it. We've started a very demanding business here. Go on at this rate there'll be nobody dead left to bury, let alone eat in this environmentally friendly neighbourhood!'

Chapter 15

Given the morbid nature of Restaurant Incarnate's origins, it was perhaps astounding that things should actually settle down, but settle down they did. The restaurant having immediately taken off, its success only continued to grow. Within weeks, numerous good and great were to be seen at tables – several famous actors, some politicians when in town – and music became an added feature, with notable jazz players enjoying a jam and getting off on the macabre atmosphere.

Against all the odds, and given his singular character, Raymond was not only becoming a chef of renown but, with Tutti as his sidekick, also a celebrity personality. Clientele waited eagerly for the few minutes he gave them as, like some Byzantine potentate, he moved from table to table. He rarely said much, but diners fell over themselves to fête him, requesting his autograph and begging his attendance at some party or social event. It was, therefore, inevitable that with such public acclaim serious food writers and critics would arrive at his court, some fawning, some more critical.

The night that one day would be written in the annals of Incarnate and New York society began, as they all did, with Raymond working frantically in the kitchen, his attention to detail never wavering, his demand for perfection ever obsessive. By the time Carmen came down, most covers were completed and the chef de cuisine was just finishing off a *tablier de sapeur* and *côte de veau*. The first person the manager met was Tabitha.

'One night of bliss; Nancy Friedland's in and just lovin' it.'

'Nancy Friedland?' Tabitha was impressed.

Carmen swirled her purple-frilled, black taffeta dress. 'You heard. Review's comin' out in *Downtown* next week. Says she's gonna sing them praises.'

'Table seven. Ready *now*!' Raymond rapped out his command. A waiter, Jerry, instantly appeared at the counter.

'Chef!' Jerry took the immaculate plates from the serving hatch.

Tabitha could barely contain her excitement. 'D'ya hear that, Ray? Nancy Friedland's here and she loves it! Gonna give us a great review.' In her ecstasy, Tabitha had grabbed hold of Raymond, who did not look best pleased. Realising what she'd done, the sous-chef self-consciously let her boss go. 'This is important, Ray. You gotta go up and see her.'

Carmen sashayed over as Raymond was busy finishing a final dish. 'Shall I tell her you'll pay a call, Mr Raymond?'

'She'll get the same as everyone else – when I'm ready.'

Carmen eyed Tabitha briefly. 'Okay. She's sittin' with some French dude, Louis somethin'-or-other. I'm sure he's in the business – seen him before.'

Raymond continued working and, having completed the dish, put it aside before looking up. A strange expression had appeared on his face.

'Make sure Monsieur Gaultier's around.'

'Will do.' Carmen swept off.

Climbing the stairs forty minutes later, Tutti on his shoulder, Raymond's mood was unfathomable. The evening had been a triumph; something was in the air as the whole restaurant stood up and applauded him. Whilst polite, he appeared neither flattered by the adulation nor affected by it. His eyes travelled round the room till he found the silver-haired head he was looking for. Blanc had his back to Raymond and, ignoring the outpourings all around him, was talking intimately to a skeletal, middle-aged woman, her dark hair swept back, her dress quiet but expensive. This was Nancy Friedland. Had she not been a renowned food writer, one would have placed her as a New York society hostess. After nodding to several people at tables, Raymond came over. Blanc looked up.

'Raymond. A very lively enterprise.' The Frenchman hadn't lost an iota of his smoothness, but he didn't stand up. In fact, he sat back.

'You won't have met my friend, Nancy Friedland.'

'Mr Babchuk – may I call you Raymond?'

Raymond smiled and as Tutti hopped from his shoulder, the chef and critic shook hands. Blanc tried to be intimate.

'Good touch – the mandrill.'

'He's a macaque. You should learn your primates, Louis.'

Attempting dismissiveness, Blanc giggled stupidly. 'In spite of these rather bizarre surroundings you've created some sensational dishes, young man. This *steak caucasien,* as you call it, has a most unusual, delicate flavour. I con-gratulate you.'

Raymond smiled and bowed slightly.

'Well, Raymond, I'm glad my competition gave you the impetus you needed.' Blanc turned back to Nancy Friedland.

'Yeah, your competition...my award apparently

rescinded. You give, you take, huh, Louis? Though your little plan backfired.'

Half-ignoring Raymond, Blanc attempted to continue his intimate conversation with Ms Friedland, who was becoming distracted. 'Youth; fanciful in their imaginings, aberrant in their creations.'

'Yeah, you're certainly a big international influence in culinary affairs, Mr Blanc.' Raymond's voice grew louder.

Carmen was passing, ushering some new customers to a table.

'Carmen, would you have the maitre d' come over please?'

Seating the diners, the manager acknowledged Raymond's request.

'How's *L'Escargot*?'

'I spend so little time there.' Blanc was off-hand; his attitude was beginning to suggest he found Raymond tiresome.

Feydor Gaultier arrived. Blanc's expression suddenly changed to one of arrogant disdain. Gaultier gave the briefest of nods to his old acquaintance before turning to his new employer.

'Mr Babchuk.'

'Monsieur Gaultier, please be good enough to repeat *Le Chat Noir's* news you told me of.'

'Certainly. Mr Chesson and Mr de Lange, unhappy about the allegation made against you, approached several of the board of Chef de France, suggesting that if the matter wasn't resolved they might resort to legal action for slander against one of their employees. Responding to their concerns, it appeared the members knew nothing of the contention and your award was reinstated.'

'Thank you. The Cat offered me chef de cuisine, which

I passed on. The place somehow had a bad taste.'

Nancy Friedland tittered.

Blanc leapt to his feet. 'You little turd! You think it clever to humiliate me, but you do so at your peril. Understand?' He spoke in a low voice, his face close to Raymond's.

'Sure do,' Raymond answered calmly and reached out to Blanc. Suddenly, the master cuisinier's face went from white to a contorted purple. There was no doubt which organs of Blanc's Raymond was squeezing.

'You're lookin' preoccupied, Louis. Don't get too excited. Then again, guess this is prob'ly the biggest turn-on you've had in a while.'

Nancy Friedland's face was incredulous. Was she enjoying herself?

'You'll excuse us, Miss Friedland.' Raymond's grip tightened on Blanc's scrotum. 'Thank you for coming by, Louis, but you're leaving now. No fuss. No bother. Nice and quiet.'

Releasing his hold, Raymond turned away, leaving Blanc doubled over, but through his pain the Frenchman suddenly lashed out and in so doing fell over. Other diners had noticed what had been happening and there was some laughter and applause. Tutti reappeared and sat down in Blanc's seat, clapping with the rest.

Utterly humiliated, Blanc staggered to the door held open for him by Raymond.

'I see that limo of yours in the street. At least you'll be comfortable on the ride home.'

'I've never been so insulted. You'll regret this.'

'Somehow I don't think I will. Get some rest now and give my regards to Pierre-Auguste when you see him. Some maestro! Phony punk!'

Blanc staggered to the limo door held open by his chauffeur and crawled into the car. Following him outside,

Raymond looked along the street. A site had been cleared awaiting construction and some hobos were sitting huddled at a brazier. An electric window in the limousine slid down, Blanc's tortured face appearing from the shadows.

'You – you upstart. You will get your comeuppance.'

'We all do in the end, Louis, but where you're concerned I've a lot to live up to.'

The car moved off. Somewhere on the Hudson a barge horn sounded.

'New York City. Nowhere quite like it.'

Chapter 16

Around the time Raymond was evicting Louis Blanc from
Restaurant Incarnate, Arnold Riseveldt, sat in an all-night
diner across town, munching a hamburger. Slouched on
a stool beside him was the incongruous figure of Jack
Grimaldi. A ringer for Jack Palance – craggy face complete
with broken nose, his greasy dyed hair swept back –
Grimaldi was dressed in an Al Capone-like wide pinstripe
suit, with spats on his feet and a fedora placed over his
violin case, sitting on the seat beside him. Experiencing a
supply problem, Arnold had hit on the idea of hiring Jack
as a possible way to resolve it. When the potential solution
came to him it had been so obvious, staring him in the
face. He'd met Jack years previously when a gangland war
was in full swing, a number of members of Grimaldi's side
ending up at RIP. A very contrite Jack had come by to pay
his last respects.

Time went by and many would now see Grimaldi as an
outdated and anachronistic killer, but in an odd way his
very obviousness only emphasised the incongruity of his
trade. If there was anything about Grimaldi that bothered
the mortician it was Jack's unpredictability; he was a schizo
good and proper – fine one minute, apparently normal,
then in the next he'd flip. Out. Gazoomed. Off on some
murderous villainy. Still, maybe that was what being a killer
did to you.

Arnold bit into another mouthful of his burger. 'Real food, huh, Jack? Real American food.'

Not eating, Grimaldi stirred his insipid-looking coffee. 'The best. Baby Face Spats – we're talkin' mean machine here. Killed forty-seven people one night back in the fifties just for scratchin' his car. Weren't the heyday, 'course, but folks had fun.' He sipped some coffee, which left a creamy line on his moustache.

'Yeah, you know, I was only saying–'

Wiping cream from his lip, Grimaldi cut in. 'And Black Jack Buchannan. He blew away half o' Detroit for murderin' 'is wife. Said he didn't mind 'er dyin' – just couldn't stand the ignominy.'

'Ignominy?'

'Embarrassment, bird brain.'

'Now, Jack, you shouldn't talk to me like that. I'm your prospective employer.'

'But the real guy – the one who put fear into every other mother with a gun – was The Tweet.'

'The Tweet?'

'Ssh! Low, huh?'

'The Tweet? Low?'

'Not the word for it. Killed women for lookin' at 'im.'

'Was he ugly or somethin'?'

'Had what they called "The Lurch"!'

'Yeah?'

'Some dame dumped him way back when. Got ter thinkin' women didn't like him.'

'Nice way to react. You know some seriously weird people.'

'Know of, Mr Riseveldt, know of. But the vital lesson of history is to learn from the mistakes guys made who went before yer.'

'They made some?'

'Got caught.'

'I can see how that would be a mistake.'

Grimaldi had another sip of coffee. 'Yer see, yer got to get into the mind of bein' a killer. It's a very particular occupation.'

'Runnin' high school classes on it now, are they?'

'May as well be. Always room for improvement in every profession.'

'Isn't that a little strong – "profession"?'

'How else d'yer want to describe it? Work? Nine to five? Goin' out all day, slayin' people. "Just got in from the office, babe. Had a busy day; blew six away." Poetry. How d'ya like that? When d'yer want me to start?'

'Tonight?'

'Let's do it.' Grimaldi stood up and placed his hat on his head.

'I'll just finish my food, huh?' Arnold stuffed some more burger into his mouth.

'Time and tide, Mr Riseveldt, time and tide.'

'Time and tide?' Arnold spoke through a mouthful of food.

'Be awaitin' for no man. So long, Rocky.' Picking up his violin case, Grimaldi strode out.

Throwing down some dollars, Arnold quaffed the beer he'd had on the go and grabbed what was left of his burger. Outside on the street the elderly killer sniffed the air.

'No city like this city.'

Arnold appeared and the two walked off along the pavement, Grimaldi striding out, the mortician scurrying along beside him trying to finish his food.

''Course, you're in the game o' death yerself, Mr Riseveldt.'

'Afterlife, Jack, afterlife.'

They stopped to look at a street mural, a giant portrait of Christ and Mohammed adorning a derelict wall.

'Afterlife. It's a thing.' Grimaldi walked on, the mortician sweating to keep up with him.

'Sure is, but I gotta get supplies, and fast.'

'I'm yer man.'

A fat youth waddled across the street.

'Wanna see me perform?'

'That won't be necessary. You come well recommended.' Riseveldt took out the keys to a nondescript van.

Grimaldi aimed his violin case at the youth. 'That I do.'

'Don't forget, I also know your work. Can I give you a lift anywhere?' Opening the driver's door, Arnold was nervous. Grimaldi opened the passenger door and placed his violin case on the middle passenger seat before climbing in. Arnold turned the ignition key.

'Must say, it's a neat way to improve yer new business, Mr Riseveldt, and you must tell me if there's any particular type you're a-wantin'. I mean, I guess you'll be needin' some fat cats, huh? Quality produce.' Grimaldi began to open the violin case.

'Hey, hey! Keep that shut!'

Ignoring the mortician, Grimaldi carried on opening it, taking out a violin.

'Yer don't like live music?' He plucked a string and slightly retuned the instrument. 'People think I'm a little crazy, Mr Riseveldt, what with my style o' dress an' all, but I'm just a guy whose intentions are...well, t'earn a livin'. Even paid taxes last year.'

They motored along.

'Tell me something. Why do you...you know?'

'Kill people? Hell now, three reasons: the money, I'm good at it, and I just love seein' that moment before. Everythin' gets real centred. Know what I mean?'

As the van moved through the traffic, Grimaldi began playing some Paganini.

Arnold was reflective. 'I can see how it could do that.'

Usually it was Raymond who was last to leave his restaurant and lock up, but that night Tabitha had also stayed late. There was so much to do, the excitement of the evening having delayed tidying and preparation for the following day.

The wall phone in the kitchen rang. Tabitha answered.

'Oh, okay...yuh. How long? Twenty minutes. Hang on.' She turned back to Raymond who was poring over the following evening's menu.

'Problem with cabs; they're a driver down.'

The chef made no response. 'Wanna share?'

'Okay.'

'How about a drink while we wait?'

'Not here.'

'Bar Mortino. They can pick us up from there.'

Ray nodded and made some menu adjustments.

'We'll just have the one cab and do a drop-off. Collect from Bar Mortino in half an hour. Thanks.' Tabitha yawned. 'C'mon, Ray, let's get outta here.'

Walking along the street, Tutti sitting on Raymond's shoulder, it began to rain.

'Quite a night.' Tabitha hated silence. Raymond only grunted as Tutti huddled into his neck. 'Amazin' how it's taken off, Ray. You passin' on that jerk Blanc's offer – did you ever think it would fly like this?'

Before Raymond could answer, a commotion ahead

caused them to look up. Oaths and curses were heard and a gun went off. Tabitha clutched Ray, and Tutti shrieked as a man came flying out of the shadows, landing on the pavement. The first to respond, Tabitha moved forward. The hobo was grizzled and stank, but somehow familiar. It was Hikey Homaster and he was in a bad way, dark rings under his eyes, his stubbled face grimy with dirt, the hand clutching a pistol bloodied. More shouts and scuffling came from inside a darkened building.

'Get the fu–!'

With Tabitha and Raymond looking at him, Homaster's eyes glazed and he fell back. Tutti hopped off Raymond's shoulder and sniffed about the tramp, who twitched away. Another shot was fired inside, accompanied by several screams and shouts.

'Let's get outta here, Tab.'

'We can't just leave him.'

'We'll call the police, but let's get out of here.'

Their attention drawn to the building, neither had noticed Homaster raise his pistol and fire. The shot passed through Raymond's jacket sleeve, nicking the flesh of his arm.

'Shi–!'

'Ray!'

'Run!'

Without a backward glance they took off down the street, Tutti screeching in fear.

An hour later, sitting on Raymond's bed, Tabitha had bathed his grazed arm and Tutti brought him a cigar. When Raymond declined the offer, the monkey took it for himself, clipped it and prepared it for smoking. Tabitha reappeared in the doorway.

'Police say there were signs of trouble – blood, but no one there.'

Raymond sank back on a pillow.

'You okay?'

Raymond sighed.

'You were lucky. Another inch, it would've been in your arm; couple of inches, in your body.' She mothered him a little, making the bed comfortable. 'Let's have that drink, huh? You could prob'ly do with it. Brandy?'

Raymond managed an affirmative grunt and Tabitha went through to the kitchen.

'Amazing, this kitchen of yours; every time I enter it I'm inspired. What are you going to do with the house?'

There was no response from Raymond's bedroom. Easily locating an array of bottles on a shelf, Tabitha began to look through them. 'Slivovitz – Hungarian brandy. Oh yeah, Hungary.' Finding a brandy glass, she poured a reasonable amount of the exotic beverage and picking up both glass and bottle, left the room. Arriving at the bedside Tabitha discovered Tutti quietly enjoying a small Romeo y Julieta, the chef de cuisine apparently asleep.

'Keeping an eye on him, huh?'

Tutti gave a little chatter. Tabitha put the glass down on a pile of recipe books beside the bed. 'That good?'

In his little monkey way, Tutti looked extremely happy. The bottle of Slivovitz in her hand, Tabitha walked around the bed into the small hall, opening the door to what had been Mrs Rinegold's landing. Stepping on to it, she lifted the bottle and looked down the stairs, the scene of Renais Rinegold's earthly departure. 'Wow!' Taking another swig, Tabitha idly descended and began wandering through the house. Starting on the ground floor, she found Renais' kitchen, which Raymond had done his best to clean up.

Next, the dining room, with its ghastly colours; white trellis covering salmon pink, and on one wall a Grecian-style trompe l'oeil depicting Renais as an exotic naked nymph. But all paled into insignificance beside the master bedroom, which was a triumph of gaudiness and tastelessness. Again largely pink, it also possessed a lurid red dressing table, a glass ceiling and black silk sheets on the bed.

Opening a wardrobe, she was almost buried by an avalanche of sex gear falling on top of her: leather basques, patent thigh-length boots and bondage chains hanging from the doors. Tabitha fell back on the bed, still clutching her bottle but draped in an odd neoprene pointy bra. She laughed.

'Whore's paradise!'

Taking another tipple of the Hungarian liquor, she put down the bottle and playfully held odd bits of the accoutrements against herself, moving her hips and sticking out her chest at various mirrors. It was in this state that Raymond found her. Finally noticing him, she turned to face him.

'What d'yer think? Swell dominatrix, huh?' Tabitha laughed and put down the crop and handcuffs. Raymond's face was expressionless. 'See you haven't done nothin' to the place.'

Raymond came over and closed the wardrobe. Tabitha gathered up the bizarre attire and placed it on the red dressing table.

'Had it cleaned – fumigated.' He seemed tense.

'Didn't she have pets?'

'Yer mean the disgustin' miniature poodles? Mr B's got 'em.'

Tabitha said, 'I should go,' but all thoughts of departure left her as Raymond collapsed in front of her without warning.

Inside, he was falling though space down a black void, his body tumbling, legs flailing, nothing to hold on to. Psychedelic colours danced across his translucent body. Tutti appeared, framed in perfect cigar rings. Then Riseveldt, a clerical collar round his neck, standing over a shrouded corpse lying in a coffin, which dropped into the abyss. And then there was a gun, its barrel huge, and behind it the grizzled face of Homaster.

Raymond sat up, screaming. A bizarre phallus lamp providing the only light, Raymond squatted, sweating and shivering, in his aunt's bed. Tabitha held him in her arms.

'It's okay, Ray. It's okay, baby.'

Raymond shook violently, his pale face a delicate shade of violet.

'I can't go in, Tab. I can't go in.'

'I know, baby, I know. You're overstressed. You need a rest.'

Raymond was still shaking.

'You want a doctor?' Tabitha could just make out Raymond's negative shake of the head over and above his body spasms.

'Riseveldt. You've got to call Riseveldt.'

'The mortician guy?'

'Yeah. I need to speak to him.'

'Why, honey? Sure you're sick, but you ain't dyin'.'

'Just get him on the phone.'

'Now? It's four in the morning.'

Lying back, Raymond shook so much it was almost as if he was having a seizure.'

'You need a doctor.'

'No! No!'

Having brought her bag into the bedroom while Raymond was unconscious, Tabitha rummaged around in it for her phone. 'What's his number?' Raymond gave it and she punched the digits into her speed dial. 'Pretty good memory. Call him a lot?'

Raymond didn't reply.

'Okay, I'll do it first thing. You need some rest now.'

Opening her makeup bag, Tabitha took out a foil sheet of pills and extracted two. Handing Raymond some water, she helped him take them. Raymond lay back again.

'That's better, baby. We'll get you well again. Now sleep.' Tabitha gently stroked his head and Raymond gradually calmed. As he entered a fitful slumber, she kissed his forehead. It was a loving and intimate action.

Chapter 17

Arnold entering RIP, the place was a hive of industry. He swept down the corridor past the Halls of Remembrance and walked quickly out toward the Preparation Centre, which was a more modern equivalent of the South Side place he'd organised for Incarnate's requirements, banks of cadaver drawers along two walls and several operating tables where clients were checked in and their bodies examined. Astonishingly, the room was full of covered gurneys and the normally controlled Manny was desperately trying to log the influx. Taking a white coat from his office, Arnold returned and began aligning the trolleys, which had been left anyhow.

'Phew! Quite an intake.'

'Yeah, killing job.'

'All of 'em?'

'Yup. Every one. And the same perpetrator.'

'How do you know?'

Manny barely looked up. 'You can always tell. This guy gives 'em the round close up, aimed into the aortic root. Either some strange ritual, which it ain't, or he's commissioned. Big calibre, too. Messy.'

Arnold's mouth went dry. There were perhaps twenty extra admissions. Surely, Grimaldi couldn't be responsible for them all. The phone began to ring...and ring, distracting him from his thoughts. 'Leave it! We've got work to do.'

Although irritated, Manny continued checking bodies and Riseveldt began assisting with the paperwork. The phone was still ringing when Julie Dominic walked in, hard-faced and severe.

'We need to talk about pulling in some more people. With this workload – there's another four in now – we just don't have the staff. Also, whatever's happening out there, the police work takes up a lot of time. Some of these have had autopsies but some bodies can't be released for embalming immediately because of ongoing enquiries.'

'Okay. Any ideas who we can get hold of?'

'There's a couple of guys we used last year in an emergency, plus I know that weird Kerj Etabrutsam is unhappy over at Kosher Crems. Nuts he may be but his work's good.'

'Let's get 'em in then.' Arnold turned to go.

'One other thing. Some girl's been calling up – a lot. Something about Mr Babchuk wanting to speak to you. Apparently he isn't making it to work today, calling in sick or something. The number's on your desk.' Julie didn't wait for a reply, returning to her massive workload.

Leaving Admissions and heading for his office, Riseveldt contemplated the situation. What was the deranged lunatic he'd hired doing, bumping off so many people? And the crazy chef calling in sick. He'd have to nail that – and fast. Was everyone goddamn crazy? Why was it always he, Arnold Riseveldt who had to sort out other people's incompetence? What failed to occur to the mortician was that these people he was so critical of were only in the positions they were because of him.

Arnold entered his office, threw off his white coat,

dropped into his chair and dialled the number scrawled on his pad.

'Arnold Riseveldt here. You've been calling.'

'Yeah, I have.' Tabitha was quite calm. Recognising her voice, Arnold sat back.

'What's this about Raymond being unwell?'

'He got wounded last night.'

'How?'

'He was shot, at close range.'

For a moment Riseveldt froze. His hired killer shot his chef? The blood drained from his face. 'Is he okay?'

'He was lucky; bullet grazed his arm.'

'Where is he?'

'Left him at his aunt's...at his house.'

Both paused.

'You at the restaurant?'

'Yuh.'

'All okay?'

'Yuh.'

'Need any help if he ain't makin' it in today?'

'He's left everything pretty much prepared.'

Riseveldt hurried on. 'Just wanting to cover my investment; it's going good there. It's got to *keep* going good there.'

'Sure.'

'Okay then; let me know if yer need anything, if I can help out at all.'

'That's very considerate, Mr Riseveldt, though I appreciate your offer of help is to cover your investment.'

'Was there anything else?'

'No. Nuthin'.'

'Goodbye, then.'

They replaced their receivers. In Arnold's case his phone was slammed down. Goddamn people.

Chapter 18

Something in Raymond had snapped. Seeing Homaster again... What was he doing, cutting up dead people to feed to his countrymen? Or maybe some of his diners weren't his countrymen? That didn't make any difference, but he couldn't go on like this. It was crazy. But people seemed to love his food – genuinely love it. They couldn't get enough of it. Tables booked weeks in advance, the good and great coming by... If only they knew. He'd be hung, drawn and quartered – no fate too bad for him. It was a dark place he was at and there was only one thing for it – the police. He'd have to go and turn himself in.

Getting up from his late aunt's grotesque bed, he dived into her en suite bathroom (walls the same shocking pink) and was violently sick. Recovering somewhat, he staggered from the room and painfully climbed the stairs to his private domain. Tutti turned from watching *Family Guy* on TV – the monkey loved American cartoon shows – and scampered over to him.

'I gotta do it, Toots. It ain't right, what's been goin' down.'

Tutti's little hand tweaked Raymond's cheek and he nuzzled into his shoulder. It was an almost human gesture. Raymond picked up the week's draft menus, still in note form, lying on the cluttered bedside table: ideas for dishes – fillet, tenderloin and rump. That was a point. Would the police believe him if he just walked in and told them about what he'd been doing?

Feverishly, Raymond went through to his kitchen and began rummaging around in his freezer, looking through the sealed bags. Finally selecting one, he stood up.

'Cerebrum: whole brain.' He found a carrier bag and placed the package inside.

Setting out for the local precinct police station, Raymond and Tutti bumped into Mr Balázs walking the late Aunt Renais' two white miniature poodles, Pussy and Hard. Since he'd had the two little dogs, Mr B had removed their pink and black studded collars (Pussy's pink, Hard's black patent). The animals being much tidied up, they would always be effete-looking creatures, something of which Mr Balázs appeared unaware. As to the coarseness of their names:

'Oh, I just call them P and H.'

Now, as he walked along, the little dogs at his heels, Mr Balázs gave Tutti and Raymond a wave.

'Haven't seen you in a while, Raymond.'

'Been kinda busy.'

'Oh yes, I heard about the restaurant. Wonderful for you.' Mr Balázs's compliment was entirely genuine, but Raymond didn't appear overly grateful.

'Yeah, well...'

P and H were checking out Tutti, sniffing and pawing him.

'You have a day off?'

'I was sick.'

'I'm sorry. Nothing serious, I hope?'

Raymond shook his head but said nothing. In the pause that followed, P and H, bored with their monkey acquaintance, began to pull on their leashes.

'You walking somewhere?'

'Er, yeah.'

'Shall we go along together?'

Obviously still below par, Raymond fell into step with Mr Balázs and they strolled off down Palmetto Street, their assorted creatures in tow. Mr B was in a conversational mood.

'You know, Raymond, when your aunt died in such, er, such an unusual manner, I was worried about you. I know you had your difficulties with her over the years – heavens, what she did to that first kitchen of yours was unforgiveable – but latterly I thought you'd both been getting on better; kind of *jobb az ördög tudja.*'

Mr Balázs's Hungarian 'better the devil you know' seemed an innocent remark. But even he had never really known how much Raymond detested, despised and hated his aunt. If she hadn't died as a result of the freak accident caused by Tutti's tail, Raymond believed he could have, would have, ended up killing her himself. Heck, he'd subsequently served up some of her remains. The canapés (Auntie's liver, moussed) had been a very good variant on chicken liver pâté and much appreciated by her mourners, of which Mr Balázs was one. When he considered why he was heading for the offices of the local police department, one of the conflicting emotions Raymond experienced was that he didn't feel bad about what he himself had done. In fact, given that Mr Balázs and others, when paying their last respects, had complimented him on the food, it all somehow had a fitting symmetry. What was Mr B saying?

'Anyway, I'm real glad things are working out for you. You goin' to stay in Palmetto Street?'

For several seconds Raymond didn't answer and Balázs

didn't seem in any hurry for a reply. They turned into Catalpa Avenue.

'Guess I hadn't really thought about it.'

'Does it bother you, living there on your own?'

'I got Tutti.'

Balázs smiled. 'You sure have. Using any of the other rooms? It's a big house.'

'Not right now.'

'Maybe you'll redecorate.'

Raymond stopped and after a few paces so did Mr Balázs.

'You going in here?' He nodded towards the Ridgewood Police Department building.

'Yeah, I got to check out some things.'

'Well, good to see you. I'm going on to the park. They love running around in Mafera.'

For several seconds Raymond and Balázs stood on the street outside the police station. Tutti looked up at Raymond, P and H strained on their leashes. Raymond picked up Tutti.

'You okay? You look kinda lost. You must have been working damned hard recently, plus all the trauma with your aunt... Maybe you should take a break.' Mr Balázs looked into Raymond's face. The day was warm now. Fiddling with his carrier bag, Raymond studied the NYPD block. Balázs caught his eye. 'Not thinking of vacationing there, are you?' He laughed. P and H pulled harder. '*Szervusz*, Radomér. Catch up with you soon.'

The elderly Hungarian walked away, pulled along by the two miniature poodles. Although they were ridiculous little dogs, somehow he didn't look silly with them, his natural gentlemanliness maintaining some style. With a look of resignation, Raymond turned back to the police building. It was now or never. He strode up to the portico and, entering the main doors, walked into bedlam.

The reception area was crammed full of the detritus of human life and most of them were complaining, form-filling or puking, whilst officers attempted to keep some kind of order. A number were shown out rapidly, their minor issues simply cluttering up police time. However, maintaining any kind of efficiency was almost impossible in the overcrowded and infinitely crazy world of the New York Police Department. Raymond had rarely had any dealings with the police or their environs and finally getting to a grilled counter, he looked balefully at a preoccupied police sergeant. When the man glanced up it was Tutti he noticed first.

'Got a problem trainin' him? Zoo's outta town, 'bout half hour up the freeway.'

'No, er, something to report.'

'Yeah? Well if it ain't rape, robbery or murder don't bother. Too much on just now.' The sergeant sounded tired.

'It...it isn't murder but...a lot of death.'

'As in life... Tell me about it!'

'Fine.'

'No, buddy, no! Just kiddin'! Look, there's shit aplenty here. Move it along, huh?'

Suddenly steely, Raymond opened his carrier bag and brought out the cellophane-wrapped package. 'You should have a look at this.'

'What the–?'

'It's a human brain. Cerebrum humanum.'

'Where d'you get it?'

'Like I said, I need to talk to someone.'

'Jeez. Yeah, yeah...' The weary police sergeant reached for an internal phone.

*

The Ridgewood Police Department interview room Raymond and Tutti were led into was the usual bleak, windowless cube, some chairs either side of a central table and a wall-mounted intercom system. A worn-looking lieutenant, with bags under his eyes (was every cop in the precinct exhausted?) sat opposite Raymond and a very young uniformed officer, a line of bum-fluff barely covering his upper lip, stood on sentry duty. Tutti Frutti sat on a chair beside Raymond, the bag containing the brain on the table.

'So, you're saying you had this accident, didn't report it because you felt compromised and since then your restaurant's been serving human flesh supplied by this mortician who put the squeezers on yer. Right?' Raymond nodded. 'How long you been runnin' this place?'

'Six months.'

'Six months? You mean to tell me you been servin' up dead people for six months?'

Raymond gave another nod.

The lieutenant was incredulous. 'And in all that time no one's queried the food?'

'This guy's a master chef. I read about it – won some award. Can't get a table. Place is a sell-out.' The sentry had been paying attention.

'Since when was your opinion asked for, Officer Cattermole?'

Cattermole adjusted his collar. 'Just trying to fill in some background. Jeez, it's hot in here.'

The lieutenant turned back to Raymond and Tutti. The monkey was fiddling with the plastic bag.

'Hey, no tampering with the evidence, huh?' The lieutenant took the bag and removed the still-cold brain.

'Holy Mother of God.' Holding up the organ, Lieutenant

Garside turned it over in his hands. 'So this is what it looks like – the human brain. Are you seriously telling me people have been eating these?'

'As *cervelle d'agneau* or *tête de veau,* and along with *coeur de veau à la hongroise* – heart; *mousse de foie gras* – liver; and all the usual meat cuts – rump, shoulder, topside...'

'Okay, okay. That's enough.'

'Wow! Are they good?'

'Officer Cattermole! That will be all.'

Cattermole actually looked disappointed. A buzzer went on a desk phone. Garside answered.

'Okay. Yuh.' He replaced the receiver, put the brain down on the table and stood up. A few seconds later a door release sounded. Officer Cattermole stood to one side as two other men entered. The first was in uniform – Captain Manifest: late fifties with iron grey hair. The second, Police Chief Giantelli, was plain-clothed, olive-skinned and heavy-set. Garside went over to them and the three briefly conferred. Odd phrases could be heard amidst their murmurings: 'That's what he says', 'Monkey', 'Cute?', 'Bizarre'.

'Okay, Lieutenant, we'll take it from here.'

Garside looked put out. 'Sorry, sir?'

'You heard me; we'll take over.'

'You're going to take over the interview, sir?'

'That's what I said.' Giantelli was already crossing the room, taking a seat.

'Er, well...'

'Thank you, Lieutenant.'

Looking from Giantelli to Manifest, Garside appeared about to speak then thought better of it. Snapping shut his file, he left the room. Giantelli watched Tutti fiddle with the brain.

'Put that thing away.' Opening the plastic bag, Tutti put

the brain inside it. 'Cute monkey. Ain't thinkin' of servin' him up, are yer?'

'I saved him.'

'From the pot? Animal lover too, huh, Mr Babchuk?' Giantelli moved his sizeable bulk on the hard chair. 'So, Mr B, what are we gonna do with you? Yer come in here with all kindsa crackpot stories and all the captain and me wanna do is get a table at yer goddamn restaurant. What are you all about, son?'

'I've been telling the lieutenant – it can't go on.'

'Hear that, Manifest? Kid's got the most successful restaurant in Manhattan and he can't go on? God, fella, I know people who'd give their eye teeth to have what you've got.'

Raymond looked flustered and dubious. Captain Manifest came over.

'So you're the head chef, huh? Doctrinal Manifest – Doc for short. Pleased to meet you.' Captain Manifest actually put out a hand, which Raymond shook hesitantly.

'But I came in here... What we're servin'...it's wrong!'

The two policemen looked at each other. It was Giantelli who spoke.

'If it's wrong, son, I'd hate to think how you'd put it right.'

Manifest leant over Raymond. 'Look, we're in the middle of a shake-down with the mayor. Your comin' by could save our bacon. He's been on about your restaurant – "Unique place", "Hopeless getting a table" – if you could get us one, we could bring him along. It'd help our corner. You understand?' The way Manifest pleaded was almost desperate.

Half an hour later, Raymond and Tutti were dropped off in Palmetto Street by a police car. Also turning into the road in his nondescript van was Arnold Riseveldt, who watched as an officer opened a rear door and Tutti, clutching a carrier bag, followed by Raymond, stepped on to the kerb. Raymond had tried to leave the human brain with the police as evidence, but was met with: 'If you're gonna serve it, you're gonna need it! I love that *cerveau au poivre.*'

This had completely done for the chef, who sank into a kind of stupor. Surely it was pure madness he was experiencing.

'And make sure we get a corner slot, huh? The mayor likes his back to the wall.' This had met with an involuntary noise from Officer Cattermole, still on door duty.

Standing in the street now, Raymond stared blankly as the officer saluted and got back into his vehicle, which swung away into the traffic. Raymond and Tutti entered their house as an agitated Riseveldt quickly found a parking space and ran up the steps. Inside, barely having closed the door, he heard a loud banging on it. Raymond walked back along the hall to reopen the front door.

'What's going down? Got a driving violation?' Arnold shot inside the house, slamming the door behind him. Raymond turned away. 'Hey! I'm talking to you.'

'Up yer ass, man! Skip out!'

'Hey, hey, hey!' Arnold virtually ran after Raymond, grabbing him by the arm. 'You tell me what this is all about. I'm workin' my butt off here, and you gotta get back to the restaurant!'

'They want a table, and nope.'

'What do you mean, "They want a table, and nope"?'

'Chief o' police, a Cap'n Manifest, and the mayor want a meal and I ain't cookin' it.'

'You're kiddin' me? The chief of police and New York City's mayor want to dine at Incarnate?'

Walking away, Raymond headed for the stairs.

'Hey, don't keep walking away from me.' Again Arnold had to run after his partner. 'What were you doing there anyway?'

'Tellin' 'em we're servin' human meat.'

'Whaaaaat?!'

'You heard me. It's gotta stop.'

'Wha– What did they say?'

'Told you. They want a table.'

'Hold it! Hold it! Yer mean yer went into the station, told them what you were doing and they want to come and eat at the restaurant?'

'You can be real quick.' Still carrying the carrier bag, Tutti began climbing the stairs. 'Even provided the evidence.'

Arnold sat down on the bottom step. 'You stupid fuckin' jerk. Crazy idiot, mother piece of sh–'

Raymond's private door swung to. Arnold's head sank forward and sighing, he rubbed his eyes.

'Jeez. That's one crazy fucker.'

He became aware of Tutti sitting down beside him. The monkey hadn't gone into Raymond's apartment and now sat gently scratching his ear, his little paw-like hands preening his fur with his nails. Although he had always expressed irritation at Tutti, Arnold now looked across at him. Almost intuitively, Tutti Frutti put the carrier bag against Riseveldt's knee.

'Whatcher doin'?' He peered into the bag and removed the brain. 'This the evidence, huh?'

Sitting up, Tutti tapped the wrapped organ.

'Tryin' to tell me somethin'?'

Tutti and Riseveldt looked at each other.

'Maybe you are, at that...'

Replacing the brain in the bag, Riseveldt stood up.

'Thank you, Tutti – you're right; we've got to get the moron back to work. Comin' up?'

In response, Tutti actually stood up and mortician and monkey began to climb the stairs. Raymond's door was half open and after knocking, he called out: 'Raymond! Raymond!' Tutti scurried past and scampered up to the apartment. Riseveldt called again. 'Raymond!' He began to climb the upper stairs and pushing back Raymond's bedroom door, discovered the chef lying sprawled on his bed.

'Jeez! Raymond, move yer butt; we gotta get you to work.'

'I ain't goin' nowhere.'

Riseveldt sat down on the edge of the bed. He looked old and tired. 'What's yer problem?'

'I told yer my problem! I do not enjoy cookin' up dead people an' servin' 'em to the great American public. It kind of gives a constraint to my talents – bein' just the one type o' meat an' all. Also, I go to the police, tell them about this bad thing we're doin' and all they wanna do is eat in the fuckin' restaurant! And as if that ain't enough, there's the small matter o' my bein' shot!'

'Okay, okay, I can see you've been under a lot lately; we both have. But we gotta stick together.'

'Phaa! The bum recognised me – I know he did. Shit, man!'

'What are yer talkin' about? So what if some bum recognised yer? Is there some crap I don't know about?'

Having sat up and spoken animatedly, Raymond now buried his face in his pillow. Arnold sighed. He hadn't bargained on all this when coming up with his ultimate business plan.

'Look, Ray, I gotta go round the corner. Little meetin'.

Let me buy you a cup of coffee and we'll talk things over, huh?'

Chapter 19

Ralph's cafe was relatively quiet as Jack Grimaldi, clad in his perennial pinstripe suit, violin case laid beside him, stood at the counter having a coffee. As has been established, Ralph seemed to know pretty much everyone in New York City, and he and Jack went back a long way, but truth to tell, the cafe proprietor had never taken Grimaldi's gangster persona seriously, simply believing him to be an eccentric musician.

'Did ya ever think of doin' any real work? I mean, with yer classical trainin' an' all, yer play beautiful. Yer could play Carnegie Hall, and yer just frig around in subways.'

'Fine way to talk about my audience. I like 'em. Besides, I ain't gonna be remembered for playin' the violin.'

'I know, I know – "Manhattan's top killer dies in hail of gunfire". I'll have 'em all round here when yer get cut down.'

Grimaldi laughed.

'Did I ever tell yer about–?'

Some other clients arriving, Ralph cut in: 'Yeah, yeah, yer did, Jack.'

Bringing up the rear of these latest customers were a tired looking Arnold Riseveldt and his bleary-eyed partner. The latter wore some strange attire – a pair of striped pyjama bottoms and a brightly coloured Mexican poncho, while his monkey chum sported a mini sombrero.

167

Finishing his coffee, Jack Grimaldi spotted his new boss reflected in the mirror.

'Mr Riseveldt, there you are. Good to see yer. Trust you're pleased with my work?'

'Yeah, yeah, great, Jack. Phenomenal. Got to keep this short, I'm afraid. I have a meetin' with my colleague here.'

'Oh, you're the chef I been hearin' about. Gather the place is goin' real good, and all thanks to my–'

'Yeah, Jack, it's going fine, thank you.' As he spoke, Arnold placed a bulging envelope inside Grimaldi's double-breasted jacket. The assassin immediately removed it, feeling its weight and thickness in his hand.

'Much appreciated, Mr Riseveldt. Plannin' on workin' across town next week. Thought maybe things'd be a little quieter over there.'

Arnold licked his lips nervously. Perhaps it hadn't been such a good idea to meet his oddball contract killer in a café. 'Good idea, Jack, good idea. Now if you'll excuse us...'

'Sure, Mr Riseveldt, sure. Just so long as you're happy with what I'm deliverin'.'

'It's great, Jack – truly great.'

Placing his fedora rakishly over his greasy, slicked-back hair, Grimaldi picked up his violin case. 'Nice monkey. Does he do tricks?'

'Shoots people and steals cigars.'

Tutti pulled out a cigar from somewhere, which Raymond removed from his hand.

'No smoking in here!'

'Ha! He's a character I can see. Smokin' monkey, smokin' gun!' Picking up his violin case, Grimaldi headed for the door. 'Gotta get back to work. So long, now.'

Wiping his counter, Ralph looked up. 'You take care now, JG. No bad notes on yer travels, huh? What can I get you gentlemen?' Ralph's glance briefly swept over Raymond's bizarre attire.

'Coupla iced teas please, Ralph.'

Raymond and Tutti wandered over to an area where the café proprietor kept newspapers for his customers to read.

'He all right – the monkey man?'

Arnold shrugged his shoulders. '*Comme ci comme ça.*'

Ralph instantly looked suspicious. 'Whatever! He was in here a while back; spewed all over the mirror. Nobody does that with Ralph's iced tea.'

'I can see how it could be insulting.'

'Insultin' ain't the word for it. Disgustin' more like.'

Two iced teas appeared on the counter.

'Raymond.'

Reading the *New York Times* restaurant reviews, Raymond didn't look up. Sighing, Riseveldt picked up the two iced teas and went over to his partner. The mortician plonked himself down on a stool nearby.

'So what gives? This bum that shot yer; why did yer say he recognised yer?' Riseveldt had a sip of iced tea. 'Look, Raymond, I can only help if yer tell me about it.'

Ignoring the question, Raymond folded the paper, came over to the counter and leaned against a stool. Tutti scampered off to explore the cafe.

'The old guy with the spats and violin case...'

'What about him?'

'Yer gave him money.'

'So? I give you money.'

Raymond sipped some iced tea. 'Workin' across town 'cause things might be a little quieter...'

'Okay, he's a bit eccentric.'

'Eccentric? Surely not! Spats, double-breasted pinstripe and fedora not being a giveaway, let alone the violin case. I mean, caricature gangster ain't in it!' Raymond had another mouthful of iced tea. He was enjoying it. 'You sure pick 'em.'

'Yeah, I sure do!' Arnold was almost snarling. He forced himself to calm down. 'So, he's helpin' with our supply problems. Deliveries already bein' received.'

'You're sick, man.'

'You really think so? I keep tellin' yer what a favour we're doin' our great American society. They should give us the Medal of Honour. Anyway, if you won't tell me what yer problem is, well, it doesn't make me feel so good. It implies you've been holdin' out on me, not tellin' me things. I don't like that.'

'Tough you don't like it, man.'

If something had recently flipped inside Raymond, it now did in Arnold. He simply sat and reflected.

'The guy who shot me; we've seen each other before.' Raymond broke the silence.

'Yeah. So what?'

'The original "evidence"...'

'The guy you killed?'

'Accidentally!'

'Accidentally.'

'It was in an alley beside the restaurant. He attacked me with this toolbar. Car clipped him and spun him. Came down through the top of the convertible.'

'I seen yer wheels. It can ruin a roof.'

'Broke his neck. Freaky.'

'And this bum was a witness?'

'There were a couple of them.' Raymond had more tea.

'So what's the big deal?'

'When he fired the other night...I know he recognised me.'

'Yeah, I'm there, but so what?'

'I ain't goin' back to work till he's out of the way.'

'Don't yer think yer unnecessarily preoccupied about this? Disproportionate?'

'Why don't yer use the old guy with the spats?'

'He's busy. I told yer we got a lot of supplies comin' in now. Twenny yesterday.'

Raymond spat tea all over the glass.

'Okay, that's it. Out! You're history!' Leaving Tutti drying glasses in the kitchenette, Ralph was round the counter and across the café faster than a dog's raised leg. Trying to mop himself up, Raymond was in a bad way.

'Banned for life, fella. Out!'

Arnold ferreted in his pocket for some change.

'As for you – I don't want yer money. Thought you knew better. Just get him outta here. Spittin' my iced tea every time he comes in. Anyone'd think I was overdoin' the lemon.'

Tutti dropped the tea towel he'd been using and hopped over the counter towards a stumbling Raymond.

'Baboons, the pair of you. Goddamn chimp's got more manners, and he's useful. Jeezus!'

Outside on the street, Raymond, drawn and a pasty green colour, tried to clean himself up.

'He's killed twenty people?'

'Prob'ly nearer double that by now. He's very...effective.' Approaching his van the mortician deactivated the central locking.

'You've been dealin' in death too long. It's flipped yer, man. You're outta your mind.'

'So you keep sayin'.' Arnold climbed in behind the wheel with Raymond and Tutti on the passenger side. 'See this?' The mortician pulled out an edition of *Downtown* folded open at the restaurant review section. A whole page was devoted to Raymond and Restaurant Incarnate. 'You're a celeb. Carmen had news crews down there lookin' to interview you.' Arnold looked across the cab. 'Yer say the single meat type is too restrictive...but you did it, kid. You're a goddamn genius.'

'I know.'

'Yeah, I know you know.'

'Still ain't goin' back ter work, though – not till this bum's outta the way.'

'Why're yer so obsessed with this vagrant? What's he goin' to do? You've already been to the police. I mean, for chris'sakes, Raymond, you've been to the NYPD and they don't wanna know. What can a hobo do to yer?'

'When he squeezed the trigger he wanted to kill me. It's givin' me nightmares.'

'So yer want our man to get specific?'

'He ain't "our" man. I didn't wanna do this shit! Anyways, don't care who does it, I ain't workin' till he's off the scene.'

Arnold sighed. 'Okay. Where'd yer see him?'

'You mean where did he try to kill me?'

'Yeah, I mean where did he try and kill yer?'

'Greenwich and Jane.'

'Near the restaurant?'

Raymond nodded.

'Jeez. Handy. This guy have a name?'

'I said. There were two of 'em – witnesses.'

'Okay, did *they* have names?'

'One was Leon. Real crazy.'

'He was the one tried to shoot you?'

'Nope. That guy's name was Kikey – Hikey – somethin' like that.'

'A kike? That's all we need. *Achat Yhudin* – takes one to know one, I guess. Better go armed with my Talmud when I lay him to rest.'

The van moved off out of Queens, heading for Lower Manhattan.

'Interestin' the police didn't take any serious interest in yer story. Guess it just wasn't wacko enough. The mayor, though; that's somethin'. What are yer gonna give him?'

'Do I have a choice?'

'That's my boy. Nice and rare, huh? He should enjoy that – dog-eat-dog. Ha! I tell yer, if we went public we'd make history!'

Tutti took out a cigar from under his sombrero.

'If you're gonna smoke that thing make sure you open the window.' Was Arnold actually talking to Tutti now? The monkey lit up contentedly. Raymond put his head in his hands.

Having motored through East Village, Raymond believing he'd seen his attempted killer/witness/hobo at least half a dozen times, the van was getting quite close to West Side when a group of vagrants stumbled out in front of it near Washington Square Park, causing Arnold to slam on his brakes.

'Goddamn bums!'

'Whoa! That's him!'

'Yeah?'

Arnold was cynical. 'You'll have us in double figures soon.' In spite of Arnold's dictum that Tutti should blow his cigar smoke through an opened window the cab was still filling up with Havana clouds.

'Ooah!' Raymond retched.

'Window!'

Raymond dropped his head down into his hands again.

'Okay, okay... Let's do a little scouting.' Not being able to park immediately, Arnold swung into MacDougal Street and a few minutes later, found a vacant slot. 'Number of nickels I spend in this town.'

The motley trio alighted and entered the park.

Less well known than nearby Central Park's square mile of Manhattan green, Washington Square Park was equally beautiful and also attracted the many citizens and tourists who comprised the potpourri that is New York City life – including some of its less desirable elements.

Arnold, Raymond and Tutti entered the west gate, the mortician's eyes darting about, those of the chef dulled, and the monkey's animated. The little curiosity Tutti aroused was caused only by his insistent cigar waving.

'Ice cream?' Raymond just stared at Arnold. 'Okay. Don't say I didn't offer.' He looked at Tutti. 'Bet you do.'

The monkey chattered and clapped. They were becoming friends. Arnold approached a nearby vendor, purchased two cones and handing one to Tutti, sat down on the stone perimeter of a fountain.

'Looks delicious.' An English voice drifted into Arnold's hearing, apparently belonging to the hobo standing nearby.

'And tastes it. Move along.'

'Couldn't spare a few hundred dollars, could you? I could do with a night at The Plaza.'

'Split, clown.'

The English tramp strolled over and sat down in a deck chair. Although his attire was shambolic, he had a kind of offbeat charm.

'Hey Raymond – tell me this ain't yer man.'

The chef was leaning against a tree reading the *Downtown* article.

'The Pierre would do.' The tramp had style.

'Will yer stop rabbitin'! Raymond! Is this the bum?'

'Hey now – that isn't nice. But if I'm not he, then who am I?' The tramp appeared mildly amused. Raymond looked up from the magazine and scoffed.

'That may be a very good question. You'll excuse us for a moment.' Finishing his ice-cream, Arnold got up and walked over to his partner.

'If you insist. You seem like nice people – and a monkey eating ice cream. Interesting. Going to give me some?'

Tutti chattered and had another lick. Arnold stood staring at Raymond.

'Not even all schnorrers look alike. Are we really gonna comb the entire town lookin' for this bum?' Fatigue was etched on both their faces. 'D'yer really think he'll just reappear? Chances are one in a million. One in ten million! Raymond, trust me on this. We gotta get back to work. Make some mazuma, make some money.'

The English tramp stood up. The three men looked at each other.

'He's right, you know. That's all any of us want – a few dollars more.'

'Listen, did you see my friend here kill someone in an alley, 'bout three months ago?'

'I'm, er, not sure...'

'Not sure ain't good enough. Yer see, if we find this guy – this witness – we gotta kill him.'

'Well now...perhaps I'm very sure I didn't.'

'Better. Look, this is a credit card I recently picked up from...someone who no longer needs it. Take it from me, it's got forty-eight hours of life. Have fun.' Riseveldt handed the credit card to the tramp.

'That's very kind. Thank you.'

'Where you from, anyway?'

'England. London, England. Home of the theatre.'

'You an actor, then?'

'That honourable profession...'

'An out-of-work actor?'

'Temporarily resting in your fine metropolis. However, this' – he waved the card – 'this can give me a new start in life; I can live like a prince.'

'For a couple of days. Look, pal, anyone dressed like you that wants to risk going into The Plaza Hotel with a dead man's credit card deserves a new start in life.'

Almost paternally taking Raymond's arm, Riseveldt led his partner away through the park.

The tramp read his plastic pay-off. 'O.B. Laden? But you got him.'

'Aw, where's Jack been findin' 'em?' Arnold turned back to the tramp. 'Maybe there's more than one.'

'Or perhaps he's been reincarnated? What a part, me playing Osama.'

He began to recite:

> In Xanadu did Kubla Khan
> A stately pleasure-dome decree:
> Where Alph, the sacred river, ran
> Through caverns measureless to man
> Down to a sunless sea.

Tutti handed the tramp the last of his cornet before scurrying after his friends. Finishing the ice-cream in one mouthful, he continued:

> And 'mid this tumult Kubla heard from far
> Ancestral voices prophesying war!

Riseveldt shook his head in disbelief. 'God bless America!'

Chapter 20

It was a Monday afternoon and pouring with rain as Raymond worked quietly away in the old South Side morgue. Having meticulously noted down the corpse's details in a little black notebook he kept, the chef began selecting cuts. One of Raymond's greatest skills was his use of offal in creating unusual dishes and it was this ability which had enabled him to make the very most from a single type of meat. Lately he'd found he enjoyed working at the old morgue: it provided a refuge from his otherwise chaotic life. Once he'd got beyond what he was actually doing to the remains of a human body it became abstract, professionalism kicking in. How good was the cut? How tender? How would it cook? Now, as he packed up the sectioned portions, sealing them and neatly stacking them for dispatch, they looked anonymous, sterile even. He con-templated the purity of his work when compared with that of an abattoir; people really were going to eat – well, defunct but beautifully-presented – people. Maybe Riseveldt was right: there was some kind of useful symme-try in what they were doing. Perhaps if someone died naturally there might be an argument, albeit a highly emotive one, for their trade, but killing people to feed other people...forget the money, forget the morals; that was tricky. How had he gotten into this? What could he do? He'd been to the police and here they were intending to dine in his restaurant that following lunchtime. And with the mayor – an individual who represented the people of New York City; the place he lived in and somewhere he loved.

His mobile vibrated.

'You okay, Ray?' Tabitha sounded concerned.

'Yeah. Yeah, I'm cool.'

'Comin' in soon? Meat supply's runnin' low. I know how you like to oversee that.'

Placing wrapped sections of gluteus maximus in a plain box, Raymond actually smiled. 'I'm on it, Tab. Say, we've got a booking for three tomorrow – lunch. Make sure Carmen has table seventeen available.'

'Window corner seat?'

'Very same.'

'Special clients, huh?'

Raymond grunted. 'See you tomorrow.'

'Ray...' Tabitha paused. 'Glad you're better.'

'Thanks, Tab.'

'*Demain, alors.*'

'*Assurément.*'

As Raymond was heading down to Incarnate with the following week's meat supply in the back of his ancient T-Bird (in spite of his increased wealth, the chef's lifestyle had changed little), Arnold Riseveldt sat in his nondescript van looking out on an area cleared for construction, just two blocks from the restaurant. Raymond had described where he was attacked and the mortician had little difficulty finding the location, surrounded as it was by occupied buildings. The front of the site was largely boarded up and, climbing out of the van, Arnold had to peer between anchored timber sheets to view the derelict yard, pitted with rubble and detritus. Although signs proclaimed the place security-monitored, Arnold could see several people sitting around inside, apparently unconcerned. Studying the scene for a minute or two, he seemed to make up his mind about something then turning on his heel, walked back to his vehicle and drove off.

Back at the funeral parlour, chaos reigned. There were bodies everywhere, stacked up in passageways, two to a gurney, the trolleys themselves several deep, making it difficult to walk past. As Arnold arrived, another batch of corpses came in, delivered by black windowless vans.

'Thank heavens you're here, Mr Riseveldt. Things have gone completely crazy.' For once the normally controlled Julie Dominic looked frayed. 'New Jersey Police have been on the phone. They're calling for a state of emergency. They reckon we're under some kind of terrorist attack.' Julie had little time for her boss, trying as she was to organise the latest intake.

Arnold said nothing. Something was going seriously awry with Arnold's business model. Of course not all the clientele would come to RIP – how could they? – but he was paying his hired man and some of Grimaldi's work was providing business for rival morticians, and that didn't suit his intentions at all. As if in a trance, he picked his way into the ER block, struggling against a tide of gurneys overflowing with the deceased like some surreal assault course. Finally he reached his office, but what little peace he could gather for himself was interrupted by the phone. Captain Manifest. Line one. Using a speaker phone, his secretary was brisk. Picking up the receiver, Arnold slumped into his chair.

'Doc – long time no hear. To what do I owe the pleasure?'

'Wanted to have a chat with you. You're gettin' a lot of extra business right now.' Doctrinal Manifest's comment fell somewhere between question and statement.

'We're busy enough.' Riseveldt was non-committal.

'Lot of homicide cases. Have your people noticed any particular pattern? Type of killing, mebbe?'

'Don't recall anything bein' said. I've been off-site, but I'll have it checked out.'

'Yer other interests...good for you; heard yer had a slice of that restaurant place. Darndest thing! Department's had a lotta hassle with the mayor recently – this and that; cuts, efficiency, results. Real up-the-butt stuff. But he's banged on about Incarnate since it opened – "Gotta dine there", "Must get a table" – so the chef walkin' in like he did, Giantelli collared him and presto.'

'That's connections for you – what it's all about.' Riseveldt paused. 'What did he come to see you for, anyway?'

'Yer chef? Some crackpot shit 'bout the kind of food he was servin'. You know what these artistic types are like. Crazy bozos – off their heads half the time. Had this brain with him, and what with the macaque...monkey brains just happens to be the Chief's favourite. Anyway, we're sailin' in the sun this end – got a table tomorrow and the mayor singin' from the trees.'

'Enjoy.'

'Oh, we will. And let me know about these homicides, huh? The Jersey boys are all up a-roarin' we're under some kinda terrorist attack or mobster hit spree, but they're always with the hysteria. So long, Arnie.'

The line clicked off. Riseveldt found himself sweating profusely. Getting up, he walked over to his window, and looked out at his morticianal empire. Another black van was turning into the rear car park as two hearses were leaving. Riseveldt sighed. Exhausted, his shoulders slumped and he felt old, terribly old. The phone rang again. 'Yeah?'

'Mr Babchuk for you.'

Arnold stared blankly at the phone's flashing light. Could he be bothered to take the call? He depressed the button.

'Got it sorted?'

'Got what sorted?'

'I ain't workin' if you ain't got it sorted.'

'By which you mean removal of your hobo witness, the current cause of your excessive paranoia.' Arnold smoothed his hair. 'How did I ever get into this?'

'Your idea—'

'Don't start that. Don't even start that!' Putting the phone on speaker, he reached for a cigar box and took out a large Havana. 'Yeah, I'm gettin' it fixed.' He clipped the end of the Cuban.

'When?'

'Tonight.'

'How will I know?'

'I might tell you, I might not. Anyway, you can serve the bastard up, for all I care! Need any more proof than that?'

The phone went silent. Arnold lit up. 'And if you ain't back in that kitchen usin' that cookie IQ fryin', brazin' and stuffin' tomorrow mornin' I'm comin' for yer. Even thinkin' about runnin' will severely displease me. You'll be at the restaurant on time and applyin' that culinary genius of yours on our very special guests. So long, Chef.'

Clicking off the phone, his cadence had a finality to it. Arnold Riseveldt took a deep draw on his cigar. It was going to be a long night.

Chapter 21

For New York City, the darkness seemed very black. Night had fallen, and Manhattan's twinkling lights shone across the city as usual, but somehow that evening their brilliance didn't permeate Lower West Side, especially the east end of Greenwich Street. Certainly they weren't casting any glow when, in the small hours of the morning, Arnold Riseveldt's van turned into the lane behind the restaurant. Parking in his car space by the darkened kitchen, his burly figure emerged from the cab, wrapped up, hooded and carrying a bag. He leaned back inside to place some items in the glove box then flicked the lock fob and moved off along the lane into the street, heading for the building site. There was movement in the shadows as he neared the place, and suddenly, without warning, he was jumped by two vagrants, who began punching and kicking him. Pumped up as he was, Arnold whipped out a knife, slashing to and fro with surprising dexterity. One man ran off, bloodied; the other's head remained trapped under Arnold's boot.

'By way of introduction' – Arnold's breathing was heavy – 'you and your friend wouldn't happen to be hangin' out just along the road here, now would you?'

'Dunno what you mean?'

'Like the clearance site a block down.'

'Not hangin' out anywhere, man.'

'Let's just you and me go an' see.' Easing his heavy boot, Arnold let the dishevelled itinerant up. The man got to his feet, gasping. 'One of these'll help.' The mortician held out a beer can. It was instantly grabbed by his assailant, who ripped the tag and poured the contents down his throat as fast as gravity would allow.

'Yer slash a knife then push a beer.' The hobo burped. Arnold held out another can which was taken, this time more slowly. 'It don't add up.'

'I'll decide that. C'mon.' He led off down the street. After knocking back most of the second can, the hobo followed. Arriving at the building site, the vagrant slid his hand through a jagged gap in the boarding and lifting what sounded like a latch, freed the barricade with no more difficulty than unlocking a front door. Entering, Riseveldt said nothing. The man closed the barrier and swayed past him, finishing off the remains of the second can. The site was L-shaped, the far end much wider and giving a hidden dimension to the location. Picking his way through bits of old brick and broken concrete, Riseveldt spied a fire and a brazier unseen from the road. Several men squatted or lay around it. Pulling a beer out for himself, he stood watching the scene as his recent attacker tossed away his empty can and stumbled into the rough encampment.

'What yer want, man?' The voice from the shadows was gravelled and deep. Unfazed, Arnold had another swig of beer.

'I'm lookin' for someone.'

'You don't say.'

Riseveldt continued not to look in the direction of the voice, gazing into the fire.

'Any particular reason?' The animosity was palpable.

Discarding his finished can, Riseveldt brought out a

six-pack and ripped off a new one, which he put to his mouth, pulling the tag with his teeth. 'Want one?' Without waiting for an answer, he tossed the remaining pack of five in the direction of the voice. It was obviously caught as it didn't clatter to the ground. There was the sound of hissing as a can opened.

'So, I'm drinkin' yer beer and you're lookin' for some-one. This drinkin' would be takin' the form of a bribe, then.' The sounds of beer being drunk and a belch followed. 'How many more packs yer got in that satchel?'

'Half a dozen.' Arnold had another swig of his own then continued.

'Yer know, I've lived in this town a long time. I seen punks make mayor, scum awarded contracts. It's greed that rules. Yer give people somethin', they always want more. The good things are written on a hand.'

'That's a truth.'

'They say Calcutta's nice this time a year, Mother.' A second voice emitted from the shadows.

'Any of you hang out near a restaurant named *Le Chat Noir*, over on Park and Seventy-Four, 'bout six months ago?' Riseveldt was still looking at the fire as a dishevelled drifter appeared, startlingly close to his face.

'*Le Chat Noir*? One of my favourites. Often dine there. Do we shit!'

Riseveldt identified the man as Second Voice. The vagrant moved away stumbling as he swigged his liquor.

'Not bad, this stuff. Info must be important.' It was First Voice again.

'Don't put too much store by it.'

'Hey, Bailey, Hikey 'n' Leon were over that way a while back, weren't they?' Second Voice was calling to the far side of the brazier.

'What?'

'I said Hikey and Leon, over Park and Seventy-some-thin'. Fancy restaurant that ways. Reckoned it was good pickins.'

'Mebbe.'

'See what I mean? Some kindness in the world.' Arnold spoke reflectively. A knife blade appeared at his throat.

'I'll put whatever store I want how I want where I want. Understand?' First Voice was a big man, swarthy and powerful. Although he didn't flinch, Arnold's eyes flitted and blinked quickly.

'Only thing you'll get outta those guys is a knife in the back. They're fuckin' nuts.' This from near the brazier.

'And greedy.' Someone else spoke; it seemed all the vagrants wanted in on the act.

'Man, they'll eat yer alive.'

'The beers. We'll be sharin' 'em out.'

Arnold released his grip on the bag.

'Very democratic. I love this town.'

'Joker. If yer ain't got nothin', any place is shit.'

Having a final swig of his beer, Arnold addressed himself to the camp.

'So none of you knows where these guys are?' There was a stirring by the brazier. The mortician moved deeper into the site. 'Any of you know this Leon, or Hikey?'

'I might. Then again I might not.' This voice from a body lying on a builder's pallet.

 Arnold addressed another bum. 'What about you?'

'Leon ain't around.'

'Know where he is?'

'Out gettin' laid. How the hell should I know?'

'What about the other fella – Hikey?'

Suddenly, Pallet Man was up and had Arnold by the throat.

'You ask too many goddam questions!'

'Okay, okay! Only wondered if they knew a friend of mine – a guy who gave them food from the kitchen. That's all.'

The hobo released his grip slightly. Moving slowly, Arnold put his hand in his pocket and pulled out a quarter of whisky. Taking a swig, he proffered it to Pallet Man who drank off most of the contents and kept the bottle.

'That's what this is all about, then. We was witness to a murder – or any rate, homicide. One fun night! This fuckin' monkey screamin' and hollerin' – it fair gave yer a thirst watchin' it. Any of that left, Leon? As dumb a question as ever I asked.'

So, Pallet Man was Leon and he was talking to Hikey Homaster. Not quite as unkempt as the others, Homaster was of medium build and reasonably spoken. But before Arnold could take advantage of this new information he was suddenly on his back, the powerful hands of First Voice pinning him down. Homaster frisked the mortician.

'I'm clean, man. I'm clean!'

Homaster removed a switchblade from the inside of Arnold's boot. 'You are now.' Homaster studied the lethal-looking knife before pocketing it. 'Serious piece. Yuh – that was some night. The guy askin' ter get wiped and yer pal tryin' to split. But he was freaked, real freaked. Been drinkin'. Bad boy!'

A sign from Homaster to First Voice, whose name was Angel, indicated he could release the mortician from his vice-like grip. Arnold sat up, dusting himself off.

'You saw him again recently – playin' with a shooter as yer were.'

'Thought I recognised the cunt. Shouldn't have got in the way.'

'And he gave yer food, provided for yer.' Arnold scrambled up.

'Just scrapin's from the table, man. Weren't no haute cuisine.' This from Leon.

'Okay, well, seein' as I'm out of liquor, guess I'll be on my way.' Arnold gently eased himself away from the group.

'Not so fast.' Homaster was nonchalant and menacing. 'A troublin' question...' He swigged some of the donated beer. 'Why should you wanna come snoopin' around plyin' us with booze to find out who we are?' Another swig. 'Why would you wanna do that?' Finishing the beer, he kicked the can into the night sky. 'Why is it so important?'

'I'm in business with him, an' it's been troublin' his sensitive nature, you pluggin' him the other night.'

'Got his own place now, has he? Your money, I guess?' Homaster helped himself to another can. 'And your comin' here to find us has what implication?'

'Thought maybe we could do some kind of a deal.' Arnold had become sullen, morose even.

'Deal? What kind of a deal would that be?' Homaster was anything but casual now. 'Must be 'cause we was witnesses that night – the chef killin' that guy.' He walked away a little. 'Only deal you're gonna want is to remove us.' This was spoken more to himself. Homaster turned back to Riseveldt and began walking round him, gradually getting closer.

'Think you're the great philosopher, huh? Lovin' New York – seein' all the life yer have. But you're naïve, man. Fat cat like you givin' us booze; you really think we don't see you comin'? We'll drink your liquor, but you're disrespect-ful to us; you think we're just stoopid illiterates. That insults us – insults our intelligence. And when things insult us, we get dangerous.'

'Who's the philosopher now?'

Homaster continued, ignoring Arnold's comment. 'Superior, arrogant scumbags; scumbags who treat us with contempt; scumbags who consider that because we're society's dross makes us idiots, thick people, un-educated people; that kinda attitude is very uninformed. It places those scumbags in an especially vulnerable position.'

New York City is never silent and distant car horns continued to pierce the night air, but if a pin had dropped at that moment...

'What have you got to say, pal? I'm waitin'.'

'I say...fuck you!' With surprising speed Arnold pivoted round and began running towards the street, but in his blind rush to escape the mortician ran straight into a metal spike held by a tramp who had stepped into his path. Impaled, Arnold Riseveldt slowly sank to his knees.

'Used to be quicker.'

'Not any more, old man.'

Homaster came up and stood over the dying man. 'You shouldn't have come messin' with the likes of us. You should've known it was goin' to lead to somethin' dumb. You gotta leave stuff like that to people who know how ter deal with it.'

Moving slightly to ease his pain, Arnold leant against the remains of a concrete block. 'Deal with it – yeah...' Blood began to ooze from the side of his mouth. 'Would yer mind movin' to one side a little? I don't wanna die lookin' at yer ugly visage.'

The mortician stared at a flashing neon sign advertising

Restaurant Incarnate, but on a Monday night it was closed. As was his life.

'The moment. It's not so good on the receivin' end, Jack.' Riseveldt's body flopped forward, his earthly mortician existence ended.

'What was that all about?'

'Don't rightly know but it's somethin' very strange and somethin' I don't like.' Homaster's voice registered concern.

'Better split, man. One dead cat equals many pigs.'

'You're kiddin'. In this town? Yer need mass fuckin' genocide to get a precinct round here activated. Only enquiries made about this piece of shit'll be made by us.' Homaster stared across at the flashing Incarnate sign.

'Are you outta your brain, man? You go askin' 'bout this jerk, you're on yer own.'

Angel finished the last of the beers and flattened the can in his fingers. Some of the vagrants were already moving off site, dispersing into the night. Leon came by and stared at the dead mortician on the ground.

'Ain't worth shit, Hikey. C'mon man. Get outta here.'

'I don't like it; somethin' weird's goin' down.'

Angel and another hobo moved off. 'Goin' down is right. This is New York City. Find me somethin' straight in New York fuckin' City.'

Having drained the last of the liquor, Leon dropped the empty quart bottle on Arnold's face. 'My hard.'

Second Voice laughed in the darkness. 'Way I heard it, yours ain't, Leon – straight, that is.'

Leon smacked his fellow hobo in the back. Second Voice wailed. 'Don't do that. Crazy bastard!'

The night swallowed them up.

Chapter 22

Even at lunchtime the restaurant was frenetically busy. Carmen and Gaultier were now a well-oiled double act managing front of house; Carmen, as general manager, ran the day-to-day enterprise; Feydor Gaultier added a touch of class as maitre d'. The combination of Carmen's exotic appearance and hands-on approach, Gaultier's elegance, the singular decor, the fabulous food and the renowned eccentricity of the chef had taken Restaurant Incarnate to New Yorkers' hearts. Internationally-known celebrities came by: Hill 'n' Bill were seen; Woody A played sax on occasional Friday evenings; P.J. O'Rourke had dined several times, along with Tom Wolfe and many other theatrical A-listers and movie people.

Restaurant Incarnate had never been a hotter venue, which rendered the window seats for Captain Doctrinal Manifest and Chief Fionn Giantelli especially privileged. Currently Chief of Queens District, Giantelli was one of the top policemen in New York. He was a giant bear of a man – powerful and charismatic. Now, as the chief sat in the best seat the house had to offer, surveying the 'in' people – movers and shakers who made the city of which he was so proud the place it was – he raised a glass of rare *Antica Distilleria Russo*, a wine created from grapes near Amalfi in the Campania region. He and the captain were doing themselves *very* proud, and Giantelli felt he had every reason to celebrate. Here they were in the ultimate restaurant Manhattan had to offer and they hadn't had to bring the mayor with them.

'To good health, family and the apprehension of all criminals.'

Raising his own glass, Manifest sipped the beautiful wine. 'Such a pity the mayor wasn't able to make it.' He managed to withhold any note of sarcasm.

'These politicos! I thought he was going to go epileptic when the governor insisted they have lunch today. Gather dining at the mansion ain't quite up to this cuisine.'

Waiters appeared, removing covers and revealing *cervelles sautées* for the chief and c*oeur de boeuf aux tripes* for the captain. The two plates were dressed magnificently. The waiters melted away and Gaultier refilled their glasses.

'*Bon appétit.*'

'I'm in heaven.' The chief chomped on his brains. 'Incarnate's sure come to life, ain't it?' he sniggered.

Manifest could hardly speak, he was in such raptures.

'If that's what it is I'm here to stay.'

That day, Raymond appeared upstairs earlier than he normally did, but to the usual acclaim. Lately this bordered on adoration, such was the esteem and cult status he had achieved within New York society. Tutti skipped about – they had their party-piece finely honed, the little monkey hopping off the chef's shoulder and, smoking not being allowed, waving his unlit cigar at the clientele. A nod to this table, a wave to that; diners were spoken to occasionally, which Raymond genuinely enjoyed. The secret of his reputation amongst the chefs of Manhattan was that, whilst conceited, even arrogant, about his abilities where culinary matters were concerned, his natural reserve in public increased as his notoriety spread to fame. Because of this outward diffidence, his appeal was somehow magnified. The clientele flocked to his feet feeling privileged to eat at a table for which he had created food.

Walking to the front of the restaurant, Raymond came over to Captain Manifest and Chief Giantelli.

'No mayor?'

'We have mercies to thank.' Obviously replete, the chief smiled. 'Called away for a meeting with the governor.' Giantelli raised the remains of his wine. 'But thank you, Mr Babchuk, for getting us this table. The mayor was in quite a state; I've rarely seen a man so torn. Desperate for one thing, bein' forced by another. It was a sight to behold.'

'Our meal – it was the greatest food I've ever tasted.' Manifest looked ecstatic. 'Which will, no doubt, blow our budget for the rest of the year.'

Giantelli smiled. 'Worth it, though. Captain Manifest hadn't eaten heart before and my *cervelles* were to die for. Both of us had the *tripes à la mode de Caen* for main – simply the best I ever ate. It was a meal neither of us will ever forget.'

Listening to Giantelli reciting their menu, it occurred to Raymond the two policemen had dined entirely from offal – and human at that. He gave a slight bow. 'Yer meal is on the house.'

'Hey, yer can't do that! We don't want no charity. Besides, speakin' with your partner recently, he'll be complainin' on his return.' Manifest appeared slightly put out.

Raymond looked round the restaurant. 'He ain't got nothin' to complain about.'

'No, guess not.'

Giantelli looked at Raymond and got to his feet.

'Anyways, let's just say one good turn... If ever you need any assistance with anything you know where to call. It was a fantastic meal, Mr Babchuk. I salute you as New York's finest chef, and when we're back next time we'll put down the plastic.'

Outside on the street, Giantelli and Manifest stood for a moment on the pavement watching other diners.

'How the other half live.' Manifest belched contentedly.

Their unmarked police vehicle glided up. The driver, a plain-clothes cop, got out and opened the door. Giantelli turned to Manifest: 'Yer shouldn't complain.'

'Oh I ain't, I ain't!'

The two men climbed in and the car moved off. As they motored down Greenwich Street, approaching the derelict site, Giantelli and Manifest noticed an ambulance, rear doors being shut and it moving off, the blue top light slowly revolving. A police car also drove away, leaving a second vehicle and several officers busy securing the barrier with extra chains.

'Somethin' goin' down.' Manifest turned to look out the rear window.

'Whatever it is, it's over. Anyway, ain't our precinct.'

'Whadya reckon with these homicides?'

'Dah! Time will tell. Just a spate, most likely.'

'The Jersey boys are all wound up.'

'The Jersey boys are always wound up.'

Manifest laughed. 'You'll be right at that. What's with the free meal, d'yer reckon?'

'The amount that boy's makin', he can afford it.'

'Thought mebbe you were gonna say he felt sorry for us poor police officers! Even so, that was big bucks.'

'Then he's one smart kid. Today was petty cash in police protection terms.'

'Reckon he needs that?'

'Manifest, everyone needs that. How else do you think this town operates?'

'Would that be the idealistic or the cynical view?'

Giantelli laughed then became more reflective as the car left Jane Street and swung out onto the Hudson Greenway. Driving alongside the water, the big river was as busy as ever and beautiful as always. 'The realistic one. God, that was one incredible meal!'

Returning to his kitchen, Raymond found his staff hard at work clearing and cleaning. The stainless steel oven and hob surfaces were already spotless, and pans and saucepans being rehung on their hooks. The whole scene was one of quiet professionalism, winding down in the break before the evening busyness. Walking over to the rear of the kitchen Raymond looked out at Arnold's van, still parked where the mortician had left it in the small hours of the morning. Taking out his mobile, the chef dialled a pre-programmed number.

Arnold's phone vibrated unheard in the glove compartment of the vehicle Raymond was looking at, having been deliberately left there along with credit cards and any other form of identification before Arnold set off on what was to be his final journey. The mortician had prepared carefully.

Snapping off his phone, Raymond turned back and went over to Tabitha who was checking some vegetables in preparation for the night ahead.

'You seen the RIP man this mornin'?' The way Raymond spoke, RIP came out as 'rip'.

'Mr Mortician himself? No, ain't seen him. His van's out back. P'raps he's got some local clients to look after?' Tabitha was indifferent. She'd never figured why Raymond had set up in business with someone she thought very strange except she knew Riseveldt had put money into the venture. Did the mortician have some sort of hold over her – she was going to say 'boss', then 'friend', but more recently she'd found her emotions somewhat confused. What did she now feel about Ray? He *was* her friend and as such had done more than anyone ever had for her, helping her career, indeed advancing it to a point she'd never dreamt of. Heck, half a year ago she'd been an assistant pastry chef, not particularly outstanding, with no great hopes for the future, and now here she was, a sous-chef in Manhattan's hottest restaurant.

But ever since that night – the night she'd stayed over at his late aunt's place – *his* place now – she'd thought differently about him. Even at this moment she couldn't quite organise her thoughts coherently. But then, she'd never let her emotions show; in their work, professionalism was everything. Watching him toying nervously with his cell phone, her pulse wasn't quite steady and her breathing a little faster than normal. Raymond appeared to reach a decision and speed-dialled another number. A voice message began with a jingle set to the tune of 'Bye Bye Blackbird':

> Pack up all my cares and woe,
> Here I go, singin' low,
> Bye Bye Byee.
> Goin' where some folks wait for me,
> Sugar's sweet, so are we,
> Bye Bye Byee.
> No one here can love or give me gala
> Like they can down at the RI Parlour…

Raymond stopped the indescribable jingle and selected a

new number. After several rings, Julie Dominic's voice answered.

'Is he there?'

'Is who there?'

'RIP Man – your boss. Who else?' Raymond could be quite rude when he put his mind to it. 'His van's outside my restaurant – been here all night. I'm checkin' up on him.'

'He's not here and when I see him I'll advise refusing any further calls from you.'

The phone call was terminated.

Julie couldn't know that, as they'd been speaking, her erstwhile boss and Raymond's partner was on his way to his own mortuary, having been diverted from Peachy Parlours, who were unable to accommodate him. It would be a fitting conclusion.

Walking to the back of the kitchen again, Raymond stared at Arnold's van before suddenly turning to his staff. 'Everyone's having the night off.'

For several seconds this announcement had no reaction. Aldo and Luke, whom Raymond had recently recruited, partly for old times' sake (neither were brilliant chefs but they worked hard) and partly because they'd begged for employment, were the first to cotton on.

'Again, Chef?'

Raymond banged a pan on a counter. 'We're takin' a night off! We're closed this evening!'

'But, er–'

'What about our bookings?'

Feydor Gaultier had already left the premises, but Carmen appeared from her kitchen office. 'What's that, Mr Raymond?' Carmen was old-fashionedly courteous.

'We're takin' the night off. Well, I ain't workin' and as no one is cookin' food I ain't prepared, we're shut. Closed. Not open.'

'But...but you can't do that!'

'Who says?'

Carmen looked at Raymond. 'Can we speak about this, please?' She turned on her heel and walked back towards her office. For a moment or two it didn't look as though Raymond would follow.

'Ain't gonna make no difference.'

As befitted Restaurant Incarnate's general manager, Carmen's office was smartly fitted out, with returned desk, and state of the art equipment. If Raymond's kitchen was immaculate, so was Carmen's domain.

'You're thinkin' you'd better call The Man. Go ahead. He hired you, Carmen. Yer do a great job but I still ain't workin' tonight. In fact, I ain't workin' again till I see my goddam partner!'

'Mr Raymond, Ray, we've got bookings for weeks ahead. We can't just stop – not now.'

'You wanna see?' Raymond turned away from the door.

'Mr... Raymond, there's people's jobs involved here. People gotta work.' Raymond stared at her dispassionately. 'Look, if I get Mr Riseveldt here tomorrow morning, will you promise we can reopen?'

'I ain't makin' no promise like that.'

'Will yer come in at least?'

With a slight jerk of his head suggesting the affirmative, Raymond walked away. Carmen sighed. What the hell was that all about? She could handle things for one night, but she'd have to get hold of Riseveldt pretty soon.

A strange relationship the chef had with his business partner. What could have sparked such behaviour? It was a pity they were both so temperamental. The chef she understood; the breed were prima donnas: the pressure, the creativity, the striving for perfection. But when the mortician had contacted her offering employment, he'd seemed a very different type: a hustling, ambitious businessman. Whilst egotistical, she hadn't seen him prone to tantrums or imbalance. Whatever he was, he'd have to get things sorted and fast. A restaurant closed for a night was never good for business, but one with such prestige, one of such renown... Heck, Restaurant Incarnate was *the* hottest ticket in town. Sitting at her desk, Carmen pressed a number on her office phone.

Although of a different temperament to her manager, Tabitha's reaction was not dissimilar. What was it all about, this sudden drastic behaviour by Raymond? Cleaning completed, the kitchen rapidly emptied, Tabitha being the last to leave. Outside in the parking area Arnold's van sat unmoved. Raymond slouched in his ancient T-Bird, Tutti Frutti beside him. The afternoon was warm and with the damaged soft top lowered, part of its tattered still unrepaired canvas hung limply across a wing.

'You okay – though I guess that's a dumb question?' Raymond looked up. 'Won't say I ain't happy with a night off, but hey, don't want to see yer business go down, Ray.' Tabitha turned to leave.

'You doin' anythin', Tab?'

'Guess not, given I hadn't planned on bein' free right now.' She smiled.

'Wanna come back to the house, chill out a bit?'

'Ha! There's an offer. Well, I ain't got nothin' else on.' She opened the car door and Tutti scampered into Raymond's lap. Starting the engine, Raymond stared at Arnold's van.

'Somethin's wrong. I know it.'

'Why d'you think so? Just 'cause he ain't been in touch the last twelve hours?'

'The mother's always at me. He's never off my case.'

'Well, what are you plannin' on doin', honey?' The term of endearment seemed natural.

'C'mon, let's get outta here.'

Engaging reverse, Raymond backed into the lane and they drove off, Tutti chattering happily.

Chapter 23

It was the end of a long day and Jack Grimaldi was heading for home, spats still immaculate, violin case in hand. Entering a subway station, he boarded a train and sat down in a near-empty compartment. Taking a small black notebook and pencil, he was poring over figures when two young guys boarded, baseball caps reversed, trousers resting on the lower portions of their asses and earphones pumping out rap music so loud it could be heard throughout the carriage. Slouching in seats opposite, they eyed the elderly killer, who looked up briefly at the disturbance then resumed his work.

'Hey, Capone! You lost? Too late at night for old folks like you to be out.' The boy's voice was loud enough to be heard above the din of the music. 'Hey! Old man! We're talkin' to yer.'

Grimaldi was leaning forward slightly, his notebook on his knee. He now sat back, revealing a very large pistol nestling in his lap. The second guy whistled.

'Hey...! Replicas're quite somethin' these days. Lemme have a look at that.' Flicking out his earphones, he leant forward.

'Have I insulted you boys? Have I been rude to yer?'

'Man, just want to look at yer gun.'

'Only way you'll see this baby is down the end of the barrel.'

The first guy burst out laughing. 'Dialogue to match the clothes, huh? You really are from another age, man.'

'When people were better mannered – even killers.'

The second youth seemed genuinely interested. 'Know them old guys, did yer – Al and the boys?'

'Matter o' fact, I did.'

'Say, if yer carryin' a piece that size, what's in the case? Thompson repro?' The first boy cackled at his own wit. The subway train pulled into a station.

'Violins are normally transported this way.'

'Get real, man.'

The train doors opened. It being late at night and quiet, Grimaldi calmly lifted his pistol and fired at a fluorescent platform light, blowing it to bits.

'Perhaps it's you kids who should do that.' He stepped onto the platform and the train doors closed behind him. The two youths turned to each other.

'Shiiiit!!'

Lying back on his aunt's bed, Raymond was in heaven. It was perhaps fitting in his strange life that his first proper sexual encounter should have taken place amidst his aunt's black silk sheets and the lurid pink decor of her bedroom. Other than the gropings of his drunken and lascivious relative, Raymond had experienced little sexual activity during his twenty-eight years, but this evening had changed all that. Returning to the house in Palmetto Street, now *his* house, that afternoon, he and Tabitha had been talking in his kitchen when she suddenly grabbed him and began kissing him passionately (admittedly he had been talking about a new recipe for syllabub), after which things got a bit blurred. He did recall Tutti clapping as they passed him going downstairs and Tabitha declaring they had to 'do it' in his aunt's lair.

'She must have been such a sex-crazed old bat – quite turns me on!'

Raymond didn't argue and the resulting experience revealed much more about Tabitha than his wildest dreams could have ever imagined. It became apparent that, whilst Raymond was little more than a virgin, Tabitha had wider sexual knowledge. Not only did she want to try on some of the unusual clothing in Aunt Renais' extensive collection, but she also seemed interested in experiencing the accoutrements. No wonder Raymond was in a daze.

Stepping out of the shower, her red hair tousled and pale body pink from arousal, Tabitha went to sit on the bed and towel her hair.

'You're beautiful.'

She laughed. 'We both know that ain't the case. Hips too chunky and these...' She flipped her pendulous breasts.

'Are amazing!'

'Ha! How d'you feel?'

'Amazing!'

She came over to him and bending over, stroked his hair. 'You were, too.'

Raymond looked up at her. 'I'm...kinda surprised.'

'So am I.'

They both laughed.

'Want to do it again?' He kissed her thigh.

'Raymond, I've just had a shower. Anyway, I thought you were tired. If you go on like this you won't make it in tomorrow.'

'I don't wanna go in tomorrow.'

'Ray, yer can't do that. Right now you're New York's most celebrated chef. Your restaurant's the most successful in Manhattan. Yer can't just walk away from it.'

Raymond looked remote.

'You got a business. People rely on yer. Me, for example.' She dropped down beside him. It was Raymond's turn to stroke and he caressed her. 'Why didn't yer want to work tonight?'

Raymond sighed.

'What's happened, baby?'

'I can't tell yer. I can't tell yer!' He abruptly sat up, burying his head in his hands.

'It's okay, it's okay. You've just been overdoing it. Sssh!'

'I can't tell yer, Tab, but I gotta get outta there. I gotta get away.'

'You need a break.' She rocked him in her arms. 'Tell yer what. Let's get things real established – real solid. Have someone trained up so yer *can* get away.'

'That'd be you.'

'I don't want it. I'm already ahead of my wildest dreams – sous-chef in the best restaurant in town. I'm not you; I could never be a maestro. Anyway, now I'd... Well, maybe *we* could get away sometime?' All at once she was strangely shy, bashful even.

'Aww, Tab.' Raymond buried his head further into her body.

'Talkin' of maestros...maybe you could train up our old friend?'

'Ha! That jerk! He can't even boil an egg. "Leetle piece of this, leetle piece of that..."'

They laughed.

'You heard he got fired from The Cat?'

'What?'

'Yeah, Frank and Alain got rid of him. He disappeared with that Louis guy who tried to stitch you up.'

'Know where they went?'

'Dunno. Disappeared off the radar.'

'Good riddance.'

'Yeah.' Raymond looked suddenly wistful. Tabitha had a change of heart. 'Hey, baby, bein' as my hair's all mussed already...'

Raymond still seemed preoccupied. His mood had diminished his ardour.

'Come on, baby...' Tabitha knew she could bring him back to life.

Chapter 24

Dawn the following morning found Jack Grimaldi at his old friend Ralph's café. The first customer in, Ralph was used to Jack's ways, regarding him as being one of his more eccentric clients. Not *the* most eccentric: that honour was reserved for a lion-taming friend the proprietor had known years previously, who had once tried to enter the premises with his charge. Leo had behaved himself quite well, till a young lady assistant Ralph had been employing tripped over some stacked chairs on the sidewalk, spilling several double espressos and splashing the poor animal. The scalding caffeine sent the lion berserk. Four people were mauled, one nearly dying, but both trainer and animal had escaped the law when the circus moved out of town. Although pursued by New York's finest, no trace was ever found of either man or beast. Some said they'd gone to another outfit, some said they'd never been in New York City. Some said Leo just didn't like coffee – which right now was smelling oh so sweet.

'Good mornin' to you, Jack. Yer welcome here as ever – unless yer meetin' up with that so-called friend o' yours and his nuts sidekick, never to be admitted in my establishment again.'

'Why, no, Ralph – though I'm sorry Mr Riseveldt and your good self don't get on. He's a great employer, and I ain't got no complaints!'

'Still the hired gun, huh?' It was well known in the neighbourhood that Ralph didn't take Grimaldi's 'profession' seriously, considering him a harmless sham – a serious misjudgement of character on the café owner's part.

'Yeah. Busy day ahead. Enjoyin' myself, though. The work's given me a new lease o' life.'

'Pleased to hear it. Old timer like you needs to be kept busy. Playin' anywhere right now, virtuoso?'

'All over town.'

'Hey – I mean a venue.'

'Music?'

'I know – yer can't find a hall big enough.'

'Hmm. The Met, mebbe.'

'You'd fill it in half an hour.'

Some other early morning customers came in and Ralph's attentions were needed elsewhere. Grimaldi finished his coffee and, picking up his violin case, headed for the door.

'So long, Jack. Have a good day, and if you're toppin' anyone make sure yer aim's good.'

'Don't worry, Ralph – my sights're set just fine. So long, now.'

Ralph served some cappuccinos to his latest customers.

'Local assassin – or so he'd have us believe.'

'Ha! Certainly looks the part. The spats...you could eat your dinner off them.'

'Not in my restaurant!'

Stepping off a subway train into the Bronx morning sunshine, Jack Grimaldi strolled along several streets, each one seedier than the last. It felt good to be alive. Work was plentiful and the old killer had a spring in his step. He'd make Mr Riseveldt proud of him; he'd be the best assassin ever employed. In his youth the bad men of the city had mocked him. They'd said he was weak. They'd said he didn't have it in him – the killer instinct. Was he showing them now, the dumbfucks. But they were all long gone, dead and buried. He was the only one to survive and he was still working – working in the profession he'd always aspired to – and treated with respect, his skills recognised at last.

Stopping on a corner, Grimaldi eyed a particularly down-at-heel, twenties apartment block. Painted powder blue, much of the colour had faded and the paintwork was cracked. Crossing the street, he approached the building. The entry phone hung loosely from the wall in the shabby portico, listing names and numbers, 1 to 20. Jack hit 13. After a few seconds a woman's thin voice answered.

'Yes?'

'Mrs Patowski? I'm Jack Grimaldi of Toonful Music, the only music company to offer a while-you-wait retunin' service. We also fix instruments an' we're givin' an introductory rate in your area. Would you have anythin' that needs mendin', need a new reed in a clarinet, piano wants fixin' – that kinda thing?'

'Well, I have an old horn...'

'Beat it!' This was a man's voice.

'Er–'

'You heard me.' The entry phone went dead.

'Shit!' Grimaldi scanned the other numbers and names, and arbitrarily pressed number 7. There was no response.

'Huh. Come on.'

'Hullo?' Another woman's voice. It sounded a little deep; certainly a contralto.

'Oh, hi, er – Miss Huxtable?'

'This is Briony Huxtable speaking. Who is that?'

'Mrs Huxtable–'

'Right the first time; it's Miss.'

'Oh, er, sorry ma'am. Miss Huxtable, I'm Jack Grimaldi of Toonful Music – only company to offer a while-you-wait retunin' service. We fix instruments, replace violin strings, tune pianos – that kinda thing. We're offerin' an introductory rate–'

'A plus for originality, but you ain't comin' in.'

'Okay, ma'am, but yer passin' up the offer of a lifetime.'

'That a threat or a promise?'

Grimaldi reckoned he might be on to something. 'Well now, Miss Huxtable, I'd say a promise.'

'Let me see yer.'

'Ain't no security camera.'

'That why yer picked the joint?'

'Kinda suspicious, ain't yer?'

A strange laughing sound emanated from the entry phone speaker. 'Step back.'

Grimaldi did as he was bid, appearing from the covered porch onto the street. Looking up, he saw the slight movement of a net curtain and returned to the building.

'Look more like an old gangster than a musician.'

Grimaldi raised his violin case.

'I'll play yer a little tune.'

'You'd better come up.'

'Yes ma'am.'

An electric door release buzzed and Grimaldi entered. Standing in the lobby of the old apartment building waiting for the elevator, he took out his violin. The dilapidated lift finally arrived and Grimaldi got in. He then hit a button and began to play 'Air on a G String'. Arriving at the fourth floor, the doors opened to reveal him playing away, intense concentration on his face. Finally coming out of his reverie as the doors began to close, Grimaldi put his foot in the gap and walked out onto the landing to be greeted by the bizarre image of Briony Huxtable. Obviously a transsexual, Briony had a python wrapped round her neck and brandished a shotgun.

'Hmm! Nice snake.'

'Not what yer expected, huh?'

'Definitely not what I expected. Careful where yer point that thing.'

'You betcha, sweetie. We're over there, aren't we Victor?' Briony indicated a door at the far end of the landing, next to a fire escape. She stroked the python.

'Pleased to meet yer. Mind if I just put my instrument away?' Grimaldi put down his violin case.

Briony waved the shotgun. 'Whoa! No tricks!'

'There won't be any, lady.' Grimaldi fiddled about with his violin and bow.

'C'mon, c'mon!'

'Say, sure you ain't got no French horns need fixin'?'

'French horns? French horns? Don't give me no French horn shit!'

'Oboe? Tuba?'

'Shut the fuck up with the musical instruments!'

'Just askin'.'

'Your type makes me sick. Musical instruments! What kind of a guy are you, anyways?'

'The musical kind.'

'You really think I'm gonna go for that shit? I mean, do yer actually believe people'll let yer into their apartments dressed as you are with some musical instrument story? Man, you're insane – outta your mind.'

'Everything all right down there?'

A woman's voice called out from above.

'Oh, yes, Miss Millichamp, everything's fine. I'm just discussing musical instruments with this gentleman here.'

'Oh, my. Doesn't tune pianos, does he? Mine needs fixin' somethin' terrible.'

Grimaldi smiled at Briony as Belinda Millichamp appeared over the fire escape stairwell. In her late sixties, her grey hair was tied back in a bun; she had a strong face with open features.

'Sure do, ma'am.'

'That's wonderful. Wouldn't care to take a look when yer finished there, would you? It's so out of tune, I can't bear to play the darned thing.'

'Be glad to. Indeed, comin' right up. Think we're about all done here.' Grimaldi raised his fedora to Briony Huxtable. 'If you'll excuse me.'

As Grimaldi began to climb the back stairs, Victor adjusted himself, slewing Briony's wig. Yanking it off, she revealed a shaved head, the razor marks through it displaying exotic patterns.

'Men! They lead a girl on. I feel like pumpin' yer!'

Grimaldi stopped and turned to see Briony wildly waving the shotgun. 'Go right ahead.'

Briony burst into tears and clutching her snake, rushed off across the landing to her apartment, slamming the door. At the top of the stairs the killer was greeted by a smiling Miss Millichamp.

'You have the look of a man who could do with a drink.'

'Not when I'm working, ma'am.'

'Coffee, then.' Miss Millichamp led him into her apartment. Given the rest of the building's state of decay, her living room was tasteful and old-fashionedly stylish, her furniture classic if a little faded. A baby grand piano stood in the corner and, obviously impressed, Grimaldi went over to it. With a sweep of his hand he rolled off an arpeggio. Several notes were off-key. Looking under the lid, he found a tuning key and locking into middle C, began working on the instrument. Miss Millichamp came in carrying a tray – coffee for two, complete with percolator. Setting it down on an occasional table, she watched the strange-looking man from Toonful Music.

'It was my father's.'

'Wonderful instrument, ma'am.'

'He gave concerts. Quite good...when he was drunk. Used to play with a bottle of bourbon inside him. Said it put fire in his belly. Unfortunately it didn't impress the concert organisers, especially when he fell off the stage at Carnegie Hall.'

'He played Carnegie Hall?' Grimaldi was impressed.

'The last time he performed Brahms on New Year's Eve, complete with sing-along. That wouldn't have been so bad, had the vocal accompaniment been the same piece of music, but "Auld Lang Syne" doesn't go so good with the "Second Piano Concerto". Been in the music business long, Mr...?'

'Grimaldi, Jack Grimaldi. All my life, ma'am.'

'How d'you take your coffee, Mr Grimaldi?'

'A little cream, thank you.'

Miss Millichamp poured his out. 'You won't mind my saying, but you're not exactly how one would figure a piano tuner to look.'

Grimaldi concentrated on the instrument. Completing an adjustment, he sat back slightly. 'How might that be?'

'Guess you're aware of how you dress – and the violin case.'

Grimaldi laughed. Miss Millichamp took his coffee over to him at the piano, placing it on a side table.

'Didn't yer hear me playin' earlier?'

'I did indeed. It wasn't the fact that I doubted your violin's existence, Mr Grimaldi; it was more your overall appearance that I was referrin' to.' Picking up her own coffee, Miss Millichamp sat down. 'I'm curious to know what other interests you have, apart from lying your way into people's apartments under the guise of musical instrument fixer – useful work though that may be, particularly in my case.'

'I fix 'em pretty good, lady.' Grimaldi was cool, if slightly harsh.

'I'm sure you do, but it's not how you earn your living. I've heard some stories in my time, but yours is without doubt the most far-fetched.'

Miss Millichamp sipped her coffee. Grimaldi picked his up.

'You know, ma'am, my rating for entry to a building's around eighty-five percent. And I never force my way in neither.'

'Pleased to hear it.'

'I'm an assassin, ma'am – a hired killer.'

'I see. Well, at least that's more what you look like.' Miss Millichamp was also cool. 'Down on your luck, are you, coming into this neighbourhood?'

'Why, no way. You'll appreciate in the particular line o' work I'm enjoyin', any neighbourhood's just fine.'

'Sounds like a pretty arbitrary contract.' Miss Millichamp put down her coffee.

'Way it works, providin' I keep killin' people I get paid, ma'am.'

'But...anybody?' Miss Millichamp's tone was conversational, if incredulous.

'Sure thing – long as they taste good.'

'Taste?'

'That's right. I'm bumpin' people off for that new restaurant over in the village. Incarnate, they call it, and by all
accounts New Yorkers are eatin' each other faster than you
can put 'em on the plate!'

'You mean...this restaurant is serving human flesh to
people as food?'

'That's exactly what I mean, ma'am. An' its goin' great!
Like I say, they can't get enough; it's why they've brought
me in. One o' the partners is a mortician and he's runnin'
outta supplies.' Grimaldi finished his coffee. 'Great cuppa
coffee, ma'am. Now, as much as I'd like to continue tunin'
your piano, time's pressin' an' I'm afraid things are gettin'
to the point where we love to come down to the real
business, if yer follow my meanin'.'

'Yes, I can see how that would have to be gotten round
to eventually.' Miss Millichamp seemed almost detached, as
though she was thinking about something else.

'Yeah, it's another busy day ahead.' Grimaldi brought
his large pistol out from inside his jacket and checked the
chamber.

'How many you been doin' a day?'

'Fifteen or so. One day last week, bumper crop, round
twenny.'

'You killed twenty people in a day...and you've been
killing around eighty a week, they all being fed into this
restaurant, In... In...?'

'–carnate. Yes, ma'am. In fact, two weeks ago I made the
three figures – a cool hundred.' Grimaldi spoke with pride.

'Incredible. Powerful handguns, those Magnums.'

'Yer takin' it pretty sweet. Know about guns, do yer?'

'My father–'

'Don't tell me. He'd shoot the audience if they didn't

applaud!' Grimaldi laughed at his own wit.

'Taught me to shoot. Like me to show you his gun?'

Without waiting for his response, Miss Millichamp got up and walked across to an escritoire in the corner of the room. Turning a key, she slid back its rolled top, removing an even larger pistol than Grimaldi's. Housed in a case and wrapped in cloth, the gun was oiled and immaculate.

'Mine's a five hundred.'

'Hey, ma'am, ma'am – no tricks, huh?'

'Think I'd try and blow you away?'

Grimaldi laughed. 'That sure would be puttin' the boot on the other foot, now wouldn't it?'

'It sure would.' Miss Millichamp cocked her pistol; Grimaldi quickly raised his own.

'Don't go messin', lady. This is serious business.'

'Which just happens to involve taking my life – something you may be surprised to learn I hold dear.'

Grimaldi fired, but the round jammed in the chamber. He looked askance. 'Ma'am, I'm just tryin' to earn a livin'; it's tough out there.'

'Not nearly as tough as it is in here, fella. You need more M-Pro 7 – that's the best oil – or maybe you've just been working that thing too darned hard. Still, your lack of maintenance gives me the advantage. Bye now.'

Miss Millichamp squeezed the trigger, blowing Grimaldi halfway across the room. He slumped over.

'You're an...unusual lady. Sorry I didn't get the opportunity of playin' to yer proper-like.'

'That pleasure will have to wait till I join you in the next world.'

Grimaldi's eyes rolled up into his head.

'And it's my intention that won't be for quite some time.'

Leaving Grimaldi where he lay, Miss Millichamp

returned to her desk and replaced the gun in its case. A sheaf of papers slid out of a compartment and fell to the floor. She casually bent down and picked them up.

'Bills, bills...'

Across town, another batch of deceased was arriving at Riseveldt's Interment Parlour, whose employees appeared, of late, to be sleep-walking. The chaos and overload were so bad that corpses were being left on the delivery porch, gurneys slewed and some bodies still on the stretchers they'd been brought in, covered only by a sheet. The admitting staff were simply unable to cope with the influx. A long-time RIP employee, Ivan – not the brightest bulb in the box, but an impressively strong porter – was now labouring, under the watchful eye of an impatient Manny, to arrange the laden gurneys in some sort of ordered rows, from which they could be logged and worked on – though what level of beautification might be possible with some of these remains was anybody's guess. A man's bloodied arm fell over the side of a trolley, causing his body to roll off its stretcher onto the floor. Ivan aligned the cadaver he'd been moving and went to deal with the fallen corpse. Looking down, even the slow-witted porter was startled.

'Hey!' Ivan called across to Manny, who was checking a toe tag. The embalmer didn't respond. 'Hey!'

'What is it, yer Slavic oaf?'

'Take a look or don't take a look.' Leaving the body where it had fallen, Ivan moved on to others awaiting his attention.

Manny completed logging the details he'd been taking and walked over to the corpse Ivan had indicated. He looked down at it. 'Shit!' It was the first time Ivan had ever seen Manny actually react to anything. 'Shit!' He rolled the torso slightly. 'You'd better get Julie – now!'

Ivan stared across at Manny who was holding the back of their late boss's head, Arnold's face a grey-white mask of death.

'Crazy, huh?'

'Get Julie!' Ivan lumbered away. Manny took control of himself. 'What the hell happened to you?' He looked down at the terrible hole in Arnold's stomach, the mortician's blood-soaked shirt ripped by the spike that had killed him. 'Whatever that was, it did for you good and proper, Mr Arnold Riseveldt, that's for sure.'

Chapter 25

Belinda Millichamp stepped out of her apartment, locking the door behind her. She looked rather 1950s, but smart and elegant, in a three-quarter-length coat with a prim little hat on her blue-rinsed, French-pleated hair. Walking to the lift, she spied Briony Huxtable peering through the back stairwell railings, still brandishing her shotgun. Miss Millichamp pressed the elevator button.

'You all right there, Briony?'

'I...I heard a shot.'

'Guns do make a noise. Mind what you do with that thing you're waving around.'

'But you're okay? That man...'

'I'm fine, dear, just fine. In fact, I haven't felt so good in a long time. Thought I might just treat myself to a restaurant today.'

'That's nice. I haven't eaten out in so long.' Briony was wistful.

'Didn't say I was eating. Just paying what you might call a business visit.'

'You gettin' into business?'

The elevator arrived.

'Could just be at that. Mind Victor, now. Have fun, dear.' Miss Millichamp got into the lift and began to descend.

Briony sighed. During her conversation with Miss Millichamp, Victor had entwined himself around the stairwell railings and was binding Briony's leg to them. In an effort to free herself, the shotgun went off. Briony fainted. The python gently unravelled its body and slithered away.

Downstairs, Miss Millichamp exited the building and stepped onto the sidewalk. A yellow cab emerged from behind the apartment block and turned into the street. Bob Patowski leaned out.

'Mornin', Miss Millichamp. Can I give yer a ride?'

'Hi, Bob. No thanks. Momma okay?'

'Fine, thank yer, Miss M. I meant, er, no charge – off the clock.'

'That's kind of you, but the walk'll do me good.'

'Say, Miss Millichamp, anyone been botherin' you recently? Hawkers? Hustlers? Seen anyone pokin' around?'

'Why no; only Victor slithering about. I just heard a gun go off. I hope Briony hasn't hurt herself. She was waving that shotgun of hers all ways a moment ago.'

'Pimp weirdo!'

'Now, now, Bob. Briony's harmless enough. Just doesn't know whether she's coming or going, poor dear.'

'Some nut was yackin' to Momma about tunin' musical instruments. The stories these guys come out with!'

'Oh, him; he was no bother. I'm going to cross here, Bob. You have a good day, now.'

'Okay, Miss Millichamp, but you just take care. You're a very special lady.'

Miss Millichamp crossed the street as the cab pulled away, Patowski still muttering to himself.

'Pimp creep sicko.'

In spite of the chaos, telephonist Anne-Marie sat in RIP's reception, her headset slightly askew, polishing her finger-nails. So clogged was the whole RIP operation, she was surrounded by gurneys. Any bereaved that came by to pay their last respects were hurried through the Halls of Remembrance by attendants with the bare minimum of ceremony. How times had changed. 'Whadya mean, yer can't see me? I don't want you to see me. I do not wish you to place yer ugly moosh in front of my eyes ever again, yer tight-fisted double-crossing louse.' Anne-Marie began to remove her headset, then stopped. 'Oh, and give my regards to *Mrs* Glickenfeigel – the lucky bitch!' Yanking out her ear-piece, the receptionist ignored the switchboard lines that were flashing and bleeping. 'Men are better off dead.'

She looked round to see Ivan, hopping from foot to foot like some preoccupied giant.

'Whadya want, Ivan, standin' there like some goddamn body snatcher?'

Ivan laughed vacantly. Even in this place there was humour to be found, though it could appear in the strangest forms. 'Lookin' for Miss Julie.'

'She'll be embalmin'. You know how she lives in ER these days.'

'Can't find her.' Ivan moved his great body ponderously.

'Well you'll have to go searchin' again, then, won't yer – unless yer think I got her here? Maybe she's in one o' those sarcopho-things outside.'

Ivan lumbered away. Looking down at her phone system, the flashes and bleeps now ablaze and shrill, Anne-Marie flicked over to speaker, then, sighing, watched Ivan's departing form. 'Try the laundry room. She sometimes goes in there for a smoke.'

Anne-Marie's voice ringing in his ears, the porter pushed open the swing doors dividing the Halls of Remembrance from the embalming rooms and, turning left into the usually quieter section of the building (though at the moment it was as crowded as the rest of the premises), he walked past changing rooms and a small coffee-making area to enter the laundry room. Julie Dominic was inside, stretched out on a pile of dirty laundry. Even to Ivan's stupefied eye she wasn't her usual immaculate self. There were bags under her eyes, and several messy smears that looked like dried blood adorned her normally immaculate white coat.

'Ivan. Come to collect the washing – which ain't done – or are you just lost?' In one sense, Julie was serene; she was certainly out of it, drawing deeply on a spliff. She exhaled the smoke.

'Manny wants yer.'

'Does he now, the anguine bastard?'

'We found sumfin'.'

'If it's a stiff I ain't interested. Diamonds, on the other hand...' She laughed stupidly.

'It's a stiff all right, but it's who it is is why I've come for yer.' Leaving the room, Ivan let the door swing shut.

'Yo, Ivan...' Julie had another pull on her joint and, finishing it, reached over to turn up the extractor fan. 'Aah – jeez.' Taking out her mobile she hit speed dial. The number she'd been calling was Arnold Riseveldt's and the attempts ran into double figures. Trying again, his phone went straight to divert. 'Aw, screw it, Daddy R!'

Snapping off the call, she took a deep breath – this time just air – got to her feet and headed for the door, swaying slightly as she crossed the room. In the corridor, Julie shoved aside the loaded trolleys and gurneys cluttering her path and made her way along the corridor. Passing Arnold's office, RIP's chief embalmer exited the building and emerged onto the admitting bay. Manny sat on its edge, his legs dangling over the side, surveying the rising tide of corpses.

'Wha–?' Julie cast a disbelieving eye over the scene. 'As if we hadn't enough to do.' She walked further along the platform.

Glancing round, Manny tossed a cigarette butt into the parking lot. 'Not anymore.'

Julie looked at him quizzically. The embalming assistant got up and, picking his way over to a particular gurney, pulled back a blanket.

At first Julie didn't react, simply staring at her late boss lying beneath her, the dead eyes of his grey face gazing up unseeing. When finally she did react, she moved back and leant against the wall.

'My God...looks like he's been here a while.'

'One of the overnights, I reckon.'

'Got any idea what...how...?'

'From the wound in the abdominal wall and subsequent tissue decay, I'd say death occurred around twenty-four hours ago, probably between midnight and four in the morning.'

'Cause?'

'Penetrating injury to the lower abdomen inflicted by a serrated instrument: large knife or spike.'

Julie smiled at Manny's love of pathological and legalese terminology. 'You mean his guts have been ripped out.'

Manny took out another cigarette. 'Probably by a pike of some description.'

'I'll take one of those.'

Manny tossed the packet over to her. Opening it, she removed a cigarette and searched her tunic coat for a lighter. Manny tossed that over too.

'Well, that's my bonus gone.'

'Whadya think we should do?'

'Why ask me?'

'Cause other people are gonna. You're chief embalmer.'

'Don't mean I know nothin' about his business.'

They smoked in silence for a while then Manny said, 'Interestin' thing is though, he was discovered on a derelict site down the road from that restaurant he'd bought into. You know, the place with the chef who was snoopin' around here a while back.'

'How do you know that?'

'Take a look at the docket.'

Julie returned to Arnold's prostrate body and idly flipped over the tag attached to his left foot. A see-through plastic bag was also clipped to his jacket, with reference numbers and codes on it; inside were several items, including some loose change and a set of car keys. Julie removed the bag and looked at it.

'What were you messin' with, Daddy R, over there in the village, huh? Out late at night...what had you been up to?' Putting the bag in her pocket, Julie spoke to the body in a way that was almost intimate. She replaced the blanket covering his face and, exhaling, stubbed out her cigarette. 'Rest in peace, Daddy R. Rest in peace.'

Chapter 26

Arriving at Restaurant Incarnate that morning, Tabitha and Raymond discovered Arnold Riseveldt's van still parked as they'd left it. This wasn't good news for the chef, who refused to get out of his car.

'I know this is bad, Tab. Something's up and I ain't goin' in there.'

Tabitha was already out of the T-Bird and stood with a set of restaurant keys in her hand. Tutti had recently taken to rolling his own cigarettes, which he did stylishly. Raymond removed the monkey's latest effort from his delicate fingers, tossing him a box of small panatellas. Tutti clapped.

Tabitha flicked the keys in her hand. 'Ray, I gotta go in. We gotta open today. We need you, the restaurant needs you, but with or without you we gotta open.'

She rocked back and headed off. Trying the door, Tabitha discovered it was already unlocked, and went inside. Raymond stared at Arnold's van, his eyes boring into the cab.

'Where are yer, yer bastard?'

He was in his usual head-in-hands position when Belinda Millichamp found him.

Julie Dominic sat on the train coming into Manhattan, her mind a blank. She'd not been close to her boss, Daddy R as she called him. Funny guy, but he'd never really bothered her and she believed he genuinely did want high standards at his parlour. She also knew it had upset him when, for reasons of business pressure, things had slipped some. More recently matters had got so out of hand, the situation so bizarre... God, it could get to you, being surrounded by death all day long. But this was a feeling she'd only lately experienced.

Sitting on the train, Julie couldn't quite remember how she'd become an artistic embalmer in the first place, except she did know, when she first started her training at the Herbert Biddlecombe School of Beautification of the Bereaved, she'd rapidly felt it to be her natural vocation. Somehow, making a smashed face lovely or handsome again gave her incredible satisfaction. The fact that the person wasn't alive seemed irrelevant. After all, what was life if it didn't include death? But Daddy R being killed had changed everything, thrown her off-balance. She'd worked for him for a year and had got to know his idiosyncrasies and little ways. She supposed in an odd way she was fond of him – his puffing and panting, his fascination with all things funereal.

How did it happen? Why had it happened? Likely he'd been visiting his restaurant, but if Manny was right about time of death, what was he doing out so late and on some derelict site?

The train stopped at 14th Street station and, almost too late, Julie realised it was where she should get off. Running for the closing doors, she just made it onto the platform. She turned down 8th Avenue onto Horatio Street and took in the surroundings; it was a nice part of town but, as Julie knew so well from her work, people could be killed anywhere and a smart neighbourhood did not rule out an untimely death.

*

Having taken a subway train downtown from the Bronx, Belinda Millichamp had also been walking around West Village, immersing herself in its environs. It was a part of the city she rarely visited. With its attractive shops and apartments, Meatpackers' Wharf was a smart district, much coveted by the trendy and high-earning movers and shakers of Lower Manhattan. Finding Restaurant Incarnate hadn't been difficult and, looking at it, she considered the place befitting for such a chic neighbourhood. Of course, she'd read in magazines it was one of *the* restaurants to be seen at.

When she happened upon Raymond, it was the sight of Tutti sitting on the car's hood smoking a small cigar that attracted her attention.

'Does he have a name?'

Removing his hands from his face, Raymond looked up. 'Tutti Frutti.'

Right on cue, Tutti blew a perfect smoke ring.

'Tutti Frutti? Blows rings, too. That's unusual. Is he yours?'

'Guess you could say so. Kind of.'

'Where'd you get him?'

Raymond sighed. 'Well, he was brought in as a delicacy at a restaurant I was workin' in. We got kind of attached to him in the kitchen, after the client he'd been purchased for cancelled. I was leavin' the joint and he just came along with me.'

'Interesting. I wonder if you can help me. I'm looking for one of the partners who run Restaurant Incarnate – guess this is the back of it – who also has an interment parlour. Do you know if he's around right now?'

Raymond involuntarily looked at his partner's van. 'Tell you the truth, ma'am, I don't know where he is.'

'You wouldn't by any chance be anything to do with the restaurant, would you?'

Raymond didn't answer. 'You're kind of askin' a lot of questions. What might be your business with Mr Riseveldt?'

'Ah, Riseveldt, is it? Could you be his partner?'

Realising his mistake and suddenly suspicious, Raymond eyed the old woman more closely. 'What if I am?'

Completely calm, Belinda Millichamp stood back holding her handbag in front of her, her fingers on its catch. 'Young man, I think you and I should have a talk – a very serious talk.'

'And why would we want to do that?'

'Given we've established you're his partner here, you'll be fully aware of the unusual nature of his activities and' – she paused and looked around her – 'exactly what you're serving. I refer particularly to the meat type.'

'We've established no such thing, and I dunno what yer talkin' about.'

Just then one of the rear doors of the kitchen opened and Aldo's head appeared. He looked across at Raymond and waved.

'Mr Babchuk, you comin' in?'

Raymond could see activity beginning in the kitchen and nodded.

'Want to tell me about it?' Miss Millichamp was not about to give up.

'Can't talk about somethin' I know nothin' about.'

'Fella, I'm sure you're very far from being stupid, but you don't know how much trouble you're in.' There was impatience in her voice. 'Now, we should go inside and have a chat. It's early yet. I'm sure we can sit at a table quietly.'

*

Walking along Jane Street, Julie reached the Greenwich Street intersection and, strolling down it, came to the derelict site now guarded by a police officer. Taking out her oversized professorial glasses, she tried to peer between corrugated iron sheets that had replaced the timber boards. Several padlocks and an electronic security device were also fitted. Managing to peek through a small gap, she saw that police tape was everywhere.

'Crime scene, ma'am.'

'Yuh. I know. My boss was the victim.' Having come across town with her feelings fluctuating from nothing to devastation, Julie now looked about aimlessly. She suddenly felt an overwhelming emptiness. 'Know if any progress's been made?'

'They don't tell us, lady. I do what I'm told and take my pay.'

'Enjoy your job?'

'Does anyone?'

'Sure.' Julie fiddled with her hair. She could be attractive. The cop obviously thought so. 'Ever been in the line of fire?'

'Most days.'

Julie looked at him.

'Joking – though every day is in this job. You should see the paperwork.'

Julie smiled.

'To answer yer question, I have had discharged ammunition aimed at my person.'

'What's it like?'

The cop laughed. 'Don't know as I can describe it, really. Usually happens pretty quick. Then time stops. Then, if it's been close, you might not feel so good.' The officer scratched his arm. 'What about yourself – type of work?'

'Senior embalmer and beautician at a mortuary. That's what he was – a mortician.' Julie nodded at the derelict site.

'Guess we all go sometime.'

'Ha! Not sure he was that keen on checking out just yet – nor the way he did.'

'He at your place now?'

Julie nodded. 'That's how I knew this location. You guys tag 'em.'

While they'd been chatting, Julie was looking around and spied the Restaurant Incarnate sign. She took off her glasses and popped them in her bag. 'Think I'll go pay a visit over there. Nice meeting you.'

The policeman tipped his peaked cap. 'Pleasure meeting you, ma'am, and if ever I need any help in that line, I'll know where to come.'

'You may be too late. Don't know what'll happen to the business.'

'Why not take it on? I'm sure you're capable.'

'We'll see. So long, officer.'

Julie wandered away up the street. She had quite a sexy hip swing, an asset not wasted on the cop.

A number of pairs of eyes watched Raymond as he accompanied a genteel elderly lady through the kitchen and headed for the stairs. Feydor Gaultier had arrived and, although not in his white tie, showed perfect courtesy to his boss and guest.

'We'll, er, be sittin' upstairs, Feydor. Some coffee, please. Coffee all right?' Raymond turned to Belinda Millichamp.

'It'll do fine, thank you. I like a little cream.'

In spite of the elderly woman's slight appearance, her voice was firm and cultured. Gaultier gave his customary clipped bow and left them to go up. At that moment, Carmen emerged from her office and watched the two depart. Tabitha also appeared, now changed into her sous-chef's uniform.

'Least he's here.' Carmen looked at her watch. 'He's okay for twenty minutes. Menu out?'

'He'd pre-written it last week.'

'Thank God. Know who she is?'

Raymond and Miss Millichamp topped the stairs and entered the deserted restaurant.

'Not the slightest idea. His mom?'

Carmen smiled. 'Ha! Chefs!'

It wasn't Raymond who chose their seating but Miss Millichamp, selecting one of a raised row of banquettes that ran along a side wall. She sat down, Raymond sliding in opposite her.

'Pretty crazy setup – the coffins and all. Ha! I'll wager nobody here suspects a thing. Dead giveaway really, but then everything's obvious when you know.' Miss Millichamp sat composed and alert. 'How did he get to you?'

Raymond was mute.

'Ray – it is Raymond, isn't it? – I know what's been happening here and I'll be able to prove it.'

'But right now you can't.'

'Son, a killer was sent by your partner to do me in. The man had the stupidity to tell me what he was up to, I guess thinking it'd make no difference, but unfortunately for him it was his end he met, not mine. His body is lying on my living room floor and when I tell the police, and they check out my story – that he was a hired gun who had killed a number of people in the service of this restaurant, and that I shot him in self-defence – even their brains'll begin to work it out, and another piece of this bizarre jigsaw will slot into place.'

'How? How will they be able to work it out, Mrs...?'

'Miss – Belinda Millichamp.' Reaching into her copious handbag – Raymond spied the handle of a revolver just visible – Miss Millichamp produced Grimaldi's little battered notebook. 'Names, dates, deliveries...' Having flicked through several pages, she returned it to her bag. 'Talented chef that you undoubtedly are, you're not going to tell me you just woke up one morning and decided to cook human flesh to serve to the public. That would show an imagination I doubt even you possess. So tell me, how did the mortician get to you?'

With impeccable timing, Gaultier appeared, dressed as the immaculate maitre d' he was, placing a tray of coffee and some delicate mille-feuilles before them. Then, lifting the pot, he poured two cups of coffee, proffering cream to Miss Millichamp and placing it beside her on the coffin-lid table. Another barely perceptible nod and he departed.

'That's got to be the smartest man I ever saw. I congratulate you on employing him.'

'You still can't implicate me.'

'Oh, for heaven's sake, grow up! Your meat freezer is full of human flesh. Want me to take a look?' She eyed Raymond penetratingly. 'No, you wouldn't want that. Let's just call the police and have them go through it, shall we?'

It was Raymond's turn to look more relaxed. 'You're welcome to try, but I've spoken to them already.'

For the first time in their encounter, Miss Millichamp appeared wrong-footed. 'You've told the police what you're doing?'

'Uhuh – the precinct chief and the captain.'

'What happened?'

'They came and had a meal here.'

Miss Millichamp was taken aback. 'Let's get this straight; you went to the police to confess and they did nothing about it?'

'Don't know as I'd say confess; just wanted to tell them about it.'

'That could be interpreted as a confession.'

Raymond shrugged. 'Anyways, what they did about it was book a table. They were desperate for one – wanted to bring the mayor. Best meal of their lives, they said.' Raymond leaned forward. 'Now you see here, Miss Millichump, or whatever your name is, I don't think you realise just what I've done here, old lady. I've created the best restaurant in Manhattan. People are queuin' up to get a table, and I'm booked out for weeks, so if you've got any issue 'bout anything, you go find Mr Riseveldt and have yer grievances out with him. A lot of things are gonna change around here, including meat supply, so I don't give a kiss-my-hand for you or your accusations.'

Belinda Millichamp listened, composed but astounded. When she spoke, her voice was low. 'Incredible...making human flesh edible.'

'Hey, that's a pretty good line.'

Carmen appeared at the top of the stairs and although she could never be anything but flamboyant, Restaurant Incarnate's manager did her sensitive best to make her intrusion as polite as possible.

'Mr Raymond, you're needed downstairs. We have one hour.'

'Edible...incredible. Ha!'

'And, er, someone's askin' for yer. Says it's urgent.'

'Yeah?'

'A young woman. She says you know her, sort of.' Raymond continued to appear disinterested. 'Says it's to do with Mr Riseveldt.'

He was interested now, as was Miss Millichamp.

'Okay, I'll come down.'

'Why not see her up here?' Miss Millichamp spoke more confidently. Raymond shrugged.

'Okay, Carmen, show her up.'

'But, Mr Raymond, we open in just over an hour.'

'Sure.'

Carmen left them. The two sat in silence for several seconds before Miss Millichamp said, 'You should be applauded for your culinary talents, sir. With only the one kind of meat, it's astounding what you've achieved.'

Carmen reappeared, along with Julie Dominic.

Chapter 27

When the history of Restaurant Incarnate – subsequently re-named Restaurant ^{Re}Incarnate – was written (at least two significant works have appeared: one by an NYC health official, pub. Deutsch: Library of Congress, ISBN 0-3334-60917-0; of the other, more later), it was asserted not only was the restaurant's inception so astounding, but also the events formulated that particular afternoon. Whilst diners had, in the short term, to be turned away, the speed at which the place reopened the following night under its new name, and then re-emerged onto the New York and global stage as it did, was truly astonishing. Few could have foretold such stratospheric heights would be reached, particularly as, at the outset, things between the various participants were so muddied.

Matters kicked off with apparent indifference in the encounter between the young embalmer/beautician and the chef.

'You'll remember me.'

Though aware of her presence, Raymond didn't respond. Because preparation work could be delayed no longer, several members of staff appeared and began to put the final touches to tables, placing fresh flowers on them (purple orchids and black lilies) and checking place settings ready for opening.

'Haven't seen you around for a while.' Julie looked for

a seat and, spying several stools, took one. 'May I...?'

Raymond continued being his unresponsive self and it was Miss Millichamp who spoke.

'Since we understand you're from Mr Riseveldt, go right ahead.'

'You are?'

'An interested party.'

Julie brought the stool over and, sitting down, addressed Raymond. 'Well, seein' the van outside, guess I'm at the right place.' She tossed Arnold's van keys on the table. 'I'm sure you'll be sorry to know that Daddy R, Mr Riseveldt, is dead.'

Miss Millichamp's attention was obvious; Raymond's was not.

'I'm afraid he was murdered not a block away from here.'

'When? Er, how long ago?' It was impossible for Miss Millichamp to keep the intensity from her voice.

'Two nights back, we reckon.'

'How d'you know he was murdered?'

'It's what the police think. At any rate, a large serrated knife or spike of some kind passed right through him. Ripped out his guts.'

'Where is he now?'

'Body's down at the parlour.'

'His own parlour?'

Julie nodded. Miss Millichamp sat back and reflected. 'Fitting, I guess. Okay, Maestro, gonna tell us now?'

Raymond sat inert.

'Because if you don't, I will.'

Raymond looked at her, his face white, his expression stony. Very deliberately, Miss Millichamp opened her hand-bag again and took out her enormous revolver. Staff members attending their various duties couldn't help but notice and there were sharp intakes of breath. This was drama.

'Okay, then.' Miss Millichamp rested the gun on her lap.

Carmen, Feydor Gaultier and Tutti Frutti appeared, the little monkey scampering up and sitting down beside his master.

'Miss...er...?' Miss Millichamp addressed Carmen, who eyed Raymond, but the chef gave her no indication as to how she should respond.

'Carmen. Just Carmen.'

'Very nice. And if I may say so, my dear, you're most striking.' Waving her pistol casually, Miss Millichamp continued, 'I need you to gather everyone together in about five minutes.'

'Mr Raymond?' Carmen looked at her boss, who gazed blankly into space.

'The announcement will not take long. Go along now.'

Carmen hesitated but turned to go.

'I'd killed a man – accidentally.' Though uttered quietly, enough people heard, or thought they heard, what Raymond had said. No one moved.

'If it was an accident, what did he have over you?'

'I was drunk.'

'You still weren't going to hang.'

Raymond sighed and told the whole story – about his repugnant aunt and her soirées, how he'd cooked up the evidence then been blackmailed by Arnold Riseveldt, how because of their success, Arnold had to hire a hitman to keep pace with supply and demand. The tale unfolding left listeners askance; it left Raymond sunken and withdrawn.

Luke and Aldo also came up and, alone in the kitchen,

Tabitha finally appeared, curious to know what all the fuss was about. Miss Millichamp then addressed the shocked staff confirming clarification. 'Yup. The meat you've been serving is human, from his partner's funeral parlour.'

At this Julie let out a hiss. 'Jeez!' Others around the room looked pale and one or two decidedly queasy.

'That's why... That's why you've always been so insistent about only you handling the meat!' Tabitha moved centre stage. 'And that's why you go off to that place – "Meat Supplies" you call it – and you're always bringin' cuts back wrapped and sealed.' Everyone was transfixed. 'But it can't be true, Ray. It cannot be true. You cannot have done this. You cannot be a part of this, you...you animal!' Now face-to-face with her lover, she began beating her fists on his chest; Tutti screeched beside her.

Initially, Raymond made no response, but when he tried to comfort her she drew back, repelled.

'Don't touch me! Don't ever touch me! You're a beast. A wicked, degenerate, evil...!' The whole staff watched as Tabitha ranted out of control, horror-struck. 'I'm going to the police right now. I'm going to tell them everything. This is all going to stop – this whole crazy thing. My God, for the last six months we've been serving human remains to people. It's sick. It's beyond sick. It's depraved!'

About to run from the room, she was brought short by Miss Millichamp firing her pistol into the ceiling, bringing down black-painted plaster, a little cloud of dust billowing out from the hole above.

'I wouldn't do that.' Coolly cradling her gun, Miss Millichamp's voice was steel. 'It would be a big mistake.'

Tabitha turned to her, shocked. 'What do you mean?'

'Maybe you didn't hear; he's already been to the police

and their response was to come and eat here.'

'I don't believe it. They can't have known what they were eating.'

'Or who.' Julie's comment struck a droll note.

'I went to the police to tell them. Tutti came with me. We took a brain with us as evidence.' Raymond stared at the floor. Several people guffawed.

'Why?'

Raymond looked at Tabitha dully.

'Why a brain? Why did you take a brain?'

Again, several people began to laugh, including Luke and Aldo.

Raymond suddenly got up. ''Thought you were going to ask why I went to the police?' He paced around. 'I don't know why I took a brain. I don't know how I've been livin' these last months. I don't know anything anymore!'

'The point is, he went to the police to confess.' Miss Millichamp looked at Raymond. 'He went to tell them and they didn't want to know. Just came here for lunch.'

'Which they said was the best food of their lives!' Raymond spoke with passion; his feelings about the food he had created somehow highlighted the extraordinariness of the situation. He turned to Carmen. 'The front window, recently. Booked for three; two came. The mayor couldn't make it.'

'The mayor?' Tabitha was incredulous.

'Yeah, the cops had financial trouble; the mayor wanted to cut their budget, but he also wanted a table here and couldn't get a booking. Them gettin' one got him off their backs.'

'Why didn't he show?'

Raymond shrugged. 'Got called in by the governor or somethin'.'

Tabitha sat down, completely drained.

Replacing her gun in her handbag, it was time for Miss Millichamp to take charge – and she did.

'Do you have an office?' She addressed Carmen, who nodded. 'Okay, I want a meeting with you, you and you.' Miss Millichamp nodded to the manager, the sous-chef and the beautician. 'The rest of you take a break. Nobody leaves here right now – especially you, or you.' This to Raymond and Tutti. 'Anyone see them trying to leave and doesn't tell me will have this to reckon with.' She gave her handbag a comforting pat.

Standing, Miss Millichamp walked over to Gaultier. 'When people come to the door, please arrange for staff to politely turn them away. Politely mind. They should be told that due to a crisis in the kitchen we're unable to open today. Then cancel all tonight's bookings, explaining the same. I believe you will do this with your customary perfect manners; I'm aware it isn't your normal job, but you'll appreciate these are not normal times.'

'But if they wish to re-book?' Gaultier remained ever the professional.

Miss Millichamp considered before continuing, 'You can advise them that they will be contacted shortly. Within twenty-four hours.'

Gaultier went over to a booth on the far side of the restaurant and began checking the day's entries.

'Ladies, if you would follow me.' Carmen led the enigmatic Julie and a withdrawn Tabitha down the stairs, Miss Millichamp bringing up the rear.

For several seconds no one moved or spoke. Then Aldo turned to Luke.

'Human meat, man – crazy!'

'Yeah. What d'yer reckon to "broken heart" or "tennis

elbow"? Bet they've already been eatin' them things.'

'And maybe throw in "spare rib", "cauliflower ear" and "brain dead" while you're about it. Ain't that the biscuit – brain-dead cops, huh, Mr Babchuk?'

Black humour was kicking in.

'Must say, Mr Raymondo sir, that's one hell of a dark tale. Let's get some coffee on.'

Aldo went downstairs. Other staff milled around, largely ignoring Raymond who sat down again, Tutti at his side. The monkey stroked Raymond's knee as if to say things would be all right, but Raymond's face was dull and death-like. In the background, Feydor Gaultier could be heard cancelling bookings, but that was not a state of affairs that would last for long.

'Why can't we? There's nothing in the constitution says it's against the law, and we know he's *been* to the law!' Miss Millichamp was matter of fact.

'You believe that?' In spite of her shock, Tabitha was cynical.

'I do.' It was Carmen who spoke. 'At least the cops were here – that I can vouch for.'

The women sat or stood in the manager's little office. Carmen, Julie and Tabitha had been astonished by what the old lady had said to them regarding her plan for reopening the restaurant. She had proposed publicly announcing that Restaurant Incarnate would *only* be serving human meat, the supply of which would result from an advertisement she intended placing in the *New York Times* that very evening, offering $500 to anyone assigning the rights to their bodies on death to the restaurant. It was outrageous. It was crazy. It was inspired.

'There's nothing to say a man can't eat another man; they

do anyways in every other sense. Have done for all time, for God's sake. Now what they were doing secretly, we'll do publicly.' Miss Millichamp was persuasive in her argument.

'But...but supposing anyone did respond, actually offer themselves; you think other people are going to come here and knowingly eat them?' Carmen was struggling with the concept.

'Why not? They have been up till now.'

'Yuh, but that was when they didn't *know*. To actually go public...' So amazed was the manager she could barely catch her breath, yet Carmen felt strangely excited.

'Why not give 'em a choice – ordinary meat or the... alternative?' Julie was business-like.

'No – understand it'll be the uniqueness of the place and its food that will bring its success.' Miss Millichamp was adamant.

'It's sick! You're all sick even thinking about it.'

Thinking hard now, Carmen ignored Tabitha. 'If produce is being brought in at five hundred dollars a corpse, what's the profit?'

'With the prices charged here...by my reckoning, about a thousand percent. But you'd know how much waste there is on the cuts?' Miss Millichamp turned to Tabitha.

'Almost nothin'; he uses everythin'. Hell, what am I saying? This whole idea is demented. It's insane. We've got to stop talking like this right *now*!'

Miss Millichamp was calm. 'Miss...?'

'McKindrick. Tabitha.' Tabitha was sullen.

'Nice name. You know, biblically you're generous and kind?'

Tabitha made no response.

'What exactly is your job here? I can see you're some kind of chef.'

Tabitha still said nothing.

'She's sous-chef; that's number two in the kitchen.'

'I'm sure you do a good job.'

'I'm okay. It's Ray who–' she stopped abruptly. The room waited, but not for long.

'Who what, dear?'

'Who's the goddamn genius! Oh my God, it's so awful, what he's done, what's been going on.'

'And what *you've* been cutting up. I guess you do work on dishes?'

'Yes, yes – what *I* did too! But *I* didn't know! *He* did. *He* did it deliberately!' Tabitha resumed her hysteria. 'He deserves to rot in hell!'

She burst into tears. Miss Millichamp came over to her, cradling her in her arms, the young woman crying into her shoulder.

'That's as may be, but he was compromised. Once he'd done what he did after the accident, he must have felt he had to co-operate in order to avoid discovery. I don't think he could figure any way out.' Letting go of Tabitha, Miss Millichamp produced an old-fashioned linen handkerchief which she handed the young woman. Neither Carmen, Julie or Tabitha spoke. Miss Millichamp continued reflectively, 'Obviously we're where we are due to a combination of things. I think Ray hated his aunt so much it blotted out a lot of what he was doing. Then when he'd done it, served up that first body, and seen what a triumph the meal was...in a way, in a dark way, he revelled in his achievement. Then when he got rumbled by your boss, the whole thing became a nightmare.'

'However crazy my boss was, what he did was little short of brilliant – marrying his business skills with the chef's talents.' Julie hadn't said much throughout the exposé and the discussion of new plans, but her voice was even in its delivery.

'Given his particular business, you're right. In the same way it could be said my own proposed intentions are, perhaps, pioneering.' Miss Millichamp preened a little.

The women fell silent again then Julie said, 'But why and how did Daddy R go and get himself killed?'

'That we may never know, but dead he is.'

'How do you propose to run things – shares and stuff?' Julie was business-like and to the point. Miss Millichamp laughed. It wasn't an unpleasant sound.

'Ha! I'm glad you got around to that. We're going to need him – Raymond. He is indeed some kind of gastronomic genius and it's through his skills that the restaurant has already achieved such great heights.'

'What makes you think he'll agree?' It was Carmen who spoke. 'My reckoning is he's gonna want the hell out.'

'Then we'll just have to employ the same tactics Mr Riseveldt did.'

'Are you all insane?' Tabitha looked at them in turn. 'Carmen's right. He's not gonna want to continue. He just wants to quit!'

Miss Millichamp came over to her again. 'You really think so?'

Tabitha was about to remonstrate, but Miss Millichamp took out her gun again and cocked it.

'What are you doin'? You really are one crazy old bat!'

'It's not pointed at you. Just shut up and hear me out.' The 500 Magnum certainly had the desired effect and the old lady replaced it in her handbag. 'Now think about it. He's one seriously fucked-up boy, but he's got himself into this and while I'm sure part of him wants to jack it in, part of him feeds off it. I reckon he actually needs it.'

'He certainly liked all the praise when folks cheered and hollered. As for the monkey...' Miss Millichamp laughed and Julie smiled at Carmen's description.

'So I think you should go and talk to him.' Miss Millichamp was addressing Tabitha.

'Me? You want me to go talk to him?'

'That's right. You love him and he'll listen to you.'

'Love him? I hate him. He's a monster!'

Miss Millichamp looked as though she didn't believe the sous-chef. 'You know, life's a funny thing. I grant you there's a lot of bad people out there, certainly some strange ones, but there's a lot of folks just trying to get by and something gets tweaked in their brain – it needn't be much – they start behaving in a very strange way. Haven't you ever wondered at how tenuous things are, how everything's held together in the world?'

'Sometimes it isn't.' Julie spoke quietly.

'That's right.' So did Miss Millichamp.

Tabitha began to pace frantically around the room. 'Oh, great! Great philosophy lecture, but it still don't justify you doin' what you're proposin', an' I'm having nothing to do with it – nothin'. I'm gettin' outta here, clearin' out.'

'Okay. And what are you gonna do? Go to the police?' Miss Millichamp was cool.

'You betcha! Not that it's any of your business, but this time they're going to believe what they're told.'

'Think so? What proof have you got?' Interestingly this wasn't uttered by Miss Millichamp but Carmen, who for the second time side-lined Tabitha. 'Anyways, with her or without her, how is this thing gonna run?'

'Like I said, we need Raymond, whatever happens. I propose equal split – either four or five ways. After all, none of us have to be greedy.'

'What about Gaultier?'

Miss Millichamp looked at Carmen quizzically.

'The maitre d'?'

'What about him?'

'Well, I think if this is gonna work it would make sense to have him in.'

'Yeah, and set up B shares for staff, stuff like that, then everyone's involved.' Julie's idea impressed Carmen.

'Agreed.' This from the manager.

'Agreed.' This from the beautician.

'No way!' This from the sous-chef.

'What's the matter, honey? You want a bigger share?'

The other two women smiled. Tabitha looked likely to return to hysteria, something Miss Millichamp quickly nipped in the bud.

'Okay, okay. Look, I suggest we take a break. You go talk to your boyfriend – he is your boyfriend isn't he? Then if you still want free and he's going to be difficult, you split. He isn't, though; I've got to tell you that. He's in this thing up to his neck and there's no easy road out for him.'

'Why? Why do you want to do this?' Tabitha's was a good question. The other women watched Miss Millichamp, who looked back at them steadily before replying.

'Young woman, a hired killer tried to do me in today. The reason you know about.' Miss Millichamp walked away from them. 'When something like that happens to you, it makes you think. This is a crazy world with crazy people in it.'

'But that's no reason why you've got to be crazy!' Tabitha cut in.

'No, it isn't. But I'm not trying to break the law. If people don't like what we're doing they'll soon tell us. And you know what? Before I die I want to make some money!'

244

'*We're* doing? *We're* doing? I keep tellin' yer, I ain't havin' no part in this!' Still looking shocked at what she'd seen and heard, Tabitha nervously went to the door. 'You're all...you're all mad – all of you. Her, coming in here like this' – Tabitha waved an arm in Miss Millichamp's direction – 'with these crazy ideas. It's okay for the old bat to be off her head, but what we've been doing... We didn't know; you and me workin' here, Carmen, and you, you at the funeral parlour. But if we get involved with this new thing, we'd *know*.'

'So would the public; that's the whole goddamn point.' Now it was Julie cutting in, vehemently. 'We ain't bein' secretive, sister; we're bein' open. We're bein' entrepreneurial. We're bein' *American!*'

Tabitha stared at them for several seconds. 'You can't really think he's gonna buy into this crazy scheme. And neither am I.'

She went out. With her, tension left the room. Carmen and Julie looked at each other. What might they be letting themselves in for?

'She'll get over it.' Miss Millichamp sighed. 'As for him, his guilt still stands, but if he gets awkward it's on his head. I've a mind he won't, though. Like I say, I've an idea he's caught in his own weird world and the adoration's a drug habit he just can't kick.'

Miss Millichamp went over to Carmen's seat and sat down.

Julie said, 'There's one thing that's causin' me food for thought.' Miss Millichamp and Carmen looked at her. 'How are we gonna pay 'em – the folks signin' up?'

It had been in Miss Millichamp's mind to use her savings, but if things went as well as she expected, they wouldn't be anything like sufficient and it would be necessary to take a loan. As long as the operation could survive the first few weeks, she didn't think that would be difficult.

'I can answer that one. The account here's a-wash. They never spent nothin'.' Carmen spoke with authority.

'Is there enough for a few weeks?'

'There's enough for a few months, unless the entire city enrols and you buy 'em all up.'

Little did they contemplate the seriousness of that possibility. Miss Millichamp turned to the manager.

'Would you happen to have the number of a local signwriter?'

'Come with me.' Tabitha walked into the restaurant and found Raymond sitting exactly as she'd left him, staring into space. Several staff were by the main entrance handling the customers who were beginning to arrive. Feydor Gaultier was working the phone and others sat about drinking coffee. Tabitha went over to Luke. 'Bum me a coupla joints, will yer?'

Luke looked around. If anyone heard they were indifferent.

'Okay.' Luke got up and went downstairs. Tabitha looked back at Raymond, who hadn't moved.

'Hey, Ray. Let's go. You' – she pointed at Tutti – 'stay here.' She surveyed the general company. 'We're goin' out back. Anyone wantin' to watch is welcome, and tell the old crone where we are.'

Tabitha led a zombified Raymond downstairs where they met Luke coming out of the changing room carrying a small pouch which he handed to Tabitha.

'Owe you.' Taking the package, the sous-chef led Restaurant Incarnate's chef de cuisine across his kitchen and out the back door. Walking over to Ray's old T-Bird and not bothering to trouble him for the keys, Tabitha reached under the torn tonneau and unlocked the car door. 'Get in.'

Raymond went round to the driver's side. Inside, Tabitha rolled two joints. She was just about to light up when Tutti appeared.

'Oh, for God's sake! Goddamn monkey.' She still opened her door. 'Wouldn't be the same without yer, I guess.'

Tutti hopped up and scrambled into the back. Tabitha lit a spliff and handed it to Raymond. 'Smoke.' It wasn't a request.

Raymond took the joint; she then lit the second. For several minutes they experienced the marijuana. Finishing hers, Tabitha rolled another.

'The crazy old woman's gonna reopen. Ha! *Re*incarnate this time. She intends placing an ad in the newspapers advertising to buy people's bodies providin' they allocate them to the restaurant on death. She's goin' public. Reckons it'll clean up!' Tabitha lit her second joint. 'You've got to be in on it. No choice, she says...and she wants me too – equal shares.' Tabitha inhaled deeply. 'It was her idea I speak to you. Me! Crazy old girl!'

'Why?' This was the first word Raymond had spoken for a while. Tabitha looked at him.

'Whadya mean, why?'

'I mean, why did she want you to speak to me?'

'Hell, I don't know!' Tabitha had another pull on her spliff. She needed it after the revelations of the morning and didn't immediately reply; when she did she was sullen. 'She said I loved you.'

A slower smoker than Tabitha, Raymond finished his joint. 'Do you?'

'You got to be kiddin'! I hate you! You're evil, bad.'

'Yeah, I guess.' He pulled back the lever to open his joint.

'Whadya doin'?'

'Tab, I haven't any choice. I've been to the police; I told you what happened.'

'Yeah, only when it all came out. Anyways, of course yer have a choice. You can go see 'em again, turn yerself in.'

'You know what? Once was enough. And about the other stuff... What was I gonna do? Fell for yer, okay? So I'm obviously gonna tell yer I've been spendin' my time choppin' up human bodies every week. Explainin' stuff like that's real good for a relationship, yer know?' His door part-open, Raymond flicked the joint butt out of the car. 'Now I don't even know who I am, what I am – I don't know nothin' anymore, okay? So you can think what yer like of me and get the hell out. I sure as hell know I would!' He moved to get out of the car. 'Oh, and I might as well tell yer – as I ain't ever gonna be seein' yer again – there was a part of me that got off on it. Because I only had this one bizarre meat to work with and people loved the cuisine. Ha! I admit it did it for me. So now you know. Sicko *and* crazy.'

Raymond got out and spoke to her through the open door. 'Whatever happens with the mad old bird, I kinda, well, don't care. At least it's public. Anyways, I got other things on my mind. So long, Tab.'

Not wanting to be left behind, Tutti hopped out and Raymond closed the car door. Tabitha watched as, with Tutti on his shoulder, he walked back across the concrete parking lot to the kitchen door. She had a last almighty pull on her joint, finishing it.

'Sicko, crazy, monkey-loving jerk, but one mother-fucker of a brilliant chef. Shit!' Tabitha punched the dashboard.

Chapter 28

An hour or so later and back at RIP Julie addressed the staff in the Hall of Remembrance, an empty sarcophagus in their midst. Still buzzing from the meeting at the restaurant and with the cop's words ringing in her ears – 'Why not take it on? I'm sure you're capable' – Julie had called Mamie Riseveldt and organised bereavement counselling for her from the parlour. It was the least they could do. She also met with Manny, explaining something of the situation to the assistant embalmer, who surprisingly received her information matter-of-factly. Julie instructed him to drive the van to an address in the Bronx where he would meet an elderly lady and collect a body. Ivan would accompany him. They were then to return. Manny slithered off on his mission, accompanied by the hapless caretaker, and now she faced the remaining nineteen employees. Everything depended on keeping them onside.

'Okay, guess we're all gathered up here?'

Julie's words were met with a quizzical rather than mournful response. Perhaps the world of formaldehyde and glaze left employees bereft of any bereaving emotions – even when it related to their own founder and employer? Everyone knew about Riseveldt's death – though not the precise details of his demise – and the staff's mood was fickle, even darkly intrigued as to what the chief embalmer might have to say. Running his hand along a sateen covered catafalque, an employee commented, 'Perfect in its mouldin', fittin' in its style. Just how Mr Arnold liked 'em.'

This brought smiles and empathy from colleagues.

'Right, well, I guess there's no point beatin' about the bush. You've all heard the sad news our founder Mr Riseveldt has gone to the other side – joining those he'd assisted so uniquely in passing from this life to the next. Irreplaceable in his devotion to all things morticianal, we will miss him.'

This met with the odd murmur of agreement.

'However, in spite of the tragedy of his loss we're all experiencin', you will of course be thinkin' about your future in these turbulent times, and likely have some questions.' Taking a swig from a bottle of water she'd brought in, Julie had their attention now, and the more she spoke the more confident she became.

'I'm sure you'll be interested to know I've been in touch with the bank, who are contactin' the legal people. Most likely Daddy R's estate will pass to his dear momma, Mamie, who many of you know. If she wishes to run the business then this will be discussed, but at her age – she's near eighty – I think that unlikely. So, what I propose is this.' Julie looked steadily at her audience's expectant faces. 'I propose we turn RIP into a co-operative, each member of staff bein' awarded shares, with the possibility of buyin' into the business and increasin' their interest. I'm nomi-natin' myself to temporarily manage things, but if anyone wishes to contest this, that's fine by me.'

At that moment no one appeared interested in doing so. Indeed, general murmurings sounded positive.

'To support this plan, I am personally covering this month's wage bill while we get things sorted out – share structures in place and the like – so if you accept this today you will be working for me in the short term. Is that understood?'

'Sure you got that much money?' This from a junior embalmer.

Opening her bag Julie took out a cheque. Little did any of them know it represented her entire life savings. 'This is a draft for $30,000 from my bank to the business. It's a loan, but if we go down I lose the lot.'

Julie had been busy. There were impressed mutterings from the audience as the would-be MD returned the cheque to her bag. An employee spoke up.

'Pretty confident are yer?'

'Aren't you?'

'I ain't puttin' the money in.'

'Mr Riseveldt was an example to us all. He certainly was to me and I feel confident we can build on the fine work he founded by continuing to make Riseveldt's Interment Parlour a byword of excellence in lapidarical perfection.'

Julie had another gulp of water.

'I wish Daddy R was standing here – but he ain't, so if you want it, there's work to do.'

The staff felt her sentiments. They were with her.

'Okay, you'll have all seen the number of murder victims comin' in to the parlour.'

'Number? Over two hundred the last time I counted,' a colleague's correction was greeted by others laughing nervously or coughing.

'I have it on good authority that this spate of violence will decline – sharply.'

'Police tell yer that?'

'In a manner of speakin'. Julie paused. 'Unless next of kin, or any other livin' relative or dependent, have confirmed an interest in any of these victims after our standard RIP search has been conducted, according to State Bylaw 3179, subsection 4F, all embalmin' or enhancement work on these bodies is to cease immediately. In fact, I want all of them crated and stacked right after we finish here. They will be removed off-site. We've now got to concentrate on the regular work we have – repairin' damage and creatin' beauty for those that need it, ready for their glorious onward journey, either in burial or cremation.'

'What about Mr Riseveldt? Wasn't he murdered? You want him set aside too?'

'Course not. Daddy R will be given the send-off we'd all want him to have.' Julie took a final look round at what was now her staff. 'All right, unless there are any further questions, I only have this to say. We've experienced some very difficult times recently – times when things have been out of control. But they'll be goin' back to a more manageable level, a level where RIP resumes its rightful place as one of the highest quality funeral and bereavement services on the East Coast – a premier end-of-life establishment.' Julie cleared her throat. 'So, cleanin' things up and gettin' the premises back to their professionally spotless state – that's what we got to do, and I'll thank you all now for your help and co-operation in this.'

Julie stopped talking. There was a second or two's silence, then a round of applause.

'Where are we gonna hold the Christmas party?'

Much laughter, over which Julie yelled, 'Summer outin' first; no more Coney Island – it's a weekend in Florida!'

More hurrahs and clapping. The deed was done.

Chapter 29

It was raining when, much later that evening, Julie, driving Arnold's heavily-laden van, made her way from RIP in Queens to the old morgue off Amsterdam Place in South Side – the premises the late mortician had leased for his abattoir-style supply operation. Alone, she'd decided on her course of action earlier that day, having got things settled with Belinda Millichamp. Sous-chef Tabitha's continuing negative attitude – probably a combination of shock and indecision – notwithstanding, the women had organised the maitre d's *Re*Incarnate share participation, along with the rest of the proposed management infrastructure, and now all was in place.

Julie couldn't quite figure the old girl out, why was she so determined to expedite her plans. The proposals were exciting, though – no doubt about that. The decision to manage RIP had been easy; she knew the business was sound, just overburdened with the crazy amount of excess clientele. Driving across the Bronx's Whitestone Bridge heading north, RIP's new MD reflected on the amount of bodily wastage that must have occurred. In a strange way it increased the respect she had for Babchuk – how he'd not only managed to avoid poisoning Restaurant Incarnate's customers but made the place Manhattan's eatery of choice. But what Belinda Millichamp was doing – making the whole thing public knowledge – that was another deal entirely. And how Julie's new role there as head of body acquisition would work out she couldn't foresee. Miss Millichamp had in mind hiring a team of junior medics to check over her anticipated meat supply, under the embalming beautician's management ('Young medics are always broke; they'll jump at the chance.'). Anyway, it wouldn't be long before the outcome was revealed and getting RIP straight would secure her future, irrespective of the restaurant's fortunes.

The van's portable sat nav bleeped and Julie turned into Amsterdam Place. Raymond's ancient T-Bird was parked outside a squat, darkened building. The chef having told her to reverse towards a roller-door entrance, Julie parked the van then took a piece of paper from her purse and read off a number. Slinging her bag over her shoulder, she opened the cab door and trotted round to a side entrance, where she tapped digits into a numeric lock. The door clicked and Julie entered. Arnold Riseveldt might have anticipated Julie's reaction to his secret storage location, but even so its macabre origins somehow took the young woman's breath away. Tutti's swinging over iron roof beams and dropping down beside her also caused her to stifle a scream. Then Raymond appeared.

'You okay?'

'Monkeys appearin' outta nowhere, rainy night, old morgue, dead bodies – I'm cool.'

Raymond turned away and after getting a grip on herself, Julie followed him along a corridor, Tutti scampering beside her. They arrived at what had been the pathology unit, where bright lights hung down over several empty examination tables. Raymond was working in an adjacent room, surrounded by nondescript boxes. He half-turned to Julie:

'Found it all right?'

'Garmin door to door.'

Raymond smiled. He had quite a nice smile, she decided.

'Checkin' stuff?' She noticed several black notebooks nearby, one of which was open, revealing Raymond's spidery handwriting.

'Gotta keep tabs.'

'Right on.'

'Everythin' in the van?'

Julie didn't reply for a minute then said, 'What did you used to call them?'

'Supplies.'

'It must have done yer head in.'

'Done? Still doin'.'

Julie sighed. 'But–'

'How did I manage not to go insane choppin' up dead people all the time?'

'Well, yeah.'

'Ha! Sometimes I'm not sure I haven't gone mad.' Raymond put down the notebook he was logging from and stood up. He too sighed. It was a sighing night. 'Cutting open the body's the worst bit, but once you get stuck in, it becomes abstract. Then when you've done a few – guess it's like any other meat preparation.'

'But the first...the first time...' Fascinated, Julie couldn't help herself asking.

'That was easy. I was so wired I couldn't wait!' Raymond checked his phone for no apparent reason. 'And anyway, apart from tryin' to kill me, he was a bad guy.'

'But you didn't have to do what you did.'

'Long story.' Raymond put his phone away. 'Got screwed by your boss.'

'What about the embalming chemicals?'

'Nightmare. I told him – all that money he paid yer to make 'em look great – criminal waste, criminal.' Before Julie could ask anything more, Raymond said, 'How many you got?'

'Forty-three...and, er, a half.'

'A half? That's novel.'

'Er, yeah – no legs.'

'Oh, wheelchair, huh.' Raymond moved away and crossed the examination area, on the far side of which was an electronic gurney with a hydraulic riser. Moving it towards the outside door, he killed several of the lights and began raising the roller. Although electric, it was old and slow. The two waited in the half light.

'Is *he* in there?' Raymond nodded towards the van. Julie looked questioning. 'The killer – Jack Grim-whatever-his-name-was? Spats, double-breasted suit. Yer original Capone?'

'Oh, yeah. Had him brought in.'

'With or without the violin?'

Julie smiled. 'Play, do you?'

'Virtuoso. You buy what the old dame's plannin'?'

'It's different.'

'Say that again. Can't last.'

'Why not? This is America!'

Raymond laughed. The roller door reached the top. 'What about your late boss?'

'Your late partner? What about him?'

Raymond nodded at the windswept van. For a second or two Julie looked distracted.

'No, he's not in there.'

'I dunno – be kinda fittin'. You got the keys?'

RIP staff having stacked the van, it took Julie and

Raymond forty minutes to empty it and begin to store the cadavers in the sliding-drawered vault. There were too many bodies to accommodate, so those that couldn't be housed in the normal way were placed on racks in the freezer room.

'Given what I do for a living, that was quite the weirdest experience of my life.' Julie stretched her back.

'Thinkin' "haute cuisine"?'

Julie laughed.

'Haven't eaten at the restaurant yet, have you?'

'No...'

'When it comes down to it, it's all just meat. Secret's in the preparation.'

'I'll remember that.' Julie swallowed. 'I still can't work out why Daddy R got it, what he was doin' on that site, what he was messin' with.'

Raymond was silent.

'There was nothin' on him – no ID, no credit cards, driver's licence, cell phone. Found all that in the glove box. Which means he deliberately emptied his pockets before goin' there. Which means he planned to go there. He knew, or thought he knew, what he was gettin' into.'

Raymond still said nothing. 'Wouldn't have an opinion on that, would you?' If Julie could have seen the preoccupied look on Raymond's face in the darkness, she'd have surmised that he might. 'Guess not, huh? Real strange, though. He was a lot of things was Arnold, but he weren't no coward.' Julie snuggled into her coat and shivered. 'Well, time to be headin' home. Busy day ahead. You lockin' up?' She could just make out Raymond's affirmative nod. 'So long, then. Mind yer don't get reincarnated – that can wait till tomorrow.'

*

Walking into his house in the small hours, Raymond didn't at first discover Tabitha; it was Tutti who did. The sous-chef had let herself in, climbed upstairs to the chef's apartment, unlocked it and now sat in the gloom on Raymond's bed. The monkey clambered up the stairs – forever remembered as the scene of Aunt Renais' particular demise – ahead of Raymond, pushed open the unlocked apartment door and making his monkey screech, scampered up to Raymond's quarters.

Being an intuitive individual, Raymond realised some-one else was in his house, and that unless his property had been broken into, that someone would be Tabitha. Having heard Tutti, he pushed open the top door and saw his erstwhile lover sitting in the half-light. Putting on a side lamp, Raymond went through to the kitchen.

'What are you doin' here?' Raymond depressed the cold water fixture of his fridge with a glass and watched it fill. Tabitha got up and appeared in the doorway.

'Guess I came to say goodbye. I owe you that.'

'You don't owe me nothin'.' Raymond drank some water. Tabitha began walking round the kitchen.

'I do. No one ever helped me like you did. I always loved this kitchen. I always thought this was the best room in the world. Now I think it's the most evil; here's where it all began.'

Raymond was preparing a bowl of mixed fruit with leaves, eggs, nuts and grain. 'This is where it started all right.' Preoccupied with his task, Raymond was quite matter of fact.

'That's why you wouldn't let me in that night.'

'Like I said, Reardon tried to kill me. There's a freak accident, my car hits him. I'm drunk, he's in the trunk. What do I do?'

'You don't serve him up.'

Completing the bowl, Raymond set it on the central console. 'No? You know, Tab, when I go down that'll be the thing that'll worry me least.'

'Still plannin' on goin' in tomorrow?'

'Do I have a choice?'

'I told you – go to the police. Again.'

'Okay.'

'Yer will?'

'Yeah, I'll go see the police. In fact, I'll call the chief right now.' Raymond reached into his inside pocket and took out his cell phone. Tutti climbed on to a stool and began to eat his supper.

'It's two a.m.'

'So? He may want another table.'

'Oh, Ray!'

Raymond speed-dialled a number.

'You always feed him like that?' Tabitha nodded towards Tutti.

'Pretty much.' Raymond listened to his phone ringing. 'Voicemail. Want me to leave a message?'

Tabitha came over, took his phone and terminated the call. 'His manners are pretty neat.'

'Yuh, better than some of the so-called humans we get at the restaurant.'

Tabitha moved into Raymond's arms. 'Goddamit, Ray, you've fucked me up!'

'It weren't deliberate, Tab.'

'Oh, why did you have to do this stuff?'

'Told yer, but it don't matter no more.'

'It does, it does – don't yer see it does?' Tabitha was passionate through her tears. 'I love yer, yer stupid bastard! I've always loved yer. Oh God...' And with this, she ran from the room.

Cleaning his teeth with a toothpick, Tutti took a cigar from the box on the counter.

'Good idea, wise monkey. Mind if I join you?'

Chapter 30

Passers-by on Jane Street early the following morning witnessed a sign-writer putting the finishing touches to the restaurant's new sign, the letters 'Re' being inserted:

Restaurant ^{Re}Incarnate

The way it had been painted was to Belinda Millichamp's specification. Some building work had also been going on. A side entrance previously unused was opened and marked 'Supply'. A small lobby gave onto stairs that ran up to a large open-plan area above the restaurant. Tables and chairs were positioned at the front of the room, with light-weight hospital-style beds and moveable screens creating cubicles behind. The whole thing had a hospital clinic appearance.

Arriving as early as her sign-writer, Miss Millichamp had been busy supervising the layout of all this, the 'clinical' side of her new enterprise. An hour or so later, restaurant staff began to appear. Raymond was in first, unloading several boxes, followed by Carmen and Feydor Gaultier. Around 10.30a.m. Miss Millichamp came into the kitchen, carrying some newspapers.

'Good morning to you.'

Kitchen and waiting staff half turned to her, murmuring greetings. Miss Millichamp walked through to Carmen's office, where the manager and maitre d' were in conference. Showing, as always, his impeccable manners, Gaultier stood up as she entered.

'Thought you'd like to see these.' She plonked the newspapers down on Carmen's desk. They were each opened at a relevant page. The *New York Times* ad ran:

> *Bodies Wanted!*
> *$500*
> *Sell the rights to your body to Restaurant ReIncarnate –*
> *the place where the food chain counts!*

The Herald ran with:

> Your body *and* your life!
> *$500 paid*
> *Assign your bodily remains exclusively*
> *to Restaurant ReIncarnate –*
> *innovative cuisine guaranteed!*

And USA Today:

> *Of Human Interest*
> *$500*
> *Commit the rights to your body*
> *to Restaurant ReIncarnate – the only*
> *restaurant to support the cycle of life!*

And so it went on. Reading the advertisements, Carmen eyed Gaultier, whose face betrayed nothing. She turned to the old lady:

'Had any response?'

'Sure. Comin' in as we speak. The other ads are for

medics to apply to screen potential clients.' She flicked through the papers and sat down. 'Hell it's employment. I've got folk up there taking calls; a young para-medic friend of mine, Joel, is handling the doctor interviews and Pansy's looking after this.' She tapped the open papers. 'Taking bookings and assisting front of house.' Pansy had been one of Carmen's assistants.

'Has anyone called in yet?'

'You kiddin'? About thirty.'

'But the ads have only been out an hour or two.'

'And you doubted there'd be any response.' Miss Millichamp's reply to Carmen hovered somewhere between question and answer. 'Look, honey, there's a lot of people broke out there. Providing they aren't just gristle and bone – got a bit of fat on them – I figure a body's a body. Plus, our maestro told me yesterday afternoon he previously had a heap of problems not poisoning people with Miss Julie's embalming chemicals – loads of waste, folks he couldn't use.'

Miss Millichamp took a cigarette from the pack on Carmen's desk. 'May I? Bad habit, I know. Maybe I'll donate myself. I've suggested to RIP we serve up their late boss – after they've officially buried him, of course.' Accepting a light from the manager, she sat back. 'As long as I get 'em all documented, so it's legal when they die of natural causes, where's the problem?'

'What about the law?'

'Which part of it? Reckon they'll need an Act of Congress when we're done. That or things will change forever.'

Like Julie the night before, the whole thing held a certain fascination for Carmen – the surrealism, the bizarreness.

'What about stocks right now?'

'Our superstar chef reckons with what we've got we're good for two, maybe three months.' Belinda drew on and exhaled her cigarette. 'Had all the recent produce delivered last night from the interment parlour to the secret processing place, an old morgue on South Side. Must say, he certainly had a dark mind did our Mr Riseveldt. Anyway, if we aren't starting to get some legit product coming on stream by then, my name isn't Belinda Millichamp.'

The whole concept was so completely outrageous as to make it funny. In fact, Carmen felt hysterical.

'New menus arrived yet? Printer promised overnight delivery.' Finishing her smoke, Miss Millichamp was all matter of fact and business-like.

'Just unpacking them.' Carmen took a batch from a box on the floor beside her desk.

The new menu was simpler and larger in format, though the number of options was considerably reduced. Given many of her ideas were gauche, when Belinda had tackled Raymond about this during the conversation they'd had after management and share issues were sorted, he hadn't seemed particularly concerned, which had surprised her, given chefs were normally so precious about the culinary options available to them. The menu design had continued with its black and purple entwined edging, and was headed:

Earth to Earth, Ashes to Ashes, Dust to Dust
Not anymore!
Restaurant ReIncarnate
Life cycles healthy option

Dishes such as 'tennis elbow', 'spare rib' and 'fingers and thumbs' were featured, along with 'hand on heart', 'broken heart' and 'brain dead', each with mouth-watering descriptions: 'A haunch of tenderloin succulently charred over a hot grill'; 'Ribs cured in marinade for a lifetime'; 'Frontal lobe delicacy lightly pan fried' – it was one hell of a menu.

Miss Millichamp stood up. 'Better get these out; otherwise, everything in hand?'

Carmen nodded. 'Our maestro seems to have calmed down. Surprisin'.'

'Maybe he doesn't think it will last.' These were the first words from Gaultier. Miss Millichamp looked at him.

'That could be it.' She smiled. 'But how d'you know I haven't got a chain in mind? Little acorns, M'sieur.'

This was beyond comment and neither Carmen nor Gaultier made any.

Walking towards the door, Miss Millichamp sighed. 'Well p'raps it won't make it long term, but there wasn't much wrong with Riseveldt's business plan, except he was too successful. It was all up for him when he hired killer boy. Whatever happens, they can't get me on that score. Hell, we're going public!' Walking back across the kitchen towards the exit, she bumped into Tabitha entering the rear door. The sous-chef seemed vague.

'You okay?'

Tabitha shrugged.

'What's the matter? Couldn't stay away from him?'

'Dunno what I'm doin' here.'

'Course you do. So long, now.' Miss Millichamp smiled and went out.

Seeing Tabitha, Aldo turned from his bench. 'Hiya. Didn't think you were comin' in.'

Tabitha looked a forlorn figure.

'Neither did he.' Aldo nodded towards a corner of the

kitchen where an intense Raymond was hard at work. 'Makin' sauces.' This was normally one of Tabitha's tasks. She walked over to Raymond and for several seconds, stood watching.

'I never put quite as much salt as that.'

'Yer mean "a leetle peece of thees, and paprika...voila!"' Raymond mimicked Pierre-Auguste.

Tabitha smiled wanly.

'Well, if yer gonna be here, just do these.' He indicated the sauce bowls. 'Yer better at 'em than I am.'

'Will yer take a look at this?' Excited, Jerry had run back in the kitchen. 'Prices're even more expensive now – advertisin' "Arm and a Leg" – ha!'

Chapter 31

Having hired extra workers the night before, the fair opened mid-morning the following day. Located in Central Park, it wasn't a big travelling outfit by New York standards, but it brought a splash of colour and bohemianism to the city's green oasis. Additional personnel were cast as clowns for a charity whose temporary fundraising licence permitted them to operate within the fair's boundaries. A sign over the alley-style marquee proclaimed:

Make a Clown Smile:
Donations for New York's Deprived Kids.

Inside, all comers were invited to throw coins into buckets held by the white-faced performers up on stage in their crazy clothes, dancing around before them. A lively affair, it appeared the public couldn't chuck their small change fast enough, the clowns frequently being hit by flying currency missing the intended target. One such clown, taking a hit, crashed through the black drape at the rear of the stage, dropping down behind the scaffold platform.

'This is fuckin' dangerous!' The clown, known to the late Arnold Riseveldt as 'First Voice', but whose name was Flam, rubbed his arm. Whilst impossible to recognise, these hired thesps were actually the hobos present at

Riseveldt's demise. Another of them, preoccupied with counting money, spoke up:

'It's makin' moolah.' This was the hobo known as Angel.

'Ain't all ours, though.'

'Who says?'

'Hey, it's for charity.'

'Our charity.'

'Yeah? Ain't seen you up there takin' it. They're throwin' fistfuls!'

'Somebody's gotta do the countin', dummy.'

One of the other two remaining clowns on stage, whose name to his friends (and enemies) was Battery, put his head through the curtain.

'One o' you get yer ass back up here.'

'Ass! That'd be sweet. Trap coins 'tween yer cheeks, would you?'

Several quarters hit Battery's shoulder. 'Jeez!'

Addressing Flam, Angel said, 'Get back on.'

'What about Leon?'

'Leon's drunk.'

'Tcha! Tell me somethin' new.' Flam staggered to his feet and began clambering up the rear of the stage. 'Just hope this is worth it.'

'Keep it comin' – and smile!'

Delighted by Flam's reappearance, the crowd threw more.

Lying outside round the back of the marquee were several other clown-tramps. Prostrate, Leon snored in alcoholic oblivion. Homaster, idly flipping playing cards, was white-faced with crosses above and below his eyes and his lips a fetching shade of vermilion. He sported a vivid, sky-blue outfit with large white pompoms down its front. A hobo clown named Arthur looked up from reading a paper.

'Hey! Yer seen this? Some restaurant advertisin' to pay if yer leave 'em yer body.'

Abandoning his card flipping, Homaster began collecting up the deck. 'Restaurant?'

'Yeah. Pay yer five hundred bucks as long as yer sign a guarantee so's when yer croak they got rights to yer carcass, legal-like.'

'What do they wanna do that for?'

'Seems like they wanna cook it.'

'Crazy notion. How're things goin' in there?' Nobody moved, so, muttering, Homaster got up and lurched into the back of the marquee. 'All cool, Angel?'

Angel turned his smudged clown face to Homaster. 'It's addin' up.'

'And?'

'Two-fifty, three hundred bucks.'

'Not bad.'

'Course, we gotta negotiate the exit.'

'Who'd arrest a clown?' Homaster gave a vermilion grin.

'Ha! You kiddin'?'

'Robbin' the poor, givin' to the poor... Some o' those out there don't look so broke.' Peering through a gap in the drape, Homaster was hit by a heavy coin. 'Time to go.'

'You bet it fuckin' is!' Battery jumped backstage, followed by First Voice. For some reason, the other clown carried on performing.

'Poifect. Let him enjoy himself.'

Dividing up the takings, the clowns put handfuls of coins in their copious costume pockets before Homaster led them outside. Approaching Leon, he kicked his leg.

'Come on, kiddo! Move it.'

Leon sighed, rolled over and didn't get up.

'Leon!'

Big security people roaming the fairground noticed the clowns gathering outside their tent walking in a strange waddling fashion. Suspecting something, the guards began to converge.

'Hey, schmuck, we're splittin',' Homaster hissed.

Leon still didn't respond.

'Don't say I didn't warn yer.'

Attempting to duck and dive between other amusements – rifle ranges, and hoopla stalls with goldfish in bowls – the hobo clowns were encumbered by their loads of heavy metal.

'Hahaha! Hohoho!' One hobo, Arthur, tried to clown his way out of trouble by making faces at kids and rocking his weighted body from side to side – 'Hohoho! Hahaha!' – until the long arm of security landed on his burdened shoulder. 'Hohoho!' The guard whipped Arthur's wrist behind his back in a deadlock. 'Aaah!'

The rest of the escaping hobos were likewise rounded up.

Chapter 32

It had been Wally Dimitrick who'd suggested it, and Julie could find no way out of bringing the old folks over to West Village, though it was upstairs rather than down the octogenarians headed for when arriving at the Jane Street restaurant. Julie had organised the people-carrier for Mamie and those of her old friends who had known her son, Arnold, to attend his lying in state at RIP. Indeed, they were almost the only mourners to visit the moticianal entrepreneur in his formal repose. One or two executives from the National Morticians' Association and its rival body, the Federationof Embalmers, had turned up to pay their respects, and a mysterious woman of indeterminate age who announced she was Arnold's palmist, and hinted at more.

Julie had done her boss proud; in death his cheeks had a fuller colour than in life, his thinning hair neatly combed and his smart funeral tuxedo, complete with its NMA lapel badge, was complemented by Cuban-heeled patent boots flashed with the RIP logo, of which he was so proud. The whole presentation made a deep impression on those who came to pay tribute.

It was when adjourning to Arnold's old office, where Julie had laid on some refreshments, that Wally produced a paper with the _{Re}Incarnate advertisement.

'Whadya reckon to this?' Wally was his usual direct self.

'What do I reckon to what, Wally Dimitrick?' Ruby

Montgomery bristled at Wally's failure to appreciate time and place.

'This restaurant operation Arnold had a share in – they're offerin' five hundred big ones if yer assign yer body to 'em when yer check out.'

'Whadya talkin' about?'

'They give yer money for yer body, maybe even yours, yer vilde old chaya.'

'Gimme that.' Ruby was forceful in her demand. Wally tossed the paper over, his arthritic arm not helping its trajectory.

'You could just hand it to me, yer dumb lurg.' She read the advertisement. 'Five hundred bucks, huh? Interestin'.' Ruby turned to Julie. 'Know anythin' about this?'

'Why would I?'

'No reason.'

Julie smiled her new cool business smile. 'I only went there for the first time yesterday, tryin' to find out more about Mr Riseveldt's other activities.'

'Whadya think happened to him?'

'Don't know. Some kind of accident, I think.'

'Seems darned funny to me. More likely he was bumped off.' The amount of sensitivity Ruby possessed could be contained in a follicle. Wilbur looked uncomfortable and Wally scowled.

Mamie Riseveldt, however, was her normal serene self. 'Why don't we go downtown and take a look?'

'You sure about that?' Wilbur was all consideration.

'You really want to?' So was Julie – genuinely so.

'Don't see why not. Whatever happened to Arnold, nothing's going to bring him back. He's gone now.' She smiled her delightful quaint smile. 'I think he'll be happy dead – happier dead than alive. He always liked death.

That's why he went into the business.' Mamie ate a cucumber sandwich. 'Yes, I think we should go pay a visit.'

And thus it was the elderly group, accompanied by Julie Dominic, headed downtown to Restaurant _{Re}Incarnate.

The film crew shooting an episode of *Upstate*, a popular drama based on New York State's politicians, had broken for lunch. Catering wagons and all the mobile paraphernalia associated with filming had parked up near Central Park's zoo. Among the props vehicles was a police car and it was toward this that a somewhat bedraggled clown made his way. Leaning against the fender, a couple of actor cops were eating their lunch from polystyrene loose fills; both were overweight with impressive pot bellies.

'Say, fancy loanin' me this baby for five, ten minutes?' The silver-clad clown leaned against the car scratching his balls.

'Five or ten?'

'Yer know.'

The clown shrugged.

'Where d'ya wanna take it? Clown City's a *long* way.' Talking through a mouthful of spaghetti, one of the actor cops drawled out 'long'.

'Aah, squeeze's bein' put on some buddies of mine. See over there?' Leon nodded towards the travelling fair. Although his clown suit had grass down its back and he looked a little dishevelled, he appeared sober enough.

'They been naughty little clowns, have they? Not makin' the folks laugh?' The second actor cop guffawed stupidly.

'Guess there's nothin' else for it, then.' Preoccupied with their lunch, neither of the two actor policemen saw Leon's swift movement, the semi-automatic pistol now pointing in their direction appearing as if from nowhere.

'Hey, hey! Whadya doin', man?'

'Hitchin' a ride. Now are you gonna play nice little cops, or is one of you gonna have a wardrobe change?'

'What exactly do you want?'

'I want you to act.' Leon was nonchalant. 'Go over there and spring my buddies.'

'What've they done? Tricks not workin'?'

'That'll be it. Now, this difficult assignment for you two fat-assed Smokeys requires just a little bit of actin', if that ain't too much for yer. Look upon it as me bein' yer director, directin' yer nice and clear like.'

Actor Cop Two actually laughed. 'Ha! More than this clown is!' He nodded behind him.

'No offence to your profession, mind.'

'None taken.'

'What about it, Lou? Clownie here just wants us to drive over there, do a bit of performin' and free up his fellow funsters.'

'Know what the penalty is for impersonating a police officer?'

'Sure do. Let's go.' Finishing his lunch, Actor Cop Two scrunched up the plastic tray, belched and threw it towards one of the many black bags pegged round the site. Missing the target it lay strewn on the ground nearby.

'Well, guess it'll be the most work we'll do today. Nothin' heavy, though, fella.'

'Just laughs all the way, good buddy.'

The two actor cops got in the front of the car and Leon in the back. Gliding away from the location, they turned the phoney police vehicle up East Drive then, dropping Leon off at the cab rank, made a left towards Central Park Driveway, where the fair was located. As they approached, Actor Cop One activated the siren and blue lights. Pulling up beside the ticket gate the two actors got out, very police-like, and swaggered over to where several private security men were holding the clowns.

'Okay, fellas. Guess we'll take it from here.'

The security guards relaxed a little. 'Didn't know Murphy'd called you guys.'

'Dunno about Murphy, but we got a 415/488.'

'You'll want our statements.'

'Sure will, but first let's get these clownie boys' details.' He turned to the hobos. 'Okay you, wizards of hilarity – over here.'

Actor Cop Two began shepherding Battery, Arthur, Flam and Homaster towards the police car as the security guards looked on. Actor Cop One turned back to the guards:

'Take five, boys. We'll see you in there. One half-caff ristretto with a mocha shot, one tall macchiato with double chip and skinny.' He nodded to a nearby coffee stand, his police Ray-Bans reflecting confidence all the way. By the car, Actor Cop Two took out his police notebook and appeared to be taking details. At the arrival of Actor Cop One, he said casually, 'Okay, fellas, if you haven't clowned yer way outta here in ten seconds I'll arraign yer for not bein' funny.'

Just then a shrill whistle could be heard coming from a yellow cab, with Leon hanging out of its window. The two actor cops got into their car and sped off, the clowns piling into the taxi. Half a minute later, one of the security guards appeared from the coffee stand.

'Macchiato double chip and ristretto... shit!'

The people-carrier bringing the four elderly men and women, along with Julie Dominic, to Jane Street pulled neatly into the kerb. As she left the vehicle, the new MD of RIP and director of Restaurant ^{Re}Incarnate turned to the driver:

'We'll re-book later.'

The driver handed her a chit pad, which Julie signed.

'Quite a crowd here. What's goin' down?'

'Haven't you heard; it's the "in" place.'

'Ah. What's with the "Supply" queue?'

'The proprietor's gonna be servin' up human meat in the restaurant.'

'You're kiddin'? How sick is that?'

'Try gettin' a table.'

The driver's short-wave radio squawked, advising his next ride. Julie moved away and gathered up Mamie and her friends. The lady herself was looking at the restaurant.

'It's come a long way since…Renais' send-off, wasn't it?'

'Yeah. Seems a while now.'

Like Mamie, Wilbur was reflective. 'It's so Arnold. He loved those colours.'

It being around midday, things were busy, on both fronts: people arriving for their meals at the reopened restaurant and people queuing for their medicals upstairs. Wally peered along the queue into the 'Supply' entrance.

'Sure you wanna go in here?' Julie was considerate.

'Yes. Why not?'

'Okay.'

A queue of about fifty people ran along the sidewalk. Belinda had posted marshals to guide folks who were joining all the time, but people were in good humour and things moved along at a reasonable pace.

'Maybe I could…' Julie implied that she would try getting them in more quickly.

'No, no. We'll take our turn.' Wilbur was polite and they

joined the line. 'No need to wait with us, ma'am.'

'It's no trouble. It shouldn't be long, but I feel...well, Mrs Riseveldt...'

'Mamie? You worried about her?'

'No...well, yes... Her son, her loss. My boss...'

'That's considerate.'

They stood in the queue. Ruby Montgomery addressed Julie. 'You parta this, then?'

'Miss Millichamp – the lady who's taken over – she wants to involve me.'

'Why's that?'

'Because of Mr Riseveldt's association, I believe.'

'Don't see as that makes any sense.'

'Did my Arnold know about this, Julie?' Looking up from studying the newspaper advertisement, Mamie eyed Julie, who didn't reply. 'I was just thinking...if this is the state of things to come, how perfect it would be – with his line of business and all...'

'By that you mean...?' Julie was cautious.

'Well, the parlour; RIP receivin' dead people then bringin' them here for...what we're signin' up to.' Mamie smiled. 'Might help out with the food chain. Imagine all those poor countries, how it would help them.'

'You mean America?' Wally's sharpness never failed. Mamie laughed. For several seconds none of the group said anything.

'Yes... I think we'll bring him here, right after the ceremony.' Julie and the octogenarians stared at their senior member. 'We could make some money and we could go to the restaurant. Just think, eating my own son.'

Julie gulped. The others – even Wally – looked a little shocked.

'That's a... That's a very particular attitude.'

'I guess. But what do we know? After we're dead, does it really matter?'

They moved on up the line.

In the restaurant, things were humming. Eager diners sat at tables; the whole atmosphere was glowing with a greater intensity even than in its more secretive days. Whilst the food then had been superb – and as far as Raymond was concerned that wouldn't alter – somehow things going public had given the place a more vibrant mood, more risqué and edgy. Leading an affluent young couple to a table, Gaultier held a chair for the girl.

'You really serving human meat?' The young man spoke a little shyly.

'As advised on the menu, sir.' The maitre d' gave his customary nod.

'Wow! Eating people – far out!'

The young woman was less fazed and more excited. 'Is it really true the chef's been approached about a Michelin?'

'Indeed, sir. Maestro Raymond is the very finest of chefs.'

'Will you look at this menu, George? Broken Back. Wow! Can't wait!'

Chapter 33

Having had to bribe the cab driver to squeeze them all in, the hobo clowns paid him off and alighted near the Tavern on the Green. After removing their clown costumes and cleaning themselves up in the washroom, the men ambled down Central Park West. Wandering into side streets they soon found a liquor store and, having stocked up, sat down in Tecumseh Playground to quench their thirsts.

'So what's with this restaurant kick?'

Having a long pull on his beer, Homaster seemed in a bad mood. 'I told yer – five hundred bucks for assignin' the rights to yer body.'

Arthur was mellower. 'Where is it?'

'West Village.' Finishing his beer, Homaster scrunched the can.

'That where we did the dude?'

'The dude did his self.' Angel was final. He also finished a can and ripped open another, as did Homaster.

'I don't like it.'

'Who gives a hen's peck what you like, Hikey?' Battery this time. There was silence, and more drinking.

'We're no gang. I'm goin' down there, anyways.' Angel got up.

'Well, I'm against it.'

'That's cool, my man. You be against it, but given we

ain't exactly flush, and it's only down to Leon we got anything out o' that last caper you got us into, I'm for some money.'

'Crazy stuff, huh? Money for our bodies. That's if they ever find 'em.' Flam was light-hearted.

Battery was reflective. 'They really give yer cash?'

'That's what it says.' Arthur finished his drink. Flam eyed Leon.

'What about it, Leon the lion man?'

Leon belched, having returned to his usual state. Angel and Battery moved off and Arthur and Flam were stirring themselves to follow. All at once Leon stood up and dropping his empty quart of whisky into a bin, looked about him. Spying a cab, he hailed it.

'Hey, Leon, what yer doin?'

Leon didn't reply.

'Where he's goin' I'm goin'.'

Flam crossed the road, followed by Arthur. Left on his own, Homaster stood on the sidewalk. From the back of the yellow cab, Leon called out, 'Get over here.'

Downing his second and kicking its empty can skywards, Homaster began to cross the street. 'Shit!'

Further down the block, Angel and Battery looked back.

'What's that all about?'

'You know Leon.'

'Not really.' Battery wiped snot from his nose. 'C'mon, walk'll do us good.'

'Yeah?'

'We got liquid, ain't we?'

Laughing, they continued their unsteady stroll south.

Chapter 34

Activity in the kitchen at Restaurant $^{Re}_{\wedge}$Incarnate was frenetic: chefs working flat out and waiters coming and going at a rapid pace. Raymond presided over the cuisine, watching his juniors with an eagle eye. Waiter Jerry appeared at the serving counter.

'Chef Luke, punter wants more dorrigo on this one.'

'Then the punter better go to Tasmania' – Luke would take no nonsense from the hapless Jerry – 'where it comes from. Didn't you tell 'em it's hot enough down under?'

Jerry obviously didn't quite get this. Perhaps he didn't know the 'down under' phrase or where Tasmania was – or both.

'Hey, don't take it out on me, man. You just gotta keep makin' the dishes. We've got people to feed up there. Goin' crazy they are – beggin' ter get tables. Eatin' humans is in!'

Aldo's head dropped; the pressure was intense.

'Not dyin' on me are yer, Chef Aldo? Have to cook the chef. Man, that would be somethin'!' Jerry grinned. Tutti hopped up on the counter as Jerry collected two beautifully presented plates. 'Outta the way, you; your delicacy days are over.'

Turning, he was confronted by Raymond holding a long sharp knife.

'Any more wisecracks...'

'Hey, hey, chef! Not me – I'm just servin' 'em.'

A slightly tenser Jerry headed for the restaurant carrying his order. Belinda emerged from Carmen's office with the manager, deep in conversation. The kitchen wallphone rang, and was picked up by Luke. Looking round he spied Miss Millichamp.

'Call for you, ma'am.' Breaking off her discussion with Carmen, Miss Millichamp came over to the phone.

'Yes?'

'Miss Millichamp, I've had the FDA on the line.' It was one of the clinic staff.

'So what?'

'Questions about hygiene certificates.'

'The kitchens have a current HHS permit.'

'ASA's also called about the advertisements.'

'Bit late now aren't they?' There was no comment the other end. 'Tell 'em I'll call back.'

'I think if you don't take it...' The caller let his phrase hang.

'All right, I'll come round.' She hung up. 'Sooner we get Death Star[1] down here the better.'

Hearing her, Aldo laughed as he finished another dish for service.

'Appropriate description, ma'am!'

Cool as ever, Miss Millichamp left the kitchen. Upstairs in the clinic she took the ASA call.

'Miss Belinda Millichamp?'

'Speaking.'

'Since you were responsible for placing the advertisements, I assume you must be the proprietor of Reincarnate Reassigned?'

'That is the case.'

[1] AT&T Corporate Logo has been nicknamed the 'Death Star' due to its appearance's similarity to the *Star Wars* space station of the same name.

'Well, ma'am, we're concerned by the content of your advertisements.'

'Why is that?'

'Let's just get this straight; you're asking people to grant the rights to their bodies to your enterprise on their death – correct?'

'Just so.'

'And you're gonna sell them to the public as food?'

'Already doing it.'

'Well, ma'am, that's illegal.'

'Not as far as I'm concerned. Now, if there isn't anything else...'

'You can't do this, ma'am!'

'There's nothing in the constitution says I can't. Bye now.'

'But no one'll eat–'

Miss Millichamp hung up.

'Try booking, pal.'

Such was the crowd surrounding the Jane and Greenwich Street intersection, Leon and his three compadres in the cab had to alight a block short. It was an amused Angel and Battery who spied them on the corner of Hudson and Horatio paying off the taxi.

'Cool move, Leon.'

'More money than sense or yer will have!'

'Five hundred bucks ain't a fortune.' Battery was realistic.

'More than we're worth, though.' Flam was light-hearted.

'Not accordin' to them.' So was Arthur.

'I still don't like this.' Homaster continued his opposition.

'Aw, shut up!' chorused the rest.

Picking their way through the crowds (not everyone was queuing; some people had come down just to see what all the fuss was about), Arthur, Battery, Leon, Homaster, Angel and Flam made their way towards the ever-lengthening line, now tailing back round the block. Those wanting to sign up and sell the rights to their bodies were, by and large, good-natured and not all were vagrants. Indeed, the best word to describe the gathering was eclectic. Some people were obviously down on their luck and some people were clearly pretty weird. Hangers-on included plenty of the usual minorities – Seventh Day Adventists, Jehovah's Witnesses and the rest – convinced those in line were not only selling their bodies for $500 but also their souls. An old-timer scowled at a well-meaning missionary.

'I ain't had a square meal in weeks, young man, and if some nut wants to give me five hundred bucks for my body, hell, I'll throw in my soul and anythin' else they goddamn want! Ha! five hundred for my scrawny carcass? They can have it.'

'You have to pass a medical.' A middle-aged professional type stood behind, horn-rimmed glasses, thinning hair. 'Think you'll make it?'

The old-timer cackled with laughter. 'What's a guy like you doin' here, anyway?'

Having made a comment the professional man was caught. 'I, er... I'm interested in the concept.'

'Interested in the concept? Ha ha! That is indeed inter-estin' in itself. So you're not here for the money?'

'No.'

'Mind if I have yours, then? A G'd be just swell.'

The professional looked at his newspaper, but the old man wouldn't let it go.

'Whatcher gonna do, then? Have a chat?'

'That was the general intention.'

'Let's get this straight; you're comin' down here 'cause you're interested in this notion of people sellin' their bodies and other people eatin' 'em?'

'Right. Any objection?'

'Why, no. You some kind of philosopher or sumthin'?'

'If you must know, I'm a professor.'

'A professor, huh? Well, Mr Professor, if you want my opinion it's a goddamn genius idea.'

At that moment Leon barged into the old-timer. Clutching a bottle, it wasn't clear if he was attempting to queue-jump or one of his so-called buddies had pushed him. Either way, the old boy was having none of it.

'Hey, pal, back o' the queue's that way.'

Leon burped and somehow still in possession of his clown's hat, raised it to the professor. The end of the line now ran across Horatio and into Granesvoort Street, two blocks up from Restaurant ReIncarnate. Arthur spoke to a marshal shepherding people to its tail. The young man held a clipboard and sported a hi-viz reflective vest with Restaurant ReIncarnate emblazoned across it.

'How quick does this thing move?'

'You're an hour off.'

'Jeez!'

'No gain without pain. If you wanna fill this out while you're waitin' it'll speed things up when you get in.' The marshal handed over several questionnaires asking for details of name, address, social security number and so on.

'Hey, what's with all this social security shit?'

The marshal turned back to Leon and Homaster's hobo group.

'No shit. You don't think they give out money without a

tab on yer, do yer? Has to be legal. Of course they gotta know who you are.'

'Nervous, Hikey, or ain't yer got one? Apart from being undesirable, maybe you really are an alien?' Angel laughed darkly.

'Stick down any old number.' Battery was dismissive.

'Can't do that; they computer-check.' The marshal was relaxed.

'I'm cash only.' Arthur chuckled.

Homaster spat. 'I don't like this shit.'

'So you keep tellin' us.' Flam took a form.

'Nobody's keeping you here, good buddy.'

The hobos began filling out their forms.

Chapter 35

Lunch was over. It was certainly the busiest session the restaurant had ever had – either in its Incarnate or ReIncarnate guise. Nevertheless, there were some serious issues. The strain of maintaining the quality of cuisine with such a number of covers had exhausted the kitchen staff who, although having had the previous day off, were already tired from working at the tremendous pace they had been prior to the new takeover. This was especially acute for Raymond.

Now everyone knew the meat was human, it was interesting to see how quickly the team of chefs had settled down to work again. When they collected a cut from the freezer, the meat was already prepared and any human aspect of it eliminated. Nothing had changed, except knowledge of what the food was.

Because of kitchen pressures, it had been necessary to approach Tabitha. Initially so squeamish about the whole thing, her expert help was needed with several dishes and the sous-chef hadn't turned a hair. Indeed, since arriving she hadn't stopped.

Other matters loomed. In its previous life, Restaurant Incarnate was a fashionable and chic establishment. This reputation Raymond cherished, and he had had no intention of relinquishing its exclusivity. Now, however, not only was there a line of people a mile long queuing up to sell their bodies, there was also a considerable queue outside the restaurant desirous of a table. Since that morning, bookings had gone ballistic and the phone system was on overload. But people coming downtown to queue – it was as if the publicity Miss Millichamp created touched some nerve in the citizens of New York. At once, the idea of human meat was grotesque yet strangely desirable. Always a sharp city, unique in American culture, this starship town had a pioneering attitude, loving the innovative and embracing the new. Rather than condemning the concept as unacceptable, people were asking themselves if it might be a solution. Added to that, the reputation the restaurant already had was making it a compelling venue for the Big Apple's populace. Picking up the story by lunchtime, radio stations were hot on it, and TV news crews were arriving en masse.

Although she was outwardly cool, a little sweat had begun to appear on Belinda Millichamp's upper lip as she fended off continual pressure from her Reincarnate Reassigned staff – medics checking people, cashiers making payments – and still the people came.

'Miss Millichamp, what time do you intend closing the queue?'

'Which one?'

'Body Assignment, I guess. Can't see you'll want to turn people away from the restaurant.' Maurice, the marshalling manager, looked tired.

'Nine o'clock.'

'What about those not dealt with by tonight?'

Miss Millichamp went over to her desk and opening a drawer, took out a box of numbered discs. 'Start winding down around seven then get your guys to give these out to people who want to come back tomorrow.' The marshalling manager took the box. 'What's it like out there? Busy still?' Belinda had been preoccupied with some paperwork.

'Busy? You're kiddin'? It's stratospheric!' Maurice was amazed at her apparent naivety. 'Ma'am, I ain't never seen nothin' like it. There's folks backin' up five blocks and countin' and there's a two-block line for the restaurant.'

'What do you mean?'

'What I said. People queuein' for Reincarnate. Yer got two lines: one you're payin' out on, one payin' you. Sweet, huh?' The marshal laughed. 'Sweeter still when there's more in the second.'

The wail of several police sirens could be heard in the distance, their piercing noise cutting through the late afternoon air.

'Miss Millichamp, there's some news people outside want to interview you.' The young female bookings assistant appeared harassed.

'Yeah? I'll see them later.'

Miss Millichamp's reply left Maurice and the girl taken aback. The marshal recovered first.

'Ma'am, maybe you're not quite aware of what you've started here?' The distinctive howl of police sirens grew louder. 'What you've done is little short of revolutionary.'

'I thought it might be.'

The marshal flicked the numbered discs in the box. 'Well, if you think that, Miss Millichamp, you'll understand folks are goin' crazy out there.' Gazing out of the window, the marshal looked down at the street below. People were queuing in both directions as far as the eye could see. He turned back. 'Creating this business you've somehow connected with people and I'm not sure things are ever gonna be the same again.'

'Well, perhaps that's because no one's done it before.'

'Say that again. And it's out now, lady, right out the box!' Maurice flipped a disc and went to distribute.

Upstairs in the supply room, Mamie Riseveldt stood in front of a young woman checking in applicants waiting for medicals. Several staff wearing white coats flitted about and people went in and out of cubicles. On the far side of the room was the accounts section, where members of the general public who'd passed their fitness tests and signed their lives away were now receiving their $500 per head.

'My son was one of the original partners; guess I might as well get a little somethin' out of the business before I go join him.'

'And we know his colleague, the chef; we were friends of his late aunt – a dear, kind woman, much missed.' Wilbur was ingratiating. The young woman looked at their completed forms.

'Alrighty. I see you folks have filled everything out. If you'd go to cubicle three, ma'am; you number seven, sir; you, madam, and you, sir, will be seen in just a minute.' This to Wally and Ruby. Ruby eyed up a handsome young medic.

'Do we get to choose the doc?'

Under Maurice's instructions, marshals on Jane Street had been distributing numbered discs to people in the 'Supply' queue who weren't going to get seen that evening, and the hobo group were amongst those who wouldn't make it. Handing them their discs, the young marshal offered to take their completed forms.

'Wanna leave those with me?'

'Do we shit!' Flam was contemptuous, an attitude the

young marshal ignored. 'Speed it up tomorrow.'

The marshal moved on down the line of disappointed hopefuls. With the police presence getting nearer, Arthur and Battery looked at each other, and at a sign from Leon the vagrants began to slip away. Their attempt at financial remuneration frustrated, their mood was dark.

In the kitchen, staff were so exhausted it was as if they'd been under attack, and in their fatigued daze they too heard the police sirens. Reducing heat under a pan (even now ReIncarnate's chef de cuisine was preparing for the evening), Raymond stood back. Seeing him swaying and weary, Feydor Gaultier, coming off duty, intervened.

'M'sieur, pihenned kell. You must rest.'

Raymond looked at the maitre d' through red-rimmed eyes.

'Ha! All those years ago. Father T at the Stan. Never figured you were Hungarian, though.'

'Half. My mother. My father was French-Canadian. They split up when I was born. She came south – like you, a Hungarian émigré in New York City.'

'Full of 'em. Must be more ghettos here than thirties Berlin.'

'Interesting choice of city. I heard our former colleague is involved in a restaurant there; he and the Frenchman.'

'What a duo. Still, guess that's what they said about me and Riseveldt.'

'Oh no, m'sieur. Your originality's in a whole different league.'

Raymond smiled thinly. The whine of police sirens approaching, Feydor regarded a drop of wine that had splashed onto his waistcoat disdainfully. With impeccable sangfroid, Gaultier produced a slim, silver cigarette case.

Flicking it open, he revealed half a dozen perfectly rolled joints. Taking one, Raymond smiled. The maitre d' indicated they should step out through the rear exit.

In spite of the front of house tumult, they lit up peacefully in the back lane. Experiencing the drug for several seconds, Gaultier turned to the chef.

'M'sieur Raymond, your attitude towards the new management and its intentions was always circumspect. If I am correct, you were right to be so.' Raymond drew heavily on his spliff, holding the marijuana in his lungs. 'As I believe you had foreseen, very shortly things will implode.'

Leaning against his car, Raymond stared at the ground.

'Whatever Miss Millichamp may say about her legal rights, the police will shut her down.' Exhaling, Raymond now considered Feydor. 'They'll find something. They won't allow people to eat each other.'

Raymond actually laughed – and it wasn't hysterical. 'Why not? They do in every other sense.'

'Very true, M'sieur but they still won't allow it.'

Raymond took another draw on his joint. 'You must be pretty appalled, Feydor. What I've done. Me, just a kid from St Stanislaus. You were a prefect, for chris'sakes!' Raymond finished the joint.

Taking a final pull on his own, Gaultier nipped the dead reefer, flicking its dying ember into the gutter. 'I admit when things came out they...disturbed me. But for a shorter time than you may think. When I considered the situation, I felt profoundly moved.' The maitre d' eyed the chef levelly. 'You are a genius, M'sieur. To do what you did, whilst some would say it had a grotesque side, you created the best food in Manhattan. You created haute cuisine.'

'Kind of you to say so.'

'But Monsieur Raymond, you must go now. The police will be here any minute. I suggest you and Miss McKindrick slip away. If you take your car, the marshals can let you out through the side street.'

'That's very considerate of you, but where I'm goin' doesn't require a vehicle.'

'M'sieur?'

'Feydor, the police can't get here fast enough for my liking. When the old woman showed up you don't know how relieved I was. Then when she announced what she was gonna do...manna from heaven.'

Tabitha appeared in the doorway holding Tutti's hand. The monkey skipped over to the two men and Tabitha walked across the lane to the rear wall, where she lit a cigarette.

'You said I didn't think it could last, but how fast it's all happenin' – amazin' and terrifyin' how folks reacted.'

Gaultier stared at Raymond. 'You're going to turn yourself in?'

'She wants me to,' he nodded at Tabitha, 'and the sleep I'm gonna catch up on in that pen... Can't wait.'

Tutti scampered up onto Raymond's car and the chef stroked the monkey's chin. 'Anyway, seeing how things are lookin', I have a favour to ask.' Gaultier waited. 'I'd like you to remove all the security video and keep it safe.' Raymond took a billfold from his pocket and, removing several notes of large denomination, handed them to the maitre d'. 'Some authority's gonna want it back sometime so please dupe and replace. Nothing sinister, I promise. You have my word.'

A slightly quizzical look on his face, Gaultier took the money, gave his habitual little nod and the two men shook hands. Gaultier then went inside and Raymond and Tutti walked over to Tabitha. The chef put his arm round the young woman, but was disturbed by a call in the street.

'Hey, mother! It's you!'

Raymond turned and looked up the alley. Led by Homaster, the vagrant villains were advancing.

'Yeah, you with the monkey. I know you. You're the drunk that did the guy that night.'

'Accidental. And you tried to shoot me. Deliberate.' Raymond stepped in front of Tabitha protectively.

'So you sent yer goon round, who we took care of. Punk!' Close now, Homaster spat out the last word.

'I know you. You're one of the guys we used to give food to at The Cat.' Tabitha showed no regard for any potential danger, and it was noticeable that whilst normally the hobos attacked as a pack, this time the others hung back, most of all Leon. 'Yeah, I remember you all right. So you did for Mr Riseveldt, huh? No coppin' a plea for that one.'

Laughing in sinister derision at Tabitha's attitude, Homaster moved in. 'It's cookie boy who's gonna swing.'

'Swing, no. But goin' down he will be. You'll have it comin' too, though, pal.'

'Big words from a little lady. Could be you ain't many more left.' A blade appeared neatly in Homaster's hand.

'Drop it!' Feydor Gaultier stood in the kitchen door, a .38 Bodyguard in his hand. 'With your buddies.'

Homaster laughed some more. 'What have we here? Dressed to kill, huh?'

'It works, and the safety is off.'

'Haha! – regular little Manson, aren't we?'

'Hikey! Outta here!' Perhaps the gentlest of the bunch, Arthur's utterance fell on deaf ears.

'Let's see if yer got it, pal.'

Shrouded by a lightning move of Angel's and Battery's, Homaster was grasped and spun up the alley with his companions.

'Yer put us in a bad place, man.' Leon was subdued.

'Shit!'

'No shit, Homaster! We didn't get no money – that's shit!' Flam spat.

'Anythin' with you's always trouble, Hikey.'

'And people know yer.'

The gang surrounded Homaster and now swung out into the irate crowd.

Surging along Greenwich Street, one thwarted body vendor spoke to another: 'Way I heard it, Chef Babchuk's liable for manslaughter.'

The man he was talking to laughed. 'Appropriate – the slaughter of man!' Chuckling, the recent queuer nearly tripped and saving himself, looked down at a dead Homaster. 'I'd check demand, pal, before keelin' over.'

Amidst the heaving throng, five remorseless hobos threaded their way into oblivion.

In Jane Street, the line for Restaurant ReIncarnate was still surprisingly good-natured. Since the place didn't reopen for another hour, Miss Millichamp had relieved Pansy of her administrative responsibilities to work the folk patiently waiting for tables. She had printed off a flyer explaining how the setup operated, and these were now being distributed.

'So why're yer not open all day?'

'Sir, the type of restaurant we are isn't like that.'

'I'll say it ain't!' The guy got some laughs for this.

Pansy smiled. 'I mean, sir, the sort of quality place we

are, we serve lunch and dinner separately – bookings only.'

'Well that, young lady, is gonna have to change, or you're gonna have to open another restaurant.' This from a more sophisticated man.

Pansy looked at him for a second then, speaking more generally to people nearby, she said, 'We're fully booked tonight. There may be one or two no shows and we'll do what we can to accommodate, but I can tell you now we will not be able to oblige many of you. I'll make a note of names and addresses, and we will advise people on availability, but folks, please don't waste your time queuing back there. I'm sorry but you've no chance of getting in.' What she didn't say was there was no chance of getting a table at Restaurant ReIncarnate for the next six months!

Emerging from the 'Supply' entrance, some of the last people to depart successfully with their bodily worth in dollars included Mamie, Wilbur, Wally and Ruby, smiling and laughing as they walked away down the marshal-controlled exit lane.

Chapter 36

Inside Carmen's little office, a crisis meeting was in progress between the manager, Miss Millichamp and Julie. Of Tabitha, Raymond and Gaultier there was no sign.

'It's gone crazy. The police are comin' and things are gonna erupt.' Carmen drew hard on her cigarette.

'Let them come. I'll deal with the police.' Belinda was unperturbed.

'Miss Millichamp, I'm glad they're here. Things are gettin' out of control and people are gonna get hurt. It's like the whole of New York either want to sell their bodies or eat themselves.'

'Eatin' each other. Who'd've thought it?' Julie was philosophical.

'Are you really surprised? You know how we always love the latest of everything, how we like to be first.' Finishing her cigarette, Carmen sat back exhaling.

'Thought we'd handed that over to the Chinese.'

'Suggestin' we open there?' In spite of their situation, Julie and Carmen couldn't help smiling at Miss Millichamp.

Feydor Gaultier put his head round the door.

'Ah the smartest maitre d' in town. Things ready for opening tonight?'

'That may be difficult, madame. Right now Monsieur Raymond is giving himself up to the police.'

'He's what?'

'Turnin' himself in, is he? I'm not surprised.' It was Julie who spoke. 'RIP, Miss Millichamp. It's been a wuz.'

'RIP be damned!' Miss Millichamp went to the door and, pushing past Gaultier, strode out.

The two crowds surrounding the ^{Re}Incarnate building had thinned a little, people responding to the arrival of the police, who would probably bring an end to the business being transacted inside. But although their numbers had marginally decreased, the people's mood had intensified. In spite of Pansy's advice to those queuing for the restaurant, the line continued to wait and now a chant started up:

'Human meat! Human meat! There ain't no other but human meat! Human meat! We wanna eat, we gotta eat – human meat! Human meat!'

It was as if something had happened to the people of New York; something had been triggered. There's a moment when people and their behaviour flip, and that had now occurred. As if on cue, Raymond, Tabitha and Tutti – the humans still in their chef's apparel – emerged onto the street. Whether it was Raymond's notoriety or that the restaurant door had been unlocked, people jostled towards them.

'You the chef?'

Raymond nodded.

'Where are you goin'? You're needed back in there, pal!'

Marshals were swept aside as things became more aggressive.

'Cook, cook, cook! Fry, fry, fry! Eat, eat, eat – human meat! There ain't no other but human meat!'

People were going wild as the NYPD came onto the

scene, overreacting as only police can. Members of the riot squad turned water cannon on the crowd, also firing smoke canisters into nearby streets. The whole area erupted in bedlam. Dogs, armed cops – it was deadly conflict, albeit one side had most of the weapons. Into this mêlée stepped Lieutenant Garside. In spite of the law-enforcing measures taken, many in the crowd were reluctant to disperse and fierce fighting arose, police using their shields and batons to force their way through and surround the restaurant building. As the situation became more secure, Garside threaded his way through the police cordon, finally confronting the two humans and a monkey seeking refuge, wet and bedraggled, sheltering in the doorway of Restaurant ^{Re}Incarnate.

'Kill that!'

The water cannon abruptly stopped. Raymond, Tabitha and Tutti emerged, dishevelled and dripping.

'Hi. We met before.' Garside addressed Tutti. The monkey chattered, though more likely through cold than pleasure.

Raymond stepped forward. 'Lieutenant, I wish to give myself up to the police.'

'On what grounds?'

'Killing Charles Reardon, sous-chef at *Le Chat Noir*, November twenty-second last.'

A man barged through the police chain, attempting to get to the restaurant. He was instantly apprehended. 'I demand to be let through. I'm dining here tonight.'

'Fully booked, pal.'

'But I reserved a table!'

'Tough! Police social. No public.' Garside turned back to Raymond. 'So you killed this guy.'

'He attacked me and I ran him down in my car.'

'Accident, then.'

'I'd been drinking.'

'You bad boy.'

Raymond smiled.

'What's so funny?'

'Strange. The bum who witnessed it used the same phrase.'

'Someone saw it?'

'He was here just now.'

'Here?'

'Out back.'

Garside looked around. 'Didn't try to remove him?' Garside looked back at Raymond, who met his gaze.

'Serve him up, you mean?'

Another customer appeared. 'Why can't I eat here?'

'Food's off.' Garside was sharp.

'Not what I heard.'

'Well, they just stopped serving it!'

'Why?'

'Look, buddy – scram!'

The would-be punter was feisty. 'This is America – land of the free.'

'Punk, outta here before I arrest you!' Garside sighed. 'Seems they like your food.'

Raymond neither smiled nor was contrite, and his reply was received in a similarly neutral fashion by the NYPD lieutenant.

'I did try and tell you.'

Belinda Millichamp appeared.

'Officer, I'm Belinda Millichamp, proprietor of this establishment. I demand to know what's happening here. You're upsetting my business and disturbing my clientele.'

'And you're disturbing the police, ma'am – violations 415 and 517.'

'Disturbance and Public Nuisance. I know my rights, young man. I'm doing no such thing. Barging in here with water cannon and tear gas; you think this is some third-world banana republic?'

'Two queues, a mile long each, in Lower Manhattan, ma'am, is what I think this is, and that's a disturbance of the peace.'

'Well, they're dissipating now, so if you'd kindly remove your officers, my people can get back to work.'

'No can do, ma'am. This gentleman's just given himself up into my custody.'

Miss Millichamp looked at Raymond. 'On what grounds?'

'On account of he killed a man some ten months ago.'

'Is this true, Raymond?'

'Sure is, Miss Millichamp.' Raymond seemed positively pleased with his admission.

'I'm sure it was an accident.'

'Alcohol was involved, Miss Millichamp, and there's a case to answer.' Garside indicated to a couple of officers, who stepped forward, one placing handcuffs around Raymond's wrists.

Thwarted, Miss Millichamp fumed.

'Don't say anything, Raymond, till I've called my lawyer.'

'Now, I'd like to take a look at your premises.' The lieutenant was brisk.

'You have a warrant?'

'As long as your arm, lady.'

'Show me.'

'Inside.' Garside turned to Raymond. 'Hey, Babchuk, both Chief Giantelli and Captain Manifest said yer food was to die for.'

The look Raymond gave Garside was long and considered, as if he was contemplating something. 'See yer at the precinct later.'

In custody, Raymond turned to Tabitha. 'Keep an eye on Tutti for me, will yer?'

'That all you gotta say by way of a partin'?'

'No. Go live in my place. Yer got keys – it's yours.'

'Yer mean that?'

'No. It's a joke. Course I mean it.'

Tabitha kissed her handcuffed man. 'Why do they always say that lawyer stuff?'

'In case yer incriminate yerself.' Raymond had a good laugh. 'Counsel should have a field day, the amount of incrimination I face.'

'I don't think so. There's a lotta mitigation.'

'Yer reckon? We'll see. Hey, Tutti!' The monkey leapt onto Raymond's shoulder and blew the biggest of bubble gum bubbles.

'Neat trick!' The softer cop was impressed.

'Should see his smoke rings.'

'Yuh? Decent Havana?'

'The best!'

Taking Tutti's hand, Tabitha prised the little monkey from the chef's shoulder.

'Don't let him smoke all of 'em.'

Turning back to Restaurant ReIncarnate, Raymond looked at the building. Standing on the step, Carmen, Gaultier, Aldo, Luke and most of the staff not only waved but saluted him.

'Maestro!'

Arnold Riseveldt never ended up on a plate in his restaurant, nor did he get eaten by his mother. The following day she and her friends paid their respects to him in just as surreal a fashion at RIP.

In spite of the fact that a court case would ensue involving the late mortician, the New York City coroner decided there was no reason to delay Arnold's being laid to rest, and Julie Dominic spared no expense putting on the full works in a glowing farewell tribute to her late boss. Still resplendent in his tux and flashed patent leather boots – he looked the business.

'Probably wouldn't have had to put him under for another six months, the amount o' preservin' chemicals in him,' Manny remarked. 'Lovely job though – he'd have appreciated the glazed finish and wax sheen. Spectacular.'

Fittingly, the ceremony was held in RIP's Chapel of Peace, presided over by Jesse-Lou Townsend, the Reverend having become friends with the mortician after laying Renais Ringegold to rest.

'Such a nice young man; such a moving service.' Mamie Riseveldt continued her peaceful ways until her own end some years hence; surrounded by a troubled world, her calm persona would always remain forever tranquil.

All Mamie's old friends were there – Wally, Wilbur, and Ruby, who sported a bizarre froufrou dress and bright multi-coloured leggings: 'Got to spend some o' that five hundred bucks!' The entire RIP workforce turned out, though whether this was from respect for their erstwhile boss or the fact that Julie decreed those who attended could have a day off work was moot. The surprise visitors were Tabitha McKindrick, bringing Balàzs Malursk and Tutti along in the old T-Bird, which thundered onto the forecourt, the sous-chef's pumps covering the gas and brake pedals and the monkey smoking all the way. It was a service to remember.

It had disappointed Mamie her son wasn't to be used

to feed people in his restaurant; having intrinsically, she felt, understood her boy's revolutionary business concept, she knew he'd have appreciated the gesture, though it was somewhat lost on her friends, who viewed Mamie's serenity after Arnold's brutal passing with some consternation. Her attempt to secure the mastication of his body by his restaurant clientele having been thwarted, Mamie decided if he wasn't to be eaten by a human mouth no worm would devour him, and Arnold Mordechai Riseveldt was cryogenically frozen in a Perspex surround, preserved for evermore and perhaps be resurrected if organ repair became feasible in decades to come! Several people exchanged glances during the ceremony, in particular Julie and Tabitha, recently briefly colleagues, each with their very particular memories.

Mamie had written a rather bizarre hymn dedicated to her beloved son, which she insisted was played. Set to the tune of 'The Old Hundredth', its lyrics included lines such as 'Eat your way to Calvary, food is on the cross' and 'Feed the babes and hungry, flesh of human carnate golden on its plate'. Such lyrics guaranteed a few raised eyebrows, but most sang lustily enough. In his closing address, the Reverend Jesse-Lou paid tribute to the unique mortician and restaurateur.

'"Embalm his name in glory,
Preservin' life for us.
Feedin' all his children,
A table booked, no fuss..." Words he would have loved, a sentiment he'd have respected.'

So it was that Arnold was placed in RIP's reception wearing his unique raiment, standing in the glass alcove, back-lit, a western boot with its RIP flash resting on a catafalques side. The inscription underneath:

Arnold Mordechai Riseveldt
Death his Inspiration – RIP

A truly comforting welcome.
'It's where he'd want to be, his presence everlasting.'
Mamie was radiant.

Chapter 37

The courthouse was standing room only for one of the most renowned hearings in American history. Jurors and the packed gallery heard of the weird, if not wonderful, goings on in the life of a brilliant young chef, compromised by a twisted mortician. But not everyone saw the late Arnold Riseveldt quite that way. Some took the view his was a profoundly innovative mind, unifying two distinct professions and creating a uniquely successful business model. That one should profit from such a bizarre enterprise was called into doubt. Relatives of the deceased whose post-mortem needs had been managed by RIP at the time Restaurant Incarnate began trading discussed exhumation, becoming aware the remains were likely to be considerably less than they would otherwise have supposed. In the early stages of the operation, Arnold had been careful to use only deceased folk due for cremation, and relations who still had unscattered ashes were invited to submit them for analysis. However, DNA and cinders are uncomfortable evidential bedfellows and any results obtained proved inconclusive. Things really began to hot up when probing the venture's murderous turn.

'Mr Babchuk, when did you come to learn Mr Riseveldt had hired a killer to, er, increase the supplies of your restaurant's very particular food type?'

'People, yer mean? 'Bout six months ago.'

'And what did you do?'

'Used 'em.'

There was dark amusement in court, which did not please the judge.

'The court will refrain from jocularity or flippancy during proceedings. This is a serious and evil crime, and one that will be dealt with appropriately during this trial. Proceed.'

The prosecution did so.

'Did you try to stop him; try to prevent your partner's actions?'

'Objection, your honour. Such a question is prejudicial against my client. Mr Babchuk is not being tried for murdering anybody. The prosecution is suggesting Mr Babchuk was involved in these killings when we know for a fact he was not.'

The lawyer Miss Millichamp had provided to defend Raymond, Mr Jeffry Marigold, matched the case he was involved with perfectly. Cadaverous, with a nasally, sonorous voice, he was very tall and his angular face and elongated neck gave him a giraffe-like appearance. The prosecution, by contrast, represented by Mr Gilbenkin Schwartz, was just the opposite; a rotund individual of medium height, Mr Schwartz had a compellingly energised presence. Both were excellent legal brains, though on occasion the prosecution would find itself lured in a particular direction only to be destroyed by Marigold in a swift and devastating, if hyenal, riposte. They were well-matched combatants.

'The case concerning the death of Mr Reardon is yet to be decided, but it has been established Mr Babchuk had no part in the deaths of the hired assassin's victims, Mr Schwartz.'

'I simply wish to establish complicity, your honour. Was the defendant aware of his partner's actions and, if so, whether he took any action to prevent them.'

'Sustained. You'll answer the question, Mr Babchuk.'

'And how would I have done that?' Raymond reluctantly made eye contact.

'I ask the questions here, sir. It's for you to answer them.'

'We were in a crisis. We were runnin' outta supplies. He said he'd do somethin' about it.'

'And you were aware he hired an assassin?' This was said with that 'between question and statement' intonation.

'Objection.'

'Mr Babchuk.' The judge was becoming impatient.

'Guess I figured he must have been doin' something like that.'

'You figured he must have been doing something like that...' Schwartz looked down at some papers.

Raymond didn't respond.

'I suggest, Mr Babchuk, that not only were you aware of your partner's murderous activities, but by your actions you provoked them.'

'Hiring Grimaldi? Why would I want to get involved with a goon like him?'

'So you know the assassin Mr Riseveldt hired?'

'No, I do not. I met him once, that's all.'

'And?'

'And nothing. The guy was crazy – dressed in spats and stuff, carrying a violin case. Thought he was Al Capone.'

'Whatever he thought he was, he also carried a powerful handgun and was responsible for taking the lives of a great many people.'

'Still a crazy old guy, if you ask me.'

'We're not asking you, Mr Babchuk.'

Raymond ignored Schwartz's interruption.

'Miss Millichamp told me he got into people's places as a musical instrument repair man, even played to 'em. Good thing she got rid of the old gangster.'

'We'll be coming onto that later.'

Raymond's performance was interesting. Prior to the astounding revelations surrounding Restaurant Incarnate, his culinary reputation had been confined to the greater Manhattan area. Belinda Millichamp publicising and launching, albeit briefly, Restaurant ReIncarnate revealed Raymond had potentially been in line for a Michelin star. He was catapulted first into national consciousness then onto the international stage.

'*The man who cooked humans; the best chef in the world!*' ran the *New York Herald Tribune*; '*The Mammon of haute cuisine – five star chef!*' said *The Times*. Nightly news bulletins of the trial had the American public glued to their television screens as the rights and wrongs of cooking and serving human flesh was debated. To some it was a heinous activity; others took a very different view. Quite apart from reaching the heights of haute cuisine Raymond had achieved, several public figures saw it as a way of potentially solving the world's food shortage. Eating human meat would have to become legalised: 'I mean, the meat tastes real good, man – I'm tellin yer, I tried it!'

'So now we come to the culinary side of the enterprise. More your sort of thing, I guess.' Marigold's reedy voice, magnified by the microphone, reverberated round the Rhadamanthine chamber. 'Can you tell the court what it's like to work with such...raw material? It must have been quite, er, particular.'

'Yer mean human flesh?'

Marigold nodded. The court attendants gawped. Raymond sighed.

'Once you've truncated the torso, separated out the limbs, it's pretty much like any other meat.'

Even Marigold, who'd heard just about everything, gulped.

'Where was this...activity carried out?'

'South Side. Old morgue lock-up, where the supplies are.'

'Does any..."stock" remain?'

'Undismembered? About seventy bodies, last count. There was a big delivery the other night from RIP.'

Somehow, the information held a fascination for the lawyer as well as for the greater public at large.

'Let's understand this. You kept cadavers in an old mortuary where you then dismembered them in preparation for use in your restaurant?'

'Correct.' Raymond was crisp now.

'How were they stored? Frozen? I mean...'

'Not the past tense, Mr Marigold. Like I said, they're still there.' You could have heard a pin drop. 'We have the highest standards. Nobody ever came away sick from one of my meals. Ask Chief Giantelli. He and Captain Manifest ate offal – starter and main – both of them.'

Marigold looked green. 'No, no further questions.'

That night, news crews were up at Amsterdam Place, from where the main bulletin was broadcast. Though much was shielded from the public and film cameras, brief images of police handling gurneys and gowned forensic specialists at work were glimpsed, the news being relayed round the world. New Yorkers dining off human flesh was becoming a global story.

*

Julie Dominic frequently attended court and as proceedings continued, revealing the increasingly dark twists and turns her late boss's life had taken, she began to fear the publicity surrounding his conduct would have an adverse effect on the parlour. She needn't have worried. The complete opposite happened. Many people became keen to bring their deceased loved ones to RIP, whose notoriety they felt to be unique. Rather than being upset by the late proprietor's behaviour, clients appeared to consider their dead relatives privileged Riseveldt's Interments would manage their earthly departure. And this in spite of Riseveldt having preceded them the way he had. Interest wasn't only confined to America, either; sheiks from Araby and gunmen from Russia queued up to fly their relatives into Long Island. Now, as she sat in court listening to Miss Millichamp being interrogated by the prosecution about her escape from the bullet fired from Jack Grimaldi's hand gun, Julie reflected on the profound legacy Arnold Riseveldt had left behind.

'But you'd nearly been shot dead by this man's hired assassin, a gunman entering your apartment under the false pretence of retuning your piano?'

'No false pretence about it. He did retune it. In fact, it's never played sweeter.'

The court chuckled.

'Even so, Miss Millichamp, this man Riseveldt hired Grimaldi to kill you. You don't condone that surely?'

'Damn right I don't condone it, but I did something about it, didn't I?'

'Indisputably.'

'Ha! Not a word I often hear a lawyer use.'

More amusement in the courtroom. Gilbenkin Schwartz continued.

'So, what led you to take the...unusual steps you did afterwards?'

Miss Millichamp considered. 'Well, discounting what he'd tried to have done to me – no small discount, I grant you – I figured he was on to something. I also had a guy who's about the greatest goddamn chef in the world.'

'I *am* the greatest goddamn chef in the world!' Raymond's outburst caused further interruption and the judge threatened to ban him from the court. 'Yer can't do that, yer honour; I'm the accused.'

'I can do what I goddamn like in my own court!' The 'goddamns' flying around, Judge Threadneedle was in an uncompromising mood. 'You'll behave in the proper manner or be removed. Continue, Miss Millichamp.'

'I'd read about the restaurant – how people had been trying unsuccessfully to get a table there; it was the "in" restaurant. Why, as we know, even senior police officers and the mayor of this fine city were begging to be allowed to eat there. And the food they were devouring...' Belinda helped herself to a glass of water. 'Till I discovered the real truth in such a...particular way, I figured me and Mr Babchuk were the only two people alive who knew what all those folks sitting enjoying their fine meals were actually paying for with their business accounts and American Express cards. Yes sir, I thought it was a mighty interesting business proposition all right.'

'And advertising the rights to people's bodies on their deaths to use as food?' Schwartz was bemused.

'Judge–!' Marigold objected.

'Er, no.'

'Okay, Mr Schwarzenegger – whatever your name is – think about it; the waste, the point of all the fuss around death.' Belinda sat back in her chair in the dock. 'I don't know whether you're Muslim, Jewish, Christian, believe in the afterlife or a cat swingin' off a tree. It's none of my business, neither. But something I do know is there's a lot of hungry people around, and I also reckon this old earth and America face big problems feeding them all. So you tell me, Mr Smart Ass Lawyer, what's wrong with giving people on the streets some money to feed themselves, and feeding them to others when they're dead and no more use to anybody – if you'll pardon the word? Now you answer me that!'

The court erupted, clapping and hollering, but Miss Millichamp hadn't quite finished.

'Sure, the mortician was out of line hiring the killer, but in every other way the guy was a downright genius!'

Things now got completely out of hand and Judge Threadneedle had to call in the wardens to calm the court. Even then people refused to sit down, and proceedings were adjourned for the day. That night's viewing ratings climbed into many millions, making it one of the most watched news stories of all time.

'As to Restaurant Reincarnate, I find the terms of closure upheld and a fine of $100,000 be effected, the restaurant to cease trading forthwith.' Judge Threadneedle moved some papers to one side and picked up others. 'In the case of the death of Charles Reardon, the court finds Raymond Babchuk guilty of manslaughter, a sentence of three years being imposed, the term to be served in a secure place of confinement for a minimum of eighteen months, at which time he may apply for parole. This sentence is passed in the judiciary of New York City by me, Matthias Thread-needle, Circuit Judge, Fourteenth district. The court will rise.'

The judge's gavel banged down; the case was over.

Outside on the step, Belinda Millichamp said she would file an appeal against the judge's ruling enforcing the restaurant's closure and would also instruct her lawyer to start work on Raymond's. As he was led away from the dock, the prisoner didn't seemed particularly distressed; indeed, had one been very astute one might have almost said he looked happy, his face bland but his eyes twinkling. Raising his manacled wrists, Raymond attempted a wave to the court, especially Tabitha who had been there every day. She now whipped out a big photograph of Tutti smoking a cigar, holding it high above her head.

Emerging into the corridor, Chief Giantelli and Captain Manifest walked slowly towards the court lobby, watching Miss Millichamp surrounded by reporters and press outside.

'Quite the most astounding case I ever witnessed.'

'Or gave evidence at.' Captain Manifest eyed his boss briefly.

'Certainly. But you know, Doctrinal, I wouldn't have missed that meal for the world. Would you?'

'Nope. Not even for the criticism afterwards. Neat move, advisin' how the mayor was so keen.'

'Why do you think it wasn't pressed?' Chief Giantelli was rhetorical. For several seconds the two policemen stood watching the scene below. Miss Millichamp wasn't alone in being mobbed for interviews; several other key witnesses and participants – Carmen, Luke and Aldo, and some representatives of RIP, Julie Dominic and Manny – were also targeted.

The Chief sighed. 'Talkin' of the mayor, even though we got rapped, he's still jealous as hell.' He took a Restaurant ReIncarnate condiment set from his pocket: a pair of hands entwined, salt ran through purple fingers, pepper from black thumbs. The scripted logo was embossed on each. Made from an inexpensive ceramic, the unusual design had a cheap charm. 'Know what this is worth?'

''Bout twenty cents.'

'You're kiddin'? Last I heard these were going for seven hundred dollars a set on eBay, and rising!'

Doctrinal Manifest laughed. Having had enough of watching the chaos outside, the policemen headed for a side exit.

'How long d'you think our boy'll be in?'

'Eighteen months, if he's unlucky.'

'Didn't look too troubled with the verdict.'

'Ha! Kid needs a break. So long, Doc. I gotta go see our illustrious government officer and give him the lowdown on all this.'

As the chief of police and police captain parted, Manifest called out, 'Keep him sweet – why don't yer let him have the condiments as a memento?'

'Over my dead body!'

A few days later, Carmen, Feydor Gaultier, Julie Dominic and Miss Millichamp met at Raymond's house on Palmetto Street. The meeting was hosted by Tabitha McKindrick, who appeared to have rediscovered her more balanced and practical attitude to life. Tabitha's importance had increased dramatically since Raymond's incarceration, the latter having given her power of attorney during his enforced absence. Her involvement was thus critical for any management decision made. It was agreed the foreclosing costs would be covered from funds still in the restaurant's very healthy bank account. In spite of the money Reincarnate Realigned had handed out during those heady few hours, Restaurant Incarnate, as managed by Raymond and Riseveldt, had been fantastically successful and there were still hundreds of thousands of dollars sitting on deposit.

Several of the meeting's participants gained a change of career during the trial. Julie Dominic established herself as chief executive of Riseveldt's Interment Parlour and was now driving the business forward. When negotiating her position with the company, Julie brought Mamie Riseveldt in as chairwoman emeritus. This masterstroke met with universal approval and global orders were now coming RIP's way. Other parlours were planned opening along the Eastern Seaboard that fall, and the international division expanded. Their new letterhead logo was inspirational – Riseveldt's cryogenic image proudly embossed, complete with motto.

Carmen acquired an agent, was a popular guest on chat shows and intended writing a book about her experience. Miss Millichamp, also now under an agent's management, had been invited onto the lecture circuit speaking on human food chain issues – Harvard, Berkeley and Stanford already snapping her up. Tabitha's romantic involvement with Raymond being public knowledge – she was living in his house, driving his car and looking after his monkey – her plans appeared vague. She'd been upset at Raymond's refusal to see her when dispatched to Woodbourne Penitentiary, a prison of medium security in Sullivan County some hundred miles from the city, where he was to begin his sentence. But he'd reassured her it was not for lack of love, more that he needed some time to himself, coming to terms with what had happened, what he'd done.

If Tabitha's plans were on hold, Feydor Gaultier's were

obscure. All he'd say was that he intended to take a break and see how things fell in the months to come. Leaving them now, Miss Millichamp looked up at him.

'One thing, Feydor: do you know anything about the disappearance of security footage from the restaurant? I was asked about it by that punk lieutenant.' Miss Millichamp's attitude toward the police and their determination to shut the business down hadn't softened any.

'I do, madam. In the turmoil, Mr Raymond asked me to keep the material safe. I've done so and the CCTV footage has now been sent to the police.'

'Why'd he ask you to do a thing like that?'

'I wouldn't know, madam. I'm sure he had his reasons.'

'I'm sure he did. So long, Feydor. Stay smart.'

A slight smile, the clipped bow and Gaultier was gone.

'He is the darndest, most attractive man I ever saw.'

'Why, Miss Millichamp!' Carmen laughed. 'Another drink?'

Chapter 38

A grey day, with grey people in grey mood. Rain beat down on the windows of the grey Woodbourne Penitentiary as Balázs Malursk alighted from the bus (also grey), gathering his raincoat collar around his neck and leaning against the weather. Arriving at the gate, Mr Balázs was admitted and conducted to the visitors' waiting area. Summoned from the TV room where he was watching still more news on the restaurant's demise, Raymond had been amazed his story continued to run.

TV stations, low on anything original the principal participants might have said, were in desperation resorting to interviews with less intimate colleagues and associates. Standing under guard, Raymond watched Frank Chesson and Alain de Lange being interviewed about his time at *Le Chat Noir*; both were singing his praises, affirming their dismissal of Chef de Cuisine Pierre-Auguste and still offering Raymond the maestro's post should he wish to consider it on his release.

In the visiting room, prisoner 978678 sat down opposite Mr Balázs, the two separated by a glass partition. Balázs spoke in Hungarian.

'Ah, Raymond, good to see you. I thought we might converse in our native tongue, if you can manage it. Give us a little privacy.'

'Rusty, but do me good. Let's give it a try.'

318

'You boys mind speaking in English?' The disembodied voice emitted from a little speaker on the dividing counter.

'Mine, it isn't so good. We...we're both from Hungary.' Mr Balázs, whose English was better than many native-born Americans, acted both hesitant and courteous. There was a grunt from the speaker.

'We'll assume that's a yes, then.' And off they went.

It was amazing how quickly Raymond was able to revert to his native tongue and soon the two were chatting away in privacy and intimacy.

'I didn't come to the court much. I found I had some issues with the proceedings and didn't want to say anything that might compromise you.'

Raymond looked at his hands. 'You'd have had to be called.'

'And I didn't want to risk it.' Mr Balázs eyed Raymond. 'Why did you decide to feed that man to your aunt?'

Raymond didn't reply.

'Did you really hate her that much?'

'Well, two reasons. Yup, I did hate her that much and I was... The night's events had left me pretty unstable. Seemed like a good idea at the time.'

'An excellent idea. Prophetic, an epiphany.' Balázs's words surprised the prisoner but not as much as his next. 'It paved the way for your inimitable place in American culture.'

'That's running it a bit high.'

'Not at all. What you've done has really had an effect on people. You think this is gonna go away? It's just the start. You created something – something unique. Not a lot of people do that.'

'But it wasn't my idea.'

'Maybe not, but you were party to it.'

'I thought he was crazy.'

'The mortician? From what I hear, your partner was a lot of things but not crazy.'

'Hiring the killer?'

'That was a little extreme, but–'

'Little? Your attitude surprises me, Mr B, and I'm the one behind bars!'

Balázs laughed easily.

'Anyway, you didn't come out here just to sing my praises.' The different tone in Raymond's voice changed the mood.

'No. No, I didn't. Miss McKindrick, she's upset...'

'Yeah?'

'She hasn't heard from you and she wants to see you.'

'She knows how I feel about her, and if she doesn't, you tell her from me, she's free. You may also wish to tell her I don't feel good about seein' her right now. I'll do my time then we'll see. How's Tutti? Smoked all my cigars yet?' Raymond stood up; he was always a very exacting character.

'Miss McKindrick did say she reckoned it would be all right to sign a company cheque to renew his supply.'

Raymond smiled; he had a pleasant smile when he chose. He could be quite an attractive man, but was devoid of any self-awareness.

'Well, I said I'd ask.'

'By the way, they're movin' me.'

'Oh?'

'Ray Brook – Essex County – up in the Adirondacks.'

'That's miles.'

'About three hundred.'

'Do you have to go there?'

'Guess so. Anyway, I'm happy with it.'

'You sure?'

'Yup. Further the better. Look, I know you came here for Tab, and I appreciate yer visit, but I gotta serve my time and how I get through it is my business. Don't worry; I ain't tryin' to punish myself any more than I'm bein' punished, but that's how it is.' He took a pace then turned back. 'She all right, as a neighbour?'

'Fine. She loves you, Ray.'

Raymond gave the smallest of smiles and left.

'So do I, you strange émigré genius.'

Mr Balázs went back to New York City, Raymond to his cell.

Chapter 39

Settling into Ray Brook Penitentiary, Raymond began prison life in earnest – the monotony and dullness of confinement. But with his plans in place, he would become the very model of rectitude. It was early during his stay in this New York State penitentiary that Raymond had one of the few visitors he would receive until his parole came through (though later he would actually reject those who wished to see him, unless they came by prior agreement). Feydor Gaultier's visit, however, was a very particular call. Having carefully kept his black log books and deposited them with the maitre d' before his arrest, Raymond asked his friend for a variety of information and in the intervening weeks, Gaultier hadn't been idle. On arriving at the prison he'd left everything with security, Raymond having arranged a meeting with the governor that evening.

'Thank you, Feydor. If everything's there, you've given me my lifeline.'

Immaculate as always, Gaultier smiled slightly.

'You were able to contact Miss Friedland?'

'Yes. She was very helpful. Since she considers you the finest of chefs, she was pleased to assist in providing much of the information.' Gaultier flicked an imaginary piece of fluff from his coat. 'The newspaper reports on our ex-chef de cuisine are interesting.' He referred to Pierre-Auguste.

'It appears he's opening a restaurant in Europe – Berlin – with Monsieur Blanc.'

Raymond chuckled. 'When?'

'The details are in your package. I think early next year.'

'You okay?'

Gaultier didn't answer directly. 'May I ask what plans you might be considering upon your departure from this place?'

'You could ask.' Raymond smiled, so did Gaultier. It was one of their bonds. 'Although Reincarnate was closed down, there was thankfully never any time to change the bank account and having assigned Tabitha chequeing rights, I've instructed a payment be made to you from the Incarnate account for twenty-five thousand. If you need more, you're to contact her. Take a vacation or something. You earned it.' Raymond stood up to go.

'You're in touch with Miss McKindrick?'

'Sure. At my level, bein' inside doesn't mean I can't have outside contact. I just don't want to see her. I ain't okay right now and besides, thanks to you, I've got work to do.'

That night, the package Gaultier had delivered lay un-opened on the governor's desk. A guard stood by, but the atmosphere was comparatively relaxed.

'We scanned it o' course. Got a packet o' photographs on those sticks, fella.'

'I want to do some work, for myself. Writin'.'

'Yuh? And what sort of writin' might that be?'

'Notes at the moment. Life's been kinda busy lately.'

Governor Appomattox laughed. 'Yeah, saw it on the news. You've had an interestin' time. Gonna write a book about it?'

'Mebbe.'

'Hmm! From your few days here you don't seem too much trouble.' The governor sat back. ''Tell you what I'll do. Me an' Mrs A got some people comin' over for supper in a coupla weeks. She don't like to cook too much. Truth is, she ain't so good in the kitchen, though when yer meet her don't say I told you.' The governor laughed, the guard smirked. Raymond didn't respond. 'Now, you cook up some real good food at this repast, and I'll see if I can see my way clear for you to have this.' He tapped the parcel. 'Then if you continue to be on your best behaviour, some free time might come available for you to start yer writin' work. How does that sound?'

'Any particular type of cuisine?'

'Haha!! Yer hear that, Mulroyd – any particular line in the cuisine stakes? Guy's a chef all right.' Appomattox shot a glance at prison officer Mulroyd, who dutifully smiled. 'Over at the shack they give me for lookin' after you bad people, we eat pretty much anything we can get usin' food stamps.' It wasn't quite clear whether this was a joke or contained some truth, but then the governor laughed. 'Course we'll be givin' yer the ingredients!'

'Whatever you say. I could make a recommendation: *Cervelle de singe*, perhaps, to start?'

Appomattox and Mulroyd eyed the prisoner quizzically.

'Monkey brains.'

In fact, Governor Appommatox allowed Raymond to begin his work before the governor's supper party which, when it came, was a triumph – at least, food-wise. Mrs A turned out to be something of a flirtatious southern belle and quite what she was doing with the prison governor of a New York State penitentiary was a mystery to Raymond, not that it was something he spent too much time contemplating.

Back in his cell, Raymond examined his package. It was an extensive assortment. First his notebooks: A5 black moleskin, page after page of names and dates in neat columns, written in Raymond's meticulous spidery hand. Mostly in code, they listed names, dates of 'supply' delivery and diner bookings; in other words, they were the complete list of who ate whom, including the particular dish partaken. Ghoulish little volumes indeed.

The second item was CCTV footage taken from Restaurant Incarnate, frozen frames of which had been dropped on to several USB sticks. Booting up a computer that had arrived in his room during the afternoon, Raymond began spooling through the still images and interesting viewing it was, the files appearing like something from a 'Who's Who' of showbiz, politics – an A-to-Z of celebs from all walks of life: sports, literary, musical and the traditional professions – even religion was represented.

The combination of the moleskin notebooks and CCTV imagery were a compelling amalgam, the potential of its content dynamite. Rock stars eating poets, Jews eating Muslims and vice versa, politicians eating everyone; one mid-western congressman, known for his gargantuan tendencies, had managed to squeeze a table no less than seven times in the ten months Restaurant Incarnate existed, eating all comers – Republicans, Democrats, Mormons and Catholics. His tastes knew no bounds.

The final enclosure was another memory stick on which were scanned downloaded newspaper clippings relating to Pierre-Auguste Etienne, otherwise known as Peter Anthony Everard, and Louis Blanc. A report filed on their recent activities, it was this enclosure Raymond spent most time studying. It appeared that, after Raymond left *Le Chat Noir* and Reardon went missing, Frank Chesson and Alain de

Lange dismissed Pierre-Auguste for being the sham he was. Not really a maestro at all, he'd relied too heavily on the skills of others. Equally, Blanc found himself exposed as a result of his behaviour in trying to frame Raymond with Chef de France. The two had headed for Europe, settling in Berlin where they currently resided, planning the opening of their new restaurant, *L'Escargot Berliner*, in a few months' time. Raymond didn't think they were lovers – not that he cared – rather two halves of a pretentious and corrupt whole. He pondered on the comparison with himself and Riseveldt then reflected he and the late mortician had at least been a wholly original partnership. What had Balázs said? They'd made their mark, actually helping people think in another way. However their extraordinary behaviour was viewed – from genius to bizarre, from radically innovative to evil – Restaurant Incarnate would stand unique in the culinary history of America. Raymond would never forgive Blanc for trying to deprive him of the prize he'd been awarded. The recollection sat as intensely with him now, in his cell, as it had done when he'd found out a year or so ago.

The governor and his wife, having judged their recent dinner party a success, bid Raymond continue his not infrequent chef's duties alongside his personal preparation work. It soon became apparent, however, it wasn't only his cooking abilities that were required by Mrs Appomattox. The one thing Raymond Babchuk had never been was a lothario; in fact, with the exception of Tabitha McKindrick, with whom he had fallen in love, women didn't really interest him very much. Sexually, he had been profoundly affected by his lascivious and sluttish aunt, whose grotesque behaviour deeply seared his psyche. To Raymond, the physical act had simply been a lewd and filthy pastime, till Tabitha's recent love assuaged that. He'd also come a long way since those early days, surviving all the crazy experiences he'd endured. A woman's advances did not now put the fear of God in him as had once been the case. In fact, he was surprised the only effect the governor's wife had on him was to make him crave Tabitha's touch, and even more surprised at how easily he was able to handle the situation, despite Mrs Appommatox's frustrated threats to have his privileges removed if he didn't indulge her.

'If you wish to have my concessions revoked, go right ahead and do so, Mrs Appomattox. The food for tonight's pretty much done now. Just bring the heat up on the poivre and dauphinoise – steak and potatoes to you lady – prior to serving and you've got a Raymond Babchuk meal. Anyway, with your culinary savvy I'm sure you'll know what to do.'

Raymond left the kitchen, the sound of pans being thrown and plates smashed echoing in his ears. He didn't care. Courtesy of him even the seductive Mrs A would provide a good meal for the governor and his guests.

Raymond's privileges were not rescinded and kitchen sink dramas at the Appomattox house notwithstanding, a short while later Prisoner 978678 was able to settle into his own personal working routine.

Chapter 40

So it was that Raymond Babchuk sat down to write his book, a volume which would become an international bestseller, topping the ratings for over a year as all denominations of race, creed and colour around the globe scrambled to read his bizarre adventures. Entitled *Recipes to Die For!*, the book was divided into three parts. The first section was little more than an extended frontispiece relating the extraordinary origins of Restaurant Incarnate. Raymond spared nothing of himself in describing the death of Charles Reardon: the accident and his subsequent dismembering of the sous-chef's body to serve to his aunt, Mrs Renais Rinegold, and her dinner party. He related how a guest of hers, Mr Arnold Riseveldt, had enquired about him after the greatest meal of his life, his confession and Mr Riseveldt's subsequent fantastic business proposition (here Raymond did take licence, omitting Riseveldt's threats of blackmail and suggesting that it was his culinary genius that had inspired the proprietor of RIP to propose their unlikely union which in one sense was the truth). There the opening of Restaurant Incarnate, and how, from its first customer, the place exploded onto the Manhattan restaurant scene, the phenomenal success which rapidly followed putting Riseveldt's supplies under pressure, leading to his descent into darker, more deadly waters. Then Raymond's 'discovery' of Jack Grimaldi,

Riseveldt's hired killer (again reality was adjusted some, Raymond merely implying his partner had to have been driven to such desperate measures because of the incessant demand for Raymond's cuisine which was also not wholly inaccurate), and Miss Millichamp's arrival at the front door; her public declaration of the food type being sold, advertising for the rights to human bodies for use as food in the restaurant on their owners' deaths and how, when this became known, there was not only a queue a mile long of donors, but restaurant bookings went berserk, people's palates going crazy for human meat. Then, ultimately, the extraordinary closure of the restaurant, in its final existence known briefly as Restaurant _{Re}Incarnate.

What a chapter! What a piece! The content of this segment alone was publishing dynamite, but it was nothing to the next section – recipes. With grim simplicity, Raymond described how he prepared parts of the body for the plate, the subtleties he created using unusual sauces and how, by extensively varying the methods of preparation, every conceivable (and inconceivable) option was brought into play. *Fricassée* became *passé*, *lyonnaise* became *bolognese*; Raymond even tried the civet principle involving passage through digestive tracts to vary his technique. Whatever he did, he pulled it off, as his restaurant's success proved.

But the final section was the longest and the real tour de force. Put starkly, it was an unalloyed list of who ate whom and with what recipe they had enjoyed their meal. Photographs of the diners accompanied each entry, and the record running into thousands, every minute detail was catalogued. Even to Raymond, as he sat writing it, the content broke all bounds of the macabre. It was frightful; it was terrible; it was irresistible!

Apart from having a certain surrealism, the idea Bill really ate Mrs Fanny Watson's fingers, or how much George enjoyed Rastus O'Hara's kneecaps somehow compelled one to turn the page. And the next. And the next. Mick had been in town checking in with Keith and they'd had a great meal off Albino Fritz's rump. Dolly'd come through, meeting up with Kenny, and they had old Ma Gretchen's elbow as a dish prepared for two. Even Barbra dropped by, eating some unmentionables (which were, of course, mentioned). The book would become a compulsive read, and break all publishing sales records for a cook book. A best seller.

Although usually a restrained and undemonstrative character, when one end of day Raymond reviewed his near-completed work, even he thought his writing would have a readership. Little did he know the storm that would be created by its publication and what a powerful effect his book would have. Perhaps it was only fitting after five months' solid work, rain sweeping across the wooded hills surrounding Ray Brook Prison, Raymond Babchuk pressed the return key for the last time and on the screen the title page read:

Recipes to Die For!
A Simple Guide to Human Cuisine
by
Raymond Babchuk

Then, whilst inscribed *To Tabitha and Tutti, with love,* there was another dedication:

Dedicated to
Louis Blanc,

who inspired my culinary ambitions
of excellence, originality and the creation
of exquisite taste

Table 12, 6/: Ms Ida Lieberwitz (deceased)
Menu: Ris de veau a l'intestin.

On the reverse of the flyleaf were printed the lyrics of Leonard Cohen's 'First We Take Manhattan'. It could have been written for Raymond, summing up his adventures and so much of this part of his life.

They sentenced me to twenty years of boredom
For trying to change the system from within.
I'm coming now, I'm coming to reward them.
First we take Manhattan, then we take Berlin.

I'm guided by a signal in the heavens,
I'm guided by this birthmark on my skin,
I'm guided by the beauty of our weapons.
First we take Manhattan, then we take Berlin

I'd really like to live beside you, baby,
I love your body and your spirit and your clothes,
But you see that line there moving through the station?
I told you, I told you, told you I was one of those.
Ah, you loved me as a loser,
But now you're worried that I just might win.
You know the way to stop me, but you don't have the
  discipline
How many nights I prayed for this, to let my work
  begin.
First we take Manhattan, then we take Berlin.

I'd really like to live beside you, baby
I love your body and your spirit and your clothes.
But you see that line there movin' through the station?
I told you, I told you, told you I was one of those.
And I thank you for those items that you sent me,
The monkey and the plywood violin.
I practiced every night, now I'm ready.
First we take Manhattan, then we take Berlin.

I am guided.
Ah, remember me, I used to live for music?
Remember me, I brought your groceries in?
Well, it's Fathers' Day and everybody's wounded.
First we take Manhattan, then we take Berlin.

After his abrupt departure from the governor's kitchen, Raymond had largely been left undisturbed by the Appomattoxes and because he was completely engrossed in his work, wasn't aware of much going on in the outside world. Interestingly, as the months went by his story faded remarkably little.

First Belinda Millichamp was in the news, wanting to reopen the restaurant, which it was decided wouldn't be possible as long as Raymond remained behind bars. Then there were various outbursts from relatives of those who had been neither murdered nor cremated, and whose remains were never found at the South Side mortuary holding unit, but had just somehow been lost; these folk bewailed the fact their relations had been eaten. However, the digesting of humans having already been established at the original trial, the judge who heard the submission ruled that the dead were dead so there was no case to answer. When he learned of this, Raymond mused these relatives would soon be in for quite some shock, discovering as they would exactly who had eaten their loved ones.

Several books were rushed out, Carmen Sargoza's *Vampires Incarnate* quickly climbing into the book charts, and Manny Underwine's *Dead and Buried – Who are you Kidding?* Manny was now head embalmer at RIP. Both gave an alternative perspective of life beyond the grave, and both were reasonable hits.

Having completed the guts of his work, and being in that exquisite period when the hard graft is over and a few days of reflection exist before the next stages of publication kick in, Raymond considered his life as a prisoner had been one of the happiest periods of his time on the planet. It was true whenever he met other inmates, infrequent though this was, while exercising or at the occasional canteen meal (throughout the months of his writing work he'd been allowed meals in his cell – an almost unheard of privilege), other lags mainly steered clear of him, considering him 'different' – not a popular label for a penitential guest. But official appraisals monitoring his behaviour whilst serving his sentence went from exemplary to glowing.

Nancy Friedland had been of some assistance in producing a publisher, the legal agreement between Radomér Babchuk and Culinaire Publishing Inc., managed by Mr Joshua Corfield, completed inside a month. Negotiations involved a six-figure amount and, to the outside world an eccentric codicil stating the book *must* be launched in Berlin. A short while later, page proofs of *Recipes to Die For!* arrived. Raymond got busy making final adjustments to the work, which took another two weeks. He then received several proof copies and it was whilst making checks on these – plate listings, credits and appendices – he sat down to write a letter, addressed to Louis Blanc, that was to accompany an advance gift copy for him.

Chapter 41

It hadn't actually suited Tabitha McKindrick to head upstate and visit Raymond when finally she heard from her alimental lover that he wished to see her. She had been planning a trip to visit her folks in Montana, taking Tutti along to meet Mom and Dad. Tutti had continued his bubble gum-blowing and cigar-smoking habits, and was known locally as The Smoking Monkey. Tabitha's initial irritation at having to look after the little fellow wearing off, Tutti and she had got themselves a great relationship, working up a nice little routine when out in restaurants.

'Cute pet.'

Tutti would remove a dormant Havana from his mouth, and blow a bubble gum bubble.

'My, he's a clever little thing.'

The bubble would grow and, as the gum had been impregnated with colour additive, the words Restaurant Incarnate would appear on the ballooned isoamyl acetate, people howling with amazement.

'You mean he's the monkey from that Incarnate Restaurant, the human meat place?'

'Very same.'

The bubble would pop and the audience would clap.

'Wow! Smoke too, does he?'

'Not inside. Blows perfect rings, though.'

'Expensive tastes, then.'

'He takes tips.'

And people would oblige. Now, as they sat in a restaurant, Tutti playing with the proceeds of their double act, Tabitha considered Raymond's request. Although she hadn't agreed with his self-imposed isolation while in prison, she'd thought a lot about it in the intervening time and, over the months, came to partially understand his attitude. Besides, she was aware things were changing. A week ago a publisher named Corfield called, saying he represented Raymond and that the chef would be getting in touch. She'd slightly bridled at hearing the information the way she had, but when he did email, it was vintage Raymond, the message running:

> *Dear Tab,*
> *I hope you are well. Come up and see me soon and bring*
> *Tutti.*
> *Raymond.*

No kiss, no sentimentality; he didn't even imply urgency, but Tabitha knew otherwise. Although she'd had reports of his condition (Feydor Gaultier had contacted her, as had Nancy Friedland) this was the first direct communication she'd received from him. Her parents would have to wait – they had for three years now, anyway.

Looking across at Tutti she said, 'Come on, monkey-brain, gather up your purse money. We'd better hit the road.'

It was a strange aspect of Arnold and Raymond's union that neither had spent any significant pelf as their enterprise grew and became successful. Whether this was because all they did was work, never having any time to part with their ill-gotten gains, or whether they were simply parsimonious, one couldn't say (in the case of the former, one would never know). Raymond's obsessive preoccupation with cuisine didn't allow for a change of shirt, let alone the buying of a new one and even when his aunt's house was officially left him he'd had an emotionally convoluted time adjusting to its ownership. Renais had tried to leave it to a dogs' home, but after she destroyed Raymond's first kitchen smart Mr Balázs got her signature on a revised will, in which he'd had a clause inserted stating she left 'all goods, chattels and the property known as 395 Palmetto Street to her nephew, Radomér Babchuk, residing at same address'. Renais signed whilst blind drunk and threatening to pee herself – she certainly would have if she'd known what she was putting her signature to. Balázs removed the document, leaving it in an old filing cabinet where he knew his neighbour kept her papers. Her sudden death couldn't have been more convenient and no one ever questioned the will.

Tabitha was also careful with Raymond's money. Running costs of the house came from his private account and she occasionally had Mr Balázs over for supper. But apart from that, the only other significant expense was Tutti's cigars.

Backing the old T-Bird out of the Palmetto Street garage, Tabitha did think they might invest in a new car; the convertible was leaking, rattling and drafty, the rip caused by Reardon's crash-landing through it patched over with duct tape. Easing out of New York City, Tabitha headed north on Route 22.

'All the way to Canada, Tutti; it's cold up there. You'll be glad of your jacket.' Tabitha had bought Tutti a little tartan jerkin which he rarely took off, adding to his cuteness. The monkey snuggled into it now as his little eyes gazed out at snow piles stacked high along the roadside.

*

The café at Lake Placid Lodge, where Raymond met Tabitha and Tutti, was set by the lake in Adirondack Park, surrounded by stunning snow-covered scenery. Raymond was dressed in new clothes – slacks, sneakers, a mountain shirt and anorak; he looked sharp. Tabitha threw her arms around his neck but Tutti held back, eyeing him quizzically.

'So how'd yer sort this?'

Raymond reached down and lifted a trouser leg, revealing a tag. 'I can be out several days now.'

'Great.' Tabitha was excited.

'They do rooms next door; I've paid for you.' He looked at her. 'But I go back later first.'

Temporarily crestfallen, Tabitha looked away while Raymond ordered coffee and went over to Tutti whom he began stroking the way he always did, a finger caressing the underside of the monkey's chin. It seemed to have a mesmeric effect, Tutti clambering inside his anorak and holding onto his chest as they returned to the table.

'Nothin', but nothin's gonna rock my parole, Tab.'

'But you're not out in time for the launch. Corfield said so.'

'That's why I had to see you. It's big – goin' global – and I need you.' She looked at him steadily. 'The book's being launched in Berlin, then other places around the world. I need you to make the trip.'

'Berlin? Why Berlin, for chris'sakes?'

As the café was nearly empty, Raymond opened a bag and took out some papers, a parcel and other bits and pieces.

'Reasons. It don't matter. The plan is, rather than open in New York, Culinaire Publishin'll make it the climax.'

A waitress came over with their coffee. Her glance fell on some of the papers strewn across the table; part of the book's artwork was visible – Raymond in prison shirt, Sabatier knife in hand, sitting at a kitchen table beside Tutti, smoking a large cigar (Photoshop had been busy). The title, *Recipes to Die For! – A Simple Guide to Human Cuisine by Raymond Babchuk*, emblazoned across the front cover caught her eye.

'Oh, my. You're the guy with that human meat restaurant. I recognise you. Can I have your autograph?'

'What's your name?'

'Mandy.'

Raymond scribbled, *To Mandy – Coffee to Die For! Raymond Babchuk x*, on a serviette and, putting a finger to his lips, said, 'Sssh!'

'Jeez! Your book comin' out soon?'

'Sssh!' Another finger, marking silence.

'So excited. Wait till I–'

'Ssssh!'

Mandy went away, clutching the paper napkin tightly.

'I can see I'm gonna have to get used to this.'

'Ha. Corfield thinks it'll explode.'

Raymond took out one of the proof copies and pushed it across the table. 'This is what all the fuss is about. It's for you. Want me to sign it?'

Opening the book, Tabitha read the inscription – 'For Tabitha and Tutti, with love' – and burst into tears.

'Hey. Mandy didn't do that.' Spinning the book back, Raymond wrote more intimately in his sprawling, hieroglyphic hand.

A party of high school girls on a trip were waiting outside the café as they emerged, wanting Raymond to sign autographs, which he did on everything from crisp packets to thighs.

'How they aren't freezin's beyond me. Nearly as cold as

this old bus.' Tabitha started the T-Bird.

'Runnin' good, is she?'

'Runnin' freezin'. With this new-found wealth, Mr Babchuk, we're buyin' a new car.'

'What about a pick-up? Good out west.'

They rattled towards Ray Brook Prison, Tabitha parking a block below as Raymond had instructed, cutting the engine.

Raymond nudged the brown paper parcel nestling between them. 'Money's all sorted. Corfield's set the schedule and he'll have tickets, hotels and stuff.'

Tabitha was reflective. 'Look, Ray, should I really be on this trip? Berlin, I mean. You've got Nancy Friedland – what am I doin' it for?'

'There's two reasons. One is you were sous-chef at the most celebrated restaurant in the world, and the second is me. Surely you wanna protect yer husband. Will yer marry me, Tab?'

This wasn't a good afternoon for Miss McKindrick's tear ducts.

'Guess not, then. Well anyway, thanks for comin' up.'

'You stupid fuckin' sonofabitch!' Tabitha was angry now. 'You ask me to marry you and you're goin' back inside there. You can fuck off – you and yer goddamn book. Go on, get out!'

Books, papers, everything that had been so neatly prepared came flying out of the car onto the snowy sidewalk. Completely taken aback, Raymond got out.

'And take yer goddam monkey with yer!' Tabitha glared at Tutti. 'You too – go on, out!'

'Yer won't reconsider?'

Gunning the engine, Tabitha's response was to burn rubber, which she did, skidding away into the twilight.

Standing on the sidewalk, man and monkey shivered.

'Would yer Christmas Eve that, Tutti? Women!' Then very carefully Raymond began gathering up everything strewn across kerb and road. 'After we've collected stuff from the governor's, looks like it'll be just you and me 'a celebratin.'

Having picked up some more papers and an overnight bag from Governor Appomattox's office Raymond and Tutti took a cab back to the lodge. There was no sign of the T-Bird.

Checking in, Raymond went to the room and began sorting through papers and proofs, repairing the package. Snow was falling hard when, much later, in the darkness of night, the old Mustang pulled up outside. Raymond had ordered a bottle of champagne and in-room dining. There was nothing left outside on the tray when, during the small hours, room service came by to collect.

Chapter 42

Always an exciting city, Berlin two weeks before Christmas had a magical quality about it. When Pierre-Auguste suggested they open *L'Escargot Berliner*, Louis Blanc hadn't initially been inspired but, as work progressed on the intimate bistro-style grill room, he'd become more enthusiastic. Walking from the apartment he and P-A shared, Blanc thought the city looked particularly attractive – baubles, decorations, fir trees, holly, sleighs, reindeer, and all the accoutrements that adorned shops at Christmas time giving them that Winter Wonderland welcome. Blanc liked Knesebeckstrasse, the side street off Kurfürstendamm, where *L'E B*, as the trades were calling it, was situated opposite a famous old bookstore; it had the intimate feel he wanted for their restaurant.

Although they'd had to delay opening, due to the interior design being more complicated to construct than originally envisaged, the soft opening that previous Saturday had gone well. The only problem was the kitchen's gas ranges, which lacked high-end pressure. The suppliers invited him for a meeting that afternoon at their showroom on the outskirts of town, where they planned to present an improved system for installation. After checking that evening's bookings and wine delivery with Bruno, his young maitre d' (efficient but somewhat Germanic), it was late morning before Blanc set off for the Treptow-Köpenick district, where the distributor was located in one of the city's industrial suburbs. Little did he know flying in that very same moment was his old acquaintance, Nancy Friedland, along with the ex-sous-chef of Restaurant Incarnate, now engaged to be married to – as Blanc saw it – the jumped-up, junk food jailbird. The women had even brought along Restaurant Incarnate's mascot, having obtained special veterinary clearance for Tutti Frutti to travel internationally.

Blanc's hoarded resentment resurfaced as he walked. That little turd, Babchuk... Thank God he was banged up. They should throw away the key. Daring to cock a snook at him, Louis Blanc, by rejecting his offer of employment in Beverly Hills. Let alone Chef de France dismissing him from its managing board – he, one of France's great cuisiniers. If Blanc had had his way, they'd have chaired the little fucker, thrown his entrails to the wolves and had his eyes gouged out by zombies.

Joshua Corfield arrived in Berlin a week previously and had been a very busy man. He'd placed an embargo on anything to do with the book and its launch until opening night, setting the whole thing up like a movie premiere. Glitterati would attend *en masse* – A-listers from all walks of life; movie and rock stars, figures from publishing, finance and the arts, even the odd retired president had been tipped off and might make an appearance. Not only was *Recipes to Die For!* going to be the hottest cook book ever, its launch was the social ticket to die for. The hype and razzmatazz would know no bounds. Those in media were aware the story was going to break, *R to DF!* being launched globally from the bear city, but for now everything was being kept under wraps until the very last moment. That being the case, the giant posters of Raymond and Tutti from the book's front cover were held in preparation, only going up at the launch, and those that were to adorn the outside of the bookshop in Knesebeckstrasse – higher than the building itself and spotted by searchlights – were black-draped, the whole moment held in secrecy till 8.00 p.m.

Blanc became aware the night would be lively when, returning to *L'Escargot Berliner* from his meeting, he was met by armies of construction and security people, erecting scaffolding and cordoning off the relevant thoroughfares. Indeed, he needed proof of his business address to be admitted to the street. They'd received a circular explaining something of the night's proceedings, but no further details. How could he run his restaurant with all this carry-on? Security were obtuse – he'd have to see so-and-so; he could file a complaint – but no one seemed to know exactly what all the fuss was about, except the launch of a new book. A new book, with this much brouhaha? It must be some story. Maybe J.K. Rowling had written a last secret *Harry Potter*? It would have to be something as potentially hot as that or the promoters would rapidly face bankruptcy. Blanc watched as red carpet was laid out and arc lights tested. It was going to be some night.

Some night indeed. Press and TV people were out in force a few hours later, preparing themselves for the onslaught. Few noticed a cab pulling up a block away on Kurfürstendamm, and a woman alighting, wearing an evening dress covered by a long cloak, a hood largely hiding her face. Flashing a pass enabling her to enter Knesebeckstrasse, the woman, clutch bag in hand and carrying a brown paper parcel, kept to the shadows on the far side of the street. At the entrance of *L'Escargot Berliner*, Nancy Friedland pushed back her cape and entered the lobby, where she was greeted by Bruno.

'*Guten abend, gnädige Frau.*'

'Hi.' Nancy could actually speak German quite well, but the painful memories recounted by her family meant it was a language she'd been uncomfortable with since childhood. 'Nice place. I've called to see Monsieur Blanc.'

'You have an appointment?' Bruno's English was as impeccable as most of his countrymen's.

'A surprise visit. My card.' She handed one to the maitre d' who studied it momentarily.

'Ah. You are famous, madam.'

'Think so?'

'Would you care for a drink?'

'Hmm. Maybe with Monsieur Blanc.'

'May I take your cloak?'

'I'll hang on to it, if you don't mind.'

'A seat, then.' With perfect courtesy, Bruno showed Nancy to a table in the empty restaurant. Looking out of the window, she watched as people were beginning to arrive across the road, admiring the theatrical set design. Limos were pulling up, camera flashes popping, outside broadcast TV presenters introducing the event, and the first guests walking up the red carpet into the building. She'd figured this would be the optimum moment for her visit and hopefully her timing wouldn't let her down.

'Nancy?'

Nancy Friedland turned and saw Blanc approaching. Wearing a suit, he was always a smart man, but his grey hair was now white, and she detected a slight stoop as he came towards her.

'Louis – good to see you.' He kissed her outstretched hand. 'This looks very...stylish.'

Blanc smiled smoothly. 'Wait till you taste our *selle de veau*, and I am optimistic Chef's *lentilles et saucisse à l'ail* will become a signature dish.'

'You're with...Pierre-Auguste, I believe.' The slight hesitation in her voice was perfect.

'Ah, *nous venons, nous tombons, nous montons*.' We come, we fall, we climb. 'He needed my help.' Blanc gave a slight shrug. 'But I'm neglecting my manners. A drink? Champagne?'

Nancy nodded.

'Would you care to come upstairs? My office is above.' Nancy stood. 'And dinner – you'll be my guest?'

His visitor not replying, it wasn't until Blanc saw her, standing, clad in evening gown, he thought her visit might be anything other than one of a friend (albeit a critic, and a very influential one at that) dropping by whilst passing through this most cosmopolitan of cities. It had been common knowledge he was opening *L'Escargot Berliner*, and that Maestro Pierre-Auguste would be chef de cuisine, so her appearance hadn't particularly surprised him, but now as he led the way upstairs he had a strange feeling her coming by wasn't casual but predetermined, planned. Entering the spacious first floor room, Bruno was already setting down a bottle of champagne in an ice bucket. With expert style, the cork was eased, a wonderful 'fzzzss' sound emanating from its neck, the pale effervescence bubbling gently into flutes. Serving Nancy first as she sat down on a large sofa, Bruno left a glass on the tray for Blanc who, somewhat rudely, stared out of the window at the noisy scene below.

'You require anything further, M'sieur?'

'No. Thank you, Bruno.'

Looking slightly nonplussed, the maitre d' left, closing the door silently behind him. For several seconds nothing was said. Nancy had some champagne and seemed perfectly relaxed, an attitude she was determined to maintain.

'So. This visit. Dropping in like this, dressed, if I may say, stunningly. You're attending a formal occasion?' Without replying, Nancy sipped some more champagne and Blanc at last turned to face her. 'Would it, by any chance, be this?' He gestured out of the window.

'You always were an astute individual, Louis.'

'There's been much secrecy surrounding the event. Care to enlighten me?'

Nancy looked at her very expensive Vacheron Constantin. 'In about five minutes, all will be revealed.'

'Why the secrecy?'

Putting down her champagne – Nancy was enjoying it – she began opening the brown paper parcel. Blanc watched, suddenly transfixed.

'Ten months or so ago I was contacted...' Nancy Friedland chuckled faintly, sighed and drank, 'by Feydor Gaultier. Why are maitre d's so wonderfully diplomatic?'

'Because they're paid to be.' Blanc's intonation was hard.

'It's more than that. The good ones have a deference, a subtlety that's just right. Not obsequious, not intrusive, perfect. Anyway, Feydor had been in touch with Mr Babchuk, who was wanting some advice.'

A crescendo of outside noise wafted into the room.

'From you?' Suddenly strained, it was only Blanc's discipline that prevented him from hurling the table, woman and entire contents of the room out of the window, such was the feeling of catastrophic premonition permeating the fibres of his being. Now Nancy turned to face him full square.

'He wanted publishing advice and I gave it to him.'

347

Silence for several seconds. She picked up the book. 'This is the result.'

Blanc leapt at her, or more precisely, for the book in her hand, but she held it tight. More noise from outside built into a roar, forcing Blanc to turn. Arc-lit, the drapes from giant posters fell away, revealing the same book-sleeve image. There, in his all his glory, was Raymond Babchuk, Tutti Frutti beside him, a thin line of cigar smoke climbing the poster.

'*Recipes to Die For!* He's dedicated it to you.'

If Blanc could have made a strangulated sound he would have, but his throat being so constricted, no noise was possible. Perhaps a heart attack? Certainly his face had visibly aged ten years in three minutes. They both released the book at the same moment and it fell to the floor. Nancy stood and picked it up, placing it on a desk. Seeing Blanc frozen, she wondered if he was still aware of anything. Approaching him, she whispered, 'There's a note.' Nancy Friedland appeared to drift towards the door, such was the surrealism of things.

'But you. You're with him?' Blanc's speech was so constrained he choked. Nancy turned.

'He's quite, quite unique.' And without another word she left.

Downstairs, there was no one around. The restaurant was empty and there was no sign of Bruno. Walking outside, who should Nancy see but Pierre-Auguste Etienne. Ladle in hand, chef's hat on his head, his jacket and Dali-esque moustaches immaculate, the phoney maestro looked the complete parody of a comedy chef. As she watched, he ran headlong at the security cordon, his kitchen utensil waving crazily, the chequered chef's trousers covering his little butt cheekily riding up and down. Nancy Friedland put her head back and roared.

Standing at the first floor window, Louis Blanc looked down at the scene. Raymond's letter was in his hand and he began to read:

Ray Brook Penitentiary, NY 12977   *October 27th*
Dear Louis,

I trust this finds you in rude health, residing as I believe you and Mr Everard now are in the great city of Berlin.

My life since last we met at Restaurant Incarnate has taken many turns, but the restaurant's closing down caused mayhem. So much so that publishers screamed at me, begging me to write a book, and I was inundated with offers. Most I rejected as being sensationalist, but having been impressed by Miss Friedland's writing (also she was about the only person in the literary world I knew), I took her advice regarding the best way forward, and with the help of our old friend, Feydor Gaultier, have been working non-stop these many months past. How time has flown!

Anyway, the book is now completed. My parole comes up shortly, but unfortunately not in time for me to be present at its launch, hosted at the bookstore right across the street from L'Escargot Berliner, but think of me as the celebrations begin. Advance orders have been considerable; in fact, they're bigger than for any other cooking title – ever!

You'll appreciate my writing the book has meant my incarceration hasn't been entirely wasted (indeed, it's given me necessary time for reflection), and Miss Friedland's kind offer of delivering this advance copy to you while she's attending the launch ceremony is also appreciated. I thought as it is signed personally by me it would be something you may like to keep and treasure as a tribute to our friendship.

You may wonder at all this effort to deliver you a copy of

Recipes to Die For!, *but if you turn the flyleaf you'll see why.*
I've dedicated it to you, Louis – you who inspired me in
all manner of ways; commitment, ability, perseverance, even
discretion. The dedication also cites the meal you and Miss
Friedland enjoyed at my restaurant; she had cervelle au
beurre noir – that of Mr Fred McKeiver, who she thinks must
have been a clever guy, and you ate ris de veau a l'intestin –
the bowels of Ms Ida Lieberwitz. I trust yours are working
fine!

Good luck with the new restaurant. I hope you know
what you're doing with Pierre-Auguste and he's not turning
out to be the fraud he was at Le Chat. With the Beverly Hills
L'Escargot, are you planning a chain?
Yours unforgettably
Raymond aspic, nettle – ça Babchuk

PS: Had a crank contact recently asking if Incarnate had
ever done take-out? The idea! RB

Looking up from the letter, the last thing Blanc saw
before collapsing was Nancy Friedland on the red carpet,
a massive poster of *Recipes to Die For!* behind her and
Tabitha McKindrick carrying the cigar-toting monkey on
her shoulder, waving. Nancy was looking straight at him.

Chapter 43

The triumphal launch in Berlin of Raymond's extraordinary book reignited people's fascination – and in some cases, obsession – with the comparatively recent revelations regarding human beings eating other human beings and how much they'd enjoyed the experience. It gave the phrase 'human interest story' a decided twist. Further, it became known Raymond Babchuk's parole was imminent. Coinciding with the climax of the global publicity roll out concluding in New York, the brilliant media strategy would peak in Manhattan where it all began.

South East Asia was the latest market to be gripped by human meat fever as the *RTDF!* bandwagon rolled through Kuala Lumpur, Singapore and Hong Kong, its juggernaut of hype increasing daily in momentum. Tutti Frutti became a veritable media star, with agents queuing up to represent him. Closer to home, however, Governor Appomattox had another issue to deal with: a potential riot. At the time of the televised book launch in Germany an elderly lag, Conrad Pfief, died in Ray Brook while serving time for rape homicide. Sadly not a rare crime, it was a generally unpopular one amongst inmates. Aware they had a media personality in their midst with, as they saw it, very particular skills, prisoners began to chant:

'Cook, cook, cook! Fry, fry, fry! Eat, eat, eat, human meat! We wanna eat, we gotta eat, human meat!'

Reminiscent of the New York street cries those months previously, the jailbird chorus added 'Pfief for the pot!' and 'Connie is cooked!' to their tin-banging lyrics, the tempo rising to boiling point. To quell the riot, Governor Appomattox and Raymond (who had been moved to a secure annexe adjacent to the governor's house, as refuge from the constant attention he was subjected to inside the penitentiary) hatched up the story that Pfief's body was found to be covered in festering sores and was therefore unsuitable for human consumption. When an autopsy was conducted, this turned out to be an understatement; Pfief's corpse was syphilitic and cancer-ridden. Some felt cheated, most relieved, and things quietened down. Governor Appomattox was amazed at the media attention Raymond's book had aroused and the public interest in hominoid food; OB units and satellite dishes now surrounded his penitential empire. At this very moment outside the front gates, ABC's anchor-woman, Connie Lombardo, was just one of many facing news cameras, as, inside, the governor sat watching the broadcast.

'Behind these gates Raymond Babchuk, the man at the centre of the story currently on everyone's mind, is just days away from parole, but exactly when he will be freed remains a mystery. With the US unveiling of his book, *Recipes to Die For!*, being held in the city ten days from now, it's believed prisoner 978678's release will enable him to be present for New York's celebration of its most famous – or infamous – citizen. To find out more about the human side of this "chef to mankind", I spoke earlier to Mandy Fitzpatrick.'

The picture went to an exterior of a beautiful lakeside hotel, with Connie as voiceover:

'Waiting tables at Lake Placid Lodge recently, Mandy

served Babchuk and his girlfriend, Tabitha McKindrick. Miss McKindrick is currently travelling the world as Babchuk's representative, being not only engaged to the culinary maestro, but one-time sous-chef herself at Restaurant Incarnate.'

Mandy stood by the café table where she'd served Raymond and Tabitha.

'He was real cool, signing autographs and stuff, like a regular guy with his monkey. Dig his restaurant ethic. Just got to be the smartest thing. And environmentally' – Mandy had that 'voice-rising end-of-sentence question-like' style – 'I mean, when we're dead we're dead, right? It could help out with world famine. When I go, he can have my body.'

There was a slight nuance here and the camera returned to anchor woman Lombardo, who played it straight.

'That seems to be many people's attitude. The world is caught in the grip of food shortages; why not use our defunct bodies to feed others? Are we really passing up on an obvious opportunity? Or is the idea of eating your friend, neighbour or relative too repulsive to contemplate? For many it appears not; practicalities outweigh sensitivities and if nothing else, Raymond Babchuk's activities, and those of his colleagues at Restaurant Incarnate, have taken the debate global. We're not talking cannibals on some South Sea island here, but our own society that's been experiencing this unique cuisine. People were enjoying it when they didn't know what it was they were eating, and not a table to be found in the place for love nor money when they did!' Connie raised an eyebrow momentarily. 'This is Connie Lombardo, ABC News, Ray Brook Penitentiary, upstate New York.'

*

Governor Appomattox stared at the screen and flicked the remote to mute. He turned to Raymond, who sat on a sofa half twisted away from the television, looking out of the study window. Silhouetted in the distance, the Adirondack Mountains were turning a deep purple. It was mid-afternoon; there was no light on in the room and the wintry sun was already beginning to wane. The atmosphere was intimate and subdued.

'Well, you came in a jailbird and go out a superstar. What have you done to people, they've been affected by all this like they have? Not that I'm trying to undermine your glory, mind, but...' The governor was serious and for several seconds Raymond didn't respond, continuing to stare out of the window.

'Reckon a lot of chat's gonna get rabbited up, most of it dumb.' Raymond scratched his cheek. 'Think maybe it's the taboo. Folk ain't supposed to eat other folks, and people identify with what I did – yer know, dog-eat-dog stuff; they're surrounded by it. Usually it's just a metaphor, but in my case–'

'You did it – and it wasn't just dog.' The governor's dark humour didn't seem to jar the very particular mood of the room. 'And they've made you their hero.' Appomattox reached for a file and opened it. 'I have here your parole. In one week you're a free man.' He dropped the file back on his desk. 'I've also had some communication with your agent, concerned about the furore that's likely to surround you when you get out. In fact, I've had a lot of correspondence about you; every one of the news companies, the mayor's office and even the state governor's been on the phone. Right now they're squabbling over where you're going when you leave here and how.' Governor Appomattox sat back. 'Well, you don't want to be walking through those

gates into that circus. Frankly, I don't want it either.' He put
on a side light. 'Having been a guest here, you know we get
a lot of chopper traffic – day and night – so that's the way
to go. The governor and the mayor of New York City want
to fly you out at tax payers' expense. How does that sound?'

Raymond shrugged.

'You've been kind of a brief visitor here, but you know,
sometimes people who are inside for years don't like going
out. Strange, isn't it? Something to do with security, I
guess. But think about where you go. Trust me, Raymond,
you don't know how crazy it's gonna be for you out there.
People like Joshua Corfield set the business up but it can
get outta control, and when that happens they never let you
go.' Governor Appomattox stood and put out his hand. The
two men shook. 'It's been a pleasure, but you know, I can't
say I envy you, fella.' He walked to the door. 'Enjoy the
quiet here. What you're going into – it'll be the last you'll
experience for a while.'

When Appomattox had gone, Raymond sat back, watching the last of the daylight fade to darkness over the distant
mountains.

Chapter 44

The Bell JetRanger touched down at Newark Airport in dead of night landing in a remote corner of the airfield well away from both the perimeter fence and terminal buildings. The modest limo meeting it glided up to the private 'copter area, dipping its lights in greeting. Two men alighted from the helicopter and a man got out of the car to stand by an opened door. All three got into the vehicle, the chauffeur guiding it out of a side gate on to the Lincoln Highway, signposted for Jersey and Manhattan. Some forty minutes later, the limo crossed the city and entered Queens, travelling along Metropolitan and Forest Avenues before turning off into Gates and Fairview. At the Palmetto intersection, Raymond looked out toward his house, which had the media camped expectantly outside it. The car didn't slow till, turning into Woodbine Street, it pulled up beside a quiet apartment block. The security men leading Raymond seemed to know exactly where they were going, riding an elevator to the eleventh floor and approaching apartment 121b with the certainty of previous reconnaissance. The bell answered promptly, Mr Balázs smiled a welcome. Raymond and one of the security men entered while the other man, drawing the short straw, returned to keep watch from the vehicle below.

'You're in here.' Mr Balázs showed Raymond the spare

bedroom, whose view overlooked the back of his own house only a few blocks away. 'So near, yet...'

Raymond had little luggage, which he quickly deposited and joined his host in the kitchen, where a pot of goulash simmered on the stove.

Mr Balázs indicated a pile of post on the counter. 'Your agent's company managed to collect these from Palmetto Street. Although Miss McKindrick has only been gone a few weeks, there was a lot of junk stuff I didn't think you'd want, but what's there I figured you would.'

Raymond cursorily rifled through the mail. The postcards had obvious interest, reading like some global travel-fest as names and images from every continent flashed before him: Cape Town, Beijing, Wellington, Samoa – a world tour. The South Sea Islands were of special interest, though Tabitha's message was cryptic:

'Unoriginal recipes/big appetites!'

'You hear from her?'

'Plenty. They're on the mantelpiece. That's yours, too.' Balázs indicated a large reinforced cardboard pack. 'Delivered here by your Culinaire publisher friends.'

Raymond went over and opened the box. Inside was an array of clothing samples – bomber jackets, T-shirts, caps – all bearing the Restaurant ^{Re}Incarnate logo. The front of the jacket read:

Restaurant ^{Re}Incarnate
The face of human cuisine

And the back:

Restaurant ^{Re}Incarnate
You were there

T-shirts bore messages like *I T-Boned @ $^{Re}Incarnate$* and *Sticks and Stones – Re-ignite @ $^{Re}Incarnate$.*

Balázs Malursk produced some glasses and a bottle of old Pálinka brandy. 'Your idea?'

Raymond laughed and made a face.

'Didn't think so.'

'The first floor landing where the old girl paid out – they're turnin' it into a shop.'

'It'll make a fortune. Does he – ?' Balázs waved the bottle toward the living room, where security man Raoul sat watching TV.

'Coffee, I reckon.'

Balázs called through and Raoul appeared.

'Man, that smells great. Wow – cool gear!'

Raymond smiled and lifted a bomber jacket. 'Yours after tomorrow.'

'You wanna coffee?' Balázs offered. The young security man nodded. 'Goulash. Homemade.' This wasn't really a question and Raoul nodded some more. The boy – he was little more than that – glanced across at Raymond questioningly. 'He didn't make it – how could he? Anyway, it's better than he can cook.' Mr Balázs slipped into Hungarian vernacular. 'A Fiatal Whippersnapper.'

Taking a mug from under the percolator, Mr Balázs handed Raoul his coffee. 'Okay, eat in half an hour. Then you trade with your friend for a while.'

Raoul smiled and returned to the living room. Standing by the stove, Raymond sampled the gently simmering stew.

'Where it all began for you huh – Budapest.'

Both men spoke in their mother-tongue.

Raymond smiled.

'Wanna know the secret? Less on the paprika, more on the peppers.'

'And add a little aspic!' Raymond cut in and Balázs laughed. 'It's a joke you don't want to know.'

Handing Raymond a glass of Pálinka, Balázs picked up his own. 'Man plans, God executes.' Then, looking Raymond in the eye: 'You added something to that.'

Raymond stirred the pot.

'If you're a culinary god now, just think what you'll be like with more varied ingredients.'

'At this moment I'm a hungry Hungarian con. Let's eat – and you're correct, yours is better!'

'Ex-con. Reckoned you'd need some food from home, after the stuff they gave you in the pen.'

'Didn't do so bad. Cooked for the governor.'

Balázs gave Raymond a long look and both men laughed some more.

Very unusually, Balázs Malursk slept in the following morning. Forsaking his normal time of 6.00 a.m., it was nearer seven when he appeared, bleary-eyed, in his dressing gown, having sunk the best part of the vintage Hungarian brandy whilst reminiscing about their homeland the previous evening. He found Raymond deep in conversation with Fraser, the other security officer.

'But...what was it like? I gotta ask?'

'Ain't you on guard or something?' Balázs was unusually grouchy.

Already wearing a Restaurant ReIncarnate bomber jacket, Fraser looked round.

'I didn't mean no offence; it's just a right-on thing. Everyone's talkin' about it and I'm here with the main man.' His walkie-talkie squawked and began communicating in the usual jargon of security people: 'A one-six birdie arrival, seven five, twelve blocks out.'

Making tea, Balázs rolled his eyes.

'You got visitors.'

'Sure. And you got tea – and one for Raoul.' Balázs handed Fraser two mugs, indicating the conversation was over. The security man went out, teas in one hand, short-wave radio in the other.

'You know they ain't going to let you alone. Folks are gonna hound you morning, noon and night. Your life won't be your own.'

Raymond smiled. 'No change there then.'

A commotion at the door – bags, gear and other travel impedimenta being dropped – announced the arrival of Nancy Friedland, Tabitha and Tutti Frutti, the latter looking like a caricature of the veteran traveller, with labels, sunglasses and a miniature headdress adorning his tiny simian head.

'That Orange Apple flight's the end – ungodly.' Flopping down in one of Mr Balázs's easy chairs, Nancy Friedland looked travel-weary.

'Ain't called the Red-Eye for nothing. Anyway, thought your services were five-star pampered.'

'Fifty stars wouldn't be enough for this old carcass, and don't start on the hominoid cuisine pun stuff. I've about done out on human meat equivoque, synonym and anecdote to last a semantic lifetime.'

Balázs raised an eyebrow.

Nancy exclaimed, 'See!' She eyed the near-empty bottle of Pálinka. 'Is that the end of last night?'

'Sure. Want some?'

'Why not? I might as well blitz the last man-eating hours left me.'

'Thought you couldn't wait for it to be all over?'

'I can't but it's still been a ride.'

Balázs handed Miss Friedland the remaining brandy and the food critic raised her glass to Tutti, who sat curled up in the other chair, Raymond and Tabitha having disappeared. Taking a large swig of the liquor, Nancy asked, 'How is he?'

'Too normal for my liking.'

'He ain't gonna know what's hit him. Crazy stuff, like he's touched some chord in people.' She gave a hollow laugh. 'They'll pull him limb from limb. Maybe that's it – all this casuistry permeating everything we do, are – it all comes back to it, what he did.'

Nancy had some more of the liquor. Balázs looked concerned. 'More would be yours if I had it, but right now you need to get some rest.'

Raymond appeared from his guest bedroom.

'Raymond, wanna know how it went?' Nancy stood up and walked over to the culinary superstar. 'It worked like you wanted.' She turned away and, raising her glass, stared at the pale drink. 'They both flipped to oblivion. Being just a lightweight phoney, Pierre-Auguste ran screaming into nowhere land, but Blanc...Blanc's more complex. We go back a long way.' She took a penultimate sip of Pálinka. 'You know, Raymond, there's a lot of stuff written about food. I've made a good living from it. But whereas Pierre-Auguste was an obvious fraud, Blanc had other issues.' She killed her drink and put down the glass. 'Anyway, the dedication did for him. Had a kind of fit and right now he's in some Bavarian mountain retreat not too far from *Berchtesgarden*, I believe. That's one dark lair to hole up in.' Nancy Friedland was grim. She caught sight of herself in a mirror. 'I gotta go. Plenty of layer-cake applied tonight – the final jamboree!' Turning towards the door, she touched Raymond's sleeve. 'That your prison shirt?'

Raymond nodded.

'Like it 'cause it's hair, huh?' The two looked each other in the eye. 'You don't have to whip yourself now. I can't figure out whether he was just blindly jealous or in love with you. Maybe a bit of both.' She kissed Raymond lightly on the mouth. 'See you later.'

Chapter 45

Massive banner posters towered high above the building, arc lights playing across them; if anywhere was going to outdo Berlin in the global launch of *Recipes to Die For!* it was Manhattan. Raymond Babchuk arrived quietly at Restaurant ^R_Incarnate (it appeared its latter name would be the one to remain) in the late afternoon, having been smuggled out of Woodbine Street and chauffeured to West Village. Dropped off at a preordained Horatio and Greenwich Street rendezvous point, he rode into Jane Street with a rigging crew who had been working on the venue's TV construction. Already, news units and outside broadcast vehicles with satellite dishes had their equipment lined up along the side street and around the block. Access was cordoned off and security tight; Raymond's pass identified him as 'Ray Brook'.

In the first floor shop, rows of garments on racks and copies of *RTDF!* were displayed, replacing the room's former clinic layout. Downstairs, the restaurant still had its coffin-lid tables and decor of black and purple livery and drapes, now augmented by large, full-colour pictures around the walls. Taken from the same CCTV imagery Raymond had used for his book, they featured the rich and famous dining at the restaurant, enjoying their repast. Interestingly, of all the areas visited, it seemed his former staff had elected to congregate in the kitchen. The behind-the-scenes atmosphere of this unique event was as fascinating as the characters who had been so much a part of the restaurant's daily life, and who now acted as if they were the cast of a stage show. Just about everyone was reunited and seemed thrilled at being so, wanting to touch Raymond as if he was some spectral figure who had influenced their lives.

The whole place was lit like a movie set, with cameras positioned strategically around the building, TV assistant directors employed to manage and choreograph proceedings. Carmen was dressed in her usual striking Spanish flamenco-style raiment – black slit skirt and a close-fitting blouse of vivid amethyst – resuming her latter-day proprietorial role; Belinda Millichamp had had a serious make-over, hair styled, smart and expensive clothes, her makeup elegant; Feydor Gaultier, in immaculate apparel, was suave and dignified. Luke and Aldo were both appropriately turned out, as were the remaining members of staff. Tabitha, her sous-chef uniform crisp and white, stood with Tutti Frutti, silken cigar smoke encircling the Restaurant ᴿᵉIncarnate logo on his tiny purple waistcoat. Raymond wore an immaculate chef's jacket with his name over his left breast, quiet chef's trousers and a black and white check neckerchief to finish off his ensemble. He looked terrific.

Amongst the internationally good and great – Raymond had insisted RIP be represented – Julie Dominic was duly in attendance, along with all the chef's reviled aunt's chums – Mamie, Wilbur, Wally and Ruby. Even *Le Chat Noir* was recognised, Frank Chesson and Alain de Lange spotted in lengthy discussion with Nancy Friedland.

Later, Raymond couldn't actually remember quite how things unfolded, the larger part of the evening being a blur, but walking up the kitchen stairs to the restaurant, his hand in Tutti's and at his insistence, accompanied by Tabitha, the trio stepped into a standing ovation and rock star reception. Things went mad; a kaleidoscope of images swirled around him – minor royalty, ex-US government officials, dignitaries from other countries, A-list actors and rock-and-roll stars – glitterati abounded from all walks of life, all in thrall to Raymond Babchuk, the man who cooked humans for the world.

And what was this? Captain Doctrinal Manifest, smart in his NYPD captain's uniform, smiling and ushering him toward Chief of Police Giantelli, resplendent in stars and medals, standing with a man dressed simply in a blue serge suit. Giantelli stretched out his arm.

'Mr Mayor, may I introduce cuisinier, chef and maestro extraordinaire Raymond Babchuk. Ray, the mayor of New York City.'

With cameras rolling, music thumping and fireworks exploding, Raymond shook the mayor's hand. He couldn't imagine receiving a more impressive reception had he saved as many lives as he'd cooked; the world had clearly gone completely insane.

Chapter 46

'Are you the most evil man on the planet?' David Betterman sat back in his chair, positioned higher than that of his guest and behind the counter which formed his TV chat show's set, a slight smile playing across his lips.

Raymond, still wearing his chef's jacket, though its mandarin collar was open, revealing his blue denim prison shirt underneath, appeared relaxed. Beside him, Tutti Frutti sat in another chair, a copy of *Recipes to Die For!* on his lap.

'Only to my customers, now the restaurant's closed.' The audience laughed.

'So what was it like, then, serving up human meat all day long?'

'Unique.'

'But was it, er, difficult?'

'Restricting. I only had the one kind.'

The audience roared. They loved it.

'Didn't it ever trouble you, serving...us to us?'

'Night and day, but you can read all about it in my new book!' Taking the copy Tutti Frutti was holding, Raymond's timing was spot-on. Tutti laughed, as did the audience again.

'Pair of monkeys, huh?'

'He's my best friend, aren't yer?' Raymond stroked Tutti's chin and the little monkey snuggled into his hand. There were 'Aaah' sounds of delight from the audience.

366

'Gather you saved him from the pot, as it were.'

'Fortunately. The client who wanted his brains cancelled.'

'So you took him in, as you did nearly five thousand people, those who actually ate human flesh.'

'If that's what they think. The cuisine I served was a little bit more than loaves and fishes.'

Betterman smiled.

Raymond continued, 'And when folks found out they'd been eating other folks, and how good it tasted, they just wanted more.'

A gasp ran round the audience.

'Now, I see you're wearing your prison shirt underneath your chef's tunic. Is that for any reason?'

Raymond stood up and took off his white chef's jacket, revealing his blue denim Ray Brook Prison issue with his ID number stencilled over the left pocket.

'Why do you continue to wear it?'

'To remind me what I did.'

'And it was because you were blackmailed that the restaurant began?'

'Arnold Riseveldt ran an interment parlour, RIP. It was his idea, using the deceased to feed us.'

'And he threatened to expose you, because you had accidentally killed a man?'

'That, and 'cause I 'fessed I'd cooked the evidence – yeah.'

'Gather Arnold met with a sticky end. Didn't serve him up too, did you?'

'His mom wanted it, but we got shut down before that was possible.'

Again, the audience chuckled, darkly fascinated.

'What about the lady who decided to go public with it all?'

'Miss Millichamp offered people money for their bodies when they leave this life, the plan being they provide a supply chain for the restaurant. Some people reckoned it was a smart idea.'

The conversation continued some while – the show was a wow. Then Betterman began to wind up.

'Do *you* think you're bad?'

'Maybe. Aren't we all, to a greater or lesser degree? I don't think there's ever been a chef in my league.'

'Nor likely there will be again. Ladies and gentlemen, the man who gave you human cuisine, Ray Babchuk, and his monkey friend, Tutti Frutti.'

The ratings were the highest ever for Betterman's show and the applause wouldn't die down. Standing in front of the studio crowd long after the commercial break began, Raymond soaked it up. As he walked amongst the audience, smiling, shaking hands and signing autographs, there was something messianic about him that night, an aura surrounding him as he passed out of the building, his chef's jacket slung over his shoulder, his little pet nestled against his chest.

Having dismissed his own security and transport, it was just Raymond and Tutti the studio vehicle dropped back at Woodbine Street late that night. The chef, carrying his monkey friend, walked directly into the underground parking lot servicing Mr Balázs's apartment block. On the lower level, Raymond headed for a smart black pick-up, complete with extended cab, its number plate reading:

Big Sky State
Tutti F
Montana

368

As Raymond approached, Balázs Malursk alighted from the passenger side rear door. The two men hugged, the older one patting the monkey's head as the V12 engine fired up. Man and primate climbed in. The other occupants were already settled; Tabitha McKindrick sat beside Raymond, with Feydor Gaultier behind the wheel. The smart vehicle rolled out of the near-empty car lot, the old man waving after its departing tail gate.

Chapter 47

Turn off Highway 15 about 80 miles south of Butte, then head out of Dillon on the 278, exiting before North Spring Creek, the little dorp of Polaris nestles deep in Beaverhead County. Just outside it, Tutti's Place lay off the smallest of asphalt tracks, its motif a cigar-toting monkey, the Havana's smoke trail spiralling into the logo. Western in style, and smarter than the usual backwoods dining establishment, its cuisine was reputed to be the finest in Western Montana, Hungarian dishes a speciality. Not that anyone ever tried to promote it; to those aware of its existence (and these included some serious celebs who liked to keep their privacy private) TP was a well-kept secret. About the only outward evidence of the restaurant's pedigree were a few copies of *Recipes to Die For!* discreetly displayed on a stand at the rear of the lobby. Did they ever get sold? The odd one did, diners interested in experiencing the adventures related between its covers treasuring their purchase.

Feydor Gaultier managed things in his calm and ever-professional way. The maitre d' wore his hair longer since taking up frontier life, exchanging his white tie and tux for a western outfit of check shirt and black bolo tie, Levi's and Frye boots. His style, whilst casual, remained immaculate. Feydor was married to Ponmi, a *Nez Percé* princess of Native American blood royal, whose first husband had been tragically killed in a space accident (Toohoolhoolzote was the first Native American astronaut), and had a young step-son, Ollokot. Their marital home was a ranch below the Incarnate spread; TF Enterprises had bought a ten thousand hectare retreat. At its centre a sprawling homestead commanded magnificent views of the Maverick Mountains, the vistas stunning in their remote beauty.

Tabitha and Raymond were married under special licence by the mayor of Beaverhead County shortly after coming out to Montana. Tabitha was often to be seen in Polaris with a young boy in tow. Little Ray's features were similar to those of his father, except for a shock of carrot-red hair – his mother's contribution. Now pregnant again, Tabitha sometimes dropped by the restaurant, but these days her visits were purely social and had no culinary significance. For the chef at Tutti's Place was none other than Manny Underwine. It appeared that, although rising to the position of head embalmer, Manny tired of beautifying the bereaved, believing his artistic abilities would be better served as a cuisinier. Julie initially considered contacting Miss Millichamp, but Manny also expressed a desire to leave the Big Apple, seeking a quieter existence. So it was that RIP's MD contacted Raymond, who surprisingly agreed to take on the unexpected arriviste as his personal pupil. The intervening years had been fruitful, seeing Manny achieve his own distinguished status in the kitchen.

And what of the man himself? Devoted to his family and largely reclusive, public glimpses of him were rare, but sightings did occur. After escaping the craziness of Manhattan, Restaurant ^{Re}Incarnate, prison and fame, Raymond removed himself from the public eye. Lucrative TV contracts and the movie rights to his life were offered, but both were rebuffed. At the last count, royalties paid to

Raymond for his book exceeded $20 million and his earnings from the ^ReIncarnate operation were also considerable, that enterprise continuing to flourish in New York City. However, preferring the more reclusive anonymity of the West, for some months after his arrival, Raymond did little except take to the woods. Usually with Tutti in tow, he'd walk for miles through the wilderness, and it took Julie Dominic's surprise call to reignite his interest in things culinary. Once Manny came to Montana, Raymond couldn't stop cooking. Pouring out all the pent-up frustration he'd had to contend with, working from a limited list of ingredients for so long, he imparted the very best of his knowledge and creativity to a man who wanted to learn: a man who could be as committed as he was and who liked the solitary life. Manny understood Maestro Raymond's particular nature.

And how did he age? Well, a few flecks of grey appeared on the sides of Raymond's temples, but otherwise he didn't alter much. Raymond remained somewhat bohemian in his appearance and when not in the separate professional kitchen he'd had built on the ranch, would take himself off to the tranquillity of the wild surrounding countryside. His culinary interests came to reside in experimentation – a new recipe for water chevrotain (fanged African deer) fired his imagination, the sauce, created from a combination of grains of paradise, amchur powder and anardana giving an especially spicy succulence to the unusual viand.

At the northern end of his property was a promontory Raymond named 'Frutti's Peak', from which was a view of the whole valley, the ranch house and tiny hamlet of Polaris in the distance. If he remembered his binoculars, Ray would sometimes catch a glimpse of his wife and boy travelling back from the village towards the restaurant he'd named after his pet monkey, their vehicle more weathered than the pristine order the pick-up was in when bringing them west.

At the height of his fame, Raymond had been bombarded with complaints from the animal welfare people, concerned about Tutti's smoking habits, but the monkey showed no sign of wanting to give up and appeared healthy enough, enjoying the great outdoors. Later, Tutti took to hanging out solo on his rock, but Raymond couldn't blame him for that; it was the perfect place to enjoy a good Cuban.

Chapter 48

It was a quiet Sunday afternoon in high summer and the family had come down from the house for a late lunch Manny'd prepared at the restaurant, which was, nowadays, closed to the public at certain times of the year. The Babchuk and Gaultier families were finished dining, and Little Ray and Ollokot gone off to play a game of pretend cowboy and very real Indian. Of Tutti Frutti there was no sign. Whilst initially he'd appeared to be happy enough with the children, the monkey had more recently become reclusive. He wasn't aggressive or unsafe with them; he just seemed uninterested at being around.

Raymond's deepening commitment to his family meant he'd been spending less time with Tutti, who started to disappear, initially for hours but later for days at a time. This troubled Tabitha more than Raymond, who hadn't apparently cottoned on to the fact the monkey, having been Raymond's exclusive friend for so long, might now be affected by his withdrawal; the little macaque was feeling jealous.

Raymond had just used the john and was walking through the empty restaurant when he spied Tutti sitting on the bar. He went over to him but the monkey appeared sulky, his chatter more of a hiss and his head jerking away when Raymond tried to stroke him.

'I know what you need.' Raymond spoke quietly and,

opening a humidor installed with his special friend in mind, removed two Havanas. Clipping them, he put one in Tutti's little fingers, but instead of lighting up, the monkey took off. Shrugging, Raymond put his own cigar in his mouth and headed outside for the terrace where his family sat enjoying the late afternoon sunshine. Entering the kitchen, Tutti hopped up on the hob and flicking a gas knob pressed the ignition switch, pushing his cigar towards the flame. Seconds later there was an almighty explosion.

Little Ray and Ollokot had been tampering with gas cylinder pipes before taking off for the woods to play in their stockade and tepee. Their meddling antics caused a leak which, when ignited, blew everything sky high including the cigar-toting monkey.

The blast destroyed the whole complex, but by some miracle the two families escaped serious harm, emerging charred, singed and shaken. All that was found of Tutti Frutti were his little tartan waistcoat and the singed stub of his Havana. Both are enshrined in a small memorial, erected on top of Frutti's Peak. Now something of a sacred site and noted for its mystical powers, pilgrims travel from far and wide to worship, the relics believed especially significant to those wishing to give up smoking.

Epilogue

So, this is the strange tale of Raymond Babchuk and Arnold Riseveldt, their unlikely combination briefly uniting the one's culinary genius with the other's crude, but perhaps visionary, business talents. Did it achieve anything? Did Restaurant Incarnate, then ^{Re}Incarnate, make any difference to our attitudes surrounding the consumption of human flesh, the idea that we might use our defunct bodies to feed others? Perhaps the jury's out. But as to it being the end of the matter, only time will tell.

If nothing else, though, it's taught us to keep a watchful eye on that new diner opened up down the end of the street. How sure are you of the origins of the meat it's serving? Did you check its source? And is that cut really tenderloin, or something else very rare?

Raymond Babchuk was a man caught in the wrong place at the wrong time. He experienced some extraordinary adventures and his obsessive dedication to his craft temporarily triumphed over activities deemed reprehensible. This twist of fate combination briefly made him a culinary superstar. But more than that, for a while people really did think differently about the idea of eating other people. For after all, as Ray said, they do in every other sense.

376

Ah, remember me, I used to live for music.
Remember me, I brought your groceries in.
Well, it's Fathers' Day and everybody's wounded.
First we take Manhattan, then we take Berlin

So he did it the other way round, but why should the lyrics inside our heads not be rewritten? That's what Ray did.

Acknowledgements

The author wishes to thank John Rosenberg for his script-writing assistance and ideas over the years. Also John Rush, agent provocateur, for his support and help, and Neil and Jill Campbell, without whom this piece wouldn't have made it, either electronically or grammatically! Thanks also to Carol Biss and all those at Book Guild Publishing, especially Joanna Bentley and copy editor Hayley Sherman for their excellent work. Finally, thanks to Seana for putting up with me whilst allowing my imagination to wander into the dark and surreal directions it sometimes does.

A touch of aspic, nettle – ca!

Barney Broom – Blakeney, 2014